ELLE MAXWELL

Us, Again

Cover illustrations by Elle Maxwell and Sandor
Szuhoterin/Shutterstock.com

Cover design by Elle Maxwell

Edited by Max at The Polished Pen

ISBN 978-1-6887-9969-1

This one is for myself, circa 1999.

You can calm down now, you ambitious little maniac.

I didn't let our dream die.

PROLOGUE

Mackenzie

Once upon a time, we were in love.

It was a big, crazy, terrifying love, but we were too naïve to know we should be scared. It was the kind of love that is only possible once, when your heart is still something whole that can be given away completely. It requires the guileless abandon of youth, the fearless confidence of an undamaged soul.

Our love was a miracle, a secret we were certain no one had ever discovered before. He and I were bound together in the knowledge of it, in this new world where only the two of us existed.

I was fundamentally changed, as though love rearranged my atoms. He created, or perhaps merely unveiled, parts of me I'd never known about before. And with every day that passed, we became more connected, until he was a vital cog in the machinery that allowed me to draw breath into my lungs.

I felt alive for the first time. Loving him made me realize that anything I thought I'd felt before this—this uncontainable emotion bigger than me, or him, or even both of us together—was merely a droplet and this was a torrential downpour. It was chaos, a madness we couldn't control, and we gave ourselves over to it.

What we had was a forever kind of love. Until forever suddenly ended.

It was a big, crazy, terrifying love, and it destroyed me. It introduced me to pain and betrayal. In the trusting naïveté of youth, I'd allowed another person to become essential to my being, to my very act of breathing, and when he was gone, I suffocated.

Once upon a time, love broke me. And I will never, ever, let myself fall in love again.

01. MARIPOSAS

Mackenzie

"So … you were home at 9:00 PM and I didn't hear any action. Great date, huh?"

I roll my eyes at my roommate, joining her on a bench outside the Psychology building, then eagerly accept the coffee she hands over. Bless her for knowing I needed this!

"How do you know I was home at nine?" I'm stalling. I guarantee she was sitting up listening for the door, like a parent waiting for their teen to come home—which is ridiculous, of course, since we're both twenty-three.

Marisa continues to sip her coffee, not bothering to respond. After a moment I give in and break the silence.

"For your information, I had a perfectly fine time with Jim. We already have plans to go out again."

The Queen of Sarcasm sets down her cup so she can use both hands to clutch her chest dramatically.

"Ooh, *perfectly fine*. I can't handle the passion! Wait a sec while I go change my panties."

I swat at her with the back of my gloved hand, hissing at her to lower the volume. Psych 101 just ended; some of the students in my section might hear her! She ducks away from me, giggling.

She finally calms down, face turning serious as she pins me with one of her no-nonsense looks that I swear can see right through me. Maybe it's a special Cubana superpower.

"But really, how long has it been? I think we need to go out this weekend and find a guy in a bar who gives you *mariposas en el estomago*. And then you can let him take off all your clothes."

I roll my eyes again and drink my coffee. She can keep her *mariposas*, thank you very much. The stomach fluttering excitement of pure attraction is not only absent from my list of requirements for a boyfriend, I actively avoid it. You can't trust those butterflies. They're little traitors.

"I'm not having this conversation again, Ris. I'm looking for companionship and compatibility, not passion. Passion is nothing but a temporary high that eats your brain cells."

So what if I've only had mediocre sex these past five years? Things have been lackluster with the handful of guys I've dated since *him*, but I've long since decided that type of passion isn't a realistic goal. Anyway, I'm sure what I experienced back then was the result of surging teenage hormones—or I've built it up in my head all these years, romanticizing the past so much that those memories have become exaggerated fantasies. I mean, nothing is ever really *that* good.

What I know for certain is that big love leads to big pain. Even now, I can't think about him without feeling whispers of that old ache inside my chest.

No, Jim is exactly what I'm looking for in a guy. Intelligent, driven, with a solid career and a refined palate for a nice Pinot Noir. He's right on schedule to hit boyfriend status in approximately two weeks, at which time I will let things progress to sex. By then we'll have gone out at least five times, giving us time to learn each other's lifestyle habits, family backgrounds, and five-year plans. Enough established compatibility to give a relationship a shot—and best of all, a high likelihood of a civil, amicable parting if and when we decide to end it.

"But are you happy?" Marisa asks.

"Of course I am." My smile is at least seventy-five percent genuine. "I've got a great life, a beautiful apartment that comes with the best friend a girl can have, a spot in an amazing grad program, and a job I love. I don't need a man to make me happy. That's just window dressing. I'm structurally sound and whole all by myself."

Marisa's face looks more pitying than persuaded, but I know she'll drop the subject … for now. We met in undergrad when the wounds were still very fresh, so she knows plenty of gory details about my history with love.

I shiver despite the coffee in my hand, the chill January wind cutting right through all my layers of clothing. I'm about to suggest we relocate to a warmer location when my eyes catch on something—someone—that makes my breath stutter and then halt. Standing across the courtyard, as though summoned by my thoughts, is a ghost. He must be a ghost, because it is impossible—*there is no possible way*—that Graham Wyatt is in the middle of the Boston College campus right now.

Marisa catches sight of him too, obliterating any possibility that I'm hallucinating. "Speaking of taking all your clothes off … who is the piece of man candy giving you the smolder eyes?"

He looks older. It's more than the normal signs of passing time; he exudes a new edge of darkness and solemnity. Back when we were together, there was still a boyishness to him, but it only takes one glance to see that whatever these past five years did to him removed any trace—he is now all *man*. The scruff covering his jaw makes him look rugged, his dirty blond hair is longer than I've ever seen it, and his eyes … even from this distance I can feel their intensity as they bore into me.

It's really him. The former love of my life. The man I gave everything to, who broke me so badly the pieces never healed back together properly.

Mariposas indeed. When I'm able to pull in another breath, they swarm my abdomen, filling every inch of my midsection with the pulsing and fluttering of their frenetic wings. It's a sensation I haven't felt in so long I'd forgotten the sheer power of it.

Right as all of my molecules start trying to pull me into his magnetic grip, reality suddenly slams back into place. The butterflies vacate my stomach to wreak havoc somewhere else. Because I remember.

I haven't seen him for five years because he's been in prison.

On murder charges.

02. DAY 3

Graham

I make it two days.

Two days of pacing my parents' too-large house, which now feels like a giant crypt, trying to convince myself to leave her alone. At least until I have my shit together. I've had this argument with myself a hundred times over the past five years, but it was different when I was locked up. It's easy to be noble and sacrificing when it's theoretical. Now that I'm out, knowing she's only thirty minutes away makes every part of me ache with a craving two hundred times worse than anything I felt while getting clean.

I'm luckier than most guys out on parole. A lot of them have to live in shitty halfway houses and take shittier jobs the state sets them up with because they have nothing to go home to. I, on the other hand, have a massive house at the edge of the idyllic suburbia of Westwood, Massachusetts, half an hour southwest of Boston. Not to mention the nearly twenty million dollars I inherited between my parents' life insurance policies, assets, and the settlement from their accident. All that money has been sitting in high interest accounts and investments all this time, multiplying, its growth tended to by the firm I've paid to handle the estate and maintain the property in my absence. So much fucking money, and I don't deserve a cent of it. I would give it all up in a second to have my parents back.

On day three, I break and set off to find Mackenzie.

To reach my old Range Rover, I have to pass the Benz my dad was driving the day they died. One of the universe's great jokes: it only cost a couple of grand to repair the car, while Mom and Dad are gone forever. Back then, I considered driving the thing off a bridge, and it's honestly a miracle I didn't do it. I was a mess after the accident, so lost that I fucked up my entire life.

If they'd died just a few months earlier when I was still seventeen, someone would have needed to take responsibility for me. Maybe the authorities could have tracked down distant relatives overseas or something. But I was eighteen, so they sent me home with empty condolences and the expectation that I handle things like an adult.

I wasn't an adult, though. I was a senior in high school; barely more than a kid. The product of a loving affluent household that hadn't hardened me to the ways of the world. I needed my parents. And they were gone.

I drive the Range Rover to Boston College like a man possessed (at the speed limit, though—I have no intentions of breaking the conditions of my parole). BC is on the line between Boston's westernmost limits and the city of Newton. The college atmosphere straddles city and suburb too; the campus is within walking distance to Boston's Brighton neighborhood and an easy trip downtown via public transportation but also stands apart on a hilltop, its many historic stone buildings creating a separate little world. I can see why Mackenzie chose this place. The sprawling lawns and clustered buildings give BC the traditional college campus vibe she prefers, unlike BU and other urban colleges whose campuses are tucked within the city itself.

After scoring a parking spot, I make my way through open courtyards lined with evergreen bushes and bare trees—I bet this place is a veritable oasis of green in the warmer months—until I finally locate the Psychology building. I find myself a seat a short distance away, where I can be discreet but still have a clear view of the entrance. Then I wait.

This is as far as my plan goes. My information is limited. Toward the beginning of my sentence, I received visits from old friends on the outside—not a lot, but a few—and Mackenzie was all I ever asked about. All they could tell me was that she's studying psychology at BC, which surprised me because when I knew her she wanted to be a veterinarian. It makes me itch to find out what else has changed.

I could have hired a PI who'd give me a nice fat folder filled with info, including her address, in exchange for an even fatter paycheck, but I hate the idea of some guy—or a woman, even—following my girl around, digging into her life, taking pictures of her. So I'm just going to watch her myself ... like a fucking creep.

I keep waiting. I have no idea if she even has classes today, or if this is the right building, but it's the only lead I have, so I'm not going anywhere. It's not like there's anything better for me to be doing. And I don't mean that in the way people throw it around, implying what they're doing is insignificant; this is literally the best and only thing I could be doing right now—*she* is the best and only thing I want to do with my life.

And then there she is. Maybe a hundred feet away, exiting the door I've been staring at for hours. I jump up from my seated position to get a better view.

In prison, I thought about Mackenzie a lot. No, that's an understatement. I thought about her constantly. Through every second of drug withdrawals, every minute of boredom, every hour of state-funded counseling, every seemingly interminable beatdown, it was the thought of her that kept me going. When I hated myself and started to wonder if it was all even worth it (which sometimes happened hourly) I thought about seeing her again and I pushed through.

All these years, I had an image in my mind of the girl I fell in love with. Despite the distance, it's clear I am not looking at that same person. While Mackenzie the girl was beautiful, Mackenzie the woman is *gorgeous*, a transcendental goddess who could inspire men to kneel in worship and gods to wage wars.

The sight of her hits me, and I am suddenly afflicted with every single romantic cliché.

Heart racing? *Check.*

Breath taken away? *Check.*

Vision narrowing until I only see her? *Check.*

Weak knees? *Check.* (And what the actual fuck? I literally have to sit down.)

With that one glimpse, I know without a doubt that I never stopped loving her—and I'll do whatever it takes to get her back.

03. I THINK I'M A STALKER

Graham

I don't approach her. I can't.

For five years I've been imagining the moment when I could finally explain and start to win her back. Now that it's here and she's within reach, I'm scared shitless.

I duck down so I'm hidden but still have a clear view of her, trying to take in every detail as she stands mere yards from my makeshift hiding place. She's chatting with a dark-haired girl in front of the Psychology building. A bulky gray coat hides most of her body from my view, but I can see her slender legs clad in black pants and her feet in shiny black boots. Her hair, twisted up with a clip, is the same mesmerizing orange-red color she informed me is called "strawberry blonde" when we were sixteen. She laughs at something the other girl says, and her smile flashes brightly enough to blind me even from afar.

When her conversation ends and she begins walking away from the Psychology building, it feels like she's taking my heart with her. I know what I do next is crazy, but there's an overpowering sense of urgency screaming to keep her in my sight that drowns out all reason. I'm not ready to lose her again. Not yet.

So I follow her.

I keep following her for days.

I even switch out cars and start driving my mom's—even though her scent still clings to the interior and brings back memories so potent it's sometimes hard to breathe—so I can continue to trail Mackenzie without the risk that she'll recognize my Range Rover.

I think I might be a stalker. Does it count as stalking if you're in love with the girl? The *lie down in the street and die for her* kind of love? I doubt that would convince a judge and jury, but ... fuck it. I suppose I can live with being *her* stalker.

At the beginning of every day, I tell myself I'm going to man up and talk to her. At the end of every day, I vow that I'll *really* do it tomorrow.

I follow her silver Toyota Camry, the same car she had when we were teenagers, from BC to a house in the nearby Brighton area where she lives in the apartment on the first floor. Her roommate is the same girl I saw before—and it doesn't take me long to decide she's good for my girl. She smiles more quickly than Mackenzie, laughs more, and when they're together that seems to rub off on her, so Mackenzie smiles more too.

One afternoon, I follow Mackenzie to a yoga studio in Newton. A bit of snooping (okay, maybe I flirted a little with the girl at the desk) reveals she teaches classes there a few times a week. A yoga instructor. How fucking hot is that?

Even though she wears her coat to and from her car, I get a few glimpses of her ass in those yoga pants—it is even tighter and rounder than when we were teenagers.

Sad that a few inches of spandex-covered ass are my primary spank bank material right now? What can I say? It's a fucking phenomenal ass.

Then one night after yoga, she comes out of the studio later than usual, and when she emerges, I can see it's because she was doing whatever is necessary to look like *that*.

She's replaced her fresh-faced yoga look with makeup. Her lips are bright red, and I don't know what the hell else she did, but it takes her hotness to a twelve on a scale of ten. Her hair is a shiny curtain of reddish gold hanging loose around her face, falling to a few inches past her shoulders. At school she works the sexy librarian look, hair tamed with pins or in a bun, so this is the first time I've seen it wild. My reaction is as powerful as that first time I saw her at BC—I want to drop to my knees at her feet and worship her. I can't see what she's wearing—*seriously, I need winter to be over already so she can stop covering up with that coat*—but those high-heeled black boots make it clear she's not headed to the library.

Of course, I follow her. It might as well be my full-time occupation at this point.

She enters a place that appears to be a restaurant/bar combo. It's busy and dark enough that I risk going in, wearing my Red Sox ball cap for camouflage, and take a seat at the bar. From my spot, I watch her greet a man who steps forward and hugs her.

Who. The. *Hell*. Is. That!?

She takes off her coat, and my indignation rises another level. My girl is dressed to kill. She has on black jeans that mold to her body so tightly there should be a picture of them in the dictionary under the definition for "painted on" and a sexy little black tank top trimmed with lace under a leather jacket. Not to mention the boots. I know about *fuck-me-heels* … are there *fuck-me-boots* too? I guess so, because I swear that's what she's wearing.

As difficult as it is to stop staring at her, I turn my attention to my new nemesis, AKA the lucky bastard she wore that outfit for. He is unremarkable. His body is scrawny, perhaps even gangly, and he only barely matches her height in the boots she's wearing. He has the face of an accountant, and I swear I spy a bald spot.

My gaze pings back and forth between them a few times. She's wearing *that* for *him*?

For the next hour, I watch them so intently I worry they'll catch me, but fortunately the bar's progressively thickening crowd provides cover. On the downside, my view is occasionally obstructed by passing bar patrons. I also have to turn away a few women who apparently smell my ex-con vibe and find it sexy. I tell them all that I'm waiting for my girl. It's the truth ... I just might be waiting a long time.

By the time Mackenzie and the guy share a polite hug and part ways to their separate cars, I'm more confused than ever but appeased that she isn't into him. I could tell from her body language at dinner: she remained on her side of the table with her back straight, never once leaning in his direction, and although she smiled a lot, the muscles around her mouth were tight.

When we were together, Mackenzie's body always spoke before her words did. She fiddled with her hair when she was nervous or excited. She had a particular quirk of her lips and gleam in her eyes when she wanted to fool around. She would cross her legs, continually switching which one was on top, when she was turned on. And unlike what I witnessed tonight, she always found reasons to touch me, reaching out for the menu at the same time I was holding it, running a hand over my arm when I said something funny. Not that she needed reasons—I was all about touching her all the time too. I didn't see any of that tonight. If anything, she looked kind of bored.

Still, I follow her all the way home and watch her walk inside—alone.

Enough of this. I need to finally find my missing balls, stop this stalking shit and start talking to Mackenzie. I can't begin groveling for forgiveness until I announce my presence. It's time.

* * *

I stand close to where I camped out that first day, but this time I'm out in the open where she won't be able to miss me. She should be getting out of class any minute. I'm so nervous that I'm sweating, even though it's freezing out.

When she sees me, her face goes from its usual pale to a deathly white. The way she looks at me—it's not confusion, excitement, or even anger. She looks like she's seeing a ghost—and not just any specter but one from whom she anticipates bodily harm. And then she bolts, running in the opposite direction with such haste that she slips on the icy path more than once. The roommate scrutinizes me for a few more heartbeats before following Mackenzie at a much slower pace.

I'm gutted; she might as well have shot a spear directly into my organs. I can feel myself bleeding out right here on this college campus.

I'm not totally delusional. I never thought she'd see me and happily run into my arms ready to start right where we left off. Her five years of silence—no letters, no visits—spoke loud and clear. I've been preparing to grovel every day since I pulled my head out of my ass, which unfortunately happened *after* I became a resident at a maximum security correctional facility. But I didn't expect her to look at me like *that* … as though she was in danger of passing out from shock and—what kills me most—fear.

For the first time, the full reality sinks in that the rift between us might be irreparable. The fear that I might not get her back squeezes me tight, making it hard to breathe as I stumble back to my car in a daze.

I lost her the moment they charged me with accessory to murder. (*Accessory* being the operative word, the one that seemingly didn't make it all the way through the town-sized game of "telephone" that transports news in Westwood.) Not that I'm trying to defend my actions—I own them and I know I was in the wrong, which is partly why I never fought the conviction or tried to clear up misconceptions—but I didn't pull the trigger. I've never even held a gun. Killing someone might be one of the only things I *didn't* do wrong back then.

Though I suppose I lost her long before that, the first time I reached for drugs instead of reaching for her. I was in so much pain after my parents died, and being the eighteen-year-old idiot I was, I thought I needed to deal with that outside of our relationship. My adolescent ego was convinced I needed to show her only the strong side of myself, be the big, tough quarterback boyfriend who never had to cry on her shoulder.

I've had time—nothing but time—to reflect back on everything, and I understand that was the single worst mistake I made. I had the best thing in the entire world, the love of an amazing girl I got to call mine, but instead of leaning on her, pulling strength from her goodness and the power of our love, I decided to jump off the deep end without her. With unlimited funds and no parental supervision, I dove face-first into self-destruction every minute I was away from Mackenzie. And gradually, I wasn't only lying to her when I wasn't with her; those minutes we spent together became tainted by thoughts of when I could score next, what I would do later to dull the pain. I was basically cheating on her with drugs.

Suddenly, it occurs to me what a terrible mistake I made never even trying to write to her. I'd thought that before I contacted her I needed to be ... not *worthy* of her, because I doubt that will ever be possible, but at least *more* worthy than when I was first arrested. Now I realize that I have no idea what she thinks happened that night, what people might have told her.

I don't know if she can ever forgive me for the lies, for any of it. But I have to try. I can't give up. Not now. Not before I've spoken to her ... maybe not ever.

04. WEAPON OF MASS SEDUCTION

Mackenzie

I make a few final adjustments to tonight's playlist and give out quiet greetings as people enter the room. The lights are already low and I have my "pre-playlist" on, slow and soothing songs playing in the background to set the mood, as students discard their jackets and lay out their mats. This is a time for quiet as they ready their minds and bodies to transition out of their hectic daytime lives and into their yoga practice. Some lie down and close their eyes to begin relaxing, and some start with simple poses to stretch and warm up their muscles.

A pang of yearning shoots through me, a longing to be down there with them—sinking into the atmosphere of the dim, warm room and letting real life drift away for a while. It's been too long since I attended a class as a student, and I resolve to fix that soon.

The wall clock shows there are only a couple of minutes left before I need to start class. A glance across the room reveals that it's a full house tonight, with all but a few spots of the floor already covered by yoga mats. I walk over to the sound system and check the settings, getting ready to turn on my wireless microphone headset and switch over to the playlist I created for tonight's class. I stick to contemporary music rather than the Eastern tunes the more traditional instructors use, collections I've specially curated over the years of melodic acoustic covers to pop and alternative songs. No one can convince me my modern version isn't equally as effective at opening the soul—any beautiful music can inspire a spiritual experience.

I go to close the studio door, signaling that class is starting, and walk to a spot at the front. Twenty faces stare back at me from yoga mats spread all across the room, quietly waiting for my instructions. I immediately note some new arrivals who slipped in while I was doing my final preparations, among them a single masculine figure toward the center of the room.

When my eyes land on him, he commands my full attention— because that is not just any male form. It is one I recognize with a part of my brain that never completely recovered from its addiction and still responds to the sight of him with an instinctual hum of mine.

Not mine! I censure the rogue synapses.

Regardless, that is undoubtedly Graham Wyatt sitting in the center of the yoga studio amidst my Wednesday night regulars. On either side of him, I catch girls sneaking peeks.

I'll admit he's worth peeking at. He's in a pair of full-length black cotton track pants and a simple white T-shirt that's a little too tight, as though his old clothes can't quite handle his new post-prison bulk. He has his hair pulled back with an elastic tie, in the smallest of sexy man buns. With slightly more scruff on his face than the last time I saw him, and the intricate tattoo of black roses on his left arm creeping out from the edge of his shirt's sleeves, he is six feet two inches of mouthwatering eye candy.

My eyes meet his for the length of a heartbeat. Shadowed hazel irises stare back at me intensely, framed in a serious face, though there's the tiniest quirk to one side of his lips indicating he saw me looking.

I tear my gaze away with an almost violent jerk of my head. Damn. *What is he doing here?!*

I clear my throat, which is suddenly dry. Unfortunately, the sound echoes through the speakers since I've already turned my microphone on. I force myself to rally, and manage to start off class the way I usually do, making sure to avoid looking at Graham. I can't risk my eyes and brain becoming moth-like again and getting trapped in his glow.

The class moves into its usual flow, starting with a few combinations in and out of Downward Facing Dog. As usual, I circulate around the room guiding them through the poses, only spending a little time at the front to demo a pose or transition. I can't completely avoid the center section where Graham is, and despite my best efforts, every time I reach that area my eyes travel back to him.

It's clear that Graham has never done yoga before, his movements slightly slower as he finds his way into the unfamiliar positions. I've found men, especially beginners, often have a hard time with certain parts of yoga because they tend to be less flexible than women. He's out of his depth tonight—this is my intermediate class and a lot of the girls here have been practicing consistently for years, so I don't pull any punches when planning their pose combinations. Although Graham struggles with some of the poses, he manages to follow along and keep up, and I have to admit I'm impressed. In certain parts of the flow, he's even able to compensate for his lack of flexibility with his strength. For instance, a lot of my girls skip or half-ass the Chaturanga pushup in their Sun Salutations, but he executes it with ease, lowering his body to the ground in a perfectly controlled slow motion with elbows tucked in tight along his sides.

We keep the studio hot, around eighty degrees, and not long into the class Graham's shirt starts to stick to his body. The clinging white fabric only emphasizes what was clear to me even in his jeans and jacket the other day: he is all chiseled muscle. His biceps threaten to rip the sleeves right off his shirt during those pushups.

And then he sits back on his heels and takes his shirt off.

This isn't unusual for male yogis—I've had plenty of shirtless men in my classes before. But none of them caused me to nearly trip over a student's mat out of sheer distraction. My throat dries up and the muscles in my lower abdomen pulse without my permission.

Graham was always in great shape—he played football and was the starting quarterback of our high school's team junior and senior years. Back then he had the body of an athletic adolescent, but now he's something else entirely. It looks like he spent the last five years doing nothing but honing that body, polishing and perfecting it into a weapon of mass seduction.

I instruct the class to continue their salutations independently for the duration of the next song, giving myself a break to get my shit together. I walk over to the corner where my water bottle is stashed and take a long drink. Inexorably my eyes fly back to the expanse of taut skin and straining muscle in the center of the room. Shirtless, the sleeve of roses on his left arm is now on full glorious display, and I can see every contraction of muscle and tendon as he goes through the poses.

I've never been so turned on by shoulder blades.

I make it through the rest of the class, but I'm running on autopilot.

At least half of my brain is caught up in totally inappropriate fantasies of being in this room with Graham alone. I would free his long hair from the tie currently holding it and run my fingers through it. Rub as much of myself as possible over every inch of those sweat-slicked muscles, slide my palms over those too-thin pants clinging to the defined spheres of his ass and squeeze, the scrape of his stubble against my skin as we kiss the soundtrack to our yoga porno.

Oh my God. I've completely lost it. I need some prolonged alone time with my vibrator followed by a lobotomy.

As the bodies before me lie prone and still for the final minutes of class in the total relaxation of Savasana, I am as far from serene as I have ever been.

Seeing him yesterday was a shock to my system. It was as though I had a delayed PTSD reaction. My hands shook for a full hour after I ungracefully sprinted away from him and escaped in my car. Marisa offered to talk, but I avoided her and holed up in my room, something the version of myself that existed before Graham's arrest wouldn't have done.

I used to be a sharer, seeking out solace from others when I needed to process pain. But Graham broke something in me that makes it hard to trust even my best friend with the innermost parts of my soul. I now retreat into myself to deal with the hardest parts of life, so I spent last night trying to ease the surprisingly deep ache of seeing him again with music and wine. The shock cracked open my scabbed-over wounds, causing memories and feelings I thought had healed long ago to bleed through even in my dreams.

While I was overwhelmed by grief and remorse and anger yesterday, lust was the last thing on my mind. I'd welcome those feelings back now, because they are less confusing and unwelcome than the response I'm currently having to him.

Seconds after class ends with a bow and group "Namaste," I dart out to the reception area, beg the girl at the desk to close up the studio for me, and exit into the night before the students have even finished rolling up their yoga mats. Running away. Again. I am not a cowardly person, but I tell myself this is strength through survival. I cannot deal with him right now.

At home, I have an emergency therapy session with my vibrator that provides only partial relief and then open bottle of wine—my second in two nights—to try and drown the shame for my weakness.

Okay, so he's hot. Painfully, scorchingly hot.

But I won't let my attraction to him erase any of the strength and independence I've found over the last few years, the self-assurance that tells me a risk this big is not worth taking. I've never been someone who needs to learn a lesson twice—I get burned once and I stay away from the fire forever.

05. HELL YES, I DID

Mackenzie

Although the freshmen in my section would no doubt disagree, I love exam days. There's something meditative about the energy of a silent room filled with active minds. Today's test is especially well-timed. I desperately need this quiet hour to think.

For as long as I can remember, I wanted to be a veterinarian. I used to play "animal hospital" with my toys when I was kid, and over the years it was always my answer in those "get to know you" games. Now when asked about my choice of major, I tell people that Psych 101—the very class I'm now a TA for—inspired me so much freshmen year that I changed my life plans. It's not a complete lie; I did enjoy the class and I am still close with Professor Marshaud, who even wrote my recommendation for grad school, but it's at least eighty percent false.

I've never verbalized the real reason I decided to study psychology to anyone but Marisa, on one of our many drunken nights of soul-sharing. I once even flat-out lied when an old friend from high school asked if my choice had anything to do with Graham.

Did I decide to study psychology because I was once blindsided by the love of my life, and now I want to learn all about the human mind and behaviors so I never experience that again? *Hell yes, I did.*

There are moments in life, as the cliché goes, that irrevocably change everything. Mine was, unsurprisingly, the night of Graham's arrest. When I got the news that he had been arrested for murder, followed shortly by the revelation of everything he'd been hiding from me as the police searched his car, I was shocked and devastated and angry at him. But more than anything else, I was mad at myself. I'm still mad at myself, even after all this time.

How could I not have known? No one actually asked me the question, but I felt it behind their eyes. Anyone who knew us, who saw us together for even a second, could tell how close we were. How did I not see how badly he was struggling? That he was engaging in self-destructive behaviors? That he was doing drugs?

It made me question not only him, and myself, but our whole relationship. Did I even really know him? If he lied to me about all these things, maybe he'd been dishonest in other aspects of our relationship, even before his parents died.

The only answer I have is that I believed him. I had so much faith in our love that when he told me he was doing okay I trusted him implicitly. I loved him so much that I couldn't see past those love goggles—and let me tell you, they can distort things even more than beer goggles.

And the even harder truth is that I didn't *want* to see. I was self-absorbed—not abnormally or pathologically so, but I was seventeen. I grieved for him, and with him, but I also wanted my life to stay the same. I wanted my boyfriend and the perfect relationship we'd had before, and when he seemed to be giving that to me, I didn't question it because I didn't want to.

What he did was unforgivable, but my actions were unforgivable too. He didn't have anyone else. I was the closest person to him, the one who was supposed to spend my life loving him, and I failed him.

After two days caught up in a whirlwind of emotions triggered by Graham's reentry into my life, I've landed in this state of contemplation and self-reflection. I've essentially relived all the stages of grief and recovery from the last five years in hyper-speed, crammed into a couple of days, and now I've returned to the place of acceptance I had finally achieved before Graham showed up on my college campus.

I know the next time I see him I won't run. I am no longer a girl who runs.

I remember encountering somewhere the use of broken bones as a literary metaphor about growing stronger after you've survived life's trials. Though it stuck with me, the metaphor is flawed—when you break a bone, unless you have metal inserted surgically, the place that was broken doesn't heal to be stronger. If anything, you are more susceptible to break or injure it again.

However, the spirit of the metaphor is spot on—it is possible to become stronger after experiencing pain. That particular spot will always be a weakness, a residual pain point, but the survivors learn how to grow strong around that weakness. You learn to protect it, to bolster the bones and tendons and muscles surrounding it to compensate, to adjust your movements and behaviors so there is less risk of danger to the past injury site.

Graham was my broken bone, but I survived him, and now I live my life with the knowledge of how that pain feels. I grew emotional scar tissue around my heart, and I cast aside my youthful naïveté. And sometimes the old wound aches, but the pain no longer feels like it's going to kill me.

The truth is that I am stronger now than before Graham's arrest because I taught myself how to be. I've spent the last five years learning exactly who I am and making sure that I will never again need another person to complete me, that I won't allow anyone to hold such power over my ability to survive. These days I'm more careful about choosing the men I date and the people I allow into my life.

But I don't lean on them. Because you know what happens when you lean on something and it suddenly disappears? You fall the fuck down.

※　※　※

I've collected the final exam booklet and stacked it neatly on top of the others in my bag. I heft the blue book laden tote onto my shoulder, trying not to think about the weight signifying all that grading I have ahead of me.

Before exiting the Psychology building, I stop to take a quick peek out the window. I may not run from Graham if I see him, but I don't want to be caught off guard again—a strong defense is a good offense and all that. But I see no head of dark blond hair amidst the small crowd enjoying the afternoon sun in the courtyard. With a sigh of half relief and half—*disappointment?*—I carry my usual schoolbag and the extra tote of exam books to my Camry to start the drive home.

I'm fumbling with the two bags and reaching for my keys as I walk up the front path to my house, so I don't see him until I'm almost stepping on him.

Graham Fucking Wyatt. Sitting on my front steps.

So much for not being caught off guard. I am one hundred percent surprised to see him here, so much so that I jerk back in shock and drop the bag of blue books. Half of them go flying over the small front yard, and I let out a curse. Graham's voice rumbles in a deep chuckle as he unfolds his long legs and starts retrieving books. I hastily set my bags down and race to get them myself.

27

"I've got it," I say with a little too much hostility. Without responding, he hands over a pile of neatly stacked papers.

I still haven't looked at his face.

Sometimes being strong is knowing when you need to pace yourself, when to take a breath from the hits before heading back into the ring. And I need to catch my breath right now—both literally and metaphorically. I take my time re-packing the bag and placing it securely next to the steps with my other one. Then with a fortifying breath, I turn around and face him, my arms crossed in front of me, guards back up in place.

"This needs to stop. My school, my work, now my home? This isn't normal behavior, Graham. Have you considered talking to someone professionally to help you deal with this transition?"

He chuckles again and his deep voice transfers frissons of static that raise little hairs all over my body.

"You offering to be my shrink, Kenz?"

06. THE PRINCESS & THE DRAGON

Graham

Well, those are definitely not the first words I thought I'd say to Mackenzie after five years.

Not that I had a speech planned or anything, but I guess I imagined an epic apology, or declaration of love, or ... fuck, just *"hello."*

Mackenzie doesn't look like she'd respond well to a "hello" right now. She's standing there with arms crossed, looking downright pissed as she glares at me with eyes that are filled with fire but also guarded.

It seems she spent these years building walls around herself, and I am clearly on the outside. She's so much more serious than she used to be, and more fierce. A tough as nails soul contained within the tiny frame of her 5'4" body.

She's the princess locked away in the castle tower, and she's also the dragon guarding the thing.

"I am obviously not offering to be your 'shrink.' That would be incredibly inappropriate given our history, not to mention that I'm not a licensed practitioner." Her words are brusque and businesslike.

"I got counseling in prison, but I haven't looked into a therapist now that I'm out. Maybe I will."

My honesty seems to take some of the wind out of her sails. Her posture becomes a little less rigid, and I see her eyes soften slightly. She is clearly surprised.

"Oh," she says. "Well, that's good."

"You look good." It's not poetry, and it's not profound, but again it's the truth.

"You look ... good too."

A slight rosy hue climbs up her cheekbones, and I bite my own cheek to keep from grinning. Reason Number 282 why I love that she's a redhead: she can't ever hide her blush. It spills out onto the pale canvas of her skin and paints her emotions for everyone to view.

So, she likes what she sees. That's good to know.

I'm definitely in the best shape of my life from my solid workout regimen in prison (though I confess that while the abs are a plus, it was really a strategic move to keep guys from messing with me). Regardless, I'll admit her yoga class last night kicked my ass. It was no joke—I am sore in places I wasn't aware existed. And I'm sure it doesn't help anything that I've been eating mountains of junk food and takeout for days, catching up on everything I missed while I was locked up. I need to get my ass in gear and start working out again.

Math problem: How many crunches will it take for me to make that blush spread all the way to her thighs?

Of course, now I'm thinking about her thighs, and the way she looked in those skintight spandex yoga clothes. *Wait, what were we talking about?* Definitely not me getting embarrassingly hard during our first conversation.

"Why are you here, Graham?" she says in a softer voice, though her arms are still crossed in front of her like armor. "What do you want?"

I clear my throat. Hearing her say my name, after all this time … it does something to me. I want to record it and play it on repeat to keep me company at night when I'm alone with the ghosts in my childhood home.

"I just want to talk."

She opens her mouth to say something, but I cut her off with a sudden sound of frustration.

"Shit." Roughly raking my fingers through the overly long hair on top of my head, I tug then grip the back of my skull with both hands. "No, that's a lie."

Her eyes widen in shock, and she takes a step back that almost looks unconscious.

"And I swore I'd never lie to you again. So, the truth? I do want to talk, but I want so much more than that. I want to know you, to re-learn every detail about you and find out all the things I've missed. I want to hold you, touch your skin, feel your hair. I want to be the guy who gets to hear your voice every night and wake up to your face every morning. I want … fuck, I want everything. I didn't plan to throw all of this at you right now, but it's the truth. I want to be … *us* again." By the time I speak the final words, my voice is hoarse with emotion.

She looks stunned, and for a moment she simply stares at me with wide eyes. I keep palming my own head in a punishing grip, hoping to hold myself together after I just spilled my guts all over her front lawn.

"Graham." God, again, my name on her lips. "That's not how it works. Maybe you've been holding on to some idea of our relationship, but *'us'* … it doesn't exist anymore. It stopped existing a long time ago. We don't even know each other now. I'm a different person, and

I'm sure you're different too. Plus, there's too much damage. It's not like you were away in a war. You were in prison. *Prison*, Graham."

She takes in a deep breath and closes her eyes for a second as though the weight of this talk is almost too much even for her ironclad will. Her gorgeous blue-green eyes are miles deep when they reopen and fix back on me.

"At this point, I'm not sure our relationship, that 'us,' was real. I don't think I even truly knew you then. All the lies. Drugs, Graham? Murder? How can I believe anything I thought we had was real?"

"It was real." My voice is even gruffer now, so much emotion thickening the surface of my throat that the three words are all I can get out.

"Anyway," she says in a totally different tone, regaining control of the conversation. "I'm seeing someone."

At that, I let out a derisive snort.

"That twerp from the other night? Come on, Kenz, there's no way he's man enough for you. That's like handing the keys to a Camaro over to a kid who just got out of training wheels."

Her hands are no longer crossed … she's got one propped on each hip and one leg cocked out to the side. One hundred pounds of pure attitude.

"One, thanks for the vehicle comparison. I was low on my objectification quota for the day. And two, what do you mean by *'the other night?'* Have you been *stalking* me?"

Yeah, so about that …

"I've been checking on you," I mutter.

"That's really crossing the line."

"I just needed to see you, to be close to you …" I take a step toward her and she backs away.

Dammit. I'm royally screwing this up. I sound like such a creeper right now.

"Don't make me call the police."

My gut churns again, the same way it did when she ran away from me the other day.

"Do you really think I'd lay a hand on you, Kenz? You must know I'd never hurt you."

"You did hurt me." It's nearly a whisper. Right now she's the most vulnerable I've seen her.

Then she pulls her chainmail back on, visibly stiffening her posture. She picks up her bags, which are so big that combined they're basically the same size as she is. I have the urge to rush forward and help her with them, but I hold back—everything about her stance and expression screams "stay away from me."

"Stop following me. And don't show up like this again. I mean it."

Then she's walking away—always away, perpetual punishment for the way I once left her. She disappears inside the front door, and I hear the click as she locks it behind her.

Drawbridge up, princess tightly secured. And me, still standing on the outside.

07. BROWNIE SITUATION

Mackenzie

"I want to know you, to re-learn every detail about you and find out all the things I've missed. I want to hold you, touch your skin, feel your hair. I want to be the guy who gets to hear your voice every night and wake up to your face every morning."

It's been twenty minutes and my heart is still beating so hard I can feel it pulsing behind my eye sockets.

"I want to be ... us again."

Those words. Oh, how a part of me has longed to hear those words for the last five years—in the small rogue corner of my brain still stuck at seventeen. I clearly remember the desperation I felt as I rushed to check the mail for weeks, longing for a word from Graham, even though my parents told me to let him go and my own mind knew he'd betrayed me. I longed for a note, a word, anything from him. *If he would only say he still loved me,* I rationalized. *If he would apologize and explain away the terrible things people in town said he did ...* but nothing ever came.

I never wrote or tried to visit him either. At first, it was because my parents forbade it. Later, I stayed away because even in the darkest depths of my heartbreak, I refused to be a girl who crawled after a boy, especially one who didn't even love me enough to tell me the truth.

But the pain in his eyes today, the raw edge in his voice …

"… *fuck, I want everything.*"

He didn't deny the accusation of murder, though, even when I brought it up point-blank. And *that* is not something I can overlook or justify as a grief-fueled mistake.

Marisa walks into the living room and reads my mood immediately.

"Wine or tequila?"

"Brownies," I reply. She whistles (translation: *oh shit*) because she knows junk food is my vice of choice for dire situations when alcohol alone won't do.

I'd say my ex-soulmate suddenly being released from prison and showing up at my house *definitely* qualifies.

"And tacos?" I add hopefully as she checks our cabinets for brownie mix.

"I'll put in an order from Anna's."

I thank her and sit back in a slump, resting my head on the couch cushion. Anna's Taqueria is a local Mexican chain, and their food is our absolute favorite. After what just transpired, I seriously need to seek comfort at the bottom of their guacamole.

Marisa joins me on the couch a few minutes later and hands me a glass. A quick sniff tells me she's mixed one of our favorite cocktails—tequila, soda water, fresh lime juice, and triple sec. We discovered this recipe our junior year of college, and it's become our preferred tequila drink since neither of us can stand syrupy margarita mixes.

"You're a goddess," I say gratefully after taking my first sip. This will be perfect as an accompaniment to our tacos and guacamole.

"So, why the brownies?" she asks.

I can smell them starting to bake—she whipped that mix up fast! You've got to love a best friend who's good in a crisis.

"Graham was here when I got home."

She darts her eyes around as though expecting to find paw prints on our living room floor. I let out a tiny laugh and shake my head.

"I didn't let him *inside*. Geez, Ris. He was on the front steps when I walked up."

"Well, you can't deny the boy is persistent."

"He is that." I take another long gulp of my drink before continuing. "I told him this isn't appropriate behavior and asked what he wanted."

"And what did he say?" Marisa prompts when I pause.

"He said he wants … everything. That he wants to be '*us again*.'"

"Shit."

"Yeah, shit."

I take another big drink from my glass, which is already nearly empty. I've consumed way too much alcohol this week—I never drink this many nights in a row! It's something to blame on Graham Wyatt along with the 1,000 calories of baked chocolate goodness I'll be consuming tonight.

I stare at our blank television screen without really seeing it, my mind once again lost in the thick blanket of contemplation that's been fogging my brain ever since he left.

"It's kind of … sweet," Marisa says hesitantly.

"It's *confusing*," I correct her. "I really want to hate him, Ris. I want to look at him and only see the guy who spent the last five years in prison. But he doesn't look like the guy who betrayed me and ripped my heart out. He looks like the guy who was the love of my life, the one I thought I'd spend forever with—only hotter, with the facial hair and the *muscles*!" I groan in frustration.

"So, you *do* want to give him a chance?"

"No!" I answer quickly. My brain gets to make the executive decision on this one, no matter how much my body and heart sulk about it. Those two have short memories—they're only concerned with how he makes us feel, but my brain remembers how those feelings lead to devastating pain. "I told him not to do this anymore. It really isn't healthy behavior. He needs to move on."

"Are you turning your Psych degree on him because you don't want to acknowledge that you still have feelings for him?"

"All I have is some nostalgia I'm more than strong enough to conquer, and the other feelings I can handle with a vibrator."

She laughs and tips her glass to mine—probably toasting to vibrators, because it's Marisa—and we both drink. My cup is officially empty, so she heads back to the kitchen to refill it for me.

I'm proud that my words sounded so certain, my voice firm and resolute. Now I need to actually *be* that strong, because inside I am not quite so certain.

I was once addicted to Graham Wyatt, and while I may be in recovery, the temptation is still there.

Here's something that bothers me: While I loved the Twilight series as much as the next millennial girl (Team Edward, thank you very much), ever since Graham's arrest I've had a new perspective. In particular, the people who swoon over that "you're my special brand of heroin" bullshit aren't thinking clearly.

Heroin, people.

It is the farthest thing from healthy to have someone in your life with that kind of power over you. The thing about heroin is that when you don't have it, your body can't function, the withdrawal so intense you are physically ill, incapacitated for days, weeks even. (I wonder if Graham went through that when he was arrested and had no access to drugs—was he addicted to *them* at the same time I was addicted to *him?*)

Addiction is not cute. It is not something to moon over or wish for in a great love story. There's nothing romantic about debilitating co-dependence. Obsession is not the same thing as love—the same way *needing* another person is not a sign of a healthy relationship or a stable sense of self. Because, just like heroin, when the person you're addicted to is gone, it's excruciating. Life-threatening.

I survived coming down from him once, and I won't put myself through it again. I am five years Graham Wyatt sober, and I'm not going to break that streak, no matter how strong the craving.

The fall isn't worth the high.

08. DEVIL'S ADVOCATE

Mackenzie

"Ooh!" Marisa squeals. "What is it today?" She holds out her arms to me and flexes her fingers in the universal gesture of "gimme gimme."

"I haven't opened it yet—here, you do it."

I toss the simple white envelope in my hand toward her, and she catches it. I'm glad *someone* is having fun with this, because all I feel is exhaustion.

Every day for the last week, I've come home to find an envelope taped to my front door, its exterior bearing only my name in handwriting I could recognize anywhere. The very sight of it smacks me in the face with nostalgia, the way encountering a scent from your past can immediately send you back to that imprinted memory. *Graham.*

Every day the envelope contains a piece of paper bearing a quote and nothing else.

"'In case you ever foolishly forget, I am never not thinking of you'—Virginia Woolf," Marisa reads aloud. "I like that one."

"Pour me one of those?" I ask her, indicating the wine glass sitting beside her at the kitchen counter. I kick off my heels and finish peeling myself out of all the layers today's frigid temperatures called for.

When I've taken my first sip of wine and pulled out the stool beside her at the counter, I tentatively reach over and slide the note toward me with one finger. I try to barely touch it as though it's contaminated. I'll look at it for a minute, drown in the letters penned by a hand that once knew every inch of me, then add it to the others in the pile on my closet floor.

"What does he hope to accomplish with this, Ris?" I groan. We've had some form of this conversation every day since the notes began appearing, but I still can't wrap my mind around it.

"It's *romantic*," she says, her heaviest accent coming out with the inflection so her "r" rolls, the syllables undulating sensuously.

"Does he really think he can fix this with clever Googling? This cutesy stunt might fix things between teenagers who had a fight, but not the kind of baggage we have."

"What's his alternative? You won't talk to him."

I shoot her my fiercest glare.

"I'm just playing devil's advocate!" she protests defensively. "I'm not saying you're wrong. I'm just pointing out there's something to be said for how hard he's trying."

"You know what would be *trying*?" I jump up from my stool as my voice rises on the same wave as my emotions. "Maybe writing me an actual letter where he explains himself ... FIVE YEARS AGO!"

Our apartment seems to echo with the reverberations from my shouting.

"Did that feel good?" Marisa asks calmly as she sips her wine. She appears completely unfazed by my outburst.

I take a big breath and then exhale it out loudly, the way I have my yoga students do after a challenging pose.

"Yes, actually."

"Okay then. Now sit your little *culo* down and drink your wine."

⁂ ⁂ ⁂

It's 10:00 PM and I'm lying in bed, willing myself to fall asleep so I can go to a 6:00 AM yoga class in the morning.

My phone chimes with a text, the lit screen a small beacon of brightness in the dark room. The message is from Jim, who I'd completely forgotten in the midst of all the Graham shenanigans. He wants to go out tomorrow night. I hesitate, experiencing a reluctance I haven't experienced in prior interactions with Jim. I enjoy his company, we have good conversations, and although he's only moderately attractive, he was a pretty good kisser the time we got that far. Before I can rethink it, I text him back accepting his invitation. Maybe Jim is precisely what I need to get my mind off Graham. Step away from the drama for a night and spend time with an adult.

I'm also re-thinking my standard dating timeline. Going to bed with Jim earlier than planned could help take the edge off some of this frustration. Dealing with Graham's reappearance during a months' long sexual drought is like going grocery shopping when you're hungry. You don't need all that food, and you end up making impulse purchases as a response to your immediate cravings rather than real life.

It takes me a long time to fall asleep. When I do, I dream of walking down the aisle of a grocery store, shoving Nutter Butters into my mouth from a ripped open package in my cart. At the cash register, a shirtless Graham scans and bags my purchases, but not before snatching a couple of Nutter Butters that he stuffs into his own mouth.

Calling Dr. Freud … WTF?

Graham

I make the now-familiar trek up Mackenzie's driveway and stop at her door. I retrieve the little roll of tape out of my back pocket and pull off a piece that I stick on the envelope clutched between my fingers. I've spent a ridiculous amount of time on my laptop at the local Starbucks this week, hours and hours of searching for the perfect quotes to give Mackenzie. Pretty words have never been my skill, so I'm hoping to get through to her with the help of better minds who've written about love.

Right as I've taped my note to the door, it swings open. I jump back to avoid being hit and come face-to-face with Mackenzie.

"I didn't think you were home," I say. Because apparently, I'm only capable of terrible opening lines with this girl.

She rips the envelope off the door and throws it at me. Then her other hand appears clutching a pile of papers that must be my other notes and shoves them at my chest with so much force it would have sent a smaller man onto his ass.

"No more, Graham. Take them all!"

I grip the now crumpled papers with both hands, searching her face to figure out what's on her mind. She looks pissed, but I can't figure out why.

"I was trying to tell you how I feel."

"By stealing quotes from a teenage girl's Pinterest board?"

Ouch.

"Babe, I don't do Pinterest," I quip, going for humor to mask that she's inflicted a wound.

"Graham, I'm serious. This is ... aren't you tired of this?" She *seems* tired all of a sudden, her body slouched and her face filled with sadness.

"I'm not tired of you, Mackenzie," I say softly. "I've waited five years for the chance to make things right. I've learned patience. I'm not good at this, I know that, but I'm trying."

I hold up the depressing pile of paper.

"Since you weren't ready to talk to me, I thought I'd write. I chose the most romantic words I could find."

"I don't want their words!" she yells, back to being pissed off. "Don't you get it? A million words from love poems couldn't tell me what I need to hear. I want *your* words, Graham. That's all I've ever wanted."

Her voice breaks a little, dying off at the end, and for a second, I think she's going to cry.

"I can do that," I agree quickly. "I'll tell you whatever you want to know. Just give me one chance. Dinner, tonight?"

"I can't tonight. I have plans."

"With the scarecrow?" The mere thought of him makes my hackles rise.

"His name is Jim, and you need to cut it out with the names. You don't even know him."

I shove the papers into my back pocket and take a couple of steps toward her, until I'm close enough to breathe in the fresh scent of her shampoo.

"Is it serious?" I ask.

"It could be." She takes a step backward as I advance further.

"Are you sleeping with him?"

Her back hits the wall of the house, and I stop inches away, taking in every detail of her that I can while I'm this close. Her hair shines with a million shades of red, orange, and gold in the afternoon sunlight.

"And what if I am?" she asks, eyes glinting with a feisty spark.

I growl and put my hands on the wall on either side of her head, so I'm bracketing her in with my arms. Her chest rises and falls rapidly with her increasingly shallow breaths, but her face never loses that fire.

I lean in, towering over her as I cage her in between my body and the wall.

"Are you sleeping with him?"

My voice has an edge to it, a roughness that I've never used with her—it's the tone I used in prison to intimidate any man who tried to mess with me. Her eyes go wide at the note of authority, but she recovers quickly, lifting her chin defiantly.

"I may just sleep with him tonight."

My reaction is uncontrollable, primal. I growl again, channeling the animalistic urges stirring with me. I drop my head lower until my lips are brushing the outer shell of her ear. I hear her quick intake of breath as I briefly scrape the scruff on my jaw against that sensitive skin right below her earlobe. Then I speak in a low, dangerous rumble.

"You go ahead and try to prove something to yourself, Kenz. And when Slim puts his hands on you, when you let him kiss you … you remember how it feels when it's right. You remember why you're *mine*."

My lips travel from her ear to her mouth, and before she can react to my words, I kiss her.

Mackenzie

This is why they call it chemistry. One second we are two stable elements, safe in equilibrium with inches separating us. In the next second, we collide, and the combination is immediately explosive.

We detonate.

At the first touch of his lips, I forget everything else as my body surges to meet his. There is no awkward repositioning or tentative exploration. Our mouths are not strangers becoming acquainted for the first time—they are puzzle pieces reconnecting, remembering exactly how to join and relieved to once again be complete.

My whole body is alive and coursing with desire. Every scrape of his facial hair across my skin sends chills of pleasure rolling through me. Everywhere our skin touches sparks with fire created by our chemical reaction. He tilts his head at the perfect angle that allows our mouths to fuse together as tightly as possible. Our tongues reconnect and explore so deeply, it's like we're trying to devour each other.

I can't get close enough—my hands fist in his shirt to pull him closer, but he is already flush against me. I feel him hard against my stomach and it adds fuel to my frenzy. His hands grip my waist, his fingers landing where my hipbone meets my pelvis, making me crazy with the teasing proximity to my pulsing core. One hand slips beneath my sweater, and my skin chills for a moment as it's exposed to the frigid air before the explorations of his wide palm and probing fingers quickly set me back on fire.

I rise to the tips of my toes, wanting more, *more*. His massive hands grab my ass and squeeze. Without a single pause, we move together, never disconnecting our lips as he lifts me and I wrap my legs around his waist. I tunnel my fingers into his hair, tugging his face closer to mine now that we're level. I twist and tug, hard enough that it must be painful, but he groans with pleasure and thrusts his hips toward me. This position lines us up perfectly. I grind down on him in shameless, mindless need.

His fingers move to the front of my jeans in an instinctual effort to get rid of the layers separating us. The loosening at my waist as he undoes the button breaks through my lust-induced haze, and I suddenly resurface to reality. I wrench my mouth from his and grab his hand with one of mine to stop him from pulling down my zipper.

"Wait," I say.

My voice is barely louder than a breath, but he hears me. His eyes open to meet mine. I watch clarity return to him as he, too, remembers where we are. Outside my house in the middle of the day in clear view of the street. In the freezing weather of January, no less.

He gently sets me down so my feet are back on the ground but keeps his hands at my waist.

"Call him and cancel your date," he demands in that gruff alpha male tone he brought out earlier. It triggers my irritation enough to clear the rest of the fog from my brain.

I place both palms flat on his chest and push. I might as well be trying to move stone, but he follows my lead and takes a step away. I remain leaning heavily against the wall that has most likely left permanent imprints on my back. I take in deep gulps of air trying to regulate my breathing.

"I'm not going to do that," I tell him, quietly but firmly.

He frowns and looks like he wants to say something else, but then he just nods stiffly.

"Dinner tomorrow, then, and we'll talk."

"Coffee," I counter.

"Lunch."

I roll my eyes but give in, not wanting to continue this any further.

"You tell me where and when, and I'll be there." He digs in his back pocket, pulls out a pen and one of the crumpled notes I threw at him earlier, and writes something on it before handing it to me.

It's a phone number. Though different from the one I remember, nostalgia assaults me all over again at the sight of those digits in his familiar scrawl.

He takes one step forward, our bodies not all the way flush but close enough that his warm breath coasts across my face.

"And Kenz? Don't sleep with him."

Then he turns and walks away, driving off in his Range Rover while I'm still frozen against the wall.

What. The. Hell. Just. Happened?

09. LOW FAT YOGURT

Mackenzie

I twirl my little cocktail straw and watch as the ice cubes dance with a slice of lime. I got here early so I could do exactly this—grab a drink and sit at the bar by myself decompressing before Jim arrives.

I feel a little tipsy, and it has nothing to do with the half-empty gin and tonic in front of me. *That kiss.* It was more potent than a shot of tequila, and I still haven't regained my equilibrium. And similar to the aftermath of complete inebriation, horror over my actions has been slowly settling in. When he touched me, I basically lost my mind. All my noble proclamations of independence and strength went MIA. I climbed him like a tree and dry humped him right in front of my house, for goodness sake!

With that thought, I drain the last of my cocktail. I give the cute bartender a polite smile and head shake declining his offer for a new one. Graham has caused a serious increase in my alcohol intake, and all the extra sugar, liquid calories, and toxins I've been putting into my body lately are going to catch up with me soon. I promise myself I'll make it to an extra yoga class this weekend. And take a break from drinking … once I'm on the other side of all this daily drama and heartache.

Jim walks in and waves, spotting me immediately. My gaze travels down to his legs and gets stuck there. His pants are bright orange and covered in a pattern of giant emerald green palm leaves. They might be the most hideous things I've ever seen. When he's standing right in front of me, I'm forced to redirect my eyes to his face, though it's difficult to break free from the pants' hypnotic spell. He smiles widely and leans in to give me a quick kiss on the lips.

"Nice pants," I find myself saying. Then immediately berate myself. *Don't be a passive-aggressive bitch, Mackenzie!*

But if any hint of irony slips out in my tone, he doesn't hear it. His smile grows and for the next ten minutes, he tells me all about them in a narrative that doesn't pause as a hostess leads us to a table and continues even as we begin to peruse the menu. These pants are not his only pair. Apparently, he collects them. They are all "limited edition" designs from his favorite brand—he even pulls up photos on his phone to show me. I focus on keeping my face politely interested, even though the urge to cringe grows with every swipe of his finger. He's so proud of his collection, oblivious to anything but his enthusiasm for these dreadful pants (which cost $150 per pair!)

I give myself another internal slap. *Stop being so shallow! Who cares that he loves gaudy expensive pants? He's a good guy!*

After a while, my mind wanders of its own volition to the pants Graham had on today ... black jeans that were perfectly worn without being grungy, the fabric so soft when I slipped my hands around his waist to run them over his beautiful ass.

"You know what you want to eat?"

I blink back to the present to see Jim and our waiter staring at me as though they've been waiting a while. Blushing, I quickly order a burger with a salad and take gulps of my ice water, hoping to lower my body temperature.

The rest of the dinner is nice and easy. The pants are safely hidden under the table, where they can't pull me back under their spell, and I'm able to focus on Jim. Jim is also nice and easy. Talking with him is always painless, and he generously makes sure to turn things back around to me so he doesn't monopolize the conversation. He asks intelligent and interested questions about the research I'm doing on neuropsychology for my internship and tells me about the newest projects going on at his biotech firm.

It's boring.

I try to focus on all the things I like about him. Jim is an adult with a steady job. He has excellent table manners and is always respectful. He's good-looking, in a very safe way. Six feet tall, with an average build he maintains with twice-weekly workouts to combat the effects of sitting at a computer all day (he's explained this to me in detail). His eyes might be a little too close together, but they're a pretty color blue, and though his hair appears to have a pound of gel in it, it's styled in a trendy uppercut I'm sure he paid a stylist a lot of money to choose for him.

With each thought, my mind rebels, summoning contrasting images of Graham.

... his defined pecs and abs ...

... his perfect hazel eyes ...

... the way his hair looked pulled back in that little bun...

Stop thinking about him, you hussy! You're on a date with Jim right now.

Fortunately, Jim is in the middle of explaining something engineer-y that I don't understand anyway—I just nod and smile, and he never notices my mind has left the building again.

When he invites me back to his place in the Back Bay for another drink, I accept. I usually wouldn't; it's too early in my dating timeline, but I desperately need to prove to myself that lust is not a commodity exclusively owned by Graham Wyatt. At the very least, I need to overwrite Graham's name in my internal records under the heading "Last Guy I Kissed."

❊   ❊   ❊

My eyes sting with tears that blur the passing lights so they become nothing but amorphous stars. I blink them away before they can leave evidence on my face and continue focusing my gaze outside the cab's window. A heavy cloak of disappointment surrounds me, weighing me down. Not disappointment in Jim—he was a consummate gentleman when I made my hasty excuses and left his apartment. No, I am the monster in this scenario, because in a day or so I'll have to call and to tell him we're done.

Every second we kissed, I couldn't turn off my awareness of how different it felt from earlier when I was with Graham. As unsatisfying as trying to curb a craving for Häagen-Dazs ice cream with low fat yogurt. And I hated myself for even making that comparison, for thinking about someone else while kissing Jim. For being stuck in my mind at all, unable to relax and be in the moment with him. Jim was so into it, his hands running over my body eagerly, whispering sweet words about how sexy I am and how much he likes me.

And I felt ... nothing. Nothing as he ran his hands underneath my shirt and cupped my breasts over my bra. Nothing as he kissed my neck in a spot where I'm usually extremely sensitive. Nothing as I desperately twined my tongue with his in an attempt to awaken my lust. Every glimpse of those pants was a shot of kryptonite to my already anemic libido. I couldn't even take his hard-on seriously encased inside those things. But I didn't want him to take them off, even to get them out of my sight.

I burn with shame for being so superficial. But more than anything, I seethe with fury toward Graham. He got inside my head on purpose and like a tragic cliché, I fell right into his trap. So much for my delusions of enlightened modern womanhood.

I focus on that external anger to avoid the overwhelming thoughts about my internal failings.

And I *am* angry at Graham. So, so angry.

Angry at him for showing up out of the blue and turning my world upside down.

Angry at him for reminding me how real passion feels.

Angry at him because he was able to reduce me into a puddle of lust with no effort at all.

Angry at him for bringing back all the chaotic emotions from five years ago I thought I'd moved past.

Angry at him for being annoyingly persistent when I've asked him to go away.

Angry at him because in my innermost self I don't want him to go away.

In the big scheme of things, Jim isn't that important. In fifty years, I'm sure I won't even remember him. But it's the undermining of what Jim represents—my pragmatic rules for dating, my vow of independence, my search for someone safe who will never hurt me like Graham did—that really has me shaken. I've grown strong over the past few years on a foundation rooted in those principles. What other critical flaws exist in the structure if its foundation is defective?

✻　✻　✻

This time, I see Graham immediately—he's once again waiting on the steps of my front porch. He's sitting directly beneath the hanging light, centered within its glow almost theatrically.

"How was the date?"

The flames of my anger climb higher, fueled by the presence of their designated target.

"How do you think?" I snap.

"Well, it's almost midnight and you're just getting home, so I don't know. You tell me."

There's a rough edge to his voice. As though *he* has any right to be pissed at *me* about this situation.

"Seriously, you might as well write the restraining order paperwork for me! What are you even doing here, *at almost midnight?*" I mock his words. "Shouldn't you be at your house instead of lurking outside of mine?"

"It's hard being there," he says in a different tone of voice. The strength and confidence of a moment ago are now absent. "All of those empty rooms, full of reminders ..."

My rage cools a few degrees as I'm hit by the raw, honest sorrow in his face. I hadn't considered what it would be like for him going back to the house where he spent a happy childhood with his parents.

"How was Jimmy Boy?" he repeats in an obvious attempt to move away from those deep waters.

"You got what you wanted—you messed with my head and ruined my date. Happy now?"

I wish I could say I throw these words at him with ferocity, but they come out lacking any bite. I'm so very tired. Seeing him human and lonely somehow makes this all even harder.

"So, you didn't fuck him?"

I see red all over again.

"That's not any of your business."

He unfolds his legs and stands to his full height. For a second, he is nothing but a dark silhouette backlit by the porch's single bulb; then he's right in front of me where I can see every nuance of his stupidly handsome face.

"Seeing as I plan to be the only guy you ever fuck again, I'd say it damn well is my business."

Oh. *Well.*

I shake off the momentary stupor.

"Go home, Graham."

"Wait! You didn't send a time and place for lunch tomorrow."

"I'm not sure that's a good idea ..."

"Please, Kenz. Give me fifteen minutes. We'll do coffee! I just want to talk."

I press my fingertips against my forehead, where all of today's emotions have coalesced into the beginnings of a headache. His ping-ponging between infuriating alpha male and vulnerable boy is tearing at my sanity.

"Fine. There's a coffee shop on campus. Meet me there at 1:00 PM after my last class."

"Thank you," he says.

I walk through the door and lock it behind me without saying anything else. I am worn too thin by this day, this whole week, to handle another second of his earnest face or his tender voice. I might do something idiotic, like invite him inside so he doesn't have to go back to that house alone.

10. 1:02 PM

Graham

By the time Mackenzie walks through the coffee shop door at 1:02 PM, I'm about ready to jump out of my skin.

I've been here for an hour and a half because I was too on edge to wait, and I still don't have anything else to do with my time. (My resume is going to be stellar ... short and sweet, a line for "MA State Prison Inmate, Accessory to Murder" followed by "Mackenzie Thatcher's Stalker." Who *wouldn't* hire me?)

I barely slept last night, or any of the nights prior for that matter, so at this point I'm hoping to absorb the shop's coffee-infused air particles directly into my pores. I've also already had two Americanos, so I'm shaking slightly as sleep deprivation and caffeine wage war using my body as their battlefield.

Mackenzie starts drifting toward the line to order, but I wave her over to my corner table instead. Before she can say anything or even take off her coat, I hand over the still hot skinny vanilla latte I ordered her a few minutes ago. Maybe I can avoid making an ass out of myself with another horrible opening line by not saying anything?

"Oh!" she breathes out in surprise as she accepts the drink. "Thank you."

She tries to be surreptitious about sniffing at the lid's opening. I can see the minute she realizes I've ordered her favorite drink when her eyes widen in pleased surprise. I'm grateful she doesn't ask me about it, though. Because, really, how many times can a guy be expected to cop to his creepy stalker behavior in one week?

No, this wasn't her favorite when we were in high school.

Yes, I know her coffee order because I've been watching her.

No, I'm not fucking sorry.

She takes a small sip before placing the cup on the table so she can peel off her coat. Underneath she's wearing a pink-ish turtleneck in a soft-looking fabric that clings to her curves and simple gray slacks. It's the world's least slutty strip show, but hell if I'm not half hard. If she thought that turtleneck would keep my mind off all the filthy and delicious things I want to do to her body, she was dead wrong.

Her hair is tied back in a loose bun that hangs low near the nape of her neck, and there are various loose strands around her ears and temple that have managed to liberate themselves from the hair tie. I'll always prefer her hair down and wild, but I do appreciate having an unobstructed view of her face when it's pulled back this way.

She seems anxious and kind of sad. One of the many things I've noticed during my weeks observing her is that she's a lot more serious than she used to be. There's a certain air of levity and mischief now missing from her demeanor, replaced by a layer of *'don't mess with me or I'll stick my four-inch heel up your ass.'* And the badass babe vibe is sexy as hell, don't get me wrong, but I mourn the loss of the girl who was always laughing and made every day seem like a fun, new adventure.

"Hi, Graham," she says softly when she's finally finished getting her coat and bag situated and taken her seat across from me.

Her eyes are completely void of yesterday's wrath, the way she looked ready to breathe fire and scorch me down to a pile of ash. Now, she looks tired. Did she lie awake last night too, replaying that un-fucking-believable kiss and buzzing with nerves about today?

"Hi, Mackenzie."

Her hands—so graceful, delicate and pale—wrap around the paper coffee cup. She breathes in a deep inhale and exhales it out, and I find myself following along the way I did in her yoga class.

Her eyes rise and lock on to mine.

"What did you want to talk about?"

Um ... everything? Why don't you start at the minute I last saw you and catch me up on the five years I missed?

I've wanted the chance to talk to her for longer than I can remember, but now that it's here I'm awkward as hell. The weight of the moment is nearly paralyzing.

"I, uh, actually thought you might have some questions for me?"

"I did. I do. It seems like I have millions, but I can't seem to think of a single one. I'm sorry ... this feels a little crazy, right?"

I smile. She always did have the gift of verbalizing things I felt but couldn't say.

"It really is." I shake my head then reach up to cup the back of my neck for a second as I think. "I'll start then ... how are Cheryl and Mike?"

I see her whole body relax slightly at the safe subject of her parents.

"They're good. Dad joined a rec league for basketball; he tries to make fun of the whole thing by calling it the 'old dudes' team,' but he secretly loves it."

I laugh lightly.

"I can totally see that. I bet Mike runs circles around the other old guys."

"Oh, he does. Mom says it's like he's getting to relive the glory days, being the team captain and MVP or whatever."

"And Petey?" I loved that Border collie. He never got tired of chasing a ball, and I was his favorite person because of my killer throwing arm.

"He died a few years ago, actually."

"Damn, I'm sorry."

She shrugs, and though I can see a little sadness I can tell she's made her peace with it.

"He had a great dog life. I guess it was his time. It's the hardest on Mom; she's been talking about getting a new puppy soon. Every time I'm home, she and Dad argue about it."

"You should just get her one for Christmas—the second he sees that thing he'll be obsessed and forget why he was against it."

Her mouth curves into a small but genuine smile.

"I might just do that."

We talk for over an hour, staying clear of the heavy stuff. She tells me fun stories about her undergraduate escapades with her roommate Marisa, and I ask questions about what she's studying (I may have done my homework by reading a few articles online so I wouldn't sound like an idiot). She updates me on her older brother Barrett (who is thankfully deployed overseas—I'm sure he wants to cut my balls off for hurting his baby sister). We talk about the Patriots, and freakish new potato chip flavors, and how Grey's Anatomy is inexplicably still on the air (she used to love that show, but tells me she stopped watching after they killed off some of her favorite characters).

We sink into an easy exchange and it's fun, comfortable, *right*. The same way that kiss yesterday felt—as though we've been apart days rather than years.

All the ways we fit before are still there, the most important pieces that connected us unchanged. Now I have to make her see it too, and then convince her to give me—us—another chance.

Mackenzie

We stick to safe topics, and for a while I give in to the comfortable familiarity, pretending I'm simply getting coffee and chatting with my best friend. Because now I'm forced to remember that's what he used to be—not only my boyfriend but my best friend too. I think I blocked that out of my mind, as I did so many other things from back then, because it made the loss more bearable.

I'm in the middle of a story from undergrad when the bubble of suspended reality suddenly pops and a wave of sadness hits me.

"We were supposed to do all of it together."

That summer we'd looked at colleges together, prioritizing the ones that had shown interest in recruiting Graham for their football teams. We came up with a list, and in the fall we planned to apply to all the same schools. We didn't have a clue that Graham's parents would die not two weeks into our senior year and normal high school things like Homecoming and college applications would fade into the background.

Graham doesn't say anything, but I can see in his eyes that he's on the same page, that he, too, mourns what could have been.

The mood is solemn now, and I'm finally ready to move on to the reason we're technically here. I remember all the things I've wanted to ask now that we're past that terrifying initial intensity. But in this moment, there's only one thing that I truly need to know, the question I need answered more than I've needed anything in my entire life.

"Did you do it?" I ask quietly, my eyes locked directly onto his. "Did you kill that boy, Graham?"

In the single heartbeat between my last word and his reply, everything stills. The very air around us is strung taut in anticipation. I am suspended in the rare awareness that this will be a critical moment in both of our lives.

"No."

It's only one word, but the conviction of his voice and the raw honesty in his eyes says so much more. *I believe him.*

This new truth slams into me immediately and forcefully. It strikes a place deep inside me with the impact of a missile hit, and a wall crumbles.

I don't even have enough warning to excuse myself and get up from the table. The physical reaction is instantaneous and irrepressible.

I burst into tears.

Big, loud, ugly sobs erupt out of me from the place they've been locked away for over five years. A dam inside me, one that held back more emotion than I even realized, has collapsed and I am swept away by the ensuing deluge.

I can't get myself under control, can't speak, can barely breathe. I rush to my feet and out of the building as quickly as possible, away from the eyes and ears of the coffee shop's other patrons who have undoubtedly noticed my hysteria.

Graham

I'm … fucking confused. I thought she'd be happy I'm not a murderer. The way she's crying is so intense, I stop for a second and think back to make sure I didn't accidentally say I'm guilty.

Nope. I'm positive I told her I did not kill that kid.

Before I have a chance to get over my shock at her reaction, she stands up from her chair and bolts out the door. That wakes me up. I quickly gather her stuff, throw our empty cups away, and go after her.

It's fucking freezing outside, and I curse under my breath as I think about her out in this without her coat. I'm already half frozen because in my effort not to waste any time, I just grabbed my coat and carried it along with hers. Luckily, she didn't go far. I find her against the back of the building, bent over nearly double as her body shakes with the force of her sobs. I reach her in a couple of strides.

"Go away!" she wails, hands coming up to cover her face.

"Not happening."

I drape her coat over her shoulders then gather her into my arms.

"What is it? What's wrong?" I ask as she cries into my chest.

"It's … I can't …" She breaks down without completing the thought.

I guess I don't need to understand why she's crying, not right now. All that matters is my girl is upset, and for the first time in years, I'm right where I'm supposed to be. Here to support her.

"Shh, baby. It's gonna be alright." I hold her and try to sound soothing.

Minutes pass as she keeps crying in my arms. When she shows no signs of stopping, it occurs to me that we might freeze to death if I try to wait it out until she settles down. My balls are icicles, and I'm seriously hoping there wasn't a real-life scenario that inspired the phrase "freezing my balls off." I need to get us both out of the cold now.

"It's too cold out here, Kenz. Let's go inside."

"Not y-yet." She leans further into me.

"Baby, I'll hold you as long as you want. I'll hold you for-fucking-ever. Just let me get you someplace warm first."

As though reluctantly, she nods against my chest and steps out of my hold. Before we can walk anywhere, her eyes zero in on my thin thermal shirt.

"You're not wearing a coat."

I hold up the black lump of fabric still draped over one of my arms.

"GRAHAM! PUT YOUR COAT ON!"

When a woman orders you to do something while bawling her eyes out, you do the damn thing. I suppose I'm lucky she didn't tell me to jump off a bridge or wear a tutu, because at the moment I'd do anything if it had a chance of calming her down.

"Where's your car?" I ask once I've pulled the zipper up to my chin.

"Why?"

"I'm gonna drive you home. You're done with classes for the day, right?"

She nods and points toward another building on campus.

"In a parking lot over there."

I wrap one arm around her back and we walk together, neither of us talking. The only sound is her crying, which has now died down to quiet sniffling.

We reach the car, and she hands over her keys. She doesn't argue about me driving but simply folds herself into the passenger seat, seeming to be in a daze.

I start the engine and turn the heat up then look over at her before pulling out of the parking spot. I run my eyes over her puffy waterlogged face. Still so damn beautiful.

"You did hear me, right? When I said I'm *not* a murderer?"

She lets out a little sound that's half sob, half laugh.

"Yes."

"And you're … disappointed?" I prod.

She laughs a little harder this time and shakes her head.

"Of course not. I'm so *relieved!* I'm sorry, I don't know why I can't stop crying!"

I bite back a smile at how cute her tearful frustration is.

"It's okay, babe. Just relax and let's get you home."

11. JUST FOUR WORDS ... BABE

Graham

We stay quiet the whole drive to her house. When she unlocks the front door she waits, silently holding it open in invitation.

We take off our boots and coats, and she sits down on the big plushy couch almost immediately, pulling a giant throw blanket over herself (she has to be tired after all that crying). I remain standing in the middle of the room, looking around.

I wasn't sure I'd ever see the inside of this place. It fits her perfectly, matching her sophisticated academic side with just a touch of the edgier vibe she's developed in the past five years. The space is bright with white walls (or cream or something) and colorful artwork hanging all over. There are plants everywhere and shelves with books ... tons and tons of books everywhere, even on the coffee table. The living room is a big open space right next to the kitchen, with only a counter and some stools separating them from each other. The couch is tan, and it has a bunch of mismatched pillows and throw blankets all over it. I smirk when I see one pillow has a design on the front showing the outline of a hand holding up its middle finger. All peach and white and girly and then ... badass. Yep. One hundred percent Mackenzie.

After I've done my visual sweep, I make my way over to the couch. She pats the space next to her, so I sit down.

And immediately face an onslaught of her little hands slapping me over and over—on my face, my chest, my shoulders—not hard enough to genuinely hurt, but not exactly soft either.

"The fuck, Kenz?" I grunt, trying to shield myself.

"You let me think you were a murderer all this time?!" she shrieks.

"I mean, I wasn't sure that's what you thought …"

"But you knew it was a possibility! Four words, Graham. In five years, you couldn't even write and give me that? Four. Freaking. Words."

She's stopped slapping at me, and now we're on opposite sides of the couch with our bodies turned to face each other. She isn't crying anymore, but her face is flushed with frustration and the exertion of the attack she just waged against me.

"*I – didn't – kill – him,*" she says, counting the words out on her outstretched fingers for emphasis. "*I'm – not – a – murderer.*"

I drag my palm over my face and up through my hair. Well, when she puts it like *that,* I do kind of feel like an asshole.

"*Not guilty of murder.*"

The smallest quirk appears at the corner of one side of her lips. She's still serious about this, but she's also clearly dragging it out to fuck with me.

"*Did not commit homicide,*" she continues sassily. "*Death not my fault.*"

I find myself on the verge of a smile too.

"*Gun not mine … babe.*" We both laugh at my lame attempt.

I stare at her even more intently and decide to keep going.

"Wrong place, wrong time."

"Just there to buy drugs." Then I curse. "Fuck, that's five words."

But Mackenzie doesn't laugh or give me grief for breaking the rules. Her blue-green eyes are a million miles deep, an ocean of sadness.

"Why?" The single syllable is filled with heartbreak. I know she doesn't only mean that night—she's asking why I did any of it, *all of it.*

"I wish I had a good answer for you—I was an idiot, Kenz. I was fucked up. I was drowning, and I chose a shitty way to escape."

"Why didn't you tell me?"

Thinking, I run a palm over the scruff on one side of my jaw, back and forth as the stubble abrades my skin like sandpaper. I decide to take the conversation on a little detour so I have more time to formulate my answer.

"Is that what the, uh ..."

I wave my hand in the general direction of her tear-ravaged face, which is red and swollen.

"Crying fit?" she fills in with a tiny self-deprecating laugh.

"Yeah. Was that about me not telling you?"

"It was ... everything," she says softly. "I've spent a lot of time not thinking about it, and when you told me you didn't do it, I guess it all came back at once."

"I'm sorry. I'm so fucking sorry."

"Are you okay now?" she asks, searching my eyes like she can do a psychic drug test.

I open my mouth to answer but don't get a chance because the front door bangs open and her roommate enters. She's calling out loudly from the second the door is open.

"Okay, chica! Tell me all about coffee with Señor McFuckHot. Do I need to start baking brownies, take a baseball bat to his *cojones*, or should we pop a bottle of wine so you can tell me all the explicit details about how he fucked you into next Tuesday in the coffee shop bathroom?"

She yells all of this while bustling around, hanging up her coat and putting away some things from a paper grocery bag.

When she stops talking, she finally notices us on the couch.

"Oh," she says. She doesn't seem embarrassed in the slightest that I overheard—she simply pops one hip out, throws a hand on it, and eyes me up and down.

"Nice to meet you, Señor McF."

"Hey. Name's Graham. Please don't attack my *cojones*."

"Marisa. And that depends why my girl's face looks like she's been crying for a week."

Mackenzie makes a little sound of horror at the mention of her face, and her hands shoot up to try and hide the evidence, even though we've both already seen it.

"I'll get you some ice and cucumbers," Marisa reassures her in a softer tone before zeroing back in on me.

"So … did you make her cry? She's one tough bitch. I've never seen her cry enough to look like *that*." She throws a hand out, dramatically pointing to Mackenzie's face, making her cringe in embarrassment once more. "Sorry, honey. So, what did you do?"

"Uh ... I told her I'm not a murderer?" It comes out as a question because, shit, I still don't completely understand her reaction. I'm not complaining about the result, though, because it got me here—and having her in my arms, even crying, is the best thing that's happened to me in a long goddamn time.

Marisa blinks, shocked enough that the attitude subsides for a second. She turns to Mackenzie.

"YOU THOUGHT HE WAS A MURDERER?! And you *HAD COFFEE WITH HIM?!"* She's shouting again.

Mackenzie shoots me a dirty look.

I mean, how was I supposed to know that was classified info? It's not exactly a secret—she could learn all about me within two seconds on Google.

"Well, I'm *not* a murderer, so ..."

She ignores me completely and speaks to Kenz.

"Should I go stay with my sister so you guys can have a reunion fuckfest?"

My girl blushes up to the roots of her hair. I can't help but chuckle.

"We're not there ... yet," I tell Marisa. "I've got more groveling to do."

Mackenzie

I use Marisa's arrival as an excuse to send Graham home. We have a lot more we need to talk about, but now that I'm on the other end of my massive emotional release—or "crying for weeks" as Marisa put it—I'm drained and my head is pounding.

I'm also a little embarrassed at how I melted into Graham like a puddle of needy, weepy woman. Marisa wasn't lying—I *do* have my shit together most of the time. It's likely been five years since I last cried that much.

"You're really okay?" Marisa asks me when Graham leaves.

"Yeah. It's a lot to process."

"Seems you told me the abridged version of this story." She raises one eyebrow at me, her expression demanding answers.

Although she's trying to cover it with some attitude, I can see that underneath she's a little hurt. Guilt rises within me, because Marisa's an amazing friend, and I trust her more than almost anyone. This is just something that's especially hard for me to open up about.

"I'm sorry, Ris."

Instead of responding, she hands me a bag of ice and a small plate of sliced cucumbers.

"So, no sex?" There's a hopeful note in her voice. *Shameless* ... she's still fishing for dirty details!

"No!" I toss one of the throw pillows at her, laughing. "Go have your own sex, bitch!"

"Oh, I do." She smacks her lips at me in an obnoxiously loud air kiss before disappearing down the hall toward her room.

I shuffle over to mine as well so I can take Advil and do some cosmetic damage control with these cucumbers.

Graham

I've got a shit-eating grin stretched across my face as I call an Uber to take me back to BC for my car. I'm still grinning on the drive back to Westwood and all through my impromptu grocery store stop. So yeah, obviously instead of buying cereal right now I'd rather be having that "reunion fuckfest" Marisa mentioned, but we're not there yet. Still, I'd say we made a ton of progress today. Though she may have kicked me out shortly after her roommate got home, I got Mackenzie to agree to have dinner with me later this week, so the day is a huge win.

As I step out of the store into the frigid wind, I hunch my shoulders and pull up the collar of my coat. I've just reached my car when right ahead of me three large shapes step out of the shadows.

"Long time no see, Wyatt."

Before I can even react, he launches a fist directly at my face.

12. SUCKER PUNCH

Graham

That motherfucker just sucker punched me. In a Star Market parking lot.

I won't let him get that lucky again. I see him coming now, so when he swings a second time I duck and throw a return punch before he can dodge it. My fist catches him in the side of the jaw, and he takes a step back to recoup.

Before I went to prison, I'd never thrown a punch. But I was far from defenseless, since I'd been through tackling and dodging drills during all the years I trained for football. Football also taught me how to take a hit. While I was locked up, I kept my head down as much as I could and never started a fight, but I sure as hell proved that I could finish one.

"What the hell is this?" My voice isn't friendly. At all.

I get my first good look at the guys. Despite this parking lot's shitty lighting, I recognize the owner of the fist that just decked me in the forehead. Back when I was buying drugs, I primarily interacted with a guy named Curtis, who was in charge of their little organization, but I remember seeing this kid a few times. Eli. I think he was related to Curtis somehow—Cousin? Brother? The details are hazy.

"This is a warning."

He punctuates his statement by spitting a glob of blood onto the pavement at his feet. I socked him hard, and I imagine his teeth cut up the inside of his cheek pretty good. I've been there. But I can't seem to find a drop of sympathy for him.

"That mean you're gonna start talking?"

He shrugs and smirks at me, cocky as hell even though one side of his mouth is already swelling. There's an overall sense of confidence to him now—in his steady, wide-legged stance, the edge of arrogance in his voice—that's new. The few memories I can conjure of him are of a skinny kid always hanging out in Curtis' shadow. Physically he's still far from intimidating—a greasy looking white guy with limp brown hair hanging past his chin. And still skinny—he's probably half my weight, even though I've only got a couple of inches on him in height. But he clearly thinks he's big shit now, and from their body language, I can tell the other guys are looking to him for their cues. Seems little Eli stepped up when the boss man and I went to prison. It's almost cute, how he wants to show off by fucking with me.

There's something else about him, though. Something that I can't quite put my finger on, a disturbing glint of intellect and madness in his unnaturally pale eyes. My gut, which is rarely wrong, is telling me not to underestimate him.

"You know all about talking, huh? I'm gonna make you eat that smart-ass tongue, Wyatt."

In high school we had to read that book *Life of Pi*, the one where a kid is stuck in a boat with a tiger (really ... nuts!). Can't say I loved it, but I've never forgotten the part where the boy manages to establish his dominance as the alpha—he proves he can make the loudest noise, and the tiger backs down from trying to attack him. That was my strategy in prison—if a guy wanted to show me how loud he was, I made sure I roared louder. Once I did that a few times, things got easier for me.

"I'm flattered you brought two guys for back up, E. But you should have brought three."

In a single motion so swift it catches him off guard, I slam Eli against the side of my SUV with a forearm to his chest. Primal satisfaction surges inside me at the fear that flickers in his eyes. *That's right, motherfucker, you're messing with the wrong guy.*

I've got my arm inches from his windpipe, and I apply some more pressure. I lean in closer to growl right in his face.

"You and me? We're done here. So you need to take your 'warning' and your little friends and get the fuck out of my sight. Permanently."

Click.

It's a sound I've only heard in person once before, but could never mistake—the cocking of a trigger. In my peripheral vision, I see that while I was focused on Eli one of his guys stepped right up to me. And he now has a gun pressed between my ribs.

Eli smirks, and for a second he flashes some teeth that show signs of rotting. At least Curtis was a professional—he knew not to sample too much of his product. This bastard looks like he eats meth for breakfast.

"You happen to be armed, Wyatt? Cause from where I stand, you're outnumbered and outgunned. For your own sake, back the fuck off me."

I step back even though what I really want is to smash my fist into his face again.

He cricks his neck side to side, trying to play off how much that must have hurt. Then he pins me with those icy blue eyes.

"My brother sends his regards from prison. You know, the place you made sure he'll be for the rest of his life?" *Brother*. "You should have kept your mouth shut. You think you can narc and get away with it?"

Well, fuck.

A couple years into doing my time, and a shit-ton of therapy sessions with the prison shrink, I gave in to her convincing and finally called a lawyer. I didn't bother back when I was arrested—I plead guilty to whatever they charged me with and just went along with it. Maybe I'd been punishing myself all along anyway, and to some degree it was a relief to hand the reins over to someone else and let them do the work.

After two years of grief counseling and a 24/7 diet of inescapable retrospection, I was fully aware that I'd been a fucking idiot. Honestly, my role in things that night looked a hell of a lot worse than it actually was, and one of my dad's fancy expensive-as-fuck lawyer friends could have easily brought my charges down to drug possession.

So, with the aid and counsel of my newly hired fancy expensive-as-fuck lawyer, I made a deal for a reduced sentence in exchange for informing on Curtis. I told the state prosecutor everything I remembered from my various interactions with Curtis and other members of his organization, including a detailed account of *that night*. They said my testimony was a crucial piece in putting Curtis away for life.

Did I believe them when they assured me no one would ever find out that information had come from me? Well, yeah, I did. Apparently, I am still a fucking idiot.

The gun's barrel presses harder into my side so I can feel it through my jacket. The pressure is forceful enough to hurt a little bit and more than enough to ensure I don't forget that any second I could have a bullet in my gut.

It's a solid intimidation tactic that would work on most people. People who have something important enough in their lives to make them give a damn about dying. Me? I've got nothing to lose. Except Mackenzie ... but, hell, she's probably better off without me.

I meet Eli's eyes dead-on and speak clearly and calmly.

"I repeat ... you and I have nothing to talk about. So have your goon pull the trigger or leave."

We engage in a silent stare off that seems endless. I sure as hell won't be the one backing down, so I keep my face blank and my eyes defiant.

Finally, he makes a little *tsk*-ing sound with his tongue then motions for his man to drop the gun and back away.

"Like I said, tonight is a warning. It was just a lucky accident that we were in the neighborhood and spotted you. And decided to say hello."

His eyes travel up to the tall light poles scattered around the parking lot, and I see that some have small cameras attached to them.

"I'm smarter than Curtis. When I end you, it won't be with a clean shot in a parking lot with witnesses and surveillance cameras."

I manage to hold back the flinch that wants to roll through me as my mind flashes back to that gas station parking lot and the image forever seared into my mind of the moment the bullet made impact with that guy's head.

Something sinister passes over Eli's face as he gets even closer, till our noses are inches from touching. I stay still even as his whispered words send droplets of spittle landing on my cheek.

"And, Wyatt? I *will* end you. I'm going to make sure you pay for fucking with my family. I'm more creative than Curtis too. I can draw things out, make sure you know exactly what's happening as you die. They'll never catch me, and no one will ever find your body."

13. GRIFF

Graham

Frustrated, I run a hand through my hair then pull it back from my temple and lean toward the bathroom mirror so I can examine the red swelling where Eli got in his one and only hit. It's not too bad, but I will definitely be wearing beanies the next couple of days until the bruising fades.

Fuck. I'm finally getting somewhere with Mackenzie and this happens?

After pacing restlessly for a while, replaying tonight's encounter, I decide it's time to reach out to my old cellmate Griff. I have no idea what to do here, and he's the first person who came to mind as someone I can trust with this. He got out a few years ago, but I don't have a way to reach him. We didn't exactly sign each other's yearbooks and exchange hugs and phone numbers before he left.

Are there still telephone books where you can look people up?

I blow out a breath and force myself to think. My eyes swing to the kitchen table and land on my silver MacBook. I've given that thing a workout recently, filling part of my nights Googling everything and anything to catch up on things I've missed the last five years. And, you know, porn.

Of course—*welcome back to the twenty-first century, idiot*—I'll check Facebook.

I've avoided the site (except when I searched for Mackenzie—her privacy settings are so high I could only see her profile picture—and yes, I have that shit saved to my desktop) because I don't particularly want to find out what all my old high school friends think about me. I bet my profile is covered with hateful comments from five years ago, maybe even more recently. When they're booking you for involvement in a homicide, they don't exactly ask if you want to shut down your social media accounts for privacy.

I pull up the site and stare at the home screen for a minute. Then instead of logging in, I click "Sign Up" and create a new profile with a different email address. I stick in a random picture of me I found on the laptop that's probably eight years old then stare at the blank page. If only it were this easy to make a clean slate for everything in my life.

I search for "Griff O'Brien" and find him within seconds. Seeing his face glaring at me from his profile pic sends a stab of something close to nostalgia through me.

Griff was my very first cellmate, which means he saw me at my lowest point. The state prison is not one of the cushy rehab facilities where stupid rich boys from Westwood usually go, but they had their own medical facilities and program in place to assist with detox. It's not like I was a junkie—I was only a few months into my relationship with drugs, and I'd been keeping things open bouncing between everything but heroin looking for a few hours of escape. So, while the detox wasn't fun physically, more than anything it fucked with my mind. Every speck of pain I'd been dulling rushed back in high-def color. Only now it was tinted with added layers of guilt and regret for the shit I'd done while high. Needless to say, I was a miserable son of a bitch for a while there, and Griff had a front-row seat to my breakdown. And for some reason he befriended me anyway.

Griff is huge, towering over me at a height of maybe 6'4" with a coarse mountain man worthy beard and a perpetual "don't-fuck-with-me" scowl. He was in for drug distribution and assault, and he'd more than earned his street cred with a criminal history going back to his early teens.

Griff is definitely not what you'd call a "good guy," but he's one of the best men I've ever known.

I peer closer at the Facebook photo and smile. He's towering over a slight woman and a child, both sheltered within his arms. The saddest thing is that right before the arrest that landed him in a cell with me, he was in the process of changing his ways. His girl was pregnant and they wanted to start a clean life for their kid. It was a big cosmic *fuck you* that he got busted right when he was taking the necessary steps to go straight.

His daughter must be almost six now. The three of them look happy, and that makes me think maybe the entire world isn't as terrible as I sometimes suspect.

I click to friend request him then type out a short message along with my phone number.

Hey Griff, I'm out. Let's catch up. Give me a call.

Then I go get some ice for my head. It's not that I can't handle the pain—I want to reduce the swelling so Mackenzie doesn't notice. It definitely feels like lying and reminds me of the shit I did before, but *I'm* not doing anything shady this time around. There's got to be a way I can get Eli to back off, right? If I can handle this quickly, there's no reason for Mackenzie to know, no reason to get her involved as I put this last little piece of that life to rest.

My phone rings in the morning while I'm on my third bowl of Lucky Charms. (They're magically delicious, okay?) I don't recognize the number, but since it's local I answer.

"Hello?"

"Pretty Boy? Is that really you?"

His low, gritty voice brings an immediate smile to my face. He gave me that nickname when I first went in because I looked every inch the overprivileged high school quarterback I was. I eventually fought back by calling him "Old Man," though he wasn't even thirty when we met.

If only he could see me now—he would be so proud of the bulk I've put on, not to mention the hair and beard growth.

"Yeah, Griff. It's me."

"Well, shit, kid. Welcome to the outside. What are you doing lookin' up my ugly mug online? Shouldn't you be screwing your way through Boston right now?"

"Not my style."

"Ahh, right. Your girl—Mackenzie, wasn't it? How is she?" I talked about her enough that I'm not surprised he remembers her name.

"She's ..." How to choose a word? "Perfect. Not exactly planning my welcome back party, though."

He chuckles, a deep sound that could only come from a man as mammoth as he is.

"Life ain't gonna throw roses at ya. I think you already learned that one the hard way. So, what's her deal? She got a ring on her finger? A live-in man? Kids?"

The very thought twists my insides. I pour the rest of my cereal down the sink.

"Nope."

"Well then, you do whatever you gotta do and get her back."

"That's the plan. Speaking of, I saw your profile pic. You've got one pretty girl there."

I grin ear to ear, waiting for it ...

He growls.

"Listen here, Wyatt. I don't want to hear you ever say another fucking word about my woman. You get me?"

"I was talking about your daughter, Griff."

"You little shit." He laughs big and long—a heartier laugh than I've ever heard from him. It's a great sound. It means he's happier on the outside, that things are working out for him.

"Hey, so, I actually have a bit of a situation I wanted to run by you. Think you could meet for lunch today?"

"What the fuck did you do? Don't tell me you're back to being a dipshit or I'll come out there and kick your pretty ass myself."

I laugh again—damn, but it's good having a reason to laugh. I also appreciate his unique way of caring about me.

"On the straight and narrow, I swear. And I want to stay that way, but I got a visit from some old friends yesterday who aren't on the same page."

"Got it. Yeah, well ... I'm still working this gig at the grocery store. I've got the ass-crack-of-dawn shift so I'll be off around 2:00 PM. Callin' you on my smoke break."

"Spending your break talking to me? Gosh, I'm blushing, Griff."

He curses at me good-naturedly.

"Text me the address and I'll be there."

* * *

We're sitting at a weathered picnic table outside the grocery store in Hyde Park. I've only ever visited this part of Boston to buy drugs, and I thought I was so tough back then. Now I don't find anything rough or intimidating about the area. One of the benefits of prison, I guess. Perspective.

"What do I do?" I ask Griff once I've finished giving him the rundown of last night.

He removes the cigarette from between beard framed lips. The beard is still impressive but more trimmed now, and I wonder if that's because his job made him do it … or his woman.

"Nothing," he replies with a shrug of his massive shoulders.

I stare at him uncomprehendingly.

"There's really nothing you can do that won't get you thrown back behind bars for breaking parole." His eyes fix meaningfully on the reddened knuckles of my right hand. "Once you're a con, there's no such thing as *innocent before proven guilty*, and no cop will ever buy it if you claim self-defense. So keep your head down, live your life, but watch your back. If those jokers come around again, the second you see them you dial 9-1-1. And—this part blows—suck it up and take a few hits if you have to, but don't let them catch you fighting back."

I nod. I'm not particularly jazzed about the idea of doing nothing but waiting, but he's probably right. It's the only thing I can do if I want to stay on the right side of the law.

"What else are you up to?" he asks after letting me mull things over in silence for a minute.

I rub a palm over my eyes, which are as dry and gritty as a desert. This newfound insomnia thing is kicking my ass.

"I honestly have no idea. All these years I obviously thought about getting out, but it seemed so far away, unreal almost, so I didn't think it through this far."

"What was the plan before your folks died?"

I shrug.

"I'd just turned eighteen. There wasn't much of a plan—graduate, go to school somewhere with Mackenzie, play college football, see if I had any shot at the NFL. Maybe spend the summers doing some internships and figuring out what I wanted to do. Now ... I have no idea. I should probably go back to school or something. But since I got out, I've been stuck in neutral. Everything seems upside down, you know? Like the whole world is a waking dream I'm stuck in—Mackenzie is the only thing that feels real."

Griff nods and flicks his cigarette butt into the overflowing garbage can at the end of our table.

"You got more options than most other people who've been where we have—lots of closed doors for people with a record can be opened with enough money. You and I know some good guys who are barely making it out here. Don't shit on all of us who don't have your luck by pissing it away. You're fighting for that second chance with Mackenzie—what are you gonna do with the second chance you already got for yourself?"

He pins me with those espresso eyes, so dark they're nearly black.

"You do what you gotta do to get your head straight and then get soul searching. Get your girl, but start doing something with your life, too. Love is fuel that keeps you going, but it's not a destination. Better figure out what road you're on or that fuel won't be worth shit."

I rub a hand over my eyes again because his words are striking me right in the feels. I don't want to risk getting eternal shit from him by tearing up and humiliating myself.

"Damn, Griff," I finally say. "You're a fountain of wisdom, Old Man. Shaina might have some competition from me if your dick is as good as your advice."

He mutters a curse and shoves a giant palm against my chest, not putting any force behind it but still making me sway backward a bit.

But the mention of Shaina puts a smile on his face I can see even through that beard.

"She's pregnant," he says.

"Congrats, man!" I reach over to briefly clap him on the shoulder, happier than I've been about anything in a long time.

"Thanks," he replies gruffly. Then his eyes cloud over with worry. His eyes stray to the rundown store behind us. "Been here years and the manager still acts like I stink of prison detergent. Might have to start knocking doors for something new if she won't give me more hours."

His words are quiet, almost as though he's talking to himself, but they get my feels going again. From what he's told me, the guy was basically upper management for an impressive criminal organization for almost a decade, but now that he's out of the criminal life he's stuck bagging groceries for minimum wage, worried over providing for a new baby. It's fucked up.

I'm filled with anger that's almost refreshing because for once in my sorry life it isn't about me and my problems.

We part after a brief man hug complete with back slaps—his paws are so big I'm going to check for bruises later. He says I should come over to meet his girls sometime soon, and I agree, actually looking forward to it. It's the first time in forever I've looked forward to anything that didn't involve Mackenzie.

On the drive home, my brain is churning. I would write Griff a massive check in a heartbeat, but I have no doubt he'd turn right around and shove it down my throat. He's too proud to take a hand out. But I've got a shit-ton of money and a road with no destination, and I suddenly want to do more with my life than not piss on Griff or the guys who don't have my opportunities. There's got to be something I can do to fill my empty road while spreading the wealth a little. I'm no businessman—I only have a GED and a partial Associate's degree I got through an online program through the prison—but maybe I can figure out a way to put all this money to use and finally do something that would make my father proud.

14. NOT A DATE

Mackenzie

GRAHAM: Dinner tonight

MACKENZIE: Is that a question?

GRAHAM: Mackenzie Elaine Thatcher, can I please take you to dinner tonight?

MACKENZIE: As friends

GRAHAM: As a date

MACKENZIE: I am free tonight and I'd like to see you, but we're still getting to know each other again. So I'll go to dinner AS FRIENDS

GRAHAM: Fine

GRAHAM: You come to dinner as a friend, and I'll be there dating the hell out of you. Pick you up at 7pm

MACKENZIE: Graham!

MACKENZIE: I'm serious about this

MACKENZIE: ??

MACKENZIE: Where are we going? What's the dress code?

GRAHAM: I'm taking you somewhere nice, but wear whatever you want. You're always gorgeous

I click out of Graham's text and immediately open a new message window.

MACKENZIE: SOS! Going to dinner with Graham tonight. Can you make it home at 5:30 to help me pick an outfit?

MARISA: I am so there.

※　※　※

"So, our goal is to make him jizz in his pants before you even order drinks, correct?"

I start choking on the sip of water I've just taken. I cough over and over and glare at her through watery eyes.

"Geez, Ris. Warn a girl when you're going to say that stuff! I almost did a spit take all over you."

Not that I'm surprised—Marisa's unique brand of colorful bluntness is one of the reasons I love her, after all.

She raises one perfectly plucked dark eyebrow.

"Well, isn't it?"

Is *that* the objective we should have in mind while choosing this outfit?

A slow smile creeps over my face.

"Hell yes."

She grins too, then exhales deeply, and cracks her neck side to side as though readying herself for a huge undertaking.

For the next hour, we dig through both of our (admittedly extensive) clothing collections. We butt heads frequently as we argue over possible outfits. The objections all fall into one of two categories:

Marisa: "Over my dead body! Now is not the time for classy subtlety—you've worked hard on that hot little yoga body and tonight we're going to show all of it off."

Me: "I can't wear this! I'm four inches taller than you—this dress is so short I might as well go to dinner in my thong since everyone will be seeing my ass anyway."

Finally, we agree on a middle ground.

We choose my black faux leather pencil skirt, one of my all-time favorite pieces of clothing. At first, Marisa argued it was too professional to be sexy and raised an eyebrow at the hem, which falls a couple of inches above my knees, but once she saw it on me she was sold. It fits me perfectly, molding to my backside and creating a sleek line that gives my legs an illusion of extra length, and the leather look makes it more badass than professorial. If I do say so myself, it does amazing things for my butt.

We pair it with a shirt I bought months ago that has since been stuck in the back of my closet because I've never found the right occasion for it. The sweater is a muted lavender color, made from thin stretchy cotton that clings to the front of my body in a flattering way. It has a boatneck and three-quarter length sleeves, and its cropped hem lands perfectly right above the waist of my skirt so that when I move the tiniest hint of skin shows. The best part, though, is that it's entirely backless. The fabric plunges dramatically starting at my shoulder blades.

Even I admit that on the surface this is a more conservative outfit than I'd imagined, but the reality of these two pieces together on my body is one of the sexiest things I've ever worn.

The problem with the shirt is that I can't wear a bra with it. I have a little more going on in the chest area than is ideal for going bra-less, but Marisa makes me try these little adhesive pads that will at least keep my nipples from showing through this thin fabric.

Of course, I pair the outfit with some fierce four-inch heels. If we're outside for any length of time, my bare legs will freeze, but I'm counting on a strict car-to-restaurant journey. I decide to wear my hair up so nothing will hinder the dramatic open back.

We even go as far as strategizing "the reveal." I pair the outfit with a coat that falls mid-thigh and plan to already have it on when he gets here so he won't get the full effect until I take the jacket off.

We are evil geniuses.

"It's not a date," I assert firmly as I stand before the mirror examining the final outfit. Even though Marisa doesn't say anything, I know she doesn't believe that any more than I do.

Nerves rush through me and my heart starts beating rapidly. I press my palm to my chest right above its pounding, as though if I hold on tightly enough, I'll be able to keep it safe.

"Hey," Marisa says softly, reading my mood shift. "Either it's a date and you're seducing him into your bed and your life and you guys will get married, or it's just about getting closure and making sure he knows exactly what he's lost. Either way, the off-the-charts sexy outfit is required. And be sure to shave *everywhere*."

✻　✻　✻

I've just started applying my makeup when my phone rings. Seeing "Mom" on the screen, I groan then reach over and put her on speaker.

"Hi, Mom."

I don't have time for this, but if I say I can't talk, then she'll just ask why. I don't want to lie to her, but I'm also not ready to tell my parents that Graham and I are—*What? Talking? Occasionally starring in amateur softcore porn for any voyeuristic neighbors I have? Sobbing my eyes out while he holds me and calls me baby?* —I still haven't figured out how I feel about any of it, so I definitely can't handle her opinion yet.

"Hi, sweetie!" her voice trills from the counter where I've perched my phone. "I haven't heard from you in a while, so I thought I'd call and check in."

I multi-task, lining and shadowing my eyes while telling her a few details about the research I'm doing with one of the tenured professors. She *hmm's* and *oh's* at appropriate times, but I can tell she's just humoring me.

My parents have never really understood my decision to get a higher degree. They're supportive, but in a placating way. Their attitude runs along the lines of: *"Oh, well, Mackenzie isn't quite ready to join the real world yet, so she's going to spend some more time in school."* It just doesn't resonate with them that my highly selective PhD track program is what most people consider the "real world."

I really love my parents, and I couldn't have survived that dark time after Graham's arrest without them, but we're not as close as we used to be. Sometimes I think they still see me as that same heartbroken seventeen-year-old they treated like a ticking time bomb wrapped in an adolescent body.

"How's your class?" I ask to get her talking.

Mom teaches second grade, and she begins regaling me with some recent stories about her students and school gossip.

I glance over at the clock—now I'm cutting it close. I have to finish my hair, and there's no way I can use my blow dryer while keeping up my end of this conversation convincingly. I cut in and apologetically wrap up the call with my mom, promising to check in soon.

For some reason, hearing Mom's voice has made me even more nervous about tonight. That same voice spent years disparaging Graham (or *"that boy"* as he became known in my house) and proclaiming I'm lucky to have gotten free when I did.

I'm still finishing my hair when I hear knocking at the front door.

"Shit! Ris, can you stall him for me?" I call out down the hall.

"On it!" she replies, and I hear her walking toward the front of our apartment as I shut the bathroom door behind me.

Only now does it hit me that I just threw Graham to the wolves.

Graham

Marisa opens their front door and lets me into the living room, but Mackenzie is nowhere in sight. My girl's feisty roommate props herself against the kitchen counter and crosses her arms while she stares me down. Suddenly I'm fifteen again, back in Westwood, picking Mackenzie up for our first date and enduring a nerve-racking ten minutes alone with her dad.

Mr. Thatcher is ex-military and seriously intimidating, but if I'm being honest I'd take him any day over Marisa. This girl is all of five feet tall, if that, yet I'll admit she scares the shit out of me. There's a lot of firepower packed into those five feet. I just get the sense that she was serious the other day, and she really might come at my balls with a bat if I fuck this up.

But she doesn't launch an interrogation. It's so much worse—she just stares me down for minutes on end until Mackenzie finally emerges from the hallway. I've never been so happy to see her. I might actually be sweating.

"Have fun, kids," Marisa says, her whole affect transformed from a moment ago. "Mackenzie, text if you need me. I'm babysitting for my sister tonight so I won't be back until tomorrow afternoon."

They stare at each other for an unnerving moment, having one of those silent girl conversations I can never translate. Then we head out to my Range Rover.

I can't read that girl. Is she on my side? Or still planning to assault me? In any case, she just made it clear we have the apartment to ourselves tonight, which currently makes her my favorite person.

❖ ❖ ❖

During the drive I find myself hoping for red lights so I can steal longer glances at Mackenzie. She has on just enough makeup that every beautiful facet of her face stands out. Her hair is up in one of those twist things so her neck and collarbone are exposed. Whenever I get the chance, I take in the view intently, mentally mapping the trip I plan to take over all that skin with my tongue later.

I valet the car when we get to our destination in the Seaport area. According to my best friend Google, Menton is supposed to be one of the best restaurants in Boston. It's French, so I'm not sure what to expect on the menu. I just hope Mackenzie enjoys it.

I made a reservation so we're led straight to our table. I'm on Mission Prince Charming, so I go way back in my memory banks and pull out the shit I learned in etiquette class, pulling out Mackenzie's chair for her then offering my help as she shrugs out of her coat. She turns to drape it over the back of her chair, and I get my first look at her outfit. I was eyeing her sexy heels in the car, but I had no idea she was hiding this under that coat.

"*Damn*, Kenz."

My voice sounds an octave lower than usual, probably because my body is in shock from the instantaneous migration of blood south. In seconds, the low-key buzz of awareness in my dick, which is always there in Mackenzie's presence, escalates to fully turned on.

All of my clothes are the same ones I bought back in high school when I was leaner, and the jeans I'm wearing are no exception. They didn't seem too tight when I put them on this afternoon, but with my sudden erection trying desperately to burst through the zipper and get to Mackenzie, the situation has become downright painful. I may need to finally suck it up and go shopping, if for no other reason than to give my poor dick some more room to appreciate Mackenzie, which will inevitably happen frequently if I keep seeing her. *Please let me keep seeing her.*

The entire back of her shirt is … not there. It's just miles of her beautiful toned back and creamy skin. When she sits down my eyes zero in on the front of the shirt. I would have seen a bra … Is she not wearing one? Or did they invent magical gravity defying bras while I was out of touch?

I stare and stare, but the pretty fabric reveals no answers to my pressing question (*pressing* … like my dick that's basically going to be permanently deformed with an imprint of my jeans' zipper.)

Her amused voice draws my eyes up to her face.

"Are you going to stare at my boobs all night trying to guess if I have a bra on or are we going to order and actually talk?"

Is she a fucking psychic or am I just that transparent?

"You say that as though they're mutually exclusive options." I shoot her a smirk in which I try to embed all of my dirtiest thoughts.

She shifts her weight and crosses one leg over the other. It's one of her tells when she's turned on. *Yeah, she got my message.*

She starts looking at the menu, but I can't take my eyes off of her. I could just stare at her all night. There are candles throughout the restaurant, but their glow is nothing compared to her. I love that despite all of her efforts to protest that this isn't a date, she clearly put in the effort to dress up.

It *is* a fucking date, and by the end of tonight, at the very least, I'm going to kiss her again.

"Anything to drink?" our server asks.

Mackenzie looks at me uncertainly. Her hand is hovering over the wine list but I see her hesitation.

"Are you … I mean, would it bother you …?"

Ahh, I get it. She doesn't want to drink if it will test my sobriety. She's precious.

"Choose a wine and we'll get the bottle," I say confidently.

When the server leaves, I reach over and take her hand, so small and fine inside my roughened paw.

"I'm not an alcoholic, Kenz. I keep things in moderation nowadays, but I'm not going to fall off the wagon."

"So, you're … okay? Are you going to meetings?" she shakes her head and laughs lightly. "I have all this training on how to have serious conversations, but I'm screwing this up royally."

I squeeze the hand I'm still holding.

"You're doing fine."

She gives me a small grateful smile.

"But no, I'm not going to meetings." I go on quickly when I see her frown. "I'm not an addict. I was fucked up back then and I abused drugs as a really stupid coping mechanism. It wasn't fun having to deal with all my shit without them suddenly, but once I started to get my head on straight, I've never craved them or anything. The prison shrink said I was basically using the drugs to self-medicate."

Mackenzie's eyes fill with tears that sparkle as they reflect the candlelight.

"I'm so sorry."

"What do you have to be sorry for?"

"I wasn't there for you. I didn't see you were struggling that badly. Maybe if I'd been more supportive—"

"No," I cut her off, my voice firm. "None of the shit I did is on you. It's not on anyone but me. You didn't see because I worked my ass off to hide it from you. You were the only light left in my world, and I wanted to keep the darkness from touching you. I was too fucked up not to self-destruct, but the last thing I wanted was to let any of it destroy you."

A single tear escapes from one of her eyes, and she dabs the corner of her fabric napkin to it self-consciously.

"Finding out you were hiding things from me, that you were hurting and I didn't help you ... *that* destroyed me." Her voice is soft and threaded with agony.

I squeeze her hand again and start to say something, but the bottle of red wine she chose arrives just then and the fancy waiter makes a whole production out of pouring it and having her taste the first sip. Thank fuck he didn't ask me to do that because I wouldn't have known to smell it and swirl it the way she does. And I wouldn't have looked half as good doing it.

When we each have a glass of wine, I raise mine in the air. She tentatively follows my lead.

"To second chances," I say.

"To staying in the light," she adds.

※　※　※

So, from what I can tell, French food is ... small. The server brings out a seemingly endless number of courses, each one microscopic. The salad is probably delicious, but I can't really tell because the three lettuce leaves are barely enough for my taste buds to register them.

The experience is a unique form of torture: having a parade of great smelling food placed before you only to find that they measure portions based on the dietary needs of squirrels.

I don't say anything because, even though I'm ravenous, tonight is about Mackenzie, and if she's loving this French shit, then I'll gladly suffer.

When the main course is on the table in front of us and the server is out of ear shot, she leans in and murmurs conspiratorially.

"Do you think we're being Punked? Or do French people just hate themselves?"

I try to smother my laugh in the fancy cloth napkin but mostly fail.

"Want to get out of here and get some real food?" she asks.

"Oh thank God."

Her laughter is light and happy and so goddamn beautiful.

"Tacos? Anna's delivers to my place."

"That sounds perfect."

15. MYTH BUSTING

Graham

Now *this* is a date I can get down with.

We're relaxing on Mackenzie's couch, the coffee table before us strewn with the leftover debris from the Mexican food we just destroyed. I've never doubted Kenz's brilliance, but this has to be one of the best ideas she's ever had. She managed to time things so perfectly that we pulled up to her driveway when the delivery guy was standing at the door. I scared the shit out of the poor guy by walking up from *behind* him when he was expecting the front door to open, but I gave him a nice cash tip to make up for it.

For the millionth time tonight, I scan Mackenzie from head to toe. She's definitely dressed for more than chilling on a couch.

"Guess I failed at doing the grand gesture fancy date thing. Sorry I'm the worst millionaire ever."

"You are a millionaire, aren't you?"

And this is just one of the ridiculous number of things I love about Mackenzie Thatcher. She doesn't say this with a single gleam of greed or opportunism in her eyes. It's a statement of fact, as calm as if she were verifying that my height is 6'2". There's no reason she wouldn't be intrigued by money—her parents have always been financially secure, but it's nothing compared to my current cash flow situation. Yet she doesn't care.

"This is nice," she says with a smile, indicating me and the couch and the takeout bags.

I'm still staring at her. For the past hour as we ate our second dinner, she's been telling me all about her internship for the semester. Her face lights up with enthusiasm when she talks about it, and I love seeing her in her element, completely nerding out about work she clearly loves.

"I'm proud of you, Mackenzie," I say then start rambling as I try to justify the words that just popped out of my mouth. "I mean ... I guess that could sound kind of condescending, or something a parent would say, but that's not how I mean it. Obviously, I'm not in any position where I even have the right to feel proud of you. But I am. Maybe proud isn't even the right word. I'm *inspired* by you. I'm in *awe* of you. I'm *amazed* by everything you've accomplished and just ... who you are."

I pause and she surprises the shit out of me by launching herself across the couch before I can even take a breath. Then she's kissing me fiercely while threading her fingers through my hair pulling my face closer to hers. *Fuck breathing.* This is better than air.

Just like the last time, we go from zero to sixty so fast we could give a Bugatti a run for its money. We may still be fumbling through learning how to talk to each other again, but there is no ramp-up needed for *this*. It's almost as though we're picking right back up where we left off. Our bodies just *know* each other.

The kiss is desperate, hungry, frantic in the best way. Our tongues are battling, teeth clashing, as passion takes precedence over finesse, our panting breaths commingling, our hands clutching at any and every part of the other that we can reach.

I disconnect our mouths and move my lips to the skin on her neck. I run a finger over the place where her skirt and shirt just barely fail to meet, finally touching the creamy strip of skin whose intermittent appearances have been torturing me all night.

"You did this on purpose to drive me crazy, didn't you?"

She shoots me a sexy as hell look of pure mischief and seduction.

I snake my hand under the shirt's edge and run my palm up her tight stomach. My hand almost spans the whole length of her torso, and she shivers when my callouses scrape over her silky skin. I continue my journey up, up, until I've reached the underside of her breasts. My fingers meet only skin.

I release a low animal sound from the depths of my throat.

"I knew it!"

I bring my other hand in to join the party, so I now have one perfect globe in each palm. I squeeze, making her squirm and shiver.

"I can't believe you *haven't been wearing a fucking bra* all night."

Mackenzie

He kneads my breasts almost roughly, maybe trying to make up for all those hours they were hiding just out of his reach. The stimulation shoots pleasure through me so intense that my thoughts disappear, and for a minute I even forget to breathe. My lungs finally protest, and I audibly gulp in air.

As his hands continue to explore, I see confusion cloud his face. In an instant he has the sweater pulled up over my head and throws it to the other side of the room. He runs a finger over one of the pale peach adhesive pads, now the only part of my chest that isn't bare.

"They come right off," I reassure him and peel one from my nipple to illustrate. His eyes are fixed on that spot.

"What did you do to my nipples?" he grates out.

"YOUR nipples?"

"Yes, they're fucking mine, and look what you did to them!"

His finger circles and caresses the slight crease and reddened skin left behind from the adhesive. Chills break out across my newly exposed torso.

Before I realize what's happening, his head is bent and he's running his tongue over the place his finger just was, laving the flesh like he's trying to soothe the skin and remove all traces of the offensive treatment. All the while his facial hair grazes my sensitive skin. I want to speak up and argue about the ownership of my nipples, reclaim my strong *"no-one-owns-me"* identity, but I find I'm robbed of the ability to put cohesive thoughts together, much less talk. I tell myself I'm not conceding, just tabling that discussion for a later time.

When he directs his attention to my other breast, he pauses and looks me right in the eye with a wicked glint. Then he *rips* the adhesive off. I release a tiny cry at the sudden sting, but after the first second, the tingles morph to pleasure, especially when his tongue moves right in to devote the same worshipful ministrations on this nipple as the other.

My fingers, made clumsy by my lust haze, fumble until I manage to locate and remove the elastic that's been holding his hair back. I toss it in the same general direction as my shirt then return my hand to his head, reveling in the way I can run my fingers through the nearly chin-length locks.

By the time he's thoroughly licked, nipped, sucked, and pinched my—no, at this particular moment they really are *his*—nipples, I'm clutching handfuls of his hair in a viselike grip, holding his head to me. My core is pulsing, ready for more.

"Come here," I gasp, yanking at his hair so he gets the idea and brings his face up to mine.

Our lips crash back together in a ravenous kiss, and within seconds he has me flat on my back on the couch and is hovering over me. My hips shift restlessly trying to get some friction where I'm aching for it, but the restrictive shape of this skirt makes it impossible to get close enough. He tries to snake a hand underneath but the fabric is too thick and too tight, the garment keeping my thighs from parting any further.

"Off," I declare, because right now my vocabulary is limited to only the important things. "Bedroom," I add when it becomes clear this couch is not big enough for the amount of maneuvering we need to do.

Without hesitation he jumps up. Then I am flying through the air in his arms as he walks us toward the back hallway. It happens so fast, his strong arms lifting and holding me effortlessly as if I weigh nothing at all.

"Which one?" he grunts, caught up in the same word-eating hurricane of pent-up lust as I am.

I point to my bedroom door, and he shoulders through it before dropping me on the bed. He's immediately right there with me, big paws searching all around my skirt for a point of entry.

"Where's the goddamn zipper?" he mutters, sounding downright angry.

I push his hands away, my mental fog of lust thinning just enough to register fear for the life of my skirt. I reach over and tug at the zipper where it's hiding just to the side of my right hipbone. As soon as I've got it pulled halfway he shoves my hands away almost savagely. His eyes are zeroed in on the sliver of skin that's just been revealed, including a hint of the string from my thong.

He finishes with the zipper and, painfully slowly, drags the skirt down my legs, leaving a trail of kisses along my skin as each new inch is uncovered. When it finally drops to the floor, I reach for him, gripping his shoulders to bring him back up to me. He comes willingly, and our lips reconnect as though starved after the few minutes of separation.

I am lying prone beneath him, his big body covering my whole frame in his heat and delicious *Graham-ness*. Then his hand moves between us, his fingers slipping beneath the edge of my panties. He peels them off so I am now completely naked. Then, without hesitation, his fingers are suddenly *right there*.

There was a time when Graham knew every inch of my body, and I knew his. At sixteen, we were pioneers exploring the uncharted territories of our bodies over endless afternoons and weekends in his bedroom or the back of his Range Rover. Hours of falling in love and making love as we unveiled the mysteries of sex together. We gladly sacrificed days to the pursuit of mastering ways to give each other pleasure.

It appears that Graham remembers. His finger caresses and strokes me and immediately zeroes in on the perfect spot, where he rubs and teases with just the right speed and pressure. Unlike what I'm used to with partners, I can completely let go and give myself over to the pleasure without having to give any direction or guidance on what I need.

If my body is an instrument, he is a virtuoso. He hasn't forgotten a single note.

I lose the rhythm of our kissing, only able to lie back and focus on breathing.

I accepted years ago that it was hard, if not impossible, for me to orgasm with a man. When my thoughts were inevitably drawn back to my relationship with Graham, I convinced myself it was a product of all those haywire teenage hormones that made it easy to climax, not replicable as an adult.

Graham is busting all the myths I've taught myself to believe. And this one is about to explode into nothing but ash.

"That's right, Z. Give it to me."

Hearing his secret nickname for me, the special ones we came up with together that no one else knows ("Z" and "Y" ... MackenZIE and WYatt), hits me right in the feels. It acts as a trigger, and I spasm through my release. All I can do is gasp and hold tight to him as I plummet over the edge.

As I wait for sensation to return to my limbs, I inwardly admit that my self-induced orgasms over the past five years have merely been pale substitutions for the real thing—the way wax figures look realistic from afar but reveal their inauthenticity when you get close. I fear I'll never be fooled by the knockoffs again.

Graham is still kissing my neck, my face, my chest, murmuring low words I can't make out. I roll over until I'm on top then reach down and grab the waist of his jeans. I slowly tug down his zipper. In no time I have released him from the constraints of his boxer briefs and have my hand wrapped around his warm, hard length.

"No, babe," he grunts, trying to push my hand away.

"If my nipples are yours, then this dick is *mine*," I breathe directly into his ear while giving said dick a squeeze for emphasis.

His whole body is tense, and his voice sounds tortured as he tries to resist again.

"It's been too long. I won't last. Wanna make you come again. Then I want to be inside you."

"You'll recover," I tell him, not releasing my grip.

I know I've won when he lies back and throws an arm over his eyes.

I stroke upwards, my core clenching when I find he's already leaking. I smirk with pure womanly power as I rub a thumb over his tip, spreading the moisture around and using it to lubricate my palm before making my way back down his length.

"Fuck."

His hips buck upward as though of their own volition, but he can't go far because I'm sitting on his legs.

He wasn't wrong—in just a couple of minutes, he's letting loose a string of panted curses interspersed with my name, hips thrusting into my hand as I stroke him through his release.

Finally, he can't take anymore and pulls my hand away. Not letting go, he threads his fingers through mine and lifts our entwined hands so they're resting on his sternum. He lies back and pants as if he's just run up ten flights of stairs, powerful chest rising and falling beneath our clasped hands.

After a moment he seems to recover, kicking off his jeans and using his boxer briefs to wipe his abs free of all evidence of his orgasm. Then he reaches for me and pulls me so we're face-to-face. He looks into my eyes with so much intensity, I fear for a moment that he's going to voice the things shimmering in the air between us, things I'm not ready to deal with yet. Instead, his free hand snakes back down between our bodies to cup me between my legs.

"One more."

He pushes one finger inside me, then two. His lips are on the skin of my neck. Then his teeth are on the shell of my ear and his voice is rasping into it.

"You have no idea how many times—hundreds, *thousands*—I've jerked myself off thinking about you ... this."

His words send a wave of desire through me, and my cheeks heat in embarrassment knowing he can feel the evidence on his fingers. He just smirks and kisses me. I'm so worked up, and his fingers play me so masterfully that he has me coming again not long after.

Myth thoroughly busted.

We lie side by side with our whole bodies pressed together, and I am suddenly horrified to discover he still has his shirt on. I sit up and straddle him, one leg on either side of his thighs, and I start pulling off the offending fabric. I'm no match for the sheer size and strength of his body, but he dutifully lifts his back and arms for me until he's bare.

I sigh in satisfaction when he's finally naked. My eyes caress his arms, one bearing the gorgeous black and gray ink of his tattoo, then travel down to his muscular thighs and the large beautiful organ (which I've just declared *mine*) that seems to be recovering nicely. I run my hands over every dip of his beautiful abs, the ones I've been trying not to think about ever since he came to yoga. My fingers trail over his pecs, and I run a fingernail over the edge of one nipple, making his chest muscles contract swiftly. Beneath me, another muscle is poking at me—and it's fully hard again.

You're not the only one who remembers the notes, I think smugly.

"I have an IUD," I say.

He just stares at me blankly.

"And, um, I've been tested and I'm clean ..." I'm suddenly awkward. Warmth creeps up my cheeks until I'm sure they're completely pink.

I watch Graham's eyes clear in recognition of what I'm saying. Then they darken with desire.

"I had a full physical when I got out. But I also haven't been with anyone but you ... ever. So, I'd say I'm good," he says.

Surprise jolts through me. I mean, I guess I could have figured that out since he's been in prison all this time, but ... *wow*. The knowledge fills my chest with warmth, and a part of me wishes that I could say the same to him.

"So?" he asks, hips thrusting lightly against mine.

"So," I respond with a nod.

Then he's pushing inside me, gliding easily through the slickness of my arousal, and we're one. The look of ecstasy and wonder on his face is a perfect mirror for what I feel. He kisses me, this time tender, and our tongues caress each other in contrast to their earlier frenzied wrestling.

We begin to move together, so in sync that we might as well be choreographed. As the urgency rises between us again, we pick up speed to the soundtrack of our heavy breathing. Then Graham is tensing and shuddering above me, eyes closed in ecstasy. He curses and apologizes that it was "*too fucking good*" and "*it's been five years.*" He promises he'll make it up to me in a few minutes.

But I can't stop smiling. I want no apology for what just happened. The only way to describe it is ... perfect. *Right*.

Regardless, he keeps his word and makes it up to me. Repeatedly. All night.

16. CONGRATULATORY HIGH FIVES

Graham

I wake up to a view more gorgeous than any multi-million-dollar oceanfront property could boast: Mackenzie Thatcher sleeping next to me, curled on her side so all I can see are copper locks contrasting vibrantly where they're spread over her white sheets and down the pale skin of her bare back and shoulders. The best part is that if I drag that sheet down, I'll have an eyeful of her perfect ass (no joke, I'm ready to make a donation to the yoga gods), and if I reach for her, as I have so often over the past six hours, she'll willingly turn to me revealing and offering the rest of her luscious naked body.

I hold back, though, and tell myself to be satisfied for the moment by caressing her with just my eyes. I'll let her sleep for now—she's going to need it if I have any say in the matter. Since it's Saturday, she has no classes or work to go to, and I have important plans to stay here and do nothing but her all day.

I suppose it's technically morning now—I can see the glow of sunshine through her bedroom window—but it feels like the night never ended. Neither of us slept much, only taking brief naps to recharge before the need for each other won out again. It's like with that first time we pried a lid off the box keeping our sexual chemistry at bay, and once opened there was no suppressing the flood of insatiable craving after five years apart.

Mackenzie drifted off a little while ago, but I can't seem to sleep.

Last night was … beyond description. And not just because I was so horny after five years I was ready to die. It's always been more with Mackenzie. Being inside her again was fucking magical—somehow, I think it even topped our first time together. This time there was that same sense of newness, the excitement and sense of exploration, but there was also the weight of history between us, a *rightness* as we tapped into and rediscovered all the ways we used to connect. And though we never spoke of it, there was an extra layer of significance created by everything we've been through that got us here.

When we were teenagers, the only obstacle we had to overcome was figuring out when my parents would be away from the house (and she made me drive to the next town to buy condoms because she was justifiably concerned the second I checked out at the Westwood CVS, the gossip mill would take off and the whole town would consider us devirginized before we had a chance to remove our clothes).

Admittedly, that first time I brought shame to every Wyatt male since the dawn of time. But really, I was doomed before it even began. Not only had it been five long sexless years, but I'd never gone bare before (later, I used some very creative persuasion tactics and got her to admit she'd never done it either, and thank fuck, because I really don't want to go back to prison and I'd probably have felt the need to track that guy down and do some damage). The second I entered that snug, warm heaven for the first time, my dick and I had no chance.

My only saving grace was that I managed to get her off twice before we got to the main event, (if I have a son and I only get to teach him one thing it will be that you always make your girl come before you take yours—maybe I'll write a children's book and start him young on bedtime stories of sexual chivalry), but I still knew I needed to redeem myself and my ancestors.

I think it's safe to say ... *mission accomplished.*

Not to sound like an arrogant motherfucker, but by round four I'd bet even cranky Grandpa Earl was wiping away a tear of pride and cheering along with the rest of the old Wyatt perverts watching from their skybox seats. I made her come so many times (with my fingers, my tongue, and my greedy unwrapped dick) that I lost count.

It's unbelievable how many options suddenly open up when you remove condoms from the equation. For instance, when we ventured out to forage for food in the kitchen at some point and on the way back to her room, I noticed the back of her couch appeared to line up perfectly with my hips; I could test my theory immediately by lifting her up and placing her seated on top of the piece of furniture. And I was completely right—I was perfectly aligned to push right between her spread legs. Standing like that, I could use my legs for stability and power as I pounded into her over and over, my tight grip on her hips and her legs wrapped around me the only things keeping her from tumbling backward through the open air on her back and onto the couch seat.

The memory turns me on all over again. *Okay, I think she's slept long enough.*

I decide that I'll be less of a jerk for waking her up if I make it worthwhile for her, so I tunnel underneath the covers until I'm staring right at the heaven between her legs. Reuniting with Mackenzie's body—her nipples, her lips, her clit—feels like being back with old friends. Her clit and I spent a lot of time together back in the day, and I sure as hell missed it. I waste no time now, diving right in to do some more catching up.

At some point she wakes up, and air washes over me as the sheet flies up and her hands come down to grab my hair (she seems to enjoy doing this, and I fucking love it—an unforeseen benefit of my haircut hiatus). Her hips start bucking off the bed like she's trying to get closer to my mouth. I reach up and hold her down with a palm flat to her pelvis, keeping her still. *Patience, babe.* I'll get her there—her clit and I are doing great work here, and we don't need her assistance. I give that perfect pink bud a nice suck, and I hear her let out a high-pitched gasping sound. Using my tongue, I share a quick congratulatory high five with her clit—Mackenzie's never been very vocal in bed, definitely not a moaner or a screamer, so I love it every time I manage to wrench a new sound from her. Soon, her thighs are shaking where they're squeezed along the sides of my head. I continue licking her through the spasms of her orgasm.

Then I crawl up to face level with her. She's breathing heavily and her eyes are barely open, but she reaches out and pulls me in for a slow, wet kiss that tastes of her release. When we break apart to catch our breath, I run an appreciative eye down her naked body, which is now fully exposed. I frown a bit when I see red marks all over.

"I guess beard burn is real," she says with a sated and relaxed smile.

What the ...

I examine her again, and sure enough, she looks as though she's been thoroughly dragged over a rough carpet, or attacked with sandpaper ... on the skin between her thighs, her stomach, her breasts, her neck, even on her chin and the skin around her mouth.

"Babe ..." My voice is laced with regret. "I'll shave it off, I promise."

But her face takes on a coy look, and she reaches up to stroke along my jaw. It's not quite to Griff's mountain man level, but it's definitely more than stubble.

"I like it," she tells me.

When I shoot another worried glance to the swaths of red marring her creamy skin, her eyes follow. And she laughs lightly.

"Okay, it's pretty bad," she admits. "But last night was pretty crazy, right? I can't imagine we'll ever be having *that much* sex all at once again, so it should be fine."

Wait ... *why won't we be having that much sex again?* I was thinking it should be an every Friday sort of deal. What was the word her crazy roommate used? *Fuckfest.* Yeah. Weekly Friday Fuckfests.

Her giggles are louder this time, and I can tell by her face that she knows exactly what I'm thinking.

"Don't look so sad. I'm not saying *never*—but I think we'd *die* if we kept at this!"

We both laugh now, and I decide to take it as a win that she's talking about a future at all.

* * *

It takes two hours for her face to take on the look I've been waiting for and dreading: uncertainty, regret, worry.

We're sitting on the couch, eating cereal. She's only wearing a pair of panties and a shirt (which is twice as much clothing as I voted for), with her legs crossed and tucked underneath her. I try to do some quick calculations to figure out if I can jump her and distract her with an orgasm, but I can't see it happening without milk spilling everywhere. Plus, though I'd never admit it out loud, I'm *tired.* The sleepless night and all the—let's say, *vigorous activity?* —has finally caught up with me.

"Okay, let's have it."

She jerks a little, like I've surprised her out of deep thought. Then with a nod, she places her bowl and spoon on the coffee table and untucks her legs, so she's sitting properly and facing me. Instantly, the mood in the room shifts to something solemn. I put my bowl down too and try to breathe through my sudden nerves.

My eyes race over her as fear rushes back in that this might be the last chance I have.

"I still have concerns," she begins hesitantly.

I nod, encouraging her to go on, even though I have to swallow down a knot of panic. If last night couldn't convince her we're supposed to be together, I don't know if anything will work.

"I'm not this reckless person who rushes into things. Maybe I was once, I'm honestly not sure, but now I think things through and weigh risks before acting, especially when I'm not totally sure about something."

Her face blushes bright red, and I see it racing down her neck and disappearing behind the hem of her shirt.

"I'm kind of ashamed, honestly. I basically forgot all logic and reason and threw my self-respect out the window. I mean, I *jumped* you."

I can't help but chuckle.

"I'm not complaining."

I feel myself smirking at her, thinking about everything that happened after she jumped me.

She rolls her eyes.

"Well, of course not. You got what you wanted."

Oh *hell* no. I'm not going to let her even pretend to believe that.

"Hey…" I take her face in my hands, forcing her to look at me "…I didn't come back into your life to get laid. I'm obviously not gonna lie and say that wasn't something I wanted—but that's not what this is about. I want *you*—whatever way you'll have me." I pause and search her eyes, looking for a sign that she's really hearing me. "I may not be in an addiction program, but I have a shit-ton of amends to make. When I was in prison, I did a lot of thinking about everything—going back through all the things I fucked up and figuring out what's really important in life. And, babe, you're at the top of every one of my lists. I know I failed you the first time around. But I'm here now to finally start on that forever I promised you. It begins right now—hell, it began the second I saw you again—and it never ends."

She blinks so fast I can't tell if that was the shine of tears I just glimpsed or merely a reflection of the light coming through the window.

"You can't promise that. You spent really crucial years of your mental and social development locked up, and you need to catch up on all of that …"

"Babe," I stop her, covering her lips with a gentle finger to soften the rudeness of the act.

"Analyze me all you want, throw me in your lab, scan my brain, assign me a team of shrinks, take out all those textbooks of yours and highlight every chapter that applies to me … *tomorrow*. Today I just want to be with you. Nothing else matters besides that."

"Great sex isn't—"

"First of all, it's *un-fucking-believable* sex. And second, you know that's not what I mean."

115

I take her hand, raising it up between us so our interlocked fingers are directly in her line of sight.

"*This* is what I mean. I get that you're probably not ready yet to admit you feel it too, but don't lie to me or yourself by denying it. It's not just sex—it's *us*. Just sitting here next to you … it's everything. My fucking heart beats for you, Z. I don't know what else to say to make you get that."

She takes a deep breath.

"Okay," she whispers, leaning over to place a kiss on top of our clasped hands.

I wrap my arms around her and pull her back on the couch with me, and then I just hold her. And, yeah … it's everything.

17. SHOW ME ON A RULER

Mackenzie

"Shift your hips a bit ... No, this way ..."

"I don't think this is going to work."

"Trust me, babe, it will."

"Oh yes! That's working. Keep doing that!"

"Shift back a little?"

"Ouch."

"You okay?"

"Yeah."

"Ready to try again?"

"It's too big, Graham."

"No, this is gonna work ... Okay, on three. One, two, three ..."

"I think I'm stuck."

"Oh, fuck. Hold on."

"... there! I told you it would fit!"

I wipe sweat from my forehead as I step back to view the king-sized mattress we just managed to squeeze through my bedroom doorway.

Yes, a mattress. A couple of days ago Graham declared he's sick of not having enough space for his long legs on my full-sized bed, and then suddenly this morning there were delivery men at my door with this mattress and in my room assembling a massive bed frame. Seriously ... *he bought me a bed.* I considered putting up an *I-am-woman-hear-me-roar* protest but decided it's not worth it. He has been spending almost every night here, and it is a nice bed. He definitely won't miss the money. Plus, he distracted me very effectively right as I was about to argue, and I may have lost some brain cells because I suddenly thought it was a great idea.

Graham has lifted his shirt and is currently using the hem to wipe sweat from his own face.

Holy mother of lickable six-packs.

"Like something you see?" he asks.

"Maybe ..."

But I lick my lips, which cancels out my attempt at being coy.

"Want to break this thing in?"

"Right now? I'm all sweaty and it doesn't have any sheets on it."

"Sounds great to me." He shoots me that mischievous boyish grin that is almost painfully adorable displayed across his manly scruff-covered face.

I respond by pulling my shirt over my head and throwing it to the floor. I mean, *what the hell,* right? And ... I can never resist those abs.

He tackles me onto the mattress within seconds.

❖ ❖ ❖

It's the strangest thing, starting to date someone you've previously been in a relationship with.

It's both new and familiar—there's a sense that it's the beginning of something but also that we're already a dozen steps down the road.

I imagine it's similar to the way I'd feel if I tried some of my old gymnastics routines now—I was a gymnast for years as a kid, but I haven't done a backflip in at least a decade. Just like this thing with Graham, I would be rusty and out of practice, certain muscles unused to the activity, but on some level my mind and body would sink right into it, remembering things I never consciously realized were still ingrained within me.

Being with Graham again is stretching all sorts of muscles that are out of practice (and not just the ones he's been giving a workout with all the sex, though that's certainly happening). My emotional muscles—ones connected to my metaphorical heart, rather than the one pumping blood through my veins—ache from the sudden use after years of dormancy.

I think I've still been half in love with him all this time, without realizing or acknowledging it, and the sudden resurgence of those feelings is overwhelming. It's something I told myself I would never experience again, that I would never fall into that trap. When I have quiet moments alone, the worry starts to seep in and remind me just how badly love once hurt me. How badly *Graham* once hurt me.

But, honestly, I haven't been spending that much time alone, and it's hard to focus on anxiety with so many orgasm-induced happy chemicals in my brain.

I can't remember the last time Graham didn't spend the night in my bed, though our sexual escapades have definitely not been limited to the nighttime. We're as bad as two horny teenagers. Though, actually, we're so much worse now than when we were teenagers because there's no impending deadline of a curfew or parents coming home to put limitations on our alone time.

We can (and do) basically tear each other's clothes off any time I'm not working or in class. All-night sex marathons, shower sex, floor sex, sex against walls, nostalgic cramped sex in his Range Rover … we've been insatiable.

Predictably, Marisa gets a kick out of providing commentary— over the past few weeks I've heard every possible variation of the phrase "fucking like bunnies." But I find that I'm merely amused by the blatant attention to my sex life—I suppose it's harder to get embarrassed when everything is being filtered through that haze of happy orgasm chemicals. I understand she only teases because she's happy for me—it's her unique way of being supportive. And to be fair, Graham and I haven't exactly been subtle. Although Marisa hasn't outright caught either of us bare-ass naked, there have been some extremely close calls.

After that first night when Graham and I "reconnected" (AKA we *connected* our bodies an insane number of times) when Marisa got home, she walked right up to me and, without a word, held out an old-school wooden yardstick.

It only took a second for me to comprehend she wanted me to *show her on a ruler* how big Graham's penis is. While I was still blushing scarlet, Graham casually walked up from behind me and pointed to a number. They high-fived. Sometimes the two of them together legitimately scare me.

I'm well aware it's not healthy to use sex as a way to push all of our issues to the side. The practical Psych major in me warns that we still have serious things to clear up and talk through, but when push comes to shove, I've let it go because I'm … *happy*. I didn't even realize that I wasn't happy before. Not that I was *un*happy, but I was living a life of contentment that lacked the glow of joy. Sometimes it takes experiencing pure happiness to recognize how long you've lived without that feeling.

Being with Graham is like basking in the sun, and I'm going to allow myself the luxury of soaking in it for a little while longer. I promise the pragmatic voice in my head that I'll go find an umbrella and sunscreen before I burn, because long-term exposure will require some moderation and protection. Just ... *not yet.*

❄ ❄ ❄

We're entwined together in bed (the new one, all set up and outfitted with sheets), just enjoying the afterglow from yet another amazing round of sex. This time it was "I haven't seen you in five hours" sex when I got home from class—because, you know, the horny teenager thing.

I run my hand up and down the tattoo on his left arm and encounter a bandage near his elbow that I didn't notice before in our haste to jump each other.

"New ink?" I ask.

After his parents died, I went and sat with him when he got the half-sleeve on his left arm that spans from his shoulder to his elbow— it's a beautiful design of roses and a clock threaded through with intricately shaded vines and leaves, all in blacks and grays. For his parents, because his mom's name was Rose.

He carefully peels the bandage back to show me five new small roses added to the design—gorgeous even while the skin is still a bit pink and swollen in the early healing stage.

"I couldn't visit them, you know? So, it's one rose for every year I didn't visit or leave flowers on their graves. My whole life, every single year, Dad bought Mom roses on her birthday. When they died it was the least I could do to continue the tradition the way he would have wanted—one small thing that would have made him proud of me. But I fucked that up too."

His voice is low and quiet, full of regret and self-condemnation. I think I have a better understanding now of why he was so desperate for the physical intimacy when I got out of class this afternoon (not that I'm complaining or was any less eager). I trace a finger around the bandage once he replaces it.

"I visited," I whisper. My hushed admission seems to linger in the air between, which is now heavy with our confessions.

"What?" He shifts slightly so he can look down at my face.

"I went to their graves."

No one knows this, not even Marisa. I hand him the secret, hoping it can ease some small layer of his pain.

"Every year. And brought flowers."

"When?"

"Hmm?" I ask sleepily as I nuzzle back into him.

"When did you go?"

I open my eyes so I can look up at his face—his beautiful, fierce, tortured face.

"On your birthday. I figured they were the only ones who wouldn't judge me for remembering it, who might understand why it still meant something to me. It seemed right somehow that we mark it together."

He pulls me back in and wraps his arms around me.

"I love you so goddamn much, you know that?"

Too soon. It's way too soon, my rational mind screams. We've only been back together for a few weeks.

And yet … I recognize this feeling. And it's so much more than still being *half in love* with him as I've tried to convince myself.

"I love you too," I whisper.

He rolls us so he's on top then takes my mouth in a slow kiss that builds the fire inside me all over again.

And then we have *I love you* sex. It's the best kind yet.

18. THAT GLOW

Mackenzie

I banish Graham from the house for the weekend so I can catch up on my schoolwork. I've got a massive pile of papers to grade as well as assignments for my own classes that I've been putting off.

He pouts and tries to melt my resolve by giving me his most potent pleading look.

"The whole weekend? Come on, Kenz, you can get your work done with me here. I promise I'll be good."

I raise my eyebrows at him and pin him with a look that says, *"Really?"*

Even if he actually kept his hands to himself—and this is a big if, because I highly doubt it—there's no guarantee that I'd be able to. When we're in the same space, there's this current of electricity between us that's undeniable. The last thing I need is to have my attention split while I fight to ignore the sexual tension that inevitably builds in his proximity.

"I just need these two days with no distractions and a couple of nights with eight or more hours of sleep."

Now hurt fills those expressive hazel eyes.

"Can't say I'm happy about it, but I'll do whatever you need. I'm just sorry I've been messing things up for you. The last thing I want is to drag you down. You should have told me you don't sleep well when I'm here."

He's so earnest, so apologetic, so dejected. I'm filled with a rush of remorse and overwhelming affection. *This man.*

I'm sitting on the couch watching him shift from one foot to the other before me. I reach for him, and he gives in to my silent request, closing the small distance between us and taking the place beside me on the couch. Now that we're almost eye level, I loop my wrists around the back of his neck and look right at him, wanting him to see the sincerity of my next words.

"Y, it's not like that." His posture softens at my use of the special nickname. "I don't *want* you to leave, but I have to get this stuff done. And if you're here, all I'll want to do is spend time with you. That's the problem—I've been neglecting my work because I just want to be with you. I'm going to hate not having you in my bed tonight. It's not at all that I don't sleep well with you here … We never seem to get a full night in because we can't keep our hands off each other. And I'm as much to blame for that as you are."

He grins wickedly. "Oh, I know, babe."

"Do you hear me? I'm sending you away to punish and incentivize myself, not to punish you."

He nods and places a soft kiss on my nose.

That tension between us starts pulling tight again, and I make myself get up from the couch and take a few steps away from him. I need the distance so I don't throw my responsible plan out the window and spend the whole weekend in his arms. *Must resist the Graham force field.*

125

"Now go!" I push futilely at his massive shoulder, trying to sound stern but failing as a little laugh slips out. "I'll see you Monday."

✵ ✵ ✵

Hours later, I've made a considerable dent in my grading pile and finished an assignment that's due next week. As a reward, I'm taking some time to sit on the couch with Marisa and have a glass of wine. I suddenly miss hanging out with her, and I realize how long it's been since we last spent time together, just the two of us.

"Sorry I've been so MIA lately."

Have I become the girl who ditches her best friend for a guy? I cringe at myself. *Worst friend ever.*

Marisa bats away my apology with a flick of her wrist and a wave of her red manicured nails.

"Nah. I was going to give you a few more weeks before I called you out on it. If I got together with a guy as sexy as Graham, you wouldn't hear from me for a month or two either. You've been through a lot—you deserve to walk around with that '*I'm getting thoroughly fucked on the regular*' glow."

I laugh, because I'm sure that's exactly how I look.

"It's been intense," I agree.

"So, he's obviously treating your body well—but we haven't talked much since this all happened. How is he treating your heart?"

I smile, stretching my mouth so wide I'm sure I look ridiculous and lovesick.

"He's been wonderful. He loves me, and I think I'm in love with him. Maybe I always have been," I admit. "Being with him feels so right. Besides that, I honestly have no idea what I'm doing. We still have a lot of things to work out if we're going to seriously do this, and I have to talk to my parents at some point, which I'm dreading, but for now ..." I shrug.

"You've been making decisions using just logic for a long time now. I'm glad you're finally letting yourself follow your heart. But it's never good to be too far on either end of the spectrum, so make sure you're not trading out one extreme for the other. Just try to find a place in the middle, where you're listening to your heart but using your head too."

I give her the closest approximation of a hug I can manage while we're both still holding partially full wine glasses.

"How did I get such a smart best friend?" I ask.

"Mine's not too bad either." She winks at me.

We drink our wine and just chat, catching up. Then she brings the conversation back to Graham.

"So ... *mariposas en el estomago*, no?"

I shake my head, grinning—with Graham I have *all* the butterflies in my stomach.

"Oh, Ris, I couldn't even begin to tell you all the places that man gives me butterflies."

With dramatically slow movements, she leans back on the couch cushion, crosses one leg over the other, and takes a sip from her glass. She is every bit as imperious as a queen on her throne ready to issue a decree. Then she pins me with her wicked gaze and demands, *"Try."*

Graham

I don't know what to do with myself.

I wander the house, doing whatever I can think of to stay occupied. Throw in a couple loads of laundry. Double my usual workout. Trim my beard. Scroll through some online college course catalogs. Call my parole officer for my weekly check-in. Go for a run.

By mid-afternoon, I'm climbing the walls. *Damn, I really need to get a life.*

I shoot Griff a text, hoping he's free.

GRAHAM: Want to grab a beer tonight?

GRIFF: Good timing. The girls are at some playdate shit so I'm free 3-5

GRAHAM: Great. Just say where.

We meet at a hole-in-the-wall bar near his place and order beers that the bartender hands to us in the bottle. I appreciate how unpretentious it is—this is clearly a place that doesn't mess around with things as superfluous as glasses.

"You get your girl?" Griff asks me.

I grin. "Yeah. I did."

He smacks me on the back with one of those giant paws.

"'Atta boy."

We tap the necks of our beer bottles together. A silent toast to love and shit.

"Any sign of those fuckers trying to come after you again?"

"Nope." *Thank God.* I've kept an eye out, but there's been no sign of Eli or any of Curtis' old crew. I've been hoping Eli has just dropped the whole thing, but the realistic part of my mind knows I don't deserve that much luck.

"I asked around a bit, wanted to see what the word is on Eli."

"I don't want you getting into any trouble or opening any closed doors from your old life, especially not on my account. You've got too much to lose."

"Nah, I didn't cross any lines. I got a few contacts, clean guys, who have ties to the old crew and hear things. And what they say about Eli … he's bad news, Pretty Boy."

"What are they saying?"

"Twisted motherfucker. Got a mean streak a mile wide. They say Curtis used to get shit done and made sure you knew who was boss, but Eli takes things too far, seems to get off on it."

I can't say I'm surprised. I recall the evil glint in his eyes that night in the parking lot as he promised to kill me slowly and make sure my body was never found. Yeah, *"twisted motherfucker"* sounds about right.

The top of Griff's bottle disappears inside his beard as he tosses back some beer.

"I know I already told you to watch your back, but watch with both eyes, hear me? Maybe bust out some of that money and hire professional security."

I shake my head. I think hiring a bodyguard would make me more visible, a bigger target. Plus, there's no chance I could manage that without Mackenzie noticing and asking questions. I change the subject.

"What else is new with you, Old Man? Getting everything ready for the baby?"

"We've still got a while. Shaina's only five months or so along. I was already locked up a couple in months the first time, didn't get to help her out the way I should've. I gotta make up for it, you know?

Her car has been acting up, so I'm trying to sell my Harley to get her a new one before the baby comes—something safe, better for two kids."

I see an opportunity and go for it without a second thought.

"No shit? I've been looking at buying a Harley."

It's basically true. I've *thought about* looking into it.

He cuts those dark eyes in my direction suspiciously.

"Don't do me any favors, boy."

I put my hands up to show my innocence, palms facing him and fingers pointed to the sky except for one index finger and thumb, which are still curled around the neck of my beer bottle.

"Wouldn't think of it. And hey, I'm not making any promises, just saying I'll take a look. I have to make sure it's in good condition."

He grunts in offense as I knew he would. I'm well aware he treats that bike almost as well as his woman.

"You ain't gonna find better."

I hide my smile by lifting the bottle to my lips for another swig. Looks like I'm buying a motorcycle.

Later we're settling up our bills and getting ready to head out. Just as I start to rise from my stool Griff puts a hand to my shoulder and halts my movement.

"One more thing. When I told Shaina where I was going, she tore me a new one for not having you over to dinner yet. And you'll learn one of these days that when your woman's pregnant, you give her whatever the fuck she wants. So, you free next weekend? Supposed to be good weather. I'm pulling out the grill. Bring your girl too."

19. NOT IN MY HOUSE, KIDS

Mackenzie

March in Boston is strange; the weather teeters unpredictably on the line between winter and spring the way a thirteen-year-old straddles adulthood, shifting weight between their new maturity and the foot that's still planted in childhood. And with even more mood swings. Only last week it snowed, but today is unquestionably a taste of spring. The sun is out in its full glory and there's not a rain cloud in sight.

It's the perfect day to hang out with Griff and Shaina in their small backyard. The adults are sitting in folding chairs, sipping beers Graham and I brought (except for Shaina, of course—we brought root beer for her), while their daughter Layla plays a few feet away. At the moment she's creating a masterpiece with colored sticks of chalk on a strip of pavement. Griff keeps getting up to check on the burgers he's cooking on the grill. We've been here for an hour, enjoying the sun and chatting as we get to know each other. This is Graham's first time meeting Shaina, and it's mine meeting both of them.

"So, what, he was the hotshot quarterback and you were a cheerleader?" Shaina asks me teasingly.

"This one?" Graham asks in a tone of exaggerated disbelief, with his thumb pointed at me. "Not a chance. She was queen of the nerds."

"Hey!" I laugh and swat at him playfully.

The look he shoots in my direction is mischievous but bathed in a gleam of adoration that still takes my breath away every time I see it, even though it happens daily. He reaches out one long arm and drapes it around the back of my chair, lazily running his fingers through my hair.

"Okay, okay. How's this—she was the smartest, hottest girl in our school. She wouldn't have had time for cheerleading with everything she did—I swear she was the president of every society, club, and council the school had—student government, honors this and honors that ... I was lucky she made time to go to my games."

And now I'm blushing. He didn't have to go into all of *that*. And he's exaggerating ... I was the *vice president* of some of those clubs.

"How did you two meet?" I ask Shaina and Griff, diverting attention from myself.

They proceed to tell us a story that I sense is highly edited, which likely means they met through Griff's old crew or some other criminal connection. Since they clearly don't want me to know, I refrain from mentioning that Graham told me about their backgrounds before we came here. He doesn't think Shaina was ever directly involved in Griff's old criminal activities, but she definitely has close ties to that world.

Today seems like a big step for me and Graham. He's openly including me in this, even though Griff is from a part of his life he shut me out of before. And it's not just that he invited me today—he also trusted me with Griff's past without trying to shield me from it. This is proof that Graham really has changed, that he's grown beyond the boy who lied and hid things from me years ago. It means that he's keeping his promise to be totally honest with me. Every day Graham chips away more of the hard shell casing I'd built around my heart—and as we sit here with his friends, I sense another piece disconnecting. There are barely any left at this point, only the smallest remnants hanging on in an attempt to protect me from completely falling for Graham again.

Our conversation has split in two now—the guys are discussing some mutual acquaintances from prison while Shaina and I talk about the new baby they're expecting.

Shaina is a little shorter than me, with thick shiny black hair that falls to just above her shoulders. I have a weird urge to reach out and touch it just to see if the perfectly straight strands are as silky as they look. There's an indistinct exotic look to her—seemingly the product of an ancestry woven together with a myriad of threads from gorgeous people all over the world. She has high cheekbones and a slight almond shape to her eyes that hints at some Asian threads in her genetic tapestry. I might have a girl crush on her.

Shaina is an adorable pregnant woman. She's so tiny that the little protrusion of her baby bump almost looks out of place in the middle of her body. Looking at her, I understand what people mean when they say a woman is glowing; she has this aura of happiness as she talks about the baby inside her, and her hand inevitably strays to her belly every couple of minutes, where it rests lovingly.

This afternoon has been wonderful so far, and I can't get over how cute Griff and Shaina are together. Griff's love for her is obvious—every time I look at him, I find his gaze on her or their daughter. He's a giant of a man, and it would be almost comical seeing them together with such a vast disparity in sizes, but they're so clearly in love that it only took minutes for me to see how they fit.

Today has actually been a bit of a reality check for me. I generally think I'm a really open and accepting person, but I can't deny that if

I'd come across either of them in another setting I would likely have been hesitant, maybe even a little afraid, to approach or interact.

Everything about Griff is intimidating. He is gigantic. I thought Graham was big, but Griff is on another level. He's way taller than six feet (6'5" maybe?) and he's not a lean basketball player type of tall, but a solid wall of bulk that is clearly all muscle. Tattoos cover every inch of visible skin from his chin down—colorful designs on his neck, hands, and both forearms where he's pushed back his shirt sleeves exposing some skin. The way they disappear beneath his sleeves and at his shirt's collar makes it clear they continue far beyond. (I wish I could somehow ask him to take off his shirt so I could see the full extent of his ink, but I'm sure Shaina wouldn't appreciate that, and Graham would lose his shit without a doubt.) Even now, relaxed and happy in his own home with family and friends, Griff gives off a palpable vibe of *"don't fuck with me."* If I'd run across him some other time, I would honestly have crossed the street to avoid the encounter even in full daylight.

In another context, I admit I probably wouldn't have chatted up Shaina either, even though she is nowhere near as intimidating as "her man" (apparently the preferred label for their relationship). She, too, has tattoos covering both arms and peeking out from the neck of her shirt, and multiple piercings on her face that gleam and flash in the sunlight, including a stud in her nose, a hoop in her eyebrow, and a full row of earrings covering the shell of one ear. But it's not just the body modifications—there's an overall sense of roughness to her; even now when she's comfortable she naturally emanates a sort of low-level hostility that I imagine successfully scares off most people at full force.

It's a moment of perspective I won't soon forget. It would be so sad if I had missed out on the chance to know these two humans because I allowed their outer veneers to scare me away. I'm already completely smitten with the two of them and their little family. Shaina is someone I definitely want to meet up with another time without "the men." She has a great sense of humor and has been so kind in her easy acceptance of me even though I'm arguably the odd one out among us. And Griff is a huge, fierce teddy bear (though I'll never *ever* say that to his face). I can see exactly what Graham meant when he told me Griff is a "ride or die" type—deeply loyal and protective and one of the most decent human beings he's ever met. It didn't take me long to verify that Griff has a heart as big as his body; it's downright endearing to see all 300 pounds of his formidable ferocity channeled into the love and protection of his family.

Still concentrating on his talk with Griff, Graham's hand reaches out to stroke my neck and shoulder lightly. It's a sweet little way of checking in, connecting with me even while we're part of different conversations. Again, I have that sense of *rightness* filling me, being here with Graham as a couple.

It's not that I was incomplete without him and now he's somehow made me whole. I wasn't lying all those times I told Marisa I didn't need a man—I don't *need* one. I wasn't waiting around for a man to come and give me validity as a person. These past few years I really have reached a place where I am whole and content as a person all on my own.

No, this is something different. I'd forgotten this feeling of being part of something *more*, a whole that's bigger than just my own. I am still me, and he is his own person, but now we're also connected in this new (or renewed, I suppose) entity that is *us*. I am here today as part of a unit, publicly making a mutual claim that we belong to each other. And it is *amazing*.

Eventually, Griff and Shaina go inside to grab some things for the finished burgers, after adamantly denying our offers to help. Once they're through the door with Layla close on their heels, Graham leans close and speaks to me in a low voice.

"I forgot to tell you—I may need you to drive the Range Rover back to my place."

"Why?"

"Griff's looking to sell his Harley and I told him I'm interested."

My eyes widen.

"You're going to buy a motorcycle?"

"I'm going to buy his motorcycle. He needs the money—he wants to get Shaina a new car before the baby comes."

I reach up and run my hand over the permanent scruff on his jaw, which is grown out a little at the moment so it's softer. *God, how I love this generous man.*

"That's sweet, Y. But have you ever been on a motorcycle?"

His eyebrows meet in a frown.

"Well, no."

"You know it's not like a bicycle, right?"

He gives me a look that says *"Please, don't insult me."*

"And you need a motorcycle license to drive it legally."

I watch his face fall in disappointment.

"Oh."

I slide my hand farther up his face until I can play with his hair. He cut it recently (I objected strongly when I first saw), but it's still long enough on top that I can run my fingers through it. I also made him promise to grow it back out, after presenting a very compelling list of reasons why he should. (Number 1: Man buns turn me on.)

"I can ride it, though."

I wish I'd taken out my phone so I could capture the look on his face—it's so shocked that I'm borderline offended.

"I have my license. I ride Barrett's bike sometimes."

A couple of years ago my brother had a six-month leave, and over the summer I convinced him to teach me to ride his motorcycle. Barrett is a Marine who works alongside some of the most badass women on the planet, so he never pulls sexist shit with me like telling me I can't get my motorcycle license. When he was deployed again he gave me the keys to his Ducati, which is parked in the garage of his apartment that he rarely stays in, and permission to ride it.

Mom was not pleased, but she knows how stubborn I am once I decide to do something. And I was determined. It was a heady feeling to conquer something so powerful and dangerous—another step in my quest to become stronger than I was at seventeen.

"You're kind of a badass now, huh?"

"Did you think I was sitting around waiting for you to come back and be strong for me?"

He's looking at me with a mixture of awed respect and something else—maybe confusion? Or fear? It's a look I see sometimes when he learns something about me that's changed. I suspect it's a glimpse into a part of him that fears my feelings for him will end up on that list.

Our conversation ends when Griff and Shaina return carrying condiments, followed by a bouncing Layla who is proudly swinging a bag of hamburger buns at her side.

* * *

"Stop it!"

"What?"

"Stop thinking about having sex on that thing."

I don't even need to see his sheepish smirk for confirmation; I already know I'm right.

"You're underestimating the logistics. *That* is not happening." I rotate my hand in a circular motion over the saddle seat of Griff's gorgeous Harley Low Rider.

I don't realize until it's too late that I've inadvertently issued a challenge.

Graham puts one large hand on each of my hips and backs me slowly toward the bike. I gulp at the predatory look in his eyes.

"You're underestimating my gift for logistics. I've got this all figured out, baby."

The back of my thighs brush the side of the bike as he maneuvers me all the way up against it. Then with a swift movement, he uses his grip on my hips to rotate me around so my back is to him. Graham moves in so close that his entire front is pressed to my back, enveloping me in his warmth and giving me a very clear idea of how hard he is as he presses his erection against my lower back. He places a palm along the middle of my spine and leans down to speak into my ear. The bristle of his facial hair lightly scrapes the edge of my jaw as his mouth moves, causing goose bumps to spread over my entire body.

"See, babe, I'll just bend you over it and fuck you from behind."

With a gentle but forceful push of his hand, he guides my torso down until I am bracing myself with forearms resting on the seat of the bike. He stands back up, hands curled around my sides right at my hipbones, the tips of his long fingers pressing into the top of my pelvis. Their placement is maddening—low enough that it causes my pulse to pound through that area and down to my sex, but not low enough to touch the place he's made ache. Behind me, he's rock hard and nearly lined up where he wants to be, pressing that impressive erection to the seam of my jeans.

"Oh," I say in a voice that's slightly faint. I swallow hard and can't help but push my hips back just a bit to rub against him. "That could work."

Who knows how far I'd have let him go if a deep throat clearing didn't sound behind us at that moment, reminding me that we're *still in Griff's garage.* I jerk in surprise and probably would have toppled to the other side of the motorcycle headfirst if Graham wasn't right there to tighten his hands at his hips and pull me backward to my feet. Griff's deep raspy voice rings out as I'm still regaining stability.

"Not in my house, kids. Do whatever you want with her once you get her home, but she's still mine until you leave."

My mouth is ready to drop open in shock and outrage before it dawns on me ... He's talking about the bike.

Graham laughs and his hands that are still at my hips give me a little squeeze. I'm certain I'm as red as a boiling lobster; it feels as though half of my body flushed in embarrassment.

"Oh, I will," Graham replies, and I smack him in his stomach. Of course, the damn thing is hard as stone so the only thing it hurts is my hand meeting zero resistance from his abs.

Griff turns to lead us back inside, and Graham's fingers graze the side of my face, moving a strand of hair so his lips have unobstructed access to my ear.

"Was that a yes?" he half whispers, half growls.

"Your house has a garage, right?"

"Yup."

I don't answer him with words. I just reach down and palm him between the legs, where he's still straining against his jeans. He curses low as I walk away from him toward the door, making sure my hips sway a little extra just to torture him.

20. KEEP THE HELMET ON

Graham

I've had a semi ever since Griff's garage. The sight of Mackenzie's perfect ass in those skintight jeans as she bent over the bike … *Fuck* it was hot.

But when she climbed onto the Harley to ride it back to my house? I almost lost it in my goddamn pants like a kid.

I can barely focus on the drive home, which is hardly surprising since all of the blood in my body is concentrated in my dick right now.

I'm so desperate for her that I can't even wait until she's climbed off the bike, or for the garage door to fully close.

"Keep it on," I growl as I stalk toward her. Her hands, which are at the sides of the helmet, about to pull it off her head, halt at my words.

I pick her up by the hips and swivel her around in the direction I want her, handling her weight with no effort at all because she's so fucking delicate. My very own fuckable china doll. No … that's messed up. *Shit.* I'll come up with a better analogy when my dick allows some blood back up to my brain.

Once she's sitting sideways on the saddle, I drop to my knees with no further hesitation. I have her jeans around her ankles in record time, and I'm running my beard along the insides of her thighs the way she likes.

"Graham ..." She already sounds turned on as fuck, which is good because I'm harder than the concrete floor I'm kneeling on.

She hisses a sharp inhale when I use my nose to rub over her folds, and her hips shift forward on the bike to get closer to my mouth. *Yeah, baby, I want you as close as possible too.* I hook my fingers around her hips to hold her to me. Then my tongue dives right inside those pretty pink petals. The smell and taste of her arousal coats my tongue immediately, and I groan, which makes her pussy spasm hard enough that I can feel it.

"You already this wet for me? Were you thinking about me fucking you the whole ride here?"

"Yes," she breathes out.

"Me too, babe. I'm gonna eat you first, and then I'm gonna bend you over that bike and come inside you." Right before my face, I watch the muscles of her sex contract. She loves it when I talk dirty to her.

I'm still not close enough, so I lift her legs and drape them over my shoulders. And then I eat her as ravenously as if I've been starving for days. From within the helmet she's still wearing, I hear her quietly chanting, "*Oh my God, oh my God.*" She's so turned on, she immediately starts bucking her hips and tugging on my hair in the pursuit of her orgasm. I'm almost disappointed by how quickly she comes ... *almost.* Because I'm beyond ready for round two.

She sags forward and I hold on to her legs to support her while she recovers from her orgasm, placing random kisses on her stomach and rubbing some of her juices off of my beard and onto her skin (which for some reason I find so fucking hot).

"You ready?" I ask her when her shaking has mostly stopped.

"Yes. Can I take the helmet off now?"

Fuck—I might be a terrible person, because it makes me so hot hearing this badass of a woman asking my permission. I'm not into that dominant Fifty Shades of Fucking nonsense and I would never want to actually hurt her with whips and shit—I mean, *seriously,* bro? — but there's something about her letting me be in control that's a huge turn-on.

"Yeah, baby. Take it off."

I let her keep her shirt on because it's cold now that the sun's gone down, and the garage isn't heated. I plan on keeping her pretty damn warm, though.

As soon as she has the helmet off, I dive in and taste her mouth with the same ferocious strokes of my tongue I just used on her pussy, and she wraps her legs around my waist. I'm still wearing my pants, which are strangling my dick, so I create just enough space that I can free him. We're not quite lined up this way, though, so I pick her up again and set her down on the floor with her back to me. Then I guide her to bend over and brace her arms on the bike's seat, recreating our position in Griff's garage—except this time her bare, luscious ass is sticking in the air before me and there's no Griff nearby to come and be a motherfucking cockblocker.

I lean over so my chest is pressed against her back, covering her body completely with mine. I reach around to knead her breasts, pinching her nipples through the fabric of her bra and clothes. She wiggles that ass backward trying to relieve the need I'm revving up. And who am I to let my girl suffer? I know how ready she is—the evidence was dripping from my mouth just a minute ago—so I don't waste any time taking her by the hips and tilting her to the perfect angle. I drag my cock through her wet folds a couple of times, driving us both crazy, and then I plunge inside the only heaven I've ever known. I'm so goddamned worked up I almost come right away, but I manage to fight it back. This is too good to let it end so soon.

Sometimes when we get naked, we make love—but this is undeniably *fucking*. It's uncontrolled, a little crazed, completely perfect. Around us, the garage is filled with the sounds of skin slapping on skin, the pants of our heavy breathing, and the occasional pleasured moan or curse.

I slam into her, burying myself all the way before pulling out fully. Then I do it all over again. With every forward thrust of my hips, Mackenzie pushes her ass back against me as though trying to take me impossibly deeper each time. With my hands still firmly gripping her hips, I pull her ass a little higher, angling her so I can reach that magical spot that sets her off like nothing else. I need her to come. I can tell that she's close—her tight inner muscles start to clench around me rhythmically.

"Come, baby," I demand, my voice rough from exertion and tight with the strain of holding back my own climax. "Come for me."

She does. Once her body begins spasming around me, squeezing my dick over and over as she rides her orgasm, I let go too. It only takes a couple of frenzied pumps into her still pulsing core before I come so hard I almost lose my footing. Her legs are unsteady as well, so I shift her back up to sit on the bike. Then I brace my arms on the bike on either side of her thighs and bury my face into her chest. For a minute or so, we simply stay there, unable to move or do anything but both breathe heavily.

"The logistics won't work, huh?" I mutter with my lips on her skin.

She laughs weakly, like I've fucked all the strength out of her. I sure as hell feel wrung out after that.

"Feel free to prove me wrong like *that* any time," she says.

We finally pull ourselves together enough to stumble out of the garage and up the stairs to my room where we collapse onto the bed. Mackenzie falls asleep almost immediately. It takes me a little longer, but I eventually join her in unconsciousness.

It's my first full night of sleep at this house in five years.

21. GHOSTS

Mackenzie

I wake slowly. My mind's transition to consciousness is gradual, the way thick honey drips from a jar. With my eyes still closed, I become aware of my surroundings one detail at a time. First, Graham—his big body is curled around mine, spooning me from behind, arms wrapped around me with a hand on my waist and the other cupping one of my breasts. My bare breasts, because the second thing I register is that I'm naked. The details are hazy in my sluggish mind, but I think I must have pulled my clothes off in the middle of the night, or maybe Graham did it (I can totally imagine Graham sleep-stripping me, the way other people sleepwalk). But I'm sure I was fully clothed when we stumbled into bed … which I also notice is not my bed. This isn't my house; something about the atmosphere tells me I'm not at home, though there's also a surprisingly potent sense of familiarity.

Finally, my eyes slide open to the sight of Graham's bedroom. I'm facing the room's large outer window through which morning light is creeping, illuminating my view of the gorgeous old trees that border the backyard. The plaid bedsheets beneath me, the sturdy wooden headboard visible in my periphery, even the smell of the pillow near my head … it all hits my senses in a sudden wave of déjà vu. It's all exactly the same as it was five years ago, down to the scent of the laundry detergent I now detect in the fresh bedding around me.

I carefully dislodge myself from Graham's grasp. He is out so deeply he merely flops onto his back and continues sleeping. Unusual muscles twinge as I step from the bed, and I remember. *The motorcycle.* My cheeks heat at the mental replay of what happened when we got back to Graham's house last night, a warmth that flows to other parts of my body as well. *That was so hot.*

No wonder I don't have any memory of how I ended up in Graham's childhood bed last night. Those were some seriously mind-scrambling orgasms.

I grab a shirt from the neatly stacked pile in his dresser—the exact same drawer where they used to be—and throw it on. Before slipping from the room to make some desperately needed visits to the restroom and kitchen, I steal one more glance back at the bed and the grown man asleep in this time capsule of his adolescence. My reaction to the sight of him is no longer a choice. It is as immediate and instinctual as breathing. *I love him.*

Padding my way barefoot over the dark hardwood floors of this massive house, I completely understand what Graham meant when he compared being here to living among ghosts. Within these walls time has stood still for the past five years, a perfectly preserved monument to a world that ended the day Graham's parents died. He's mentioned there was some paid cleaning service that took care of things all these years, and they did a hell of a job, because I don't see a single speck of dust as I run my eyes along the various framed photos decorating nearly every wall.

My heart squeezes as I stand before a photograph taken just months before the accident, from a charity benefit Graham invited me to: we're standing in our formal wear next to his parents, looking so very young and in love. The four of us are captured in a moment of happiness that makes me ache now.

I can only imagine the power of Graham's grief over the loss of his parents because I've mourned them deeply in my own way and my connection was trivial in comparison to his. The Wyatts were always good to me. They welcomed me with open arms from the moment Graham first brought me home and always welcomed me like a part of the family, treating me with love and acceptance. They weren't just good parents. They were good human beings, people I would have wanted to know even if I weren't dating their son.

In the kitchen I gulp down a glass of water and pop some dry cereal into my mouth (Lucky Charms … typical Graham). Every room of this house holds memories for me that seem to play out before my eyes. I can see Mr. Wyatt sitting at the kitchen barstool, reading on his iPad and drinking coffee. There were a couple of mornings he caught me sneaking out (it turned out he was a very early riser), but he just went back to reading and always pretended it hadn't happened, earning eternal cool points in my book.

It must be so hard for Graham to be here. I hadn't truly appreciated it until now.

Back in Graham's bedroom, I'm trying to be quiet as I collect my clothing from the floor when a large hand wraps around my waist, pulling me back onto the bed. I laugh and shake away the hair that flew across my face during his assault.

"There you are," he murmurs, gazing at me with sleepy hazel eyes and a smile that makes my insides quiver. "I don't know how you do it, but you make everything better. Even this place."

I run my hand along the overgrown scruff on his face, as always loving the rough scrape of it against my skin.

"You hate it so much here, why stay? Sell it. Or if you're not ready for that, just buy something else. You could get a place in the city.

You've got the money. There's nothing keeping you from doing whatever you want."

"Is that an invitation to officially move in?"

"No! *Graham!* We've only been together a couple of months."

His mouth tips up at the corner as his eyes take on a devilish glint.

"By my count it's been almost eight years."

I stare at him, unamused.

"I mean, we never actually broke up, so I've decided we were together the whole time."

I maintain my stern look but add in a little eye roll for good measure.

"Do you remember a break up conversation?" he continues, undeterred. "No, 'cause it didn't happen. So, technically, we never stopped dating."

He looks so proud of himself. A war wages inside me, frustrated exasperation wrestling against the pull of his charming irreverence. Frustration wins.

"I do remember a conversation, actually. It was when my dad woke me up in the middle of the night because he got a call from Chief Duluth that you'd been arrested in connection with a murder and were being booked without bail."

The cocky glint in his eye disappears, replaced by an all too familiar remorse that casts a darkness over his features. He opens his mouth, probably to apologize again, but I stop him with a finger to his lips. I'm not going to let him distract me from my point. I return to the original topic of this house.

"It's not your fault they died. You don't need to torture yourself in this house as some sort of penance."

"It's not my fault they died, but everything I did after is."

I stare at his face, trying to read him. He's lying on his back, and I'm right beside him with my head propped on one arm, looking down at all of his tragic, rugged beauty.

"You did your time, Y. Don't you think you've been punished enough? It's time to start believing you deserve good things again."

"Z, you're more of a good thing than I could ever hope to deserve."

The melancholy beneath his words tugs at me, and suddenly there is too much space between us. I sit up and swing a leg to his other side, straddling his stomach. I reach down to run my hands over his sculpted chest.

"Don't hope. Just do it. Keep waking up every day and being the man you really are, the one your parents always saw in you. Work on being your own good thing. I'll be right here every step of the way."

"Kenz." Graham's voice mirrors his face, a mosaic of pain and love and need.

His hands come up to my hips, and he slides me slightly backward, the motion also pushing down the sheet at his waist so I can feel his now uncovered erection nudging at my backside.

"I love you," I say. I haven't uttered the words much since that first time. I'm still wrapping my mind around the complete capitulation of my resolve. Somehow not saying it aloud made it easier to lie to myself, to keep believing I'm not in this so deep that I've passed the point of no return. But it's a lie. There's no going back, and it suddenly seems important to make sure he knows that.

I lift up slightly, angling myself just right, then take his hard length in one hand and position him at my entrance before lowering back down slowly. Like this I can take him in so completely he's hitting the farthest depths of me. I was already slick for him, but the feel of him warm inside me and the way he jerks once we are fully joined makes my core flood with arousal. He groans, his hands flexing where they grip my hips. I lean forward and brace my hands on his chest. Then I rock back and forth, the perfect angle causing my clit to rub against the base of his erection each time.

"Do you hear me?" I whisper, voice low and measured as I continue the slow undulations of my hips. "No more punishing yourself."

"Is this a new type of therapy, babe? Sign me up—but I gotta say I don't like the thought of you using this tactic with other patients." He pushes out the words in a voice gravelly with need.

"Don't deflect with sarcasm, *babe,*" I chide in the same soft voice as before, swiveling my hips on the last word and making him groan again.

"But no, this isn't for anyone but you. Only you."

His hands tighten at my sides, and I see his jaw clench. I'm torturing him—he needs me to move, to pick up the pace—but he's letting me do this my way. The sight of this powerful man, who could so easily use all that muscle to take control, shaking beneath me with the effort of restraining himself sends a fresh surge of lust through me that pushes me close to the edge. My movements become choppier, losing rhythm as I chase my release.

Sensing that I'm getting close, Graham begins to thrust upward while his hands hold my hips down to meet him. His powerful legs propel him forcefully despite his limited mobility in this position, and as he pushes up into me again, he hits that place that causes my whole body to begin tingling.

"Right there?" he asks, hips suspended off the bed as he rotates them, making lights dance before my eyes.

"Yes," I gasp out.

With his next thrust he hits that perfect spot again, and that's all it takes for me to shatter into a thousand blissful pieces. He holds me through the largest waves of my release before flipping us over in one powerful movement, still connected, so he is on top. His carnal grin is almost enough to push me over the edge again.

"My turn. You play patient now, babe—the doctor is in."

�֍   ✖   ✖

"Oh my God, why are these better than any other pancakes ever?" I groan around my mouthful of syrup covered fluffy blueberry goodness. I give the fork an extra swipe with my tongue, using it to hide my smirk of satisfaction over the way Graham's eyes darken with desire.

"It's the sex," he says matter-of-factly, reaching over to spear another huge section onto his own fork.

I almost contradict him before silently conceding that he's probably right. For all I know, there is absolutely nothing special about the blueberry pancakes, scrambled eggs, and home fries at this little diner near our old high school. But this was always our place, our special tradition: he would order pancakes, I'd order eggs, and we'd put our meals in the middle of the little table and share. And yes, we inevitably ended up here after burning a ton of calories with a night of sex.

I haven't been back here in years, and it fills me with a nearly overpowering sense of nostalgia and sadness, as his house did. But mostly I'm filled with food—amazing, grease and sugar loaded food paired with nearly toxic black coffee that somehow compliments it perfectly. I'm so grateful that my memories of this meal live up to the reality (similar to sex with Graham … though with him the reality is ten times better than I'd allowed myself to remember).

We even have our favorite table—the one that's debatably too small for two people, but perfect if you're two people who can't keep your hands off each other. There's no choice but to be right in each other's personal space, legs linked beneath the table, arms touching constantly while we eat. As teenagers we were shameless. A lot of times we'd just end up taking breaks from our food and making out right here over the table. I'm low-key tempted to go old school and give that a try now—Graham looks particularly delicious this morning in his too small Henley and his dark blond hair tousled in the same messy bedhead he woke up with.

I'm still eye fucking my—*boyfriend?*—when I hear a voice that should never be paired with fucking of any kind.

"Mackenzie? What are you doing?"

I don't need to turn and look, but I do and confirm what the pit of dread in my stomach already knows. It's my mom—standing right next to our little corner table with my father at her side.

"Mom? Dad?"

"Hello, Mr. and Mrs. Thatcher." Graham tries to get up but struggles to untangle his legs from mine and squeeze his large frame out from the tight corner seat.

I peek over at my dad and wish I hadn't, because he looks ready to turn this diner into a crime scene.

"Get the hell away from my daughter."

22. RUINER OF SUBURBIA

Graham

We just *had* to do the cutesy couple shit and sit over here at the smallest fucking table ever found outside a preschool.

It's bad enough that my first encounter with Mackenzie's parents is happening like this. (Seriously, take your pick of the unfavorable circumstances: it's unexpected, in public, and we were so hungry this morning we left my house without showering or making much effort to hide the *well-fucked chic* look we've both got going with our disheveled hair and clothes.) And just adding insult to injury, I'm over here idiotically fumbling to stand up like a giant trying to climb out of one of those clown cars and getting stuck halfway. The harder I try to free myself, the more I end up just banging my legs against the table's metal frame and hard edges. At least I manage to salvage a small sliver of my pride by swallowing back the curses that rise to my lips every time my shins or knees make impact.

It's a shit show. The whole scene only lasts a few seconds, but under the stone-faced stare of Mackenzie's father, every painful millisecond lasts an hour. I finally free myself and stand in front of the man who still pins me with eyes that look uncannily like Mackenzie's—except for their murderous expression.

I glance over to check on Mackenzie, who has made no move to leave her seat. She's frozen, face as pale as the paper napkin on the table.

"Did you hear me?" Mr. Thatcher growls.

I give our surroundings a fast visual sweep.

When we arrived, the diner was almost empty, but now nearly all of the tables are occupied. In my quick glimpse, I catch many pairs of curious eyes peeking in the direction of our little drama. The air in here was previously filled with the low-key white noise of quiet Sunday morning conversations underscored by sounds drifting out from the kitchen, but at Mr. Thatcher's raised voice the room's atmosphere suddenly picked up in volume and intensity. I swear I can almost make out my name among the dozen or so conversations happening around us. Maybe it's narcissistic to think they're all talking about me—hell, I hope I'm wrong—but I know this town. The blended sounds of every voice in here is reminiscent of buzzing bees, and Mr. Thatcher just poked their dormant nest, which will no doubt unleash a hoard of resurrected gossip and suspicions.

Yep, folks. That's right. Your friendly neighborhood murderer is back in town. Favorite scapegoat and Ruiner of Suburbia, right here.

I try to focus on the man I hope will one day be my father-in-law and ignore the sensation of all those eyes sneaking glances at me. And now I'm cursing my own stupidity ... Did I really taunt Fate a few weeks ago with that flippant thought that I'd prefer a confrontation with Mr. Thatcher over Marisa? Get that Latina fireball over here ASAP, because I am officially changing my stance on this issue. Mike Thatcher appears to be barely holding himself back from picking up the fork I just dropped and shoving it straight through my eyeball and into my brain.

Okay, God, I get it. You've called my bluff ... I'm ready to wake up from this nightmare now.

I break our staring contest by speaking first.

"Why don't we talk outside, sir?"

Mr. Thatcher nods stiffly and turns around to march out the front door. I grab some bills from my pocket and throw them on the table before following, not paying much attention but sure it's more than enough to cover our meal (in fact, there's a strong chance I just left $60 for a $15 tab, but if I can't take advantage of the whole millionaire thing in this moment of crisis then what is even the point?).

In the parking lot, the four of us cluster in something of a face-off: Mr. and Mrs. Thatcher on one side with me and Mackenzie facing them, the space between us teaming with tension and a sense that lines have been drawn.

I look at the older couple I haven't seen in five years. It's easy to see Mackenzie in Mrs. Thatcher's appearance. Although my girl's blue-green eyes came from her father, her mother is the one who passed on her slight stature and red hair (though I'd bet hers is dyed now because it's much darker than Mackenzie's natural strawberry hue). They both gave her the pale skin and proclivity to freckle, clearly inherited from a background of Irish and Western European ancestry.

Cynthia Thatcher turns to her daughter and speaks in a harsh tone that sounds like she's trying to whisper but failing.

"What are you doing with that boy? He *murdered* someone, Mackenzie."

Kenz makes no effort to keep her voice low. Apparently, she's rallied from her initial shock.

"No, Mom, he didn't! You don't know the real story ..."

She still doesn't know the whole thing either. I experience a twinge of guilt that I've been putting off having that talk, too caught up in how good things have been. Regardless, it feels amazing that Mackenzie is defending me right now.

"I hadn't even heard he was out ..." Mrs. Thatcher says faintly, almost as though she didn't hear her daughter at all and is just continuing a conversation with herself.

"I was released on parole the beginning of January," I say to the woman who still won't look at me. It seems she's going to pretend that she's having a private conversation with Mackenzie.

"And how long did it take you to track down my daughter?" Mr. Thatcher barks.

Three days. But I don't think my honest answer will help this situation. I square my shoulders and try to channel my sixteen-year-old self, aiming for some semblance of *"trustworthy boyfriend material."*

"I love her," I say firmly, looking first at him and then his wife. Mackenzie's small hand bumps the top of my leg, and I reach out to take it in mine. An overwhelming sense of relief fills me as our fingers twine together.

Both of Mackenzie's parents train their eyes on our joined hands and stay there. I give her hand a little squeeze of reassurance (I hope it works, because I certainly don't feel very reassured). Mr. Thatcher still looks ready to rip me in half, but now he turns that scowl on Kenz.

"He's a criminal, Mackenzie. A murderer, a drug addict ... nothing but a thug."

"Dad, I understand there's been a lot of gossip and you've heard terrible things, but it's all exaggerated."

"So, he *didn't* go to prison for murder?"

"Accessory to murder!" she retorts.

His face turns beet red in anger, that fair skin he passed to his daughter broadcasting his emotions the same way hers does.

"Do you hear yourself? Jesus. We taught you better than this. The daughter I raised is a strong woman who is smart enough not to let a boy make a fool out of her ... twice."

Okay now. That's enough. I step forward and slightly to the side so my body blocks Mackenzie from her father.

"With all due respect, sir, your problem is with me. There's no need to attack Mackenzie."

"You think you can tell me how to speak to my daughter?"

"No, sir. I think that I will protect my girlfriend from being mistreated, even by you."

Mackenzie, too badass to hide behind me, steps around and returns to standing by my side.

"You're *dating* him? Mackenzie!" Mrs. Thatcher immediately accosts, speaking in a universal disappointed mother tone that fills me with an instinctual fear even though she's not talking to me.

"I love him, Mom," my brave girl says in a quiet but steady voice.

"So, it wasn't enough to ruin her life once, you're out to do it again?" Mike asks me—we used to be on a first name basis, which I'm guessing is no longer the case.

"That is not my intention, sir." I try to keep my words even and respectful.

But he's apparently done with me because he turns back to Kenz. This is less a conversation than a tennis match the way words are rapidly pinging back and forth among the four of us.

"Go home," Mr. Thatcher orders his daughter.

"Graham drove."

"Okay then, I'm taking you home. Go wait at my car. I'll be there in a minute."

In my peripheral vision I see her stance straighten. Her voice is firm.

"No, Dad. You're wrong about this, and I'm not letting you and Mom keep me from Graham anymore by filling my head with half-truths. You might be disappointed in me right now, but I'm disappointed in you too. For not even taking a second to consider that you haven't gotten the whole story, to hear me out. *Me*. You don't have to believe him, but I expected you to at least listen to me. To have some more faith in me." She looks up and I see the slightest sheen of emotion in her eyes. "I'll be in the Range Rover."

I hand over the keys and she walks across the parking lot at a fast pace, her mother close on her heels speaking rapidly though I can't make out her words.

"She's too good for you," Mr. Thatcher spits at me when we're alone.

"I know, sir." I look him right in the eye, gaze steady and face serious so he will be able to see how much I mean my words. "But if she'll let me, I plan to spend every day of the rest of my life trying to be worthy of her. I'll devote everything I have to taking care of her and being the man she needs me to be."

I think I see the smallest flicker of respect in his eyes, but it's gone too quickly to tell for sure.

"You left a whole mess behind when you were arrested."

"I know that too, sir."

"No, you don't know. You weren't here to listen to that precious girl cry herself to sleep for months. To watch her light dim. You lied to her and broke her heart, and because of your poor decisions you weren't even here to witness the consequences of your actions. So don't think you can just pick things up now and forget. I never forget. Ever."

He reaches inside the pocket of his jeans, and for a split second my heartbeat pounds in my temple as I think he's going to produce a weapon. Instead, he removes his wallet. He flips open the plain brown leather billfold and produces a small white square that he holds up between two fingers. It appears to be a tightly folded sheet of white notebook paper, well-worn crease marks and faded blue lines giving away its age.

"I've been carrying this around for five years. I found it in Mackenzie's garbage bin six months after you went to prison." He hands it to me solemnly. "I'm giving this to you now because your father was a good man, and I have to believe some of that goodness is still in you, and that when you read this, you'll do the right thing. Finally face what you did, see how you killed my little girl's spirit, and be the man your father raised you to be. Let her go."

✳ ✳ ✳

Graham,

Ugh, I never thought I'd be this girl who starts bawling at just the sight of your name. Or the girl who has to take a break from writing a letter because she's crying too hard to write. (Can you see the tear drops? Those aren't added for effect.)

I wasn't ever supposed to be this girl. I looked at all the drama and heartache of my friends and pitied them, because I knew we were a forever thing. (Was I wrong? Please, if you could only say one thing to me ever again, give me that answer.)

I think about writing you every day. This isn't the first letter I've written, and just like the others I probably won't ever send it. At what point am I no longer writing to you and only writing to an imaginary friend? If a letter falls in the forest and no one reads it, does the girl who wrote it even exist?

I feel very alone. I am very alone. Anyone willing to listen stopped being patient months ago. Mom and Dad don't get it. So, with them, and at school, I pretend I'm okay. "Yes, all healed up, fine now!" And everyone buys it because that's what they expect.

I can tell they don't take it seriously. I mean, we're just teenagers. It's only a high school relationship. It's not the end of the world. It couldn't possibly be real love! I see it in their faces when I slip and forget to act like I'm happy. It's impatience, like they're all thinking, "What a drama queen. Is she really still milking this Graham thing?"

But you and I know they're wrong. We know that our love is as real as it gets, no matter what age we are. So, I let them look at me and assume I'm just infatuated with the hot quarterback, a "high school sweethearts" thing. They don't understand what it's like. How when I look at you, I see my future, the other half of my soul. Our love is the thing people spend lifetimes looking for, you know? It is the kind of love that inspires epic poetry and the greatest of love songs.

Or ... was. Our love is a was now, Graham. And it's all your fault.

Why did you do that? Why haven't you written to me? Do you just think I'm a huge naïve idiot because I thought we were in this together, while you had a whole secret life on the side without me?

Why didn't you tell me what was going on? You could have. You could have told me anything. Why didn't you trust me? Was there ever a second, a minute we spent together where you felt anything less than one hundred percent confident in my love for you? No, it's just not possible. You couldn't have failed to feel my love, because I gave you everything, let you inside my body and every part of my heart and handed you so much of myself that I have nothing remaining now that you're gone. I'm empty because you have all the best parts of me and you left without giving them back.

What the hell, Graham? How can you not get how lost I am without you? Or do you know and you just don't care? Are you really just the manipulative thug my parents want me to believe you are?

As I walked through the halls at school, I used to be astonished that no one noticed the bright glow of love I felt shining around me. Now I can't believe they don't all stop and stare, call an ambulance or something, because I'm bleeding out slowly right in front of them, the way you would if you were cut in two. It hurts so much sometimes I can't breathe. And the only person I want—to hold me and talk to me and make it all better—is the very one who is making me hurt.

X X X

I wrote all that a while ago. I'm doing a lot better dealing with all of this now. I'm not crying every day anymore, which is something. I've decided it's pathetic that I'm writing these things to you, that I'm still holding on to the idea of you as my person, my safe place. Because you're not, are you?

So, this is the last time I'm going to write. But there are a few more things I need to say, even though you'll never read them.

I tell everyone I'm okay, and sometimes I even feel okay. But most of the time I physically ache from missing you. I looked it up online, and I am totally suffering from phantom limb syndrome—of the soul.

I hate you for making me feel this way. I want to shake you and scream at you. (I want to kiss you and hold you.) I want some closure, to clearly sever ties so I can be free. (I want the hope of becoming entwined tighter together.) I am conflicted.

My heart desperately wants you to be my future, although my brain tells me that you are in my past. And my parents, and everyone else in Westwood ... they're saying terrible things, and I have no choice but to believe them because you haven't said anything to the contrary. You haven't said anything at all.

It's time for me to grow up, to try and start figuring out what it means to survive without you (the way a person can live with only one kidney.) I just have to learn to look at the world differently. Because Mom is right—that boy who was my great love and future? You're not him. Maybe you were never him.

Where did he go? What did you do with him? Where is the boy I loved, the person who was my best friend, who I cherished with my whole heart? You can't be him. He wouldn't be in prison on a murder charge. He never would have been at that gas station in the middle of the night with drug dealers. He said he'd never leave me.

This is where I get to be the one who walks away.

Goodbye.

Mackenzie

�֍   ✷   ✷

"What's that?"

I nearly jump out of my skin at Mackenzie's voice right behind me.

I've been sitting on her bed reading the letter over and over while she showered. The drive back to her place was silent, and every one of the quiet tears I watched trail down her face seemed to land in my soul like burning acid.

I haven't decided yet how to bring this up to her, but she takes the choice out of my hands the way she swipes the letter from me with deft fingers. I watch her face go through a cycle of recognition, confusion, and anger as she recognizes what she's looking at.

"Where did you get this?"

"Your dad."

"My *dad*? How does he even have this? Wait—does that mean he read it!?"

Her whole face is bright red with a combination of anger and embarrassment.

"He said he found it in your trash. Kenz … we need to talk about that letter."

Her eyes pool again with unshed tears.

"No. You were never meant to see this. No one was. Why did my dad even have it with him? Why did he give it to you?"

"You meant everything in there?" I ask with a nod toward the letter, ignoring her words for now.

"Yes." One rogue tear escapes her eye.

I drop my head down to rest on my hands. *That letter.* I feel gutted, on the verge of tears myself.

"I knew it was bad, but … fuck, Kenz. Maybe your dad is right."

"What are you saying?"

"Maybe I am a murderer because I killed your spirit. You deserve so much better. Maybe I should walk away now before I do more damage."

23. MARTYR MOVE

Mackenzie

"No."

"...No?" Graham asks slowly.

His face is haunted, overcome by the same darkness that often casts shadows at the edges of his eyes. I won't let that sorrowful look distract me from my current frustration. I don't know what my dad said to Graham that brought all of his self-loathing and guilt to the surface, but I'm pissed off at both of them right now.

This morning was hard. I knew my parents wouldn't be happy when I first told them I'd reconnected with Graham, but of all the ways I could imagine it going, this was pretty much the worst scenario possible. I was always a good kid; I got in trouble with my parents sometimes but nothing big, and I certainly never did anything that made them speak to me the way they did this morning. I've also never outright defied them before. I'm drained after that confrontation, and I could really use some time doing something comforting, like watching TV in Graham's arms … not *this*.

"Just … no. You are not pulling this *'I'm leaving you to save you from me'* bullshit. If you don't want to be with me anymore, we'll end things … at some point in the future, because if you try to claim that right now, I will call you on that bullshit too."

I scan the page now permanently creased along the fold lines. I don't need to read the whole thing because I remember well enough to recognize that this piece of paper is an X-Ray image of my soul, a vivid snapshot of my insides at the time I wrote it.

I can't believe my father had this letter on him. It's something I'll need a lot more time to process and wrap my mind around, because it brings into question the way I've always thought my parents trivialized everything I went through after Graham was arrested.

All of this passes through my mind rapidly in the brief moment that I allow myself for reflection. Then I return my attention to Graham.

"This?" I wave the paper around emphatically. The motion creates a flapping sound that seems to accentuate my ire. "This is not a reason to try and pull a martyr move. You already did enough of that in the five years you didn't write or call. I'm guessing you had some noble intention of *'denying yourself'* because you didn't *'deserve'* me. Well, I hate to break it to you, but your concept of selflessness is flawed. In trying to punish yourself, you made me suffer the consequences too, and while supposedly shielding me from hurt, you caused me more pain than you can imagine."

I glance back down at the letter in my hand, filled with handwriting I can easily recognize—though my penmanship has changed over the years. The words my eyes skim over are so familiar and yet foreign. This letter is from another life, a completely different version of me.

"The girl who wrote this? This girl doesn't need you to protect her. You're five years too late. She doesn't exist anymore—she grew up and learned how to save herself. So, babe, I love you, but please stop trying to save me. I don't want a hero. I want a partner. I want *you*.

Every day I make the choice to be with you, complete with all of our past baggage. I need you to do the same, so we can carry it together."

I squeeze my eyes shut. My whole body is suddenly heavy with exhaustion. "Do you get it? Because if you don't ... I'm tired, and I can't do any more of this today. So, if you're planning to say more of that nonsense, I'm going to have to ask you in advance to just ... not. In fact, you're banned from speaking unless it's to say, 'Yes, Kenz, you're right. I'm a goddamn idiot and I'm so lucky to have you back in my life.'"

I'm certain my whole face is red from how worked up I just got. I've created new lines in the paper from how my grip on it tightened as I spoke. It felt good to say all that, though. Because I remember the seventeen-year-old who wrote this letter, even if I'm not her anymore, and I want to do her justice.

Graham is quiet for long moments, and I watch his face carefully. That face used to be as familiar to me as my own, maybe even more so. Even now, those features are much the same as the ones I once memorized, despite the changes the years have wrought. Along with the scruffy beard, there is a new strain to his features—the difference between a teenager who has never known tragedy and a man who has seen the dark depths of grief and lived among the sinister side of humanity.

He closes his eyes and takes in a deep breath, hiding whatever thought or emotion he finally settled on, then opens them and walks to me. He wraps his arms around me but stays far enough away that he can still look me in the face.

Then he speaks with dead seriousness, eyes and voice so full of sincerity I would swear the words are spontaneously coming from his own brain.

"Yes, Kenz, you're right. I'm a goddamn idiot and I'm so lucky to have you back in my life."

24. ALL THE WOMB THROBBING

Mackenzie

"Well, I think I've reached a new low," Marisa declares. "Perving on hot man candy at a six-year-old's birthday party. Not to mention those are two incredibly taken pieces of ass."

Marisa, Shaina, and I are seated facing the little group that's here to celebrate Layla's sixth birthday—though honestly, we're mostly looking at Graham and Griff.

"We can hardly blame you. Our men are one hundred percent fine. Look all you want," Shaina assures her.

It's a beautiful sunny day in May, perfect for hanging out at Layla's favorite park. The party required very little setup; Griff and Shaina took over a couple of tables right next to the playground earlier, covered them with bright purple tablecloths, then set out pizza and juice boxes for the kids, and of course the cake. Besides us, Layla invited five friends from school (three little girls and two boys). After they were finished with the "official" birthday party business of cake and presents, the kids all ran off to play with Griff and Graham, and the three of us dragged our folding chairs over to this side of the park (well, Griff carried Shaina's despite her adamant protests that it isn't even heavy). We've been camped out ever since in our primo spot under a shady tree where we can watch them playing but have enough distance to discuss things that might not be suitable for the ears of five and six-year-olds. And, of course, we have a perfect view of the two huge attractive men currently putting themselves at the mercy of six children.

"You're not the only one perving. I think Kenz is fixing to drag Graham off for a car quickie any second now," Shaina adds, and they both laugh.

You'd never guess I only introduced them a couple of weeks ago; Marisa and Shaina hit it off instantly, and the three of us have been hanging out whenever we can manage it. We've already started counting down the days until we can go out drinking together once Shaina's son is born.

I give my friends a shrug and my best impression of a Graham smirk. I can't argue with Marisa's assessment of the view, and I have no defense for Shaina. I have been very distracted by the "man candy." Though while I suppose Griff is hot, I only have eyes for a certain dirty blond with hazel eyes. Even now I can only tear my gaze away for a moment before locking back onto him. And yes, I am more than a little hot and bothered.

Today Graham is wearing an outfit we picked out together last weekend, when I finally took him shopping to get clothes that fit (I admit I'll miss those tight shirts he was wearing, but he kept complaining he could barely move his arms so I took pity on him). Those new jeans do things for his ass that should be illegal, and the olive shirt he has rolled up to the elbows makes the green in his eyes stand out beautifully. But it's not his physical appearance that has me legitimately considering Shaina's "car quickie" suggestion—it's watching him with Layla and her friends. At the moment, Graham is lying flat on his back in the grass, letting Layla and her little squad attack him with foam swords. I think he's supposed to be a dragon and they're slaying him. It's hard to tell what he's going for with the dramatic "dying" sounds we can hear from all the way over here, but the kids are eating it up. Occasionally the sound of their high-pitched giggling travels over to us in addition to Graham's wailing.

The thing about Graham is that he is six feet of pure contradiction. He is as manly as they come: ruggedly unshaven, muscled, athletic, and prone to caveman tendencies. But he is also the man I'm captivated by right now, able to put aside all sense of ego and sacrifice his dignity for the children's happiness (he never looked even a tiny bit embarrassed wearing the crown Layla put on him earlier). They have his full attention, and he's not half-assing anything. I can tell even from this distance that he's putting his whole heart into playing with them.

Seriously, who knew watching Graham with kids would turn me on this much? I've spent plenty of time around kids over the years, and even had chances to witness a couple of my ex-boyfriends with them, but it never once inspired any urgent yearning and certainly no sexual arousal. Until today. I'm only twenty-three, so there's no biological clock ticking here … It's just Graham. The idea of having his babies is too potent, and I am helpless to fight my body's primal reaction. My womb is sending every possible code red, SOS, and smoke signal to the rest of my body with the message to get Graham over here, stat, so we can start with the baby making.

"So, should we expect a mini Graham any time soon?" Shaina asks, hand resting on her belly. I swear it's twice the size as the last time I saw her, and I have absolutely no idea how she's lugging that thing around with her otherwise tiny body. Not to mention she still has a few months left! It seems cosmically unfair that such a small woman should be carrying a giant's spawn.

"Oh, no," I respond immediately. Do I want to jump his bones right now? *Hell yes.* But as for actual procreation, I'm definitely not ready. "We're not there yet. Don't listen to Graham's 'eight year' theory about how we 'never broke up.' We've only been back together for four months. It's way too soon to even think about kids. Plus, I have an IUD that's got a few years to go."

I've never been so glad I went for that IUD at the end of undergrad. Considering the way my ovaries are screaming watching Graham give Layla a piggyback ride, I doubt I'd be able to stay strong if he started campaigning for a baby. Not to mention the serious likelihood of an "oopsie" caused by getting caught up in the moment and forgetting a condom. We'd be parents in no time.

"I don't know," Marisa says with a quirked eyebrow. "If we're talking a battle between modern science and Graham's sperm, I think I'd put my money on him. If anyone could fuck a baby into you through sheer force of will—and by *will* I actually mean *hard and repeated penetration*—it's that man."

"Thanks for that," I say sarcastically as Shaina bursts out laughing. "And you sound awfully familiar with my boyfriend's sexual prowess. Anything you want to tell me?"

I'm kidding. I'm confident the two of them would never do that to me. But it's too fun poking at my bestie.

"We share a wall, chica," she reminds me with a significant look and a raised eyebrow. She doesn't stop there, though, turning to Shaina. "Our apartment is like that *Friends* episode where Joey and Chandler find a 24/7 porn station on TV."

When we stop laughing at that, we lapse back into silence for a little bit, and I keep watching Graham and the kids. *I want that.* I do. I never really had a doubt that I envisioned motherhood as a part of my future, but during those years Graham was gone, it seemed such an abstract concept, easily put out of mind in the category of "someday." When I pictured that future, there was always a fuzzy and obscure partner beside me who I'd be creating and raising those children with. I figured he was just some forever guy I hadn't found yet. It's crazy how quickly Graham's face has resumed its former place in that picture, especially today when my mind keeps superimposing images of our children over the kids he's playing with. And again ... all the womb throbbing.

"Was he planned?" I ask Shaina, nodding my head toward her baby bump.

"I don't think anything about me and Griff has ever been planned," she says with a little eye roll. Then she splays both palms over her stomach as though trying to cover her unborn son's ears; she has small hands and the bump is gigantic, so she barely spans half of it, but I still find the effort cute. "Honestly, it isn't the best time to be having another kid. Griff won't actually say it, but I can tell he's already worried about money even without a new baby. It's going to be a stretch suddenly having to buy diapers and baby stuff, especially since I'll have to be out of work for who knows how long."

Marisa and I make sympathetic noises but don't say anything, because there's nothing we can say. We may share a similar dirty sense of humor and have fun spending time with Shaina, but neither of us can truly understand the position she's in. She's only five years older than us, but sometimes she seems much older than that. At our age she already had Layla, a baby she had to care for on her own because Griff was in prison. Marisa and I simply don't have the life experiences to empathize with the sort of burden and responsibility she and Griff have. I secretly strengthen my resolve to help Graham with his goal to help them out financially.

"We're happy, though," Shaina says. "Griff and I traveled a long hard road to get here, but having what we do now somehow makes all that shit in between worth it. And I wouldn't trade Layla for anything in the world, even though she came at a rough time too. A rougher time, actually," she laughs.

This woman amazes me and continues to do so every time I'm with her. She's so strong and so incredibly resilient. And when she says she's happy, I can tell she truly means it. I have no doubt that she and Griff will make it work no matter what comes their way. I've only heard little bits of their story from Shaina as we've spent time together the past few months, but it's enough to know she's not kidding that it was tough. Maybe because of that, I get the sense that they are even more appreciative of what they have together and will fight to survive anything that tries to get in their way. I can only hope Graham and I will hold up under the test of time the way our friends have.

"I can't even begin to tell you how much better this pregnancy is. Griff got arrested when I was only a few months along with Layla, so this time he's going almost too far being sweet and helpful. I love it, but don't tell him, because I like giving him shit. And being pregnant makes me horny all the time, so having him nearby is very helpful." She gives us a little wink and waggles her eyebrows.

"So glad you're mentioning it, because I've been meaning to ask about those logistics ..." Marisa says. She makes some insane hand motions that I think are meant to represent Griff's giant 6'4" form and Shaina's 5'2" petite frame.

Proving why they became instant friends, Shaina doesn't so much as blink or blush at Marisa's question. She just leans forward a bit and smiles wickedly.

"Well, first of all, yes ... it's *huge*."

25. NO ADDITIONAL FOREPLAY REQUIRED

Mackenzie

Graham and I help clean up the tables, which looked like a hurricane had blown through by the time the last kid's mom came to pick her up. We fill a garbage bag with all the scattered wrapping paper, empty juice boxes, and plates of frosting smeared cake, then collect Layla's presents neatly in a second bag. Once we finish, Shaina pushes her camping chair next to the picnic table and sits down with a sigh, propping her feet up on the wooden bench seat. She closes her eyes for a moment, tipping her head back to soak up the late afternoon sun.

Layla, who still has tons of energy, is on the other side of the picnic tables animatedly chatting with her new BFF Marisa (well, she might be tied with Graham for that title. I'm not going to mention this because the two of them would have way too much fun arguing about it). I smile remembering the first time Shaina brought Layla over to our place. Before they arrived, Graham asked me (adorably hesitant and obviously choosing his words carefully) if Marisa could behave around a kid. I wish I'd gotten my phone ready to snap a photo of his jaw nearly hitting the floor when I informed him that Marisa—my sassy foul-mouthed roommate infamous for her sexually explicit comments, who calls Graham "Señor McFuckHot"—is actually focusing her studies on childhood and adolescent psychology. He's now admitted that she's basically magic with kids or a "kid whisperer" as Shaina calls it.

"Heads-up!"

A football flies into our area, and Graham immediately moves in and catches it midair. He does this gracefully and makes it look so simple, filling me with a little glow of pride. I'm reminded of so many great times in high school watching him play. *I wonder when he last touched a football?*

A guy who looks a little younger than us—maybe an undergrad? —comes running over from the open field on the far side of the park.

"Sorry!" His eyes widen slightly as Graham throws the ball back to him with the same easy perfection. The guy's friend comes up to join him and together they walk closer to our group rather than going back to the field.

"Nice arm!" the second guy says to Graham in an appreciative tone. The two wide-eyed boys look Griff and Graham up and down.

"Ooh, I've read this one like fifteen times! This is a classic romantic comedy Meet Cute ... they are *soooo* going to end up together," Marisa narrates quietly so only Shaina and I can hear. We try to smother our laughter so the guys don't notice and ask us to explain.

"Uh, we could use a couple more. You guys want to play?" the first boy asks.

Griff and Graham's heads simultaneously swing in our direction, looking for all the world like two kids asking their mom for permission. I lay a hand over my mouth, faking a little cough as I struggle to hold in another bout of giggles.

"What do you think? It's up to you, babe," Griff asks Shaina, aware she must be tired from the long afternoon.

"Twenty minutes," Shaina consents with a look and tone that screams 'mom' that I've seen countless times from my own mother. Perhaps it's part of some standard hormonal programming that's automatically downloaded into women when they give birth.

Layla jumps up and down, even more excited than the men. We collect all of our things and follow the boys over to the field, which is just beyond a cluster of trees that mostly obstructed it from our view before. We set out our chairs along the sideline and get comfortable to watch, laughing about how it truly feels like we're here to watch our kids at sports practice.

The boys cluster around Griff and Graham then break off into two groups. It seems each team got one of our guys since Graham walks off in one direction and Griff in the other. I hadn't noticed before, but now I see they must be playing "Skins versus Shirts," because the boys on one side of the field are bare chested. I've just registered this when something flies at me so quickly I don't have time to duck. The fabric lands square in my face, covering my whole head and obstructing my vision. I instantly identify it as Graham's shirt—I could recognize his scent anywhere)—and when I remove it, Graham is indeed now standing in the center of the field with every glorious dip and ridge of his chest on display. He smirks at the sound of Marisa and Shaina's obnoxiously loud whistles and cheers. Layla joins along, although she is too young to understand that we're celebrating her Uncle Graham's hotness. I add a "whoop" of my own, and he winks at me before turning his focus to the other boys on his team as they begin the game.

It's immediately apparent that Graham is on a totally different level than the rest of the guys, and even with Griff's formidable presence on defense, the Shirts team has no chance. Our guys stand out from the pack and are always easy to spot, not only because they are taller than almost every boy playing (Griff the tallest by far), but there is no question that they are *men* among a group of *boys*.

This is without a doubt my favorite football game of all time. I obviously see Graham naked frequently, but I'm now determined to find more opportunities to have him remove his clothing outdoors, because the natural sunlight really shows off the masterpiece that is his body better than any lightbulb. I give up trying to follow the ball, too fixated on watching the way the muscles in Graham's back and shoulders twist and contract as he runs and the sculpted finesse of his arm as he throws the ball. He works up a light sweat and the glistening moisture serves to highlight the definition in his chest and abdomen, a natural version of that oil photographers use on male models.

Holy mother of sweet panty soaking views. The car quickie is no longer optional (and no additional foreplay will be required).

For twenty minutes, our little group of four on the sideline is the world's strangest cheering squad. We cheer for both teams indiscriminately, but for our men especially. Layla, not really understanding the rules of the game, claps and yells at completely random moments and screams "Go, Daddy!" basically any time Griff moves. Marisa ruins more than one play by distracting the players with her unique exclamations of encouragement. We can only hope Layla's too busy in her own little world to pay attention because it wouldn't be great if she parroted any of this at school.

"Hey, someone on Skins switch with Gingerbread. Show us the goods! Yes, I mean you, Carrot Top!"

"*Aye Papi,* get those hands on it!" (To a boy wearing a Red Sox jersey with 'Big Papi' on the back.)

"Ooh yes, Abercrombie, way to get on top of him. Don't be afraid to grab a little flesh!" (When one boy tackles another to the ground to prevent a touchdown.)

When their twenty minutes is up, Shaina signals to Griff, and after some manly handshakes and back slaps, our sweaty men join us on the sideline. Layla, who finally seems to have run out of steam, immediately flies into Griff's arms so he can carry her to their car. We say goodbye in the parking lot and all exchange hugs before dispersing to our own vehicles.

Thankfully, Marisa drove herself.

I fix my eye on Graham and watch his face change as he takes in the expression on mine.

"Think you can find us a more private parking spot?"

26. SHRINK SHADY

Graham

"Good to see you, Doc. It's been a minute."

"It's good to see you too, Graham. I was surprised—pleasantly— to see you on my calendar. I still don't understand how you managed to get the front desk staff to make this appointment, though. It's very … unconventional."

"Oh, you mean Beth? We're old pals." I shrug and try to tone my grin down to a smirk.

Did I make a dozen calls just trying to find the woman I only knew as "Dr. Shady" and then another couple hundred to her office in order to end up in this chair? Yep. I won't admit it to her, though.

"You're something else," Doc replies with her own version of a smirk and a shake of her head. "But then you always were."

Turns out it's not so easy to track down your old shrink from prison. I finally found the woman we all called "Shrink Shady"—whose full name I've now learned is Dr. Sade Hadiyah—in this little professional building in Roslindale where she rents an office twice a week for appointments with her patients who aren't in prison. As I've now heard many times, it's not standard practice for her to have contact with the inmates she counsels in prison once they've been released, but I managed to convince the lovely receptionist Beth that I am not "standard." She finally decided I'm not a threat to the doc's safety after I showed up a couple of times with donuts and coffee for the whole office staff, looking my most civilized with my beard groomed and wearing some of my dad's expensive dress clothes.

"So, tell me what's been going on. How are you finding life on the outside?"

Her voice is more familiar to me than most in the world, and I immediately settle in my chair and sink into the old routine of spilling my guts to her. She looks the same too. Her shiny straight black hair is closely cropped around her face—a look that she totally rocks, Audrey Hepburn style. She's the opposite of Audrey in every other way, though, from her short curvy frame to her skin that's the color of spiced apple cider. She's a good-looking woman, which the inmates definitely noticed. It's her face, however, that always draws and keeps my attention. There's something … *serene* about it, this calm quiet strength that became something of a touchstone for me over the years I met with her, a steady constant that I drew comfort from the way some people do the North Star.

At first, I just stick to the good stuff. She saw me through my darkest times, and I want to show off a little by sharing how well I'm doing. I tell Doc about being back with Mackenzie and how great things are going with us and even the online course I'm taking on founding and running a nonprofit.

"I want to do some good with all this money Mom and Dad left me, you know? I certainly don't need all of it. All I need is a place to live, funds to keep Mackenzie supplied with tacos and chocolate whenever she wants, some savings in case things go to shit, and enough to send our kids to college."

She gets a look in her eyes, the one that means she approves of something I've said.

"That's an extremely responsible and healthy vision for your life, and it seems you're on track to accomplish that. You should be very proud of yourself, Graham. *I'm* proud of you."

Honest to God, I almost tear up hearing that from her, especially since the doc isn't someone who throws around empty compliments. For so long I've felt like nothing but a fuck up, a part of me sure that I'd always be a fuck up. I can't remember the last time I was proud of myself or thought that I might be worthy of anyone else's pride.

Unfortunately, she hasn't heard the whole story. I wish I could just leave it here, on a high note, but the stuff I haven't told her is among the more important reasons I came here today.

"There's some other shit I wanted to talk to you about too," I finally make myself say. "This is still confidential, right?"

"Of course." She leans forward slightly in her chair, alert to the seriousness in my voice.

"There's a situation, and I've … had to keep some things from Mackenzie lately."

Fucking Eli. After months of hearing nothing from him, he popped back into my life and now seems determined to deliver perpetual reminders that he isn't done with me.

It started toward the end of April, a couple of weeks before Layla's birthday. I walked out of my house one day to find that my Range Rover, which was sitting right there in my driveway, sporting a new cosmetic feature: it had been keyed, the word SNITCH scratched along the entire driver's side of the car. That's when I called Kenz and had to lie to her for the first time since I've been out—my first real lie, not just an omission—as I cancelled our plans by claiming car trouble and convinced her she didn't need to come get me. Griff was my second call, and he referred me to a guy he said would do the body work for me quickly and discreetly. Those two days of driving around in my mom's car were hell, a constant reminder that I was lying to my girl.

Since then a week hasn't gone by without at least one incident, though it's often twice. It started with petty pranks, juvenile shit that was annoying but didn't worry me too much. My car getting keyed. A dead rat left at my front door. A shattered window on the first floor of my house. It was creepy they were at my house, rubbing it in my face that they know where I live, but all basically harmless. Just intimidation tactics that I suppose Eli sees as a way to play with his food before he eats it. His food being me and the eating being … well, I've tried hard not to remember the chilling calm in his pale eyes when he threatened to kill me that night in the parking lot.

Then a week ago things escalated. I started getting text messages from a blocked number with photos attached, straight up surveillance style photos like you see in the movies. It's so cliché that at first I wanted to roll my eyes, but when I looked closer it stopped being funny at all. The pictures are of me, and they're not all from the past few weeks … they seem to go back months. A shot of me leaving the bank. One of me inside the grocery store taking a box of cereal off the shelf. Filling my car with gas. Leaving Target with a bag that had Layla's birthday presents inside.

The red x's drawn over my head in all the pictures—probably done in Snapchat or some phone app with someone's finger—are loud and clear. He wants me dead, and he knows where to find me. There are no words included, but none are needed. They are watching me, clearly following me, and I never even noticed. Thankfully,

Mackenzie never shows up in the photos, which all appear to be taken in the Westwood area.

I've gotten paranoid, always watching the cars around me trying to figure out if I'm being followed and taking ridiculously out of the way routes every time I drive to Mackenzie's place in Brighton. I was actually grateful when Mackenzie went on a yoga retreat for some sort of teacher training because I didn't want to add to all the lies I've already told her. But she'll be back tomorrow.

I scrub my hands over my face as I finish telling Doc all the gory details. I even admit to lying to my parole officer just the other day.

"It's just so fucked up because things with Mackenzie are amazing, and at the same time this shit is happening. But they're totally separate, two different lives … the way it was before."

Doc nods slowly, brows furrowed a bit but face still calm.

"And this is about revenge? You're certain he found out that you gave testimony against his brother?"

I nod at her. Eli hasn't exactly been subtle, what with keying "SNITCH" onto my car and leaving the rat. Message received. I'm a snitch, a rat, a narc.

Yeah, I've heard the whole "snitches get stitches" shtick, but that's not my code, not my world. I never swore any type of loyalty to Curtis. I wasn't part of his "crew," and I certainly owe nothing to his psycho little brother. I honestly don't regret helping Curtis get the maximum sentence and being locked up for life. The way I see it, Curtis is a bad guy, and he did bad things. I watched him sell to minors, and met him at his warehouse once where he kept every type of product imaginable … not to mention how he *fucking shot a guy in the head while I was standing right next to him.* I did my time (and then some) for the illegal shit I did, and he's having to deal with the consequences of his own actions. Now I just need to get his little brother off my back.

"I'm glad you recognized yourself sliding into old unhealthy patterns and came to see me. Next time, we can talk through the reasons you feel the need to lie to Mackenzie. But as for these threats to your safety, that's a problem I'm afraid I'm not qualified to help you with. You need a different type of professional. Have you called your lawyer?"

"Not yet," I tell her with a shake of my head.

"You should. The situation sounds serious, and I'm worried for you. Please don't try to handle this on your own or open yourself up to more danger."

Far too soon, my hour is up and it's time for me to leave. Shady gives me her warmest smile and clasps my hand as we both stand up. I reach inside my back pocket and pull out the envelope I've been carrying, handing it to her. On the outside I've simply written her name. Inside is a check made out to her for five grand.

"What is this?"

"I figure they can't pay you nearly enough at the prison, so I wanted to give you something for everything you do and all the help you gave me." I don't understand how she does it, having to counsel some of the guys at the prison who are the scum of the Earth and still keeping her cool. I admire the hell out of her.

"This really isn't necessary—"

"You saved my life," I cut her off, voice dead serious. "You remember what a mess I was ... I don't know where I'd be without you, and I mean that with my whole heart. This is the absolute least I can do. It's yours. Use the money to help more people if you want, or take a vacation that you really fucking deserve."

"Thank you, Graham." I nod and take her hand again. She squeezes it briefly to emphasize her final words. "Be safe."

27. TACOS AND FUCKBOYS

Graham

I'm staring at the television without really seeing it, chilling on the girls' couch waiting for Mackenzie to return from her yoga retreat. (I have my own key now, which Marisa pretty much threw at me one day with a comment about stopping with the "sad puppy dog porch troll thing—presumably referencing the way I used to wait for Kenz to get home by sitting on their front steps.) I'm both psyched to see her, because I've missed the hell out of her this week, and anxious because I don't think I can hide all this Eli shit from her much longer.

I jump up as soon as I hear her car pulling up the driveway and go out to meet her. When I hear the click of her doors unlocking, I grab her duffle bag out of the backseat before she can. She walks around the car to my side and shoots me a grateful but tired smile before balancing on her tiptoes and giving me a quick close-mouthed kiss. I follow her inside, smiling a little to myself. I'd probably lose my Man Card if I ever admitted this to anyone, but sometimes I think I cherish those little "hello" pecks even more than our deep tongue-filled kisses. Those little pecks are a milestone of sorts, a sign that we've reached a place where being together is just a normal part of our lives. We can show quick affection now because there's no hurry; we both know there will be a later. It's amazing. A place I dreamed of reaching with her but doubted I'd ever get to experience again.

Which isn't to say I wouldn't be down (or, more accurately, up) for some naked affection right about now.

I watch as she kicks off her little hipster canvas slip-ons at the door and slumps onto the couch. I look her over: zero makeup, hair up in a bun she obviously didn't spend ten minutes arranging to perfection, gray spandex leggings that end mid-calf and leave absolutely nothing about her toned legs and ass to the imagination, and a white tank top that's open in the back to show off the straps of her light blue sports bra (just one from her collection of hundreds. I swear these new sports bras are on my list of the craziest changes that happened while I was out of touch. Each one seems more complicated than the last, with overlapped crisscrossed straps in the shape of a spiderweb or some shit. Like normal sports bras weren't already hard enough to take off a girl.) She's Natural Yoga Girl right now and this side of her, like every other one, is perfection.

"I'm so exhausted," she declares, as though her posture on the couch and drooping eyes aren't enough of a giveaway. "It was amazing, don't get me wrong, but we were up with the sunrise every day and they worked our asses off. I swear I burned 3,000 calories just during this morning's session. All I want is to eat and go right to bed."

"I've got Anna's Taqueria for you. Let me grab it." I head to the kitchen where the food I recently ordered for her is waiting.

"Bless you," she nearly moans as I put her beloved tacos, chips, and guac onto the coffee table in front of her. "You have no idea how badly I need this. All the food there was super healthy vegan stuff. I've been starving for days."

I sit down next to her while she digs into the food. Her phone, sitting face up on the coffee table right in front of us, starts vibrating. The word "Mom" flashes across the screen above a photo of Mrs. Thatcher.

"You gonna get that?" I ask carefully.

"Nope," she replies, stuffing chips into her mouth as though emphasizing her answer.

I hold back a groan. I hate that she isn't speaking to her parents and hate even more that I'm the cause. Her dad is the silent stewing type, as his daughter can sometimes be, and hasn't reached out since that clusterfuck at the diner, but her mom has been calling consistently for weeks. I keep trying to encourage Mackenzie to talk to them. Her solidarity is sweet, but I don't want her to freeze them out on my account. But one look at her tired face tells me that conversation will have to wait for another day.

When she's finished eating, she sits back with a contented sigh. I run my hand up and down the part of her back that's not pressed against the couch.

"Missed you," I murmur as I place a kiss to her temple, then one farther along her jaw. It feels like it's been forever since I've seen or talked to her. That place is no joke. They even take away cell phones so the yogis at the retreat can be fully "in the moment" or whatever without distractions from the outside world. Mackenzie gives me another tired smile and lifts her hand to run it through my hair.

"I missed you too. But I'm even too tired for sex right now. I swear if my libido were on the outside like yours, I'd be sporting one seriously limp flag. Closed for business."

"That's fucking disturbing," I groan, trying to banish the image from my mind. I also have to send some signals to my own 'flag' to chill the hell out because after more than a week without sex, all I want to do is take her right here on the couch.

"Sorry." She laughs at whatever expression is on my face right now. "Just let me sleep, like, seven hours, and I'll try to be horny for you in the morning, babe."

I chuckle and start cleaning up, gathering the empty bags and food containers.

"I've got this. You go shower or whatever you need to do and get into bed."

"You don't have to stay if you don't want. You could just go home since you're not getting any sex tonight," she calls to me while beginning to move toward her room.

"Hey, who are you talking to, Kenz?" I ask, prompting her to turn and look at me. "It's me, babe. I'm not just here for sex, and I'm not going anywhere."

"Right, sorry," she concedes, face flushing slightly before she darts down the hallway.

I shake my head a little at her retreating back. Every now and then I have to remind Mackenzie that I'm not one of her little fuckboys and not to treat me like one. (Okay, so I confess that I have no idea what "fuckboy" actually means, but I heard Marisa say it once and it cracks me up, so I get a kick out of using the term to describe guys Kenz dated while I was gone.) When it happens and she slips, I see how different she was with those guys, always keeping them at a distance, staying in control by setting and maintaining clear lines. Basically, from what I can gather, in these "relationships" she dated wimps of the Jimmy Boy variety, who she had wrapped around her little finger. Not that I encourage this particular topic of conversation—I seriously don't enjoy hearing about her with other guys, who as far as I'm concerned don't even count—but occasionally we can't help but avoid them in conversation. I've collected each little tidbit and filed it away, until I now have the lineup figured out.

According to Mackenzie, after I was arrested, the male population of our high school basically treated her like a pariah the rest of senior year. She said she figures half of them saw her as damaged goods, slapped with an eternal "recently dumped girl" label, and the other half thought if they touched her, I would somehow murder them from prison. I can't exactly say I'm mad about it. At least my reputation was good for something.

So, it wasn't until she went to college that she started "dating." The first guy was Stefan, an international student she saw for a couple of months before she broke things off because (as told by Marisa) he was "pretty" but "couldn't tell a clit from his own asshole." Loser.

Next, she was with some kid named Earnest (I shit you not) for over a year. Earnie was a med student, and from what I can gather, I think the thing lasted as long as it did mostly because he was too busy to spend much time with her, so the "relationship" was low maintenance. They went on seeing each other a few times a month (even though he also sucked in the sack) until he graduated and got placed at a program in Iowa. When he asked Kenz to move there with him, she responded by giving him the old "hell no" heave-ho.

She went on dates with some guys who didn't make the cut for a while before meeting Bobby, who Marisa describes as being "boring as khaki pants." Piecing together the little tidbits Mackenzie has dropped here and there, it seems she used him as a prop more than anything else, a little cardboard "boyfriend" stand-in … her built-in date for awards banquets, someone to drag to parties she didn't want to attend, a safe suitor to bring home to meet the parents. Easy, uncomplicated, dull. They were together until he apparently fell in love with her, a crime for which she set him loose.

Most recently there was an older guy named David, a business executive of some kind, who came into the picture at the end of her senior year and lasted through the start of grad school. Mackenzie's too classy to say it outright, but I get the impression he had a big bank account and a small dick.

So, four. Four guys I'd honestly enjoy wiping from the planet, but I suppose I'm ultimately grateful to them for keeping her busy but uncommitted until I came back. Good riddance to them all. I chuck those thoughts, along with the last of the taco remnants, and head back to the bedroom.

Even though it's only 9:00 PM, I crawl onto the bed beside my freshly showered girl, tucking my body around hers and inhaling the scent of shampoo clinging to her damp hair.

"Love you," she mumbles. Her body melts against mine and her breathing evens out, asleep before I have a chance to say it back. But she knows.

✳   ✳   ✳

My phone vibrates from the back pocket of my jeans, waking me. I'm not sure what time it is; I don't even remember falling asleep. I slowly pull away from Mackenzie's sleeping form and step out of the room before retrieving my phone and unlocking it so I can see the contents of the message. It's from a blocked number, which means it's Eli. A familiar little bubble of dread rises in my stomach while the photo loads, and I wonder what he's got for me today. In an instant that bubble bursts and I am flooded by fear.

I struggle to wrap my mind around what I'm seeing, because this photo isn't of me. It's Mackenzie, hair up with some books in her arms as she walks past a building I recognize as part of the Boston College campus.

Fuck. *Fuck.* This can't be happening. I bend at the waist, taking in a deep breath as the terror threatens to take over me. Focus. Think.

I really never thought Eli would turn his attention to Mackenzie. I'm the one he has the grudge against, the one who snitched. I'm an idiot. I press the heels of my hands to my eye sockets, digging in so hard it's almost painful. What do I do? I'm waiting for a lawyer to return my call—not the one I used before, but a close friend of my dad's, the guy I should have called in the first place back when everything happened—but I need to do something now.

I click out of the text message, find the right contact, and press "call." The sound of ringing has my hand clenching around the edges of the phone. Please be awake. Please. Unable to stay still, I walk through the house and out the back door into the humid warmth of the night.

Finally, a curt voice answers. "Yeah?"

"You have any contacts in private security?" I ask without wasting time on preamble. "I just got another text, but the photo is Mackenzie. He's watching her."

"Fuck," Griff growls quietly. I hear shuffling, and I imagine him moving through their house, trying not to wake Shaina who is now almost nine months pregnant. "Yeah, I know a couple people. I'll text you the info. Graham ..."

"I know. Fuck, I know."

I nearly hold my breath until his text comes through, and then I start making calls.

28. SEVENTY-YEAR PLAN

Graham

"Babe, I'm pretty sure we've passed that exit twice already. Are you sure you know where you're going?"

"Of course. Just keeping you on your toes." I shoot Mackenzie a wink and a grin that I hope looks cool and casual.

Of course, I have to be in love with a woman who's not only beautiful but also smart and observant. Though there's really no way I could hide or justify that the trip from her place to our destination in Newton, just a little over two miles, is taking forty minutes in the middle of the day. I have to tell her—and soon—about the situation that's making me drive like a guy who's paranoid as fuck. We're in Mom's Beemer again, which I explained by claiming to be "giving the engine some exercise," but really, I've just been rotating vehicles constantly trying to make myself harder for Eli and his guys to follow. In addition to my attempts at evasive driving, which Kenz just noticed.

Not that I know the first thing about spotting a tail, but I've been keeping a vigilant eye on the road, and I don't think anyone is following us. I haven't even seen the private security guy whose team I'm paying to keep eyes on Mackenzie 24/7, and I can't decide if that makes me more impressed or worried. I did specify that I want him to be discreet so Mackenzie doesn't catch on, but I wonder where he is.

Hopefully she'll let this go and just assume the circuitous route is all part of my secrecy about where we're going. Still, I decide against doubling back a fourth time and actually take the correct exit. Minutes later, we finally arrive. I pull into the driveway of the two-story house, stopping even with the "For Sale" sign in the yard.

"Graham?" Mackenzie's voice is a bit lower than normal, laced with suspicion. "What are we doing here?"

I don't answer and just beckon her from the car, leading her down the paved walkway toward the front door. I enter a code onto the hefty lockbox that's attached to the doorknob, retrieving the key. I might have needed to flirt a little with my realtor to get that code, which is really only meant for agents, but I figure it was a small sacrifice for the larger cause. When I put an offer on a place (hopefully this one) it won't hurt to have her on Team Graham.

I lead Mackenzie through the front door and across the foyer with its small hanging chandelier I only saw for the first time yesterday. I'm actually kind of nervous because I'm pretty sure this house is perfect, and I want her to agree. The well-maintained exterior is a classic early 1900's New England style that Mackenzie prefers, and throughout the interior some of the original charming details have been preserved. Everything else on the inside, though, has been recently renovated and updated: newly installed central air and heating, a modern state-of-the-art kitchen, brand-new bathrooms, and even new windows.

I watch her eyes trace along the polished wooden staircase right in front of us that still has the original wooden bannisters with beveled details I knew she'd love. Again, she follows me through the doorway to our right, which brings us to the large open-plan living room and kitchen. She's quiet but her head is on a swivel taking everything in, especially once I flick on the lights. From here we have a great view of the fireplace and most of the kitchen with its stainless-steel appliances, off-white marble granite countertops, separate island, and counter with bar stools. This angle even gives a glimpse of the backyard through the glass panels of the French doors.

"Do you like it?" I can't help but ask, even though she's barely had a chance to look.

"Is it...for you?"

"Well, I'm hoping you'll move in with me when your lease is up in September. Or, you know, next week, and just let me make out a check to cover the rest of your rent."

She rolls her eyes, and I can tell she's getting ready to start one of her "we're moving too fast" speeches, so I start talking again before she has a chance.

"I know what you're going to say ... something about rushing, or that it hasn't been enough time. But hear me out. We're not two kids that just fell in love and are still getting to know each other. There's not one molecule in my body that doubts you're it for me, that we're meant for forever. I don't want to wait, and I don't think we should. When Mom and Dad died..." my voice gets a little hoarse, because it's still hard to talk about sometimes "...I lost it for a little bit. I started thinking that life was pointless, that nothing really mattered. But I was so wrong. I wish back then I'd realized that what happened to them, how they were just gone in an instant, doesn't mean that nothing matters. It means *everything* matters. Every single day, every single second is the most important thing in the world. That's why there are all those cliché posters with cats or whatever that say 'live in the moment' and 'today is the first day of the rest of your life.' We literally don't have any time to waste, and, baby, I don't want to spend another second pretending that loving you isn't my five-year plan, my twenty-year plan, my seventy-year plan. You want me to find you a cat poster that says it better?"

"You said it just fine." Her smile is a little wobbly as she shakes her head at me. As though needing a second to collect herself, she abruptly turns and picks up one of the little flyers from a stack the realtor left on the coffee table. She flips through the glossy pages, checking out the photos and specs.

"Why do we need five bedrooms?"

We.

Hell. Yes.

Deep breath. Keep your cool. Do not give in to the urge to do a 'Breakfast Club' jumping fist pump.

"One for us, one for your office, two bedrooms for our kids, then a guest room slash backup in case a third baby happens."

A little laugh bubbles out of her.

"Think maybe you're getting a little ahead of yourself? When did we have two kids with an 'oopsie' baby on the way?"

I shrug.

"I'm about forever with you. I figure it doesn't hurt to plan ahead. Decide your objective and then take steps that will lead you to that destination, right?" (Okay, so I stole that from an online course I'm taking, but based on her face I think she bought it.)

She steps over and wraps her arms around me, her head against my chest. I think I feel the soft touch of her mouth right over my heart, but I'm not sure because the fabric of my shirt is in the way. She tilts her face up to mine, chin propped on one of my pecs.

"Show me the rest of it?"

Mackenzie

My mind is still blown by that house, even though we left hours ago after spending a ridiculously long time walking through every room dreaming up our future. Not only did he find a place that's basically my dream home, but he even chose one with an easy commute to BC. Not to mention the great schools where we can send our two (or three) kids that he's apparently already decided on. I didn't explicitly agree to move in right away, but when I told him to make the owners an offer they can't refuse, I think we both knew I'll be talking to Marisa and packing my things sooner rather than later.

Graham is lying on my bed intently focused on his laptop, and he doesn't even look up when I enter even though I just got out of the shower and only have a bathrobe on. There's an open book beside one of his legs, one from the pile he's been reading and using for reference while working on the initial business plan for his nonprofit project. We've been discussing this and bouncing ideas around for months now, with varying degrees of seriousness, but now it's getting closer to a reality every day. He has a meeting with his lawyer soon and some calls set up with people who can help him get this thing started. It's been amazing watching him work so hard.

This new serious Graham? Incredibly sexy. My body starts to pulse in all the places I want him to touch me, preferably soon. I sit down next to him on the bed, and he finally spares me a glance and a small smile.

"Have you talked to Griff about Wyatt House yet?" My question pulls him from whatever he's doing so I now have his full attention.

"It's not going to be called Wyatt House. I get that I'm a little cocky, but I'm not *that* egotistical! What about Mackenzie House?"

199

"I was thinking Wyatt ... for your parents."

His eyes soften and he nods thoughtfully. "Maybe."

"But have you told Griff?"

"Not yet. It's still in the super early stages, and he's got so much going on with his current job, and Layla, and Shaina due pretty much any minute at this point."

"She's got a few weeks, at least!"

"Still. I don't want to put this in front of him until I have something solid, until I can make him a legitimate job offer that isn't just some agreement we write on a coaster. I want to show him I'm serious, and that he doesn't need to worry about putting his family's future at risk on some whim I had."

That's it. I can't handle any more of this man being perfect today. I reach out and lift the laptop off of his legs, gently setting it on the bedside table with the screen still open so nothing he's working on will be disturbed.

"What are you doing?"

The final syllables get rougher and lose volume, because while he's speaking, I pull down the waistband of his sweats to free his cock. And promptly wrap my lips around it. I suck, one hand gripping him at the base while the other cups his balls.

"Fuck," he groans as he quickly hardens, growing impossibly big inside my mouth. "What's this for?"

I give the round swollen head a slow lick then release him for just long enough to tell him the truth.

"Everything."

29. FOUR MINUTES, TOPS

Mackenzie

Is there anything quite as satisfying as a to-do list with every item checked off?

I've got mine on the empty passenger seat beside me, covered in thick black lines indicating everything I accomplished today (because, yes, I'm the nerd who carries her physical list around along with a black Sharpie). I dropped some things off at the dry cleaners, got my hair trimmed, went grocery shopping, and even squeezed in a trip to Target where I bought some cute galaxy print leggings I can't wait to wear to my next yoga class. I'm basically winning at adulting.

But it wasn't *all* responsible adult stuff … I was so excited about the watermelons I'd splurged on that I decided to send Graham a picture. He seems a little stressed lately, probably about everything that has to be done for the nonprofit, and I figured he could use a midday smile. So I propped my phone on top of my car, set the timer, and posed—right there in the parking lot with people staring; I held up two watermelons, balanced them against my chest like boobs, and pulled a goofy face.

It's something I never would have done five months ago. But that's the effect Graham has on me — I give fewer fucks about the stuff that doesn't matter, like the dirty look an old lady shot me for my display.

What matters is that Graham will get a kick out of it, and making him happy makes me happy.

In fact, I'm pretty damn happy in general. As I drive home, I don't even try to hold back from grinning like a fool, letting that happiness sink in and warm me along with the beautiful sunny day shining through my windshield. It's been one of the best summers I can ever remember. I'm not taking any classes and only working a few times a week at the yoga studio, so I have lots of time to spend with Graham. We've been making the most of it, doing couple-y things like going to movies and having picnics in parks, and riding the motorcycle everywhere (I even let him drive sometimes, since he has his license now).

Every time I look in my rearview mirror, I catch sight of all the brown paper bags stuffed with groceries, so many that they're filling my backseat door-to-door, and I even had to put some in the trunk. The visual just makes me think of Graham, since he's the reason my grocery hauls have gotten bigger now that he "visits" at our place nearly every day. (I still won't let him officially move in. It's the principle of the thing.) It won't be long before the whole "visitation" pretense falls apart completely, since I've already committed to moving into the house in Newton with him once my lease runs out. I still can't believe that beautiful house is going to be his — *ours*. Graham made an offer right after we left last week, and the current owners accepted it two days ago.

Even the watermelons now tucked into one of those grocery bags increase my happiness—watermelon just *tastes* like summer and good memories. We are definitely cutting these babies open tonight— maybe we'll even infuse one with liquor like we used to do in college, when we'd cut a hole in the melon and stick an upside-down bottle of vodka in it for a day. We could even try tequila this time! Now I can barely wait until Graham and Marisa get home. I check the clock on my dash; Marisa should get out of work soon, and Graham is probably already on his way back from meeting with his lawyer.

I park my car in our driveway. The other spots allotted to our apartment are empty, which confirms that neither of my "roommates" are back yet. For a moment I wish Graham was here to help carry these bags inside, but I quickly chide myself for the codependent thought. *Shame on you, Mackenzie! You don't need a man to carry heavy things for you!* I won't let a man—even Graham—make me forget or undervalue my own strength.

It's so hot that sweat forms on my skin the second I step out of the car. I move around to the back door and open it, but just as I've started reaching inside for the groceries, I suddenly feel a solid presence at my back. An arm wraps around me from behind and a voice—a man's, unfamiliar—speaks right at my ear.

"Hello, Mackenzie. Good to finally meet you." My entire body stiffens.

"Who are you?" Panic rises within me as his grip tightens, and he starts pulling me away from my car. "What are you doing?"

Though I try to turn around to see his face, I only manage a glimpse of longish brown hair and pale blue eyes. What I do see clearly is something dark and metallic clasped in one of his hands—a gun.

"We're gonna get in my car and go someplace we can have a little more privacy."

My limbs come unfrozen as I snap out of my initial shock, and I try to struggle against his hold. Although his arm is thin, it's surprisingly strong as he maintains his grip on me.

"Let me go!" I gasp then start to yell for help. He cuts off my attempt, slapping a rough hand over my mouth—the same hand that's holding the gun, so I can feel its cool metal surface against my skin.

"Nuh-uh," he growls.

I have to get away from him. What do they always say about self-defense? *Go for the balls.*

The positioning is awkward with my back still pressed against his front, but I kick backward blindly as hard as I can hoping to connect with the crown jewels. I miss, clipping him in what feels like the shin. He hisses in pain as he whirls me around and pushes me back against the side of my car.

He's facing me now, leaning in far too close and sneering at me open-mouthed, so I have a clear view of his uneven rotting teeth. I try to shrink away from him, repulsed by his acrid breath and the disturbing rage twisting his sallow features.

"Listen up, bitch. I don't wanna do this here, but if you're gonna be trouble then I will," he barks into my face.

There's a crazed look to his creepy eyes, made worse by the way his pupils are so dilated the ice blue of his irises are just a small ring around the black. Fear floods me all over, and I start struggling again. This time, I manage to lift my knee high enough to strike him in the nuts. He curses loudly, and I tense, hoping the pain will make him let me go and give me a chance to escape. Instead, he lashes out.

Before I can even process what's happening, much less duck, he hits me across the face with the body of his gun. My ears ring as the deafening crack of the impact reverberates repeatedly through my brain. Splitting pain along the right side of my face causes my vision to waver. The world tilts sideways and I stumble, falling backward so my head slams against my car before meeting the hard asphalt of my driveway with another nauseating crack.

Blackness flickers at the edges of my vision, but I fight to stay conscious. I watch him through squinted eyes as he tucks the gun into the waistband of his jeans before crouching down close. He pulls a large switchblade out from somewhere and caresses the dull end with a finger as he eyes me with sudden unnerving calm.

"Pity. I wanted to have some more fun with you. But I do like the thought of Wyatt finding you here."

He grins and maintains eye contact as the knife descends and searing pain blazes in my shoulder. I scream, but the sound comes out hoarse and pitiful. In my peripheral vision I see a glint of sun along his blade, and I tense waiting for the next wave of pain, but it doesn't come. I hear another man's voice from somewhere close by just before my attacker abruptly disappears from my line of sight. I can hear the two male voices yelling from somewhere above me.

The intense pain in my arm has cleared my mind a little, and I realize I need to try to take advantage of this opportunity while he's distracted. Running is probably out of the question—I doubt I could stand up right now, much less make it very far without passing out. Instead, I start scanning the area around me looking for my phone. I can't see my purse, but I do spot my keys on the ground where I must have dropped them. Figuring it's better than nothing and not knowing how long I have before he comes back, I reach for them with my uninjured arm and close my hand around the bundle of metal.

A shadow falls over me as a large male body kneels down to my level. I use every bit of strength I can muster to swing at him with my good arm, hitting him in the face with my keys. He grunts but doesn't move away, so I try to scream, still flailing and trying to strike him with the keys again.

"Hey, hey, it's okay!" The hands on my shoulders are larger than before, and the voice is different. My vision is blurry, but I think I make out unfamiliar brown eyes.

"I'm not going to hurt you. Mr. Wyatt sent me." The new voice repeats this a few times before the words register.

My head is swimming. *Mr. Wyatt? Why would Graham's dad send him?*

"Mr. Wyatt?" I croak.

"Yes, ma'am. I'm private security. Graham Wyatt hired me to protect you."

At the sound of Graham's name, I give up trying to fight. My whole body goes limp, my arm falling back to my side. I've exhausted every last drop of energy. I squeeze my eyes closed, but it doesn't help the dizziness making my head feel like it's floating, somehow not connected to the rest of my body.

"Hey, stay with me. I just called him. He'll be here soon."

With those words, my body gives up the fight and the blackness pulls me under.

Graham

My phone vibrates with an incoming call. I already have a ridiculous grin on my face as I pull it out of my pocket, expecting it to be Mackenzie. That photo she sent earlier was so damn cute. I immediately made it my phone's wallpaper.

"Hey."

"Mr. Wyatt?"

My grin disappears the second I hear the voice on the other end, which is male and not immediately recognizable. Definitely not Mackenzie. I'm driving so I don't want to pull the phone from my face to check the caller ID.

"Yes?" I say in a tone far different from the warm way I answered.

"It's Sam, from Gold Dome Securities."

"What's up, Sam?"

"How far are you from Brighton?"

"Five minutes. Talk to me. What's up?" I can't interpret the tone of his voice, and he's never called me unscheduled before. It's making me agitated and impatient.

"Eli was here when Mackenzie got back from the store. He grabbed her when she got out of her car—"

No, no. Shit!

"Is she okay? Where is she?" The intense pounding of my heart echoes in my temples.

"Probable concussion, possible other injuries but none immediately visible. I'm with her now. I was waiting to call an ambulance until I spoke to you."

"How did he get to her? WHERE THE FUCK WERE YOU?" *Concussion?* Fear makes my chest squeeze painfully.

"I had to circle the block to find parking. I only had eyes off her for a couple of minutes, four tops." *Four minutes.* Apparently, that was more than enough time for Eli. "I came up on them as soon as I could, drew my gun on him, and disarmed him of his knife and gun before he ran off—"

Knife. Gun.

I look down at the dashboard and realize I'm speeding as my foot has instinctively pushed down on the gas pedal during this call. I want to press the thing to the floor and race to her, but getting pulled over won't do her any good right now, so I reluctantly ease off to get back down to the speed limit.

"Should I call an ambulance?" he asks.

"Should you?" I growl, not trying to hide my frustration. He's the one there with her, able to assess her condition. Goddammit. I thought these guys were professionals.

"I think she can wait a few minutes."

"Then I'll drive her. I'll be right there. Don't fucking move."

I hang up on him because I need the next two minutes to get my shit together so I don't strangle the guy.

I pull to a lopsided stop in front of the house and jump out almost before the car is fully in park. Sam is walking up to me as I get out, his usually stoic face revealing signs of stress as he tries to apologize. I push right past him without a word, running over to where I can make out Mackenzie's form on the driveway. She's so still, lying there prone beside her parked car with her mass of golden red hair spread out. It's shining as the sun hits the silky strands directly from above, inappropriately beautiful in this situation.

I drop to my knees in a single motion, not even noticing the impact on the concrete beneath me although it's hard enough to bruise. It's nothing compared to the bruising sensation spreading through my chest. I reach for her as gently as I can, not sure where exactly she's hurt. As I brush her hair away from her face, I see a large bruise, red and angry, spreading across her right cheekbone.

"How long has she been out?" I ask Sam. *It can't be good that she's unconscious, right?*

"She was conscious when I got here, just passed out a couple minutes ago, right after I hung up the phone."

Fuck, what do I do? *This can't be happening.* It doesn't seem real.

"Z," I say, conscious to keep my voice light even though I want to roar in anger at Eli for doing this—and at the idiot hovering a foot away for not stopping him. "Baby, wake up."

Her eyes drift open slowly, slowly, and for the first second she seems to stare through me instead of at me, eyes blank and lacking recognition. Then the haze clears slightly and I see realization sink back in.

"Graham," she whispers. "There was this guy ..."

She shifts, trying to get up. I place my palm on her chest, silently urging her to stay where she is.

"Hold on, maybe you shouldn't move yet. Can you tell me where you're hurt?"

She looks confused, which worries me even more.

"My head hurts," she says after a moment, wincing as though the very mention of it increases the pain. I find myself wincing along with her in sympathy. The helplessness of not being able to take her pain away is killing me.

"...Is he still here?" she asks suddenly, her voice rising and eyes widening in fear. I turn my head to see she's caught sight of Sam's form behind me.

"No, he's gone," I reassure her. "That's Sam. He's the one who called me. What hurts besides your head?"

"I don't know," she says a little slowly, trying to lift her head like she's going to do a visual inventory of herself but quickly putting it back down with a grimace.

Feeling totally clueless and wishing I had medical training of some kind, I start prodding different areas of her body lightly to check for any injuries she might not be aware of at the moment, anything that would make it a bad idea to pick her up. That's what they do on TV, right? She sucks in a breath when I run a hand over her left shoulder. Looking closer, I see a tear in the fabric at the very top of her short sleeve that I didn't notice before because the shirt is black. It's the same clingy athletic material as her yoga clothes, so the blood seeped into the absorbent fabric as sweat would, keeping it from dripping down her arm—but there's a lot of blood. The fabric is fully saturated—I see a small patch of red blooming on the driveway beneath her, and my hand comes away covered in it.

That cut worries me, but there doesn't seem to be any reason I can't move her to my car and drive her to the hospital, so I pick her up and start walking. Trying to keep my movements as smooth as possible, I place her in the passenger side of the Range Rover. She moans softly in pain as I slowly roll up her left sleeve to get a better look at the wound.

"Shit," I whisper. It's deep, and it looks like it was made with a blade.

"I'm so sorry, Mr. Wyatt," Sam says from right behind me. He must have followed us down the driveway, but I didn't notice because I'm only focused on her. "It was only a couple of minutes—"

"Look." I turn around, putting my back to Mackenzie for a moment so I can stare Sam down. He's around my same height and weight, but he looks smaller at the moment. He knows he fucked up. "You aren't my priority right now. Stick around until her roommate gets home. Make sure she's safe. We'll talk later. Oh, and call your boss. He and I will be talking as well."

Without another word to him, I turn back to Kenz. Without the sleeve to absorb it, a stream of red blood is now running down her arm. There's more than I would have thought possible, since I only looked away for a minute. *That motherfucker came at my girl with a knife.* I tamp down the rage, reminding myself that she needs my entire focus.

I grab a shirt from my gym bag in the backseat and tear it in half. I use the first half to wipe up the blood on her arm and tie the other half around the wound. My stomach turns with nausea as I hear her gasp in pain when I pull the fabric tight. I hate hurting her, and I have no idea if I'm doing this right. I buckle her in carefully then start driving to the hospital as quickly as I can without making too many sudden turns that could jostle her. Her eyes are closed, and I try talking to keep her awake because she might have a concussion, and I remember something about it being dangerous to sleep too soon with a brain injury.

Fuck. *A brain injury.* My insides feel as gashed as her arm, my soul bleeding out because she's hurt. And it's my fault.

At a red light I pull out my phone and stab my finger at Marisa's name. It rings enough times before she answers that my voice comes out as a bark, tight with anxiety, the second I hear the call connect.

"Marisa. Are you safe?"

I hear her sigh. It's definitely Marisa because no one else can pack so much sass into a single wordless sound. But my concern isn't fully alleviated.

"McF. Is this going to be a contraception joke? Because you know I'm usually down, but I'm in the middle of s—"

I cut her off.

"It's not a joke. Where are you right now?"

"About to head home." I can tell from the uncertainty in her voice that she's picked up on my unusually serious tone.

"Good. When you get there make sure all the doors are locked."

"Okay …" She draws the word out into multiple syllables. "What's going on?"

I shove a hand through my tangled hair and look over at Kenz, whose eyes are still closed. I can't see how her face looks because the injured side is facing away from me, but she's bled through the shirt I tied around her arm, making the previously white fabric completely red.

The light turns green, and I step on the pedal.

"I'll tell you when you get here. I'm taking Kenz to St. Elizabeth's ER. We're pulling in now. A guy named Sam is going to meet you at the house. I hired him. You need to go in and pack an overnight bag for yourself, and one for Mackenzie, then come to the hospital."

"The ER? *What is going on?* Tell me right now. I mean it!" Her voice is both demanding and frightened.

I switch on the turn signal and wait for a car to get out of my way so I can enter the hospital parking lot.

"Can't now. About to park. I'll explain when I see you. Be safe, okay? Keep your eyes open and don't make any extra stops."

"You're freaking me out …"

I hang up on her. I'm sure I'll face her fury later. But since there's a very real chance Mackenzie will never forgive me for this, I might even welcome the chance to go out via Latina firing squad.

30. "START TALKING. NOW."

Graham

Kenz is a little more alert once I park the car at the hospital, even trying to argue that she can walk on her own. Of course, I ignore her and sweep her back up into my arms. I carry her in through the emergency room doors, radiating so much agitation that we're processed in record time. She's assigned a bed in one of the ER's closet-sized rooms. There's a flurry of activity as people come in and out of the room, examining her and asking questions. I get quite a few suspicious side-eyes, though Mackenzie repeatedly tells them I'm not the one who hurt her.

"Are you sure you don't want to call your mom?" I ask for the hundredth time when we have a moment alone.

"I'm sure."

I'm tempted to call her parents anyway but decide to respect her decision.

After a while another nurse comes with a wheelchair to take Mackenzie away for CT and MRI scans, saying they're checking for bleeding in her brain and making sure the knife didn't cut any nerves or cause damage that might require surgery. Both possibilities make my pulse race with panic. Despite my efforts to follow, the nurse firmly tells me to stay behind. Before they're fully out the door, I hear Mackenzie calling for me, and I'm at her side in an instant with my pulse pounding in renewed anxiety.

"What's wrong?" I ask, scanning her body as though expecting to see some new injury.

"The groceries," she says, making me frown in confusion. Her eyes are a little glassy, and I'm not sure if it's because of the concussion, the painkillers they gave her, or both.

"What, baby?"

"The groceries … they're in my car. It's hot. They'll spoil."

I would have sworn nothing could make me smile right now, but my lips tip up at her genuine worry over this in the midst of such an intense situation. She's so fucking cute.

"Don't worry. I'll make sure they're okay," I assure her, which apparently calms her enough that she allows the nurse to wheel her away. I'll probably just end up buying more food to replace whatever goes bad because there's no way I'm leaving her to go check on them. But she doesn't need to know that particular information now—or ever.

Once Mackenzie is gone, the room becomes too small, the walls too close, reminding me of a prison cell. After pacing restlessly for a couple of minutes, I can't stand it a second longer, so I walk out the door and lean against the wall to wait for her. As soon as I'm in the hallway, I can breathe a little easier, even though I'm also breathing in that uniquely dismal hospital scent of chemical sanitization that never fully masks the underlying aroma of bodily affliction.

A quickly moving figure in my peripheral vision draws my attention to the ER entrance. Marisa is barreling toward me with Sam close on her heels.

"What the fuck, Graham?" She's seething as expected. "Where is Mackenzie?" She tries to move around me to force her way inside the room.

"She's not in there. They took her somewhere to get a CT scan and an MRI."

Marisa stops short, and I know her well enough now to detect the fear beneath her front of fury. She pokes me hard in the chest with a finger.

"Start talking. Now."

I gesture to Sam to wait for me and lead Marisa back into the room where we can have a little privacy. Not wanting to make her wait any longer, I start right in explaining Mackenzie's injuries and what happened. Marisa's caramel skin pales as I talk. I can relate. I have the image branded in my mind of what that fucker did to the woman I love. One side of her face is fully swollen now, covered in a colorful bruise that stands out in ghastly contrast against her pale skin. Not to mention the "laceration" (as the nurse called it) on her upper arm that they cleaned and stitched up first thing while Mackenzie winced and I held her other hand.

"Well, what are you doing here?" Marisa demands when I'm done. "Shouldn't you be off tracking that guy down and beating his ass?"

I guess it's a fair question. I can't say the thought hasn't already crossed my mind a time or twenty.

"A few years ago, I'd already be on my way to do just that," I tell her honestly. "But as much as I want to make that asshole hurt, it wouldn't be the right move. Because if I went after him, that means I wouldn't be here with Kenz. She's my first and only priority. Plus, I don't want to leave her by getting thrown back in prison."

I sound so reasonable, even though on the inside I'm vibrating with rage and the desire for retribution. He is not going to get away with this. I will do whatever it takes to make sure he can never hurt Mackenzie again. But not right now because she needs me here.

Marisa's eyes soften in silent approval and understanding. She takes in a deep breath then looks down at the floor, nodding her head like she's trying to process everything. Then she straightens and scrutinizes me. "Do you know who did this? Did you have anything to do with it?"

I nod and swallow down the lump that rises in my throat.

"Eli. He's after me for revenge because I gave the cops information on his brother that helped put him in prison for life."

Her eyes narrow.

"How long have you known he's after you? Did you have any idea Kenz was at risk?"

It all pours out of me—the abridged version, anyway, because I'm not sure how long those scans will take. I tell Marisa about the confrontation in the grocery store parking lot, the pranks on my car and house, even the creepy surveillance photos. I didn't intend to dump so much on her, but once I start talking, I can't stop. I'm compelled to confess my sins, although I'm not expecting or looking for absolution.

"At first I really thought she didn't need to know any of this. When things got worse, I knew I had to tell her, but I was … a coward, I guess. And selfish. I couldn't stand the thought of losing her when I'd just gotten her back. So, I convinced myself I'd be able to figure this out on my own." I duck a little so she can see the dead seriousness on my face. "But I swear to you, I never thought he'd come after her directly. He only sent those pictures a few days ago, and I hired the bodyguard right away. I talked to my lawyer and was trying to make a plan. But I wasn't fast enough."

Both of my hands go up to my hair. I've been doing this a lot over the past hour, tugging at it as an insufficient outlet for the powerful emotions threatening to overwhelm me.

"I get it," Marisa says quietly, causing me to swing my eyes back to hers in shock. That was not the reaction I'd been expecting.

"You … get it?" I repeat slowly, my tone incredulous.

"I mean, you fucked up, no doubt about that. But I believe your intentions came from a good place. A naïve, hardheaded place, but a good one." She tips her lips up in the smallest of smirks, though her eyes are sad.

It almost feels like a physical blow, as though she actually did slap me across the face the way I'd sort of expected her to—and would have almost welcomed. I definitely don't deserve the rush of relief her words bring.

"You have to tell her everything."

"Yeah. I will."

She sighs, looking thoughtful.

"I've gotta be honest, I'm not sure if she'll forgive you." I nod again, heart sinking even though this isn't news to me. "And no matter what happens, I have to be on her side. But for the next couple of minutes, I'm on yours, okay? I know all you want is to take care of our girl."

"Thank you." My words are uneven, shredded by the sharp edges of my emotions. Then I surprise the shit out of both of us by hugging her. She's stiff for a second before her much smaller arms wrap around me, like she understands I need this moment of comfort.

Mackenzie returns, wheeled in by the nurse. Marisa immediately rushes up and hugs her, not caring that she has to hunch over awkwardly because of the wheelchair. Mackenzie's face is paler than I've ever seen it as I help her into the bed, expression tight with pain as she settles back against the pillows. Noticing my concern, she gives me a weak smile.

"My head is killing me. The MRI was ... loud." I can tell from the look on her face that she's downplaying it.

Once the nurse is gone, I leave the girls to have some alone time, telling Mackenzie I'll be right outside the door if she needs me. I see Sam as soon as I step out, and my mouth tightens grimly. We step to the side so we have a view of the room but will be out of the way of nurses and patients traveling through the hallway. I notice Sam has a bandage on the side of his face, and tip my chin toward it.

"Eli get one in?" I ask.

"This was your girl, actually. Hit me in the face with her keys."

I think back, and now that I'm not tunnel focused on getting Mackenzie to the hospital, I can recall that Sam had blood running down his face earlier. I can't help smirking at him a little, proud as hell of Mackenzie and a little glad he didn't get out of this too easily.

"I talked to my boss," he tells me after a moment. "He's calling me off the assignment and tripling your security at no additional cost. He said you can call him whenever you're ready, no matter the hour."

I acknowledge his words, slightly appeased. After talking for another minute, ensuring he has no further information, I send him on his way with a handshake (he did save her life, after all) and return to my girl.

While we wait for the doctor to arrive with results from the scans, Marisa goes to find some coffee.

"Apparently the police are coming to talk to me," Mackenzie says almost as soon as the door closes behind her roommate. "What do I tell them?"

"Whatever you remember."

"I mean ..." Setting down the ice pack she's been holding to her bruised cheek, she looks up at me. She scans my face with her swollen slightly lopsided gaze. "Is there anything you don't *want* me to say?"

I swallow hard and can't seem to form any words, but I force my eyes to remain locked on hers. I hate the uncertainty and wariness I see there.

"You hired me a bodyguard," she almost whispers.

"Yes." The word is a confession, a curse, a plea. My head drops but my eyes don't leave hers.

"Which means you knew there was something I needed to be guarded from."

"Yes."

Sadness and worry war with the pain still apparent in the tight muscles of her face.

"He knew our names. What's going on, Graham? Can this lead back to you?"

I push aside my own fears about getting the police involved. I don't want her getting caught up in this, at least, not any more than she already is. And I certainly don't want her lying to the authorities for me.

"Don't worry about that. You tell the cops every single thing you remember so they can get the guy that did this to you." I take a deep breath. Squeeze my eyes closed for a second as remorse threatens to pull me under. Give her the full eye contact she deserves. "I'm so sorry—you have no idea. There are things you need to know, and I promise I'll tell you everything, anything you want to kn—"

An assertive knock interrupts me. The door to the small room opens, and a guy walks through in a black Boston Police Department uniform he doesn't look old enough to be wearing. He's followed by a female cop who's probably in her mid-thirties. I breathe out through my nose, tamping down my instinctual panic at the sight of them. I remind myself that this isn't about me. Not yet, at least. Directing my focus where it belongs, I step closer to Mackenzie and give her hand a reassuring squeeze.

I'll accept whatever comes next. Anything. As long as she is safe.

31. THE PRECIPICE

Mackenzie

The too white walls of this tiny room were not meant to hold four people, especially not when two of them are very large men. The officer who entered first is almost as tall and broad as Graham, and he's surprisingly young, probably not much older than us. He's cute in a very clean-cut way, with a smoothly shaven face and closely cropped brown hair that's a few shades lighter than black. He smiles kindly, a smile that I notice travels all the way up to his blue eyes, and introduces himself as Officer Derek Schwartz. Then his more stoic partner introduces herself as Officer Dean, offering no first name. Her blond hair is pulled back in a sleek bun, tight and flawless without a single hair out of place.

I can sense Graham's tension as he stands next to me, rigid and unmoving from his position next to my bed. Both officers have already eyed him suspiciously, Officer Dean in particular radiating antagonism from the second she spotted him. It's been this way all afternoon, everyone immediately assuming my injuries are the result of a domestic abuse situation. It's understandable, but incredibly frustrating. I'm so tired of repeating myself, continually having to tell every person who enters this room that Graham isn't the one who hurt me.

After I resist their efforts to send Graham from the room, the cops ask me to tell them what happened earlier. I take a deep breath to steady myself. Going back through the whole encounter is the very last thing I want to do right now. Really, I want everyone to leave me alone so I can close my eyes and sleep. The pounding ache in my head is slightly better than before, a percussion that's now more of a punk band than a college drumline. But it's still intense, almost making it hard to hear my own thoughts.

Just get it over with! I tell myself, so I start talking. Graham maintains his place beside me the whole time as I recall the incident. I watch the muscles of his forearm get progressively tighter as I describe what happened, his body nearly vibrating with the effort of restraining his emotions. This is the first time he's hearing all the details, and it's probably almost as hard for him to hear as it is for me to relive it.

My heart pounds furiously as I talk, the whole thing replaying vividly in my mind.

His weight pressed into me, trapping me against the car.

The butt of the gun slamming into my face.

The bone jarring impact of my body hitting the driveway.

His ice-cold eyes gleaming with a sickening mix of hatred and excitement.

The knife slicing into me.

"And then there was, uh, a guy who came and scared him away." I barely manage to keep my eyes away from Graham as I stumble over this part. I suddenly don't want to mention Sam, though I'm not entirely sure why.

222

Officer Dean's eyebrows try to climb up to her hairline.

"A guy?"

"I think he's one of my neighbors? I live in one of those college neighborhoods, so it's hard to keep track of everyone. Lots of turnover." *Stop rambling.* "Anyway, I called Graham and the guy stayed with me until he got there."

"Did you get this guy's name? We should get a witness statement from him to go in our report." The skeptical way Officer Dean says "this guy" makes it clear she's not fully convinced by my story.

"No, but I might be able to ask around and see if any of my neighbors know him," I say noncommittally.

"Why didn't he call an ambulance? Or the police?"

"I don't know," I say honestly. My shoulders lift in a shrug that I immediately regret when pain flares in the stitched knife wound and travels through my whole arm.

"So, the man who attacked you. Had you ever seen him before?" Officer Schwartz asks. I'm glad he seems to be taking me seriously.

"No."

"Are you sure?" Officer Dean pushes. She checks the little notepad she's been scribbling in. "You said you're getting your Master's at BC? Could he have been a student in one of your classes?"

"No, I'm sure I would remember that. He knew my name, though. He called me Mackenzie." Again, I force myself not to look at Graham as I say this.

"Did he give any other indication that he's familiar with you or your life?"

"No," I lie.

"I wanted to have some more fun with you. Though I do like the idea of Wyatt finding you here."

I swallow back nausea at the memory of his voice. I have no doubt that he intended to kill me, and the reason has something to do with the man standing guard next to me. My heart sinks.

Oh, Graham, what have you done?

Officer Dean keeps asking questions, pulling every possible detail out of me about the guy—voice, height, weight, clothing, hairstyle. I feel drained at the end, as though she's literally sucked me dry in the process of extracting all of those details.

We're finally done, and I've just given them all my contact information in case they need to follow up, when Marisa barges back through the door. She stops short at the sight of our two visitors in their BPD Department uniforms, eyes swinging back and forth between them before landing on Officer Schwartz and staying there.

I watch her eyes widen minutely, the reaction so subtle it wouldn't be noticeable to anyone who doesn't know her as well as I do. *Interesting.* I wouldn't have pegged Derek Schwartz as her type.

There's a buzzing sound, and Officer Dean bends to pull a phone from her pocket. "I need to take this. Excuse me. Take care, Miss Thatcher. Schwartz, meet me outside in twenty." She steps out the door and leaves with no further ceremony.

"Marisa Perez. I'm Mackenzie's roommate and BFF." My best friend wastes no time stepping right up to Officer Schwartz, hand extended.

His eyes and lips crinkle in a small smile.

"Officer Derek Schwartz," he replies, taking her hand and shaking it.

"You need to take a statement from me?" she asks.

"Were you there? Do you have any information about what happened?"

"No," Marisa concedes. "But surely you need *something* from me?"

I can't believe she's shamelessly flirting with a policeman on duty. No, scratch that. I can totally believe it. It's exactly the kind of crazy thing she'd do. To my surprise, the young officer doesn't rebuke her, his smile actually widening. As though unable to help himself, his blue eyes track down her form, taking in her dark curly hair and the curves of her body.

"I was getting ready to head downstairs and grab a coffee. Maybe you can walk with me and share any possible insights?"

I glance at the still hot cup of coffee Marisa just brought back with her. She deftly stashes it on the table behind her but then pauses and glances at me in obvious conflict. I wave her off with the icepack still clutched in my right hand, silently encouraging her to go with him. I have no idea how long we'll be here waiting for those scans to come back.

"Lead the way, Officer Guapo," she purrs.

"*¿Crees que soy guapo?*" he asks, smoothly responding to her in Spanish with a perfect accent. *You think I'm handsome?*

A small laugh bubbles up inside me at Marisa's shocked face. It's not every day I see her stunned into silence.

"That was interesting," Graham comments when they leave. I murmur in agreement. Then we both remain silent for a long moment. The unspoken words hanging between us are deafening in this small space.

I just lied to the police.

"Do you know who he was? The guy who … attacked me?" I finally ask.

I can't help the flinch that constricts my muscles at the word "*attack*." It's a stark reminder that this is all real and not some dream. Not a horrible thing that happened to someone else. Graham briefly brushes his hand over mine to offer comfort. Then he nods, features heavy as though weighed down by his remorse.

"His name is Eli."

"Eli," I repeat. The syllables taste foul on my mouth, and I shudder. Somehow giving him a name makes it all even more real.

We're interrupted again, this time by the arrival of the doctor. As the gray-haired man talks, my attention is split between his assurances that I can go home tonight and Graham. Every time I look at Graham over the next couple of hours as I'm discharged and we get into his car, I catch him staring at me with a look I've never seen before. It is a mask of shame and fear, anger and sadness. It fills me with dread more powerful than I can ever remember experiencing. I can't quell this overwhelming sensation that we're balanced on a precipice and any second we'll tip over the edge. And deep inside me I sense that once we do, everything will change.

Graham

We check in at a hotel nearby, where I've gotten a room for Marisa and one for me and Mackenzie. I don't want the girls going back home tonight, even with the three new guys from the security company on duty.

When Mackenzie is settled on the huge bed that takes up most of our hotel room, I sit on the edge of the mattress beside her. Bending to rest my elbows on my knees and shoving my hands through my hair, I force myself to breathe through the anxiety trying to choke me. I can't avoid this talk anymore. I've already put it off far longer than I should have.

"So, about Eli—"

She stops me when I've barely begun, laying one delicate hand on my forearm.

"Wait," her soft voice implores. I stare at her in surprise.

"What is it?"

"It's bad, isn't it?" she asks somberly in that same quiet tone.

I nod.

"Will I be mad?"

I nod again.

"Will it change everything?"

"I don't know," I tell her honestly, my voice cracking with emotion. *Please God, don't let it change everything.*

"I don't want to know yet, not tonight."

"Kenz ..."

"No," she argues more forcefully. A single tear escapes from her eyes. "Today has been too hard, and I—I just want to put off reality. At least for a few more hours. We can talk tomorrow. But tonight, I really need you to hold me. Please."

I look down at her huge imploring eyes after she says the final word in a wavering voice. One of my hands lifts to her face, and I use my thumb to catch another tear. Whether she was putting on a strong front

227

at the hospital or whether everything is just now hitting her, Mackenzie suddenly seems on the verge of crumbling. I've never seen her like this. She's always been so independent, never one to cling or beg, and seeing her vulnerability kills me. And makes me want to kill Eli. My normally unshakeable girl is visibly shaken by what he did to her, and in spite of everything she's turning to me for strength and comfort. I would die before telling her no.

"Okay, babe. Whatever you need."

I settle myself back against the pillows and hold out my arms for her. She immediately shifts over and curls herself against me. We don't talk. We simply lie there, and I hold her as she asked. For over an hour I simply soak in her closeness, running my hand through her silky hair and down her back over and over. I try to commit this moment to memory, wanting to make every second count, this time an unexpected gift that I don't deserve. I think she's asleep, so it surprises me when she suddenly speaks.

"Graham?"

"Yeah?"

"Make love to me?"

Her head tilts up so she can look at my face, hers sad and imploring and so, so beautiful.

"We can't," I remind her gently. "Because of your head. Remember the doctor said you need to take it easy for a few weeks?"

Her pale hand drifts down my body until it rests over my crotch. Unconcerned with the protocols of concussion treatment, my dick responds immediately to the prospect of her attention.

"You can be gentle," she whispers. "Please. I need you." Her voice is unsteady again.

I know we shouldn't, but I am powerless to turn her down when there is so much desperation in her voice, in her eyes. I am simply not strong enough to deny the girl I love when she's begging me to make love to her.

I move to reposition us so she's lying flat on her back and I'm kneeling beside her. I gaze down at wide eyes filled with a trust I'm going to greedily accept even though I'm not worthy of it.

"We'll take it slow. Tell me if your arm or your head hurts and we'll stop, okay?"

"Okay."

I pull off my shirt, then my pants, watching her eyes track every movement I make. When I'm down to only my underwear, I start undressing her. I tug at the waistband of her stretchy yoga pants and slide them down her legs. Then I begin unbuttoning her pajama top, kissing her sternum and each one of her breasts before continuing down her stomach as each button exposes more skin. I leave the shirt like that, spread open but not fully removed so she won't have to sit up or pull it over her injured arm.

I sit back on my heels, taking a second to look at her laid out beneath me, and I breathe out heavily. *Damn.* I am no less affected by the sight of her body than that first time we slept together back in January. Finally, I slide off her panties. Once they're gone, I return my hand between her legs and slide two fingers inside her, pumping unhurriedly. Her hand comes down and grabs my wrist.

"I'm ready," she breathes. "I want you inside me now. Please, Graham." Her voice is still uncharacteristically needy, almost pleading. And I still can't deny her.

I grab one of the white pillows from the head of the bed and slip it beneath her, right where her spine meets her ass, so I'll have a better angle. Gently, I grab hold of her near her hipbones, my dick swelling at the sight of my huge hands against her creamy skin. I keep my hands there to hold her in place so I can try and limit any jostling that could hurt her head. Then I line myself up to push inside her. When I enter her, we both suck in breaths at the same time. I move my gaze from her hips up to her eyes, and we maintain that eye contact as I start moving, still going as slowly as I can manage. Her body welcomes me as I slide in one hard inch at a time, her wet warmth squeezing my length tightly in its embrace. It's so good that for a moment I see stars at the edges of my vision and have to focus so I don't come.

I continue to fill her until it's impossible for me to get any deeper. Our pelvises are pressed together, the base of my dick rubbing against her clit. Still buried deep, I angle my hips and swivel them slightly until I see the pulse in her neck jump and her eyes widen, signs that I've hit the right spot. I stay right there and grind against her for long seconds before pulling back out (slowly, so slowly) until I've removed all but the very tip. My gaze drops, fixated on the place where we're joined, and I watch as my dick slowly disappears inside her again.

When I look back up to her eyes, I see them shiny with tears, wetness already sliding down her cheeks. I freeze in place as my brows furrow with worry.

"Are you in pain? Is this too much?" I start to pull out, but her voice stops me at the same time her legs come up to wrap around my waist.

"No, don't stop."

I remove a hand from her hip and skim my fingers through her tears, my touch lighter than a feather as I trail along the bruised side of her face.

"I don't want to hurt you, baby. If you need a release, I promise I'll get you off with my mouth or my fingers. That might be easier on your head." I try to pull away again.

"No!" Her thighs squeeze in and clamp around me, halting my progress with those leg muscles that are so incredibly strong for such a small person. "Please don't stop. I need this. I need you."

Her voice is a little broken, tears now streaming down her face faster than I can wipe them away. There's no way her head isn't hurting, and I know we should stop. I'm probably a huge bastard for doing this in the first place instead of insisting she rest and take care of herself. But I'm not that good of a man, and my body wants her with a desperation that matches the need in her eyes. I don't have it in me to be noble right now.

I sink within the cradle of her body again and again. Occasionally I lean in to kiss her, my tongue caressing hers with the same slow strokes as my hips. I don't think we've ever had sex this slow before; we both usually want it a lot faster and harder, tending to get caught up in passion. But this … what we're doing now is something else entirely, something deep and intense. The rhythmic movement of our bodies is almost hypnotic. The world around us disappears, narrowing until there is nothing left but this moment and the two of us. Our eyes are still locked together, exchanging professions of love and hope and fear and sadness even though no words leave our lips. Tears still trickle down Mackenzie's face, but her hands on my body and the tight grip of her legs around my hips urge me on with a silent plea not to stop.

I'm barely holding back tears myself. Because we're both pouring every ounce of emotion into our lovemaking, as though for the last time. It feels like goodbye.

We come together. It's powerful, drawn out, and so intense that her tears turn to sobs. I can't hold back a few tears of my own that I let fall onto her skin as I bury my head in her neck. Then we stay unmoving, just clinging to each other for a long time, until her body goes slack and her breaths even out in slumber.

I carefully disentangle myself and go to the connected bathroom. I lean over the sink, splash water onto my face, and run it through my hair. Now that the sex haze has faded, my chest and throat are tight again with worry. The fear is crippling, thinking about what happened to Mackenzie today, what could have happened, and dreading what will happen to us tomorrow.

I catch sight of the little orange pill bottle on the counter, full of pain pills the doctor prescribed for Mackenzie. I reach over and pick it up, fiddle with the top, fingertips tingling with the sudden urge to open it. My heartbeat picks up in anticipation of the relief from this unbearable pain inside me. *I could take a few and she would never notice.*

In the large bathroom mirror, I can make out a sliver of the bedroom through the ajar door, enough for a small glimpse of Mackenzie's bright red hair standing out against the fluffy white sheets. *She almost died today.* I have to make this right, have to make sure she's never in danger again, and I won't be able to do that if I'm fucked up on pills. Although my hand shakes, I release the grip my fingers have on the pill bottle and drop it back to the counter.

※　※　※

I let Mackenzie sleep in. (I, on the other hand, was up most of the night and have been out of bed since the sun came up.) I greet her sleepy face with a kiss to her forehead and a cup of coffee, waiting until she's more awake to return with a bagel, coffee, glass of water, and her meds. I can barely look at them as I shake a couple of pills out and place them on a napkin for her. I'm disgusted at myself for what I almost did last night. It was one of the many things I stayed up stewing over.

She swallows the medicine and a couple bites of the bagel before taking a deep breath and patting the bed beside her in invitation. She seems more like her usual self, only a hint of yesterday's vulnerability visible. When I sit down, I find her looking at me directly with determination in her eyes.

"Okay," she says, face and voice resigned. "Now, tell me everything. Start with the night you were arrested five years ago—what exactly happened?"

32. THAT NIGHT

5 years earlier...

Graham

If you asked me a few months ago, I would have insisted, adamantly, that I'd never be caught dead in this sketchy part of town. Certainly couldn't have imagined I'd ever willingly be standing around in the parking lot of this rundown gas station in the middle of the night. A bitter wind hits me, and I duck back a few steps, hoping the graffiti covered pole will help shield me from it. No such luck. High above me, the pole has one broken bulb that causes it to cast a lopsided glow over the empty lot. The station's small row of gas pumps sports more handles with scribbled "out of order" signs than ones that don't. Everything about this place screams "dirty" and "wrong." Myself included.

Curtis is late, and I'm ready to crawl out of my skin with impatience. I bounce on the balls of my feet, whole body agitated. Restless. I can't figure out what to do with my hands, shoving them inside my coat pockets and then removing them repeatedly. Every time my right hand enters the fleece lined pocket, my fingers brush against the cash stashed there, the roll of bills held by a rubber band totaling more than a grand. Money for drugs.

If Curtis would fucking show up already.

So, yeah, I never thought I'd be here, but that was before. Before my parents died. Both of them gone in an instant, killed in a car accident on a completely normal day that shouldn't have born witness to such tragedy. It was the middle of the afternoon on a quiet Sunday, for fuck's sake, the sun shining brightly, and they were driving a route they'd taken a million times before on their way to the grocery store. But they never made it. Never came home. Never will again.

I don't know who the hell came up with those stages of grief, like they come in some sort of linear sequence. My experience of grief is more akin to a pinball machine, my emotions the helpless little sphere ricocheting erratically from place to place. But whether I momentarily land on denial, or grief, or anger, one constant remains. The pain. Since the moment I answered my phone and a voice on the other end told me Mom and Dad were dead, there's been this—I can't even explain it—this *pressure* inside my chest. Day in and day out. It kind of feels like when you're submerged in water for too long, when your lungs run out of air and your whole body buzzes with an overwhelming urgency, survival instincts screaming at you to get oxygen, to breathe. The difference is that for me there doesn't seem to be a surface. No air just above waiting to remedy this pervasive agony inside me.

Everyone is quick to share a sympathetic word, a pitying look, a bit of advice about how they've "been there." So many people have told me "it gets better." That "time heals." *Time.* If we're talking time here, then the truth is that this second is unbearable, the next hour daunting, and tomorrow seems impossible. So, promises of feeling better within the vague parameters of "time" does more to hurt than help me. It does nothing to quell that urgency inside driving me to seek relief. The same drive that brought me here, to what is undoubtedly my lowest of low points.

I didn't jump into drugs right away. First, it was alcohol. I started with Dad's extensive bourbon collection. I definitely blame the anger stage for sending me to Dad's prized liquor cabinet, chugging that covetable aged bourbon as though it was ten-dollar shit from the bottom shelf at the corner liquor store. After I drank the last bottle, I wept like a baby, my overwrought emotions pinging suddenly to devastation that another piece of my father was gone. But running out of the fancy stuff didn't stop me from drinking. I drank anything and everything I could get my hands on. And it worked—at least at first. Drunk was okay for a little bit. Drunk put a dent in the suffocating pain and helped me sleep. Until it didn't. Until it left me with nothing but a headache and sluggish muscles that made it hard to keep up at football practice.

After that, my descent into drug abuse was predictable, almost inevitable. Nothing you can't find in any cautionary tale about the slippery slope of drugs.

It's fucking pathetic, really. In the end, I'm nothing but a cliché. Just another poor little rich boy buying drugs with his dead daddy's money, popping pills and sniffing powder to take the pain away for a few hours.

Speaking of, I could use a couple pills right now. Thanks for nothing, Curtis, you motherfucker. I'm going to take some as soon as I leave here tonight, one or two to loosen the knot inside my ribcage and help me sleep. I generally let myself have more at night, because the nights are the hardest, and also because during the day I'm walking a thin line making sure to keep my little habit a secret from my classmates, coaches, teammates, and most importantly, Mackenzie.

When was the last time I took something? My mind isn't sure, but my body is certain it's been too long. Lately the days are getting harder, my attempts to stay sober at school less and less successful.

Today, at least, a little midday orgasm took the edge off. A smirk tips at my lips remembering how I talked Mackenzie into some oral in the back of my Range Rover during lunch. My girl would never have agreed to that shit three months ago, but she's been giving me pretty much whatever I want lately. Kenz probably thinks I'm using excessive amounts of sex to cope with the grief. Shit, I wish that were true. It might even work, if I could somehow keep my dick inside her twenty-four hours a day. I'd even give her a break every now and then, let her rest as long as she put it in her mouth or even her hands. If only.

My Mackenzie. Guilt hits me hard. What would she say if she saw me right now? No, I don't want to think about her, not while I'm here. I don't want her near any of this, not even in my thoughts.

"Wyatt."

I nearly jump a foot in the air, cursing at Curtis for sneaking up on me. He gives me an unapologetic grin and pulls a plastic bag from his back pocket.

"Went through that last batch fast, huh?"

I grunt and shrug, eyes focused on the bag in his hand. I pull out the cash. His gaze lands on it, and the greed gleaming in his eyes is so clear he might as well be a cartoon with dollar signs popping from them. We make the exchange, each pocketing our respective treasure.

Suddenly, there's a commotion on the other side of the parking lot. Curtis and I both look up to watch a short Hispanic man stalking toward us, ranting in rapid Spanish.

"You sold to my baby sister?" he yells at Curtis when he's perhaps a car's length from us.

"Nothing personal, *amigo*." Curtis sneers in a mocking tone, butchering the Spanish word by drawing out the vowels (*ay-mee-go*). "*She* came to *me*. I guess her big brother would deal to everyone else but wouldn't share with her, so she had to look elsewhere. I simply obliged."

Curtis has been smug, almost combative, but when the guy raises his hand revealing a gun, his whole body language changes. He tenses beside me, and before I can blink, he's pulled out his own gun from somewhere.

Holy shit. I blink. Is this really happening?

"Don't compare us," the man growls, literally spitting onto the pavement in disgust. "We don't sell to kids. And we don't move bad product. The shit you sold her was laced!" He's now waving the gun around as his hands gesture with his words. "She's in the hospital in a coma, on a fucking respirator!"

His pain is palpable, the manic shine in his eyes making him look unhinged. I'm pretty sure he didn't bring that gun for show-and-tell—he looks ready to use it. *Shit.* I want to run, but I make myself stay put. I don't move or speak, not wanting to draw his attention.

"Hey now, it's not on me if she doesn't know her limits." Curtis uses a placating tone now, obviously sensing the danger of the situation. But even though he's put on a false friendly demeanor, he doesn't put his gun away. In fact, I think I see the muscles of his arm tighten.

"No!" The man's shrieked denial is broken, his voice cracking with the force of his emotion. He steps closer to Curtis with determination, gun still clutched in the hand now hanging by his side. "No, she didn't overdose. The docs said they found fucking Fentanyl."

Fentanyl? I think I've heard that word thrown around in the news. Something about dealers increasing their profits by lacing heroin with it? I remember the reporter saying it's cheaper and gives a more intense high than heroin, but it's also far deadlier. *Fuck.*

He takes another step forward, eyes fixed on Curtis. Beside me, there's movement then a click that seems to echo through the gas station. Before I can process what's happening, a deafening crack sounds. I flinch back, instinctually expecting pain that doesn't come. Instead, not five feet in front of me I see the other man jerk back. Blood and God knows what else sprays from his forehead where the bullet hit and lodged. It doesn't look real, the blood too red, the spray and unnatural movement of his body making me feel like I'm in a Quentin Tarantino movie. Then he drops, a pool spreading out beneath his head far too quickly, his face too pale, body too still. I feel moisture on my cheek and reach up a finger to swipe at it. My world narrows as I stare fixated at the red staining my finger, my ringing ears supplying the soundtrack to my shock.

Oh my God. Curtis just fucking shot him. I have a dead man's blood on my hand.

Then something hard slams into my chest, snapping me out of my stupor and back to reality. Looking down, I see that what I felt was Curtis' gun, which he's now pointing right at my chest. He yells in my ear.

"Wake the fuck up, Wyatt. We have to get out of here. Your car. Now." He presses the barrel of the gun harder against my body for emphasis, a clear message of what will happen if I don't comply. So I do.

My mind goes fuzzy again, and I move in a daze. Walk to my car. Unlock it. Get in and sit behind the wheel. Look to my right, seeing Curtis already in the passenger seat.

"Drive!" he orders. I do.

The next few hours have a dreamlike quality to them. Everything moves slowly and disjointedly, flashing before me in choppy images. The ringing in my ears persists, a monotonous underscore. All other sounds are muted. My body feels far away, and I watch its actions in a state of detachment. My hands turn the wheel. My foot instinctually presses the pedals. Gas, break, gas. Red and blue lights in the rearview mirror. High-pitched siren breaking through the white noise in my head. Officers in black. My body slamming against the side of a car, metal closing around my wrists, rough hands digging through my pockets. A bag of unmarked pills shoved in my face. A monotone recitation of words that resonate through my fog with vague familiarity. *Do you understand?* The question repeated loudly until I nod.

Then a car, walking, finally left in a room that's too bright. The door opens, closes. Angry voices that blur into static. Faces. The bag of pills again, thrown onto the table. A laptop slammed down right in front of me, screen showing a scene that looks familiar but strange. It hits me that what I'm seeing is the gas station, from security footage taken by a camera that must be on top of the building. I focus on it, rapt. Recognize my own form from behind, then Curtis facing me. The quick movement of the other man appearing. Curtis shifting so we're standing side by side, both turned away from the camera. Movement as Curtis' hand raises. The sudden spasm of the man's body as the bullet enters his head. His body crumpling to the ground. Somehow, it's even more horrifying to watch the second time. Then two dark shapes walking away together toward a dark SUV. My form disappearing on the driver's side. Curtis on the passenger side. Driving away.

They leave me alone in that room for a long time, the hard steel chair beneath me and the metal cuffing my hands cold. That coldness slowly spreads throughout my whole body until I start wishing they would give me back my coat. My ass goes numb from being pressed against the hard seat for so long, but I don't get up. The discomfort brings me back into myself. Slowly. The ringing in my ears fades, replaced by the earsplitting silence of this room.

Hours go by. I'm aware of time passing only as it's marked by the burn in my tired eyes and the rising protests of my empty stomach. And the return of that internal ache, that pressure. I try to search my pockets with still bound hands until I remember they've been emptied. My throat thickens as awareness that I have no pill or powder to give me relief makes the pain intensify twofold. It makes my situation finally sink in, as nothing else has been able to.

Mackenzie.

I think about her for the first time in hours. She's right there at the top of my mind as soon as I fully shake the strange haze of shock. Her beautiful smile, smooth white skin, silky pale red hair, her hands on my body. The clear mental image sends a sharp stabbing sensation straight through me, compounding the agony already gripping my insides with crushing force. My thoughts darken.

This is all my fault. I'm a fuck up. She's better off without me. I don't want her to see me like this. If Mom and Dad could only see me now. Worthless fucking idiot.

I will myself to slip back within the fog. I decline my phone call, agree to charges I barely hear. The officers leave me in that same room to wait to be transferred to jail. The door slams shut, the sound too loud as it reverberates through my bones. This room might as well be a coffin, that door clicking shut a lid closing on the life I once had.

33. ARE WE OKAY?

Mackenzie

I'm crying, though I couldn't say at what point in Graham's story it started. I wipe at the tears with my bare palms, breathing in and out through my nose to slow the tide. He's finally finished talking, caught up through the events of yesterday, and we're sitting in silence letting it all slowly settle around us like a cloud of dust. I can barely wrap my mind around all the things he just told me, every revelation and clarification. On top of that, everything hurts. I woke up to find every minor bump and bruise and strained muscle from yesterday's altercation had coalesced and become an ache I feel throughout my whole body. Not to mention my throbbing head, which makes the knife wound on my arm seem nothing more than a minor scratch.

A knife wound. Is this my life? I would laugh if I didn't think it would open the door for a flood of tears that might never end.

"I still don't understand how our entire town—the sheriff, my parents—ended up believing you killed him?" I try to grasp onto something tangible. Facts, details.

While he was talking, Graham remained seated and still atop the bed, making eye contact with me most of the time but occasionally looking off toward the distance as though lost in thought. Now he rises and starts pacing, his legs eating up the hotel carpet for a couple of long strides before pivoting and retracing his steps in the other direction. His path is not long, his position always as close to the bed (and me) as it seems his agitation will allow. He looks like a lion trapped in a small cage, powerful muscles meant for open spaces. I'd bet anything he's dying to run a couple of laps full speed right now.

"Accessory isn't as gossip worthy as full murder, or as easy to whisper, I guess. And the exact charges were hazy for a little bit, because the position of the security video made it look like we were in it together. I seemed complicit in the whole thing, and they thought I willingly offered to drive the getaway car." He stops and shrugs a little helplessly, sad eyes meeting mine. "It's not like I was correcting anyone. And later I talked to the state police, so the Westwood Police likely weren't updated. If that would have even mattered."

I don't think Graham has slept at all. He's messing with his hair, pulling at the locks that have grown back out to nearly the length of my fingers, then pushing it away as it falls in his face. I reach over to the bedside table and rifle around in my purse until I find an elastic hair tie then toss it at him. He gives me a little sheepish smile, barely there on his otherwise grim face, before reaching up and fastening his dirty blond hair into a careless knot on top of his head.

I watch his every movement, tracing the taut muscles on his raised arms with my eyes. Savoring. I've been doing this since last night, trying to capture mental images of every beautiful feature, memorizing all of his motions and expressions, cataloging each sensation of his skin on mine when we made love. I have that sensation in my stomach again, the one you get when the roller coaster is approaching a steep drop in the track ahead and your muscles tighten in anticipation of the plummet.

"Why didn't you ask for a lawyer? You could have afforded a great one." There's no point in going over this again now. It won't change what happened five years ago, but I can't help myself.

"Doc Shady says I have some self-destructive tendencies." The upward twitch at the corner of his lips lacks humor, and I easily read it as wry self-deprecation.

You think? I silently respond with a roll of my eyes, and his almost-smile grows a fraction before disappearing.

"I know I'm repeating myself, and it doesn't do any good now, but I'm so sorry, Kenz. I'm so sorry I didn't tell you sooner, and that it got you hurt ..." His hazel eyes are glassy, the remorse clear in every inch of his body.

"I don't blame you, not for this." I reach up and lightly tap at my bruise mottled face then the bandage on my arm. "You wouldn't have put me in danger if you could help it. You tried to protect me, and I'm sure you would have done more if you could."

I watch his face as he processes my words, obviously surprised by this bit of absolution. Hope enters his eyes for the first time this morning, and my heart drops a little.

"Are we—?"

He doesn't finish his question, but the unspoken words hang in the air between us.

Are we okay?

Are we going to get past this?

Are we still together?

I carefully slide my legs off the bed and stand, dismissing him with a firmly held out palm when he rushes to my side offering assistance. I walk slowly but steadily over to the window. There's not much of a view, only the dismal cloud-filled sky and the hotel's parking lot far below.

"Are you sure you shouldn't be in bed?" he asks.

I wave him off. "I need to think for a minute. Just give me a minute."

Silence signals his agreement to my request, and I assume he's sat back down on the bed when I hear its springs depress beneath his weight. He gives me the quiet I asked for, leaving me alone with my thoughts as I continue to stare out the window.

My heart hurts after hearing his whole story. I understand better now what he went through back then, and even how he managed to hide it from me, from everyone. We all chalked up any unusual behavior to grief, considering it a normal response to his parents' death. Grief and depression share many symptoms and characteristics, after all. But what Graham felt was deeper than the average person's grief, darker. It is clear to me now, as it was to the "prison shrink" as he calls her, that he was clinically depressed. It's understandable why he turned to drugs, but I wish with everything in me that he'd sought professional help. A doctor could have prescribed him antidepressants to treat the chemical imbalance he was trying to combat with illegal drugs. I'm only grateful he never used heroin and managed to avoid a long-term addiction to the drugs, but who knows what might have happened if he wasn't arrested then? If he'd gone on with his drug use for more than those few months, he might have spiraled further. Likely would have.

But it's so hard to fathom. I can't seem to reconcile *my* Graham with a boy so broken he gave up and accepted charges far greater than he deserved. Had he pled and proven his innocence for involvement in the murder, his sentence would have been a couple of years for purchase and possession of the drugs, probably less with good behavior, and an expensive lawyer might have even gotten him off on community service with court mandated rehab. But he didn't speak up. All of my years studying psychology are proving insufficient to help me personally relate to that mindset, to being in a place so dark you would throw your whole life away.

I can only thank God the therapy in prison helped him enough that he eventually gave evidence in exchange for an early release. He probably helped a lot of people too, making sure Curtis stayed off the streets. By sharing every detail of that night, he gave the police the information they needed to check hospital records and find the sixteen-year-old girl who died from the Fentanyl-laced heroin Curtis sold her. Curtis won't ever get out, not with her death added to his charges. I'm so proud of Graham for that, for giving at least some justice to that poor family who lost both a son and a daughter within days of each other.

That was the past, though, things I've long since accepted even before I knew the specifics. But now there is this whole business with Eli. *What has Graham really done wrong?* There is this part of my mind that keeps asking, wanting to clear him. Graham assures me he hasn't turned back to drugs, that he hasn't engaged in any illegal activities. It would be easy, almost, to forgive him. To let his good intentions and my love for him outweigh his lies. But would it be the right thing to do? For *me*?

I suddenly recall a long-ago conversation with my mom, back in junior high when I was angsting over one of my early experiments with "boyfriends." The pre-adolescent infatuation didn't last long, of course, but I've never forgotten what she said when I came to her complaining about some small flaw of his.

"Well, is it a deal breaker?"

"A deal breaker?" I ask.

"You're always going to find some flaws, or less than favorable characteristics, in a boyfriend. Do you think your father is perfect?"

"No." I giggle and roll my eyes.

"Right. But we've been together for almost twenty years."

I nod, now totally engrossed in her words. Twenty years is an unfathomable amount of time to my twelve-year-old mind.

"You'll never be happy with a boy, or have a lasting relationship, if every time you find something you don't like, you just give up. You have to decide what's most important to you, and what behaviors or traits you absolutely can't live with. The automatic relationship killers ... the deal breakers. So, this boy's breath, for instance. Is it part of a larger problem? Is he generally bad about taking care of his hygiene?"

I scrunch my nose. "No. I think it's because he eats Doritos at lunch."

I watch her bite back a smile.

"So, if you really like him, if everything else about him is good— you enjoy spending time with him, he treats you well, he's a good person—could you fix it by carrying around gum or mints to offer him?"

I grin and nod. I never realized before, but my mother is a genius.

"So, it's not a deal breaker. What would be a deal breaker for you?"

"I guess—if he was mean to someone. The way Mitchell Helvey picks on Jennie Maither because she has a stutter."

Mom hugs me.

"As always, you never fail to surprise me with your maturity. I'm proud of you, honey. You have a good heart and a good head on your shoulders. I have faith you'll make smart choices as you grow up, and that you'll be strong enough to recognize a deal breaker and do the right thing even if it's not easy."

I didn't understand her then. Why wouldn't it be easy to do the right thing? It was beyond my capacity to imagine at the age of twelve. But oh I understand now.

Are we okay?

It might be easiest in the short term to forgive him, to give in to my craving for him and fall back into his arms. To let love blind me to his flaws. It's so tempting. A part of me is screaming insistently that only his arms, his love, will ease the sharp ache in my heart that's currently making it hard to breathe.

How did I let this happen? How did I get here?

I promised myself I would never experience this pain again. I made an internal oath to stay away from the kind of love capable of ripping me apart from the inside out. I was determined to be stronger, to be smarter, to always love myself first. And all it took was a couple weeks of Graham Wyatt's presence for me to forget all of that, to eschew self-preservation and self-respect and jump back into bed with him, back into *life* with him.

But I didn't do it completely blindly. I let him back in with a condition, one filled when I believed he had changed. He promised he'd never lie to me again, that he would never keep anything from me. And he broke that promise.

I think I've known the truth all along but wouldn't admit it to myself. *This is a deal breaker.* The deal breaker to end all deal breakers.

I walk slowly back over to the bed and sit down beside him, keeping an arm's length between us. I lift my eyes to his and find them already glassy. His pain and fear hurt almost as much as my own.

This is where I have to be strong, even when it isn't easy.

Are we okay?

I shake my head slowly, the slight motion enough to make a sharp pain lance through my skull that I try to ignore.

"No," I tell him softly, not pulling away from our eye contact even though it's breaking my heart. "No, we're not okay."

I drop my eyes to watch his Adam's apple move as he swallows hard, adding his thick neck covered in a day's growth of scruff to my mental snapshot gallery.

"What does that mean?"

"You lied to me," I say. My voice isn't harsh or angry—it's resigned. Sad. "You promised things would be different, and then you went and did the exact thing that ruined us the first time."

"I'm so sorry. Please—" he begins to plead in a hoarse voice. But I stop him with another painful shake of my head.

"You've said you're sorry. I heard you, and I believe you. That's not what this is about. I don't think you lied about Eli because you were doing anything wrong or because you were trying to hurt me."

"Never," he agrees fervently.

"So, you didn't tell me because … you were ashamed about the reminder of your past? You were scared and didn't want to show me that weakness? You were afraid that it would scare me away?"

His nod is slow, so slow, and paired with a heavy-lidded blink.

"And that's what it comes down to. The deal breaker. You don't trust me."

"That's not true!" He closes the space I'd left between us and takes my hands in his, eyes and voice beseeching. "I do trust you, more than absolutely anyone else. You have to see that."

Tears gather in my eyes and quickly overflow to cascade down my cheeks. My lips tremble with the effort to keep myself from breaking down completely.

"But you thought I wouldn't stand by you? Thought I wouldn't want to be with you if I knew?"

"I was scared."

I squeeze his fingers in my own, wrapping them around his large hand as far as they can reach.

"And your response to fear—again—was to shut me out, to hide things from me, to lie. To have this whole separate life going on while I was falling in love with you even deeper than before, letting myself believe this was the beginning of our life together." A single sob breaks through my efforts to control it, and as though my emotions are connected to his, magnetized, my anguish pulls the first tear from his hazel eyes.

"It is the beginning. I've been right here with you, falling so fucking deep. None of that is a lie. I still mean every word I've said to you. The way I love you, the life we're planning, that isn't a lie. Please, Z."

I'm crying harder now, my vision almost too blurry to make out his tortured face mere inches from mine.

"I believe you. But you weren't letting me in on the whole story. Even when you knew—you knew—how badly you hurt me before, how I was breaking my own rules to let myself love you again. You don't trust me, and now I—I can't trust you either." My voice breaks with the force of my emotion, and I have to pause until I'm a bit calmer.

"I can't build a life with you never knowing when the next hard thing will come up and you'll compartmentalize again, build a wall to keep me out from part of you. I can't give you all of me when something in you isn't willing to do the same."

He leans in. I close my eyes briefly at the sensation of his hands cradling my face, his big callused thumbs swiping at my collected tears.

"Don't do this. Baby." There's a desperation in his voice I've never heard before, so heart-wrenching that my next breath comes out on another sob. "It won't happen again. I swear it. You have to believe me. I'll never lie to you again."

I cover his hands with mine, hovering for a single heartbeat to take in the feel of our skin together. Then I remove his hands from my face. He's so much stronger than me, he could easily resist my gentle push, but he doesn't. He lets me move away, and I scoot back until I'm as far from him as I can get, now perched at the very edge of the bed.

Strength, Mackenzie. Love yourself more.

"Fool me twice," I whisper. I try to smile, but I'm sure it looks as sad as my soul is right now. "You mean that now, but this is a toxic pattern I'm not sure you even have control over. And I can't risk it. There's no third strike here. I won't survive it. I need to choose myself now."

"I love you," he says in a low, broken voice that's almost more than I can bear.

"I love you too."

Then I close my eyes, breaking the eye contact. Breaking us.

"I want to go home. To Westwood," I whisper. Suddenly, I need my mom and dad. I need to feel safe in their house.

"I'll take you."

"Marisa could—"

"Please. Let me do this one last thing."

"Okay."

34. MR. FUCKING CONGENIALITY

Graham

Seconds after I watch Mackenzie disappear through the doorway of her childhood home, tucked beneath her mother's arm, Mike Thatcher emerges and stalks toward me.

"This is how you *take care of her*?!" he roars.

Mr. Thatcher comes at me hot. Maybe back in his active duty days he could have caught me off guard, but now I can see exactly when and where he's going to swing. I don't make any move to retreat or duck. I lock my legs a bit, brace for impact, and let him smash his fist into my cheekbone. He may not be at the top of his game, but his hit is still as powerful as a sledgehammer.

My face is throbbing, and I resist the urge to lift my fingers and touch the spot. *Fuck, that's going to hurt for days.* But I can't really bring myself to care all that much. No hurt could be half as bad as the pain in my chest where his daughter ripped my heart out this morning.

I make myself stand still, waiting to see what he'll do next. A few seconds pass as we stare each other down on the paved walkway outside the Thatcher's house. I keep my face and posture purposefully calm, while before me his gaze is murderous, his chest heaving with the force of his anger. When he doesn't move closer or raise a hand to hit me again, I finally speak.

"Mr. Thatcher, I need to talk to you. It's important."

His nostrils flare angrily. Smoke might as well be pouring from them.

"What makes you think I give a damn about anything you'd have to say?"

"I don't, sir. But it's about the man who hurt Mackenzie. Right now, her safety is the one thing I'm certain you and I can agree on. I have an idea, but I need your help." He continues glowering at me. I take a slow step forward, letting him see the sincerity in my face. "Please. It doesn't mean you have to stop hating my guts. You can even hit me again first, if you want."

"You have two minutes," he finally grumbles.

I don't waste any time. I start talking.

✲ ✲ ✲

Mike Thatcher glares over from his seat beside me, and I try to still the frenetic bouncing of my leg. I've been bursting with nervous energy ever since we walked through the doors of the Westwood Police Station, a building I'd hoped to never see the inside of again. Now we're sitting in tense silence, waiting for Chief Duluth to return to his office where he left us almost twenty minutes ago.

The door swings open abruptly. Police Chief Edward Duluth enters and immediately makes his way over to the massive chair on the other side of his desk, where he sits heavily. He drops two folders from his hands that make a smacking sound as they land on the sturdy surface. I don't really remember him from before—so much of *that night* is a

254

blur in my memory—but the man before us now is a bit overweight, with gray hair that's well on its way to balding. These signs of aging do nothing to decrease the man's domineering presence. He manages to carry the extra weight with purpose, and beneath thick, nearly black eyebrows, his dark blue eyes are shrewd. It's not hard to see how he ended up in this position of authority and kept it for so many years.

"You've got a pretty shiner there yourself, Wyatt," Duluth comments suddenly. His eyes zero in on the swelling that's encroaching on my eye, the area surely a nice purple by now. "How did that happen?"

Not letting my gaze stray to the man sitting beside me, I give the chief an easy smile—the kind Mackenzie calls a smirk.

"Would you believe it? I clocked myself in the face with a kitchen cabinet door! One of many reasons I should probably just stay out of the kitchen."

He doesn't laugh or so much as crack a smile. *Tough crowd.* He brusquely moves on from the topic, obviously not too concerned over whoever hit me. He doesn't open the folders before him, but as he begins talking, he continually pokes at them with a single raised finger.

"Okay, so I talked to the officer who gave you his card—Schwartz—and he was willing to share the file with me even though it's a Boston matter, out of my jurisdiction. I did a little reading to update myself on your case too." He cuts those sharp blue eyes to me. "Seems there have been a lot of developments since my office last handled it."

He pauses to let his words hang in the small room. It's not an apology. It's barely an acknowledgement that he was wrong and far short of any recognition that he unfairly slandered my name around town. But it's something. I nod and work to keep the muscles in my face loose. I need to be Mr. Fucking Congeniality right now, because I need these men to help me. For Mackenzie.

"Boston's already got a warrant out for the assault on Mackenzie. She's a good girl, and I hope they catch the son of a bitch." He nods soberly at Mr. Thatcher. "There's not much I can do down here, though."

"We know who it was, sir. His name is Eli Markum, brother of Curtis Markum. He's recently vandalized my property and stalked me here in Westwood too. I wrote it all out and included screenshots of some phone messages." I produce the packet of notes I put together a few days ago.

His dark brows move closer together as he flips through it.

"Why didn't you bring this to us sooner?"

"Would you have listened?" I shoot back before I can stop myself.

Duluth makes a little grumbling sound that I choose to interpret as grudging acknowledgement. He and I both know damn well no cop in this precinct would ever take me seriously. The Westwood Police are not exactly my number one fans. I can only imagine the response I'd have gotten if I walked through the doors of the WPD station without Mike Thatcher at my side. Let's just say, I wouldn't be in this seat right now with the chief willing to hear me out. I'm only here because of his friendship with Mr. Thatcher—and, of course, Mr. Thatcher's devotion to the girl we both love being stronger than his hatred for me.

"I also hired a PI to get dirt on Eli," I continue. "It's only been a few days, but here's what he found so far. If he comes back with anything else, I'll pass that on to you as well."

Two gray heads bend over the desk. The men pore over the contents of the new folder I've laid there. I don't need to look; I am all too familiar with the details they're reading. I've already read it myself a dozen times and have almost memorized the veritable grocery list of shady shit Eli's got his fingers in. Moving heroin. Dealing to minors. Drug trafficking across state lines. Likely import and distribution of synthetic Fentanyl from Mexico. Not to mention a bevy of assault charges and a suspicious number of missing persons reports surrounding him and his operation, though so far, no evidence has been found to tie them to him directly. Eventually Mike Thatcher leans back, scraping at the hint of stubble on his chin as he breathes out a low curse before pinning me with an accusatory stare. I didn't discuss all of these details with him earlier.

"What the hell is wrong with you, getting messed up with someone like this?"

I grit my teeth and try to maintain a relaxed tone.

"With all due respect, sir, I bought drugs from his brother more than five years ago. I've served my time for that, and even contributed evidence to the state's case against Curtis. I never personally sought out Eli and have no ties to the shit—uh, I mean the *stuff*—he's done while I was locked up."

Mr. Thatcher lets out a little *"hmph"* and sits back in his seat, appeased but not willing to offer any verbal concession or apology. Geez, these are two stubborn old men.

Ignoring our little exchange, Chief Duluth is still flipping through the pages. For long minutes he scans the information my expensive private investigator dug up.

"None of this would be admissible in court or enough for a search warrant." Duluth muses. "But I think I could run it by an old buddy from the service who went to work for the DEA."

Now we're talking. I'm all for setting the Drug Enforcement Administration loose on Eli's ass. Those guys don't fuck around.

"The Feds have a hard-on for opioid dealers right now," the chief says. Then his eyes flick up to me as though remembering I'm here, that he's not just talking casually to his pal Mike. He clears his throat. "It's something to work with. I'll keep you both apprised if anything changes. In the meantime, be sure to give his name to the BPD so they can have Mackenzie ID him."

"I want to be involved," I say firmly. "Eli wants revenge for his brother, so I have the best connection to him. He'll come after me again."

"Hmm." He eyes me thoughtfully. "I'll get back to you after I put in that call to my friend at the DEA."

"I'll hold you to that, sir," I tell him as we shake hands. I meet his eyes straight on and think I see a small glimmer of respect. Good. I want him to see I'm not fucking around with this. If I don't hear from him in two days, I'll be back in this office following up in person.

The love of my life may have just dumped my worthless ass, but it's not time to crawl into bed and fall apart. Not yet. First, I need to make sure Eli Markum never has the chance to hurt her again. After that, who knows what the hell I'll do with myself, but at least she'll be safe.

35. TIME TO GET UP

Mackenzie

Three vigorous knocks pull me from the comfortable half-asleep state I've been floating in. I hear the door open mere seconds before the bedsheet is ripped off my body. I have a good guess who it is even before I drag open my lids.

Yep. Those are definitely my best friend's deep brown eyes staring down at me.

"Ris!" I groan feebly. "I'm sleeping."

"As I hear it, all you've been doing for the past four days is sleeping. Time to get up." Marisa flips on the light switch and makes herself comfortable in my childhood room, plopping her butt down on the bed nearly on top of my feet.

I squint in the sudden brightness and glare at her.

"Did my mom call you?"

"Actually, *I* called *her* when you didn't return any of my texts or phone calls."

"I have a concussion. I'm not supposed to look at screens."

She raises a single eyebrow.

"Bullshit. You could look for the fraction of a second it takes to see my name and fabulous face and swipe to answer."

"I need a little more time," I whine, sounding petulant even to my own ears.

"You've been through something hard, *chiquita*. I get it. Your body and your mind need to recover. But somewhere in there you know *this*…" she waves her hand over the bed I've barely left in days "…isn't healthy anymore. You're welcome, by the way. I'm the one that gave you four days—your mom thought I should come and storm the gates after two."

"I broke up with Graham," I whisper, staring at the white dresser and matching shelves on the other side of my room. I try to focus on remembering what, if anything, is still in those drawers. The pitiful attempt at distracting myself from thinking about Graham fails miserably. *Graham.* One great thing about sleep is that it gives me a reprieve from thinking about him, worrying about him, *missing* him. My chest tightens with pain that seems to be radiating out from my heart. This pain is so much worse than my residual headache.

"I know," Marisa responds softly, placing one of her hands on my leg and patting me over my comfy sweatpants. "He told me."

That gets my attention. Suddenly alert, I turn to her so quickly it makes my still sensitive head throb in protest.

"He told you? You've talked to him?" I sound a little desperate, too eager, but I can't help myself.

"I told you, I was worried. I called him, and he told me you were here."

Beyond my control, a rogue tear slips out. It tickles my face on its way down to my chin.

"You want to talk about it?"

"Not yet."

"Okay. You need to talk to someone, though. A professional."

"Ris–" I start to protest.

"Kenz, step outside your own viewpoint for a second—if you were assessing a patient or studying this as a test case, you *know* you would say the same thing. You went through something traumatic, even without the..." she stops herself from saying his name "...the McF situation. Be as smart about taking caring of yourself as you would if I was the one in that bed."

I sigh, and she recognizes it for what it is, a sound of defeat. Because of course she's right.

"Now," she says in a brusque no-nonsense tone. "First things first, you need to shower. I hate to say it, but you look like hell and stink even worse."

"Gee, thanks. Your bedside manner is fabulous." I can't help but laugh a little.

"Please, you've seen how I can soften it up when necessary. But what you need is tough love, so that's what you're getting, even if you hate me for it at the moment." She waits a moment for me to respond or move from my position on the bed. When I don't, she stands up and plants both hands on her hips.

"So, are you going to get in the shower, or do I need to haul your scrawny ass in there myself?"

"My ass isn't scrawny!"

"It might be now, considering how little your mama says you've eaten the past few days."

"Seriously, how much have you two been talking?!"

"A lot," she says more seriously. "We're worried. We love you. Now get out of that bed and shake it for me so we can see if you have any booty left."

I pull myself to an upright position. My momentary dizziness is confirmation that I haven't eaten enough the last few days. I've been embracing the melancholy and sinking into a funk, not fighting against my desire to sleep most of the day or make myself do more than pick at the food my mom brings me. Mom has actually been really great since I got here, not asking too many questions and letting me be— except for a few times a day when she comes in to give me food or fresh water or help change out the bandage on my stitches.

Apparently, she's only been biding her time, placating me while conspiring with my bestie all along.

Marisa's Shawn Mendes ringtone fills the room, and I lean over to nosily glance at the screen at the same time she does. I spy the words "OFFICER GUAPO" before she hits "ignore" and shoves it back inside her pocket.

"Is that who I think it is?" I ask, perking up a little. For the first time in days, a small buzz of interest, of life, courses through my veins.

"Mmm," she mumbles evasively, shrugging.

"Come on, Ris, take my mind off things. Is that the hot cop from the hospital? Derek … Schwartz, right?"

"Es posible." Maybe. I swear if she could blush with that golden complexion, her face would currently be bright red.

"Tell me everything!"

"Okay, I will. *After* you shower!" She punctuates her command by grabbing a towel from the top of my dresser and tossing it at me.

"Okay, okay. I'll shower." I actually laugh a little and feel a bit more like myself.

✳ ✳ ✳

"So ... Officer Guapo is calling you. Have you gone out with him?"

I'm clean and changed into a fresh set of clothes, perched on the edge of my bed ready for some gossip.

"No, not since we had coffee at the hospital. He wants to take me on a date, though. He texted to ask me out the same day we met, and now he keeps calling."

"And ...?"

She shrugs, eyes darting to the side.

"He's a hot as hell police officer who speaks Spanish! I see no problem here. Why are you ignoring his calls?"

"When we got coffee, I feel like he spent more time looking at my hand than my ass."

"Like he's got some sort of fetish?" I half-whisper. I wouldn't put it past my mom to be listening at the door right now.

"*Dios,* no!" Marisa lets out a quick trill of laughter. "I mean that it seemed like he was imagining putting a ring on this." She holds up her left hand and waggles her ring finger at me.

I roll my eyes.

"Only you could manage to have commitment issues with a guy you haven't started dating yet."

"Okay, so maybe I was imagining the ring finger ogling. The man spent an appropriate amount of time checking out my fantastic T&A. But I still don't know if I want to get involved. I doubt he could do casual. Everything about him screams 'looking for a girlfriend to bring home to mom.'"

"And would something more than casual be so bad?" I ask, more gently.

She shrugs, and I catch a rare glimpse of her deeply hidden vulnerability. When we met back in freshman year, one of the things we instantly bonded over was the fact that we both happened to be nursing broken hearts. I suspect that even after all this time, hers hasn't recovered much more than mine has.

"Girls?" Mom calls from outside the door. "Are you coming out for lunch?"

Marisa peeks at my face before answering. "We'll be there in a minute, Mrs. T!"

We sit in silence listening to my mom's footsteps as they retreat in the direction of the kitchen.

"What's up?" Marisa asks when Mom is out of earshot. She knows me too well and can clearly read my hesitation.

"I was so childish," I admit. "I haven't talked to them for *months*. I ignored so many of my mom's calls. And the last time we spoke …" I cringe, remembering the confrontation in the diner parking lot. That partly seems like it was a hundred years ago, while my memory of the disquiet it created inside me is still as fresh as if it happened yesterday. "I think the worst part is that I was basically choosing Graham over them. Standing up for him, standing *by* him, because I believed in him. But I guess they were right after all."

I will not cry. I will not cry. Another tear slips out.

Marisa doesn't say anything right away. She tilts her head, thinking. The movement makes her beautiful black curls swing to one side and drape over her shoulder.

"Do you think they'll rub that in your face?" she eventually asks. "Is your mom an 'I told you so' person?"

Will they? Is she? We've never had this kind of fight before. I've always been the good daughter—obedient, respectful. But do I really think they'll hold a grudge against me?

"No. I don't think so."

"Well, *chica*, your pride is hurt along with your body and your heart. But you're going to walk out there anyway. You are Mackenzie Motherfucking Thatcher, the biggest badass I know. You're a fighter. You are *not* a girl who hides out under the covers feeling sorry for herself."

I sit up a little straighter. Honestly, at the moment I feel pretty damn far from "Mackenzie Motherfucking Thatcher," but I can take this first step toward being her again. When we stand up, Marisa immediately reaches back to give me a light swat on the ass, like a sports coach telling her player to *"go get 'em!"* I yelp a little and step farther away from her.

"Now find the giant lady *cojones* I know you've got inside those leggings somewhere and let's go have lunch. If it gets awkward, think of dessert. Abuela made a huge batch of cookies she insisted I bring you."

That does the trick, propelling me to rise and turn the doorknob. Marisa's grandmother makes *the best* chocolate chip cookies, and I suddenly want to eat a mountain of them. I'm well aware there's no magic cure for a concussed head or a broken heart, but chocolate seems as good a place as any to start with the healing process.

36. ALL DRESSED UP, NOWHERE TO GO

Graham

"Do you think you're depressed, Graham?"

I shrug. "I don't see how that matters."

The doc's eyebrows draw together in a small frown. "Of course it matters. How have you been spending your time? Are you doing anything productive?"

"Until Eli is in jail, taking him down is my only focus."

Shady waits for me to say more. When I don't, she prompts me again. "Have you moved into the new house?"

"No. I figure it's better to live with the ghosts of the past than the ghosts of what could have been my future."

"That's quite a bleak perspective."

"Things are pretty fucking bleak right now, Doc."

"I want to keep seeing you weekly. And you have my cell number—use it if you need to talk in between sessions. You're not alone, Graham. Please remember that."

❖ ❖ ❖

Rays of sun hit my closed lids, signaling to my body that it's time to wake. I roll over to my side to get away from the light, trying to go back to sleep, but consciousness has its hold on me and I'm soon alert no matter how tightly I squeeze my eyes shut.

I guess my dick missed the memo that we have nothing to get up for, because underneath the sheets I'm hard as granite. *Yeah, I see you're all dressed up, but we got nowhere to go, buddy.* Not long ago, I would have been able to reach over to the other side of the bed and make use of my morning wood with Mackenzie. But that side of the bed is cold and empty, as it has been for weeks now.

My phone buzzes and I answer it with a single grunted word. "Update?"

It's the lead guy on Mackenzie's security team. I'm not worried. He's only doing as I've instructed, calling and checking in with me every twelve hours.

"All clear," he replies.

I hang up without another word. I figure he's in no position to be offended, not with what I assume is the astronomical salary he's pulling. If the security company asked for payment in organs, it would probably be cheaper than what I'm paying them, even with the hefty discount I received as an apology for their failure to keep Mackenzie from harm. As though saving some cash makes anything about what happened better.

There has been no word on or from Eli since he attacked Mackenzie nearly a month ago, but I still have three guards assigned to her 24/7. I'm also keeping a guy on Marisa and another on Griff and Shaina's place, just for good measure. Who knows how far Eli is willing to go to make me suffer? I won't let him surprise me again. The guards are out in the open now, and I couldn't care less if the girls don't like it. I want those guys free to shadow as closely as necessary to protect them. Griff isn't aware of his guard, of course, because he'd lose his shit thinking I'm questioning his ability to keep his family safe. But I couldn't stand it if anything happened to them. It's not worth the risk.

At least paying for the security makes me feel like I'm doing *something*. I'm going out of my goddamn mind here, waiting for Duluth to get back to me about involving the DEA. I'm sure by this point the chief and the station's front desk lady are sick of me calling and dropping in to ask for updates, but it's all I can really do right now. It seems as though nobody is taking this seriously. I mean, it's been more than THREE WEEKS, and they've got *nothing*. I've even dropped off more dirt that my PI found, including some leads he acquired through legal sources, public records and shit that might be admissible in court. (And yes, I've been researching "admissible evidence" and "police jurisdictions," because I can't just fucking sit here doing nothing.)

The only other person who seems to be on top of this thing with me, shockingly, is Mackenzie's dad. He has never told me to chill out, never gotten annoyed with my persistence. We exchange updates a few times a week via text. He won't tell me much about Mackenzie, of course, but even getting that small personal confirmation that she's okay means everything to me.

Knowing I won't be able to get back to sleep now, I throw off the bed sheet and walk buck naked into my attached bathroom where I take a piss then turn on the water in the shower. My shower is a nice big walk-in one with enough space for a guy my size to move around. Unlike the shower at Kenz's place, which is so small I always end up banging my elbows on the walls when I try to wash my hair or basically make any movement. Somehow, though, we still managed to have sex in there a couple of times.

The memory of Mackenzie naked and wet has my dick standing at attention all over again, like an eager puppy who hasn't realized its master isn't coming home. Not that the memory is necessary, because I honestly think about having sex with her all the time. The only time I'm *not* thinking about sex with her is when I'm remembering everything else about her. All the millions of tiny things I love about her. The way she looks when she's all serious, curled up on the couch studying. Her adorably over the-top-obsession with guacamole and all things chocolate. The light freckles on her face that come out of hiding during the summer then fade away again in winter. A fucking movie style montage of her ass in all thousand pairs of yoga pants she owns. And ... we're back to sex. But it's still Mackenzie on my mind. Always Mackenzie.

* * *

In the early afternoon, I get a text message.

GRIFF: Want a beer?

GRAHAM: I'm in.

GRIFF: Got some in my fridge. Come over whenever.

The real reason behind Griff's invitation becomes quickly apparent when he answers the door looking straight up frazzled—a word I would usually never associate with him. He has a wailing two-week-old baby boy slung over his shoulder, and he waves me in with one hand as the other huge paw sporadically pats his son's back. He follows me inside slowly, stopping every few steps to bend his knees in a bobbing motion like he's trying to mimic something he's seen Shaina do and failing miserably.

I don't laugh, but it's hard.

Shouting to be heard over his son's continued shrieks, Griff explains that Shaina went out with Layla for a couple of hours for some special "girl time" since baby Harry has been getting so much attention. It turns out this is the first time Griff has been left alone to care for Harry since the baby was born, and he's not doing a great job of hiding the fact that he's freaking out.

Griff is a big tough guy hardened by life and the streets and prison, and he's generally not ruffled by much. Even when he is stressed or upset—like those first few months we were cellmates, when he and Shaina were having serious problems—he's more of a strong, silent brooding type. So it's actually a little shocking to see him this way. His eyes are wide with panic, his beard in disarray as though Harry has been pulling at it, and there's some unidentifiable substance in his hair and on his shirt that could be puke, poop, pee, or milk (most likely some combination). His giant tattooed hands are currently gripping his son as though he's never held a baby before, which he definitely has—he's seemed calm and competent the other times I've visited since Harry's birth.

Again, I try not to laugh. I guess I'd be out of my depth too if I were in his shoes.

I do *not* let myself stray to thoughts of Mackenzie and the children we won't have if she never takes me back. I have to be here for my friend right now, so I can't let the sorrow drag me down.

I hold out my arms and Griff hands the kid over so fast he nearly throws him. As soon as his hands are free, he begins pacing agitatedly around the living room and rambling as though he's been waiting to pass the baby off before losing his shit.

"He won't stop crying! I changed him and fed him, and I've tried everything Shaina does and he won't stop. I'm a fucking shitty dad!" His hands tug at his unkempt beard. "Ah, *fuck!* I'm not supposed to curse around the kids!"

This is one of those moments when I'm reminded that Griff wasn't around for the first couple years of Layla's life. This baby business is all as new to him as though Harry were his first kid. Actually, I'm kind of flattered to be the one he called for backup.

"Hey, little guy," I say to the screaming infant, holding him the way Shaina showed me. I keep my voice calm, trying to model good behavior for both of the O'Brien men. "Sit down, Griff," I say in the same tone.

Griff sits on the edge of the couch and runs his hands over his face, barely blinking when some of whatever is in his hair ends up on his fingers.

"Okay, first of all, you need to calm the fuck down," I tell him evenly. He glares at me and I roll my eyes. "Language is the least of your worries right now. He doesn't understand anything at this age. Layla's the one you need to watch it around."

He seems to relax a tiny bit, shoulders lowering from their tense position up near his ears. I go on.

"So, I don't have much experience with babies, but I figure they're not that different from dogs, right? You know how animals can sense your mood, smell fear and all that? I bet you being stressed out isn't helping him calm down."

His face shifts from the stormy glare that appeared as I compared his kid to a dog, and I see his brows lift in consideration.

"Go clean yourself up and … I don't know, take deep breaths or something. Chill out and then come back. Harry and I will be fine here."

We both turn to the tiny hurricane, whose cries have remarkably lessened a bit since his dad sat down. Griff nods, trudging down the hall to his bedroom after giving Harry a quick kiss on the top of his head (giving no fucks if it makes him look soft, which honestly makes him a bigger badass in my eyes).

Ten minutes later Griff is back in a new shirt, beard and hair neatly brushed and slightly wet from a shower, looking more himself, which is to say gruff and intimidating as hell. I smile at the welcome sight.

While he was gone, I've managed to distract Harry with some stuffed toys I found, which I've been dangling above him one at a time making them dance with my free hand. I've been using my best baby voice to tell him a story that bears a strong resemblance to the rules of American football. Now I hand him over to his dad, and right as we complete the pass, a loud fart comes from the little guy, closely followed by the foulest stench I've ever smelled.

❖   ❖   ❖

Three hours later—hours during which the two of us fumbled to deal with a poop explosion while Harry literally laughed at us and pissed in our faces, attempts at baby talk that can never be spoken of again, and some truly trippy children's television—an O'Brien boy is finally fast asleep. Of course, it isn't Harry. No, it's Griff who is passed out cold on the couch, head tipped back and mouth wide open in a deep exhausted sleep. Harry is still awake but cheerful and calm for now, so I leave Daddy Griff to his well-deserved nap and decide to bring the baby out to the backyard. I quietly maneuver open the back door with Harry in my arms then take a seat on a patio chair.

The sun is still out although it's nearly 7:00 PM, but the scorching hot day has cooled and there's a slight breeze. I sit back onto the chair, bouncing my knee as I hold Harry low on my chest with both hands the way I would a football. Around us, the neighborhood is quietly alive. These long summer days in late June always bring the people of Boston flocking to the outdoors to soak up the warmth. From beyond the fenced area of the little yard, I can hear the murmurs of people talking and laughing and smell a hint of charcoal from someone grilling for a barbecue. Above our heads, a low rumble of bass starts up from the apartment on the third floor of Griff's building.

Harry begins to shift around restlessly, so I start talking in the soft voice that seems to soothe him. Of course, when I open my mouth, the words that come out are about Mackenzie.

"I messed up, little man," I tell him quietly. "I hope when you find the girl of your dreams you don't make the kinds of mistakes I have. I messed up so bad I don't think I can ever fix it. And I don't have a clue what to do with myself if that's true."

I hear the door open behind me then Shaina's soft voice.

"Are you imparting words of wisdom to my son?"

She walks over and stops at the side of my chair. I look up at her, though she's so short I don't have to raise my gaze all that far.

"Honestly, I think it's the other way around," I admit.

She makes a little "hmm" sound of acknowledgement and reaches out to trail the tips of her fingers over the soft black fuzz on the baby's head.

"And has Harry helped you figure anything out?"

"Can't say I have any more answers, but I'm sure going to sleep well tonight."

She laughs lightly. "Let's see if we can get him to stay asleep all the way to his crib."

She's still recovering from the C-section and not supposed to lift things, so I keep Harry in my arms as I stand and follow her inside the house. We pass through the living room where Griff is still out. I see nothing but love in the smile Shaina aims at her sleeping man. Still carrying Harry, I walk behind Shaina toward the bedroom she shares with Griff, where they've also set up the baby's crib. When we're halfway down, the hall a door opens and Marisa tiptoes out of Layla's room.

"She didn't wake up," Marisa whispers to Shaina, who responds with a quiet "thank you" before Mackenzie's roommate turns to me and gives me a sad little wave. I nod at her but keep walking because I don't want to wake Harry.

Once I've laid him down in his crib, I ask Shaina, "Did Mackenzie come with you guys today too?"

She gives me a sad smile, very similar to Marisa's, and nods. My body tenses and my heart races at the thought of Mackenzie waiting for Marisa in the car, right outside. As though she can read my mind, Shaina puts one small hand on my arm and shakes her head at me.

"Give her time."

37. EVERYONE DIES SOMETIME, RIGHT?

Mackenzie

Love is just a chemical reaction in the brain. All of these feelings we put so much stock in are really nothing but science—the biological mechanisms of our bodies motivating us to procreate so the species doesn't die out.

Love isn't real. This is my mantra. The words I repeat to myself daily, when the heartache gets too big.

Marisa doesn't approve of my coping methods. She may choose to avoid dating in favor of casual hookups, but not far underneath that sass she's a true romantic at heart. I used to be one too. Growing up, I was all about chick flicks and romantic comedies. I swooned along with the rest of the audience when it came time for happily ever after. *Romance.* I believed in it, wanted it, dreamed of it. But after Graham went to prison, I became more realistic—Marisa would say cynical. Returning to that mindset has helped me put everything in perspective, to zoom out from my tiny desolate corner of the world and try to look at matters more clinically. I try to imagine that instead of living it I'm observing animals in the wild and taking research notes.

Maybe I tend to zoom out too far, but honestly looking at my life from up close hurts way too much lately. Most days it seems that even moving my little observation deck out to the moon wouldn't be far enough to get away from the Graham-sized ache in my chest and the empty void I see when I try to envision my future.

"Would you say devoting yourself to schoolwork was how you coped after Graham went to prison and perhaps that became a learned avoidance strategy you now use habitually?"

"I don't think I'd necessarily say that."

"Well, if I say it, will you agree it's true?"

I glare at Dahlia and she grins. It figures I'd get this kind of sass from a psychologist recommended by Marisa.

"I'm here to talk about the attack," I remind her a little stiffly.

And it's true. My body is healing fine—I'll even be able to start practicing yoga again soon—but my mind isn't processing things quite so cleanly.

I stayed with my parents for two full weeks. Mom and Dad have been really supportive, and I'm grateful that we were able to move past our recent conflict—even if they only let it go out of pity for me. I hid out with them for longer than I should have. The truth is that I was afraid to go back home to our apartment. The fear was irrational and I knew it; I am well aware of the *three* bodyguards Graham is still paying to protect me. And yet when I thought of returning there, I felt a surge of panic that had me burrowing back under the blankets of my childhood bed. I'm not proud to say that when I finally did return, I needed my dad to come with me, and he slept on the couch for three days until I stopped bursting into tears every time he tried to leave.

That's right. I no longer have the right to call myself a tough, grown ass woman. Apparently, I'm a weak little girl who needs my daddy to hold my hand.

So, I'm back in my own bedroom in my own apartment. But I've been having nightmares, and some days I still have to circle the block a few times before I can make myself park my car in the driveway and go inside.

And so ... therapy.

"You're here to talk about whatever is going on with you, how you're feeling. We won't discuss Graham today if that's what you want, but I think you need to deal with those feelings soon."

Therapists. I swear. Nosy little busy bodies, every one of us.

※ ※ ※

"Earth to Mackenzie!"

I look over to Marisa and Shaina who are just a few feet away playing with baby Harry. It appears I've gotten lost in my thoughts again.

"Sorry!" I smile and pull a face at the baby.

I have to say that Harry is pretty freaking cute. The first time I saw him, I honestly thought he looked the same as any other newborn, with his squishy face and unformed features. I smiled and nodded when Shaina and Griff—and even Marisa—declared fervently that he was the most beautiful baby alive, but on the inside, I was rationalizing with science. My brain cited research on built-in biological responses to the baby—happy chemicals like oxytocin and increased activity in the brain's reward centers—that incentivize new parents to keep their offspring alive.

And then Shaina put Harry in my arms and the second he looked at me, research papers flew out of my head. When no one else was around, Harry and I had a heart-to-heart, during which I shared my suspicions that my adoration was the result of his brainwashing and admitted that I was letting it happen.

"I still can't believe you named your son after Harry Potter!" Marisa says suddenly, laughing.

"Oh, I can totally believe it," I jump in. Once you get to know Shaina, underneath the ink and piercings, she's actually a huge nerd. "What I can't believe is that Griff *let you* name your son after Harry Potter!"

Shaina snorts out a little laugh and shrugs. "I was doped up after the C-section, and when I saw Harry, he was so cute with the black fuzz on his head, and there's that little birthmark on his forehead! I mean, how could I not name him after Harry Potter? As for Griff, I think he was so traumatized by the whole experience by the time Harry was actually born, the man would have given me anything I wanted."

"Not true," Griff argues in his deep gravelly voice as he enters the living room. He drops his massive frame down onto the floor beside Shaina, and I swear the whole house shakes a little bit. "If you'd gone for Albus or Sirius I would have shut you down. And we don't have to tell anyone you named him after a wizard. There are lots of Harry's! Like ... uh ... Harry Connick Jr."

"Harry Truman," Marisa suggests.

"Prince Harry," I say.

"Harry Styles," Shaina adds in an appreciative tone. Griff's brows draw together.

"Who the fuck is Harry Styles?"

We giggle. Griff loses patience and produces his phone. His fingers poke the screen for a moment, then his frown gets deeper.

"Seriously? He looks twelve!"

Shaina smirks at him a little. "No shame in my cougar game."

Our laughter over that is raucous, but Griff remains unamused. Shaina scoots over and wraps her arms around him.

"You're the only man for me, babe. But you sure are cute when you're jealous."

"I'm not *cute*, woman," he scoffs.

I'd have to agree that cute is one of the last words I would choose for Griff O'Brien. Let's be honest: if he were a Harry Potter character, he would definitely be Hagrid, though … less friendly.

"Stinky diaper alert!" Marisa calls out then motions for Shaina to stay put. "I've got it."

Shaina smiles at her gratefully as she darts off down the hallway.

"I gotta go to work," Griff says. "I'll pick Layla up from that party on my way back. You be good." He gives Shaina a goodbye kiss so hot I turn my head away to give them a little privacy. I'd bet anything that if I asked her right about now, Shaina would say, "Harry Styles who?"

When we're alone, Shaina joins me on the couch. She rests her head against the cushion and turns toward me.

"Graham was here earlier."

I can't help the full body jolt of my reaction. Of course, I'm aware he's friends with Griff and Shaina—I mean, he's the reason I met them in the first place! —but still, hearing his name and thinking about him here only hours ago …

"Oh." I gulp and catch my bottom lip with my front teeth. I want to ask her how he's doing, but I'm also not sure I want to hear it. I'm trying to quit him cold turkey and I fear any exposure will hurt my progress. But the craving is incredibly strong.

"Is it harder to hear about him or not hear about him? Which will drive you more insane?

"You read my mind." But I still don't answer.

"It's still very fresh, isn't it?"

"Sometimes it hurts so much I think I'll die from it," I whisper. It's something I've never said out loud.

We let the truth settle in the air for a moment before Shaina asks me another question.

"Have you considered calling him? Maybe getting back together?" My heart pounds in my throat at the question, but I don't think she's trying to pressure me one way or the other. She's simply asking. I blow out a deep breath and answer honestly.

"All the time. But the reasons I ended it haven't changed. I just wonder sometimes … if I did the right thing, should it hurt this much?" I huff in frustration then wave my hand at her. "Any sage advice?"

"I wish my extra years gave me some magical piece of wisdom, but honestly? Life is hard. Getting back together with Graham will be hard. Getting over Graham will be hard."

"Geez, make me feel worse, why don't you?"

"Sorry! I mean that there isn't one choice or path to take that will be one hundred percent right because nothing is. You just have to figure out what is most right for you, then work through the hard to get to the good."

It's the truth. And like life, the truth is hard.

Graham

If I was hoping to find redemption once I got out of prison, I'd say I've done a pretty shitty job of it so far. It seems like I haven't so much redeemed myself as added to the list of things I need to make up for. But that changes now.

The chief and Mr. Thatcher care about ensuring Mackenzie's safety, but there are some things only I can do. At this point no risk is too great if it makes Eli disappear forever—no risk to me, that is. I'm not going to risk anyone else. Never again.

But I have a couple of matters to take care of first.

My lawyer is confused when I show up at his office unannounced. When he reads the paper I've just handed him, his eyebrows creep up toward the crown of his balding head.

Really, I think it's pretty self-explanatory. I kept it simple. A single piece of paper with my signature on it and a bullet point list of things I want him to use to make my will. In short, Mackenzie gets everything except for Griff's Harley, which goes back to him, and an immediately accessible trust for Harry and Layla. Mackenzie will also receive control of the Rose and Tyler Wyatt Foundation, which is officially a thing, according to the paperwork that came in the mail yesterday. It shocked the shit out of me, because it feels like a lifetime ago that Mackenzie and I filled out that application together, back before everything went to shit. It seems fitting to leave it in her hands. She'll probably do a hell of a lot better than I would making it worthy of my parents' legacy.

"Graham," my lawyer says slowly, "as your lawyer and your friend, I have to say that I strongly advise against whatever you're about to do that has you coming to me asking for a will."

"Just thinking ahead. Everyone dies sometime, right?" I keep my voice cheerful, as though I'm really only here to be responsible.

"At twenty-three years old I'd hope that thought wasn't so urgent you'd come to me with *this*." He holds up the piece of notebook paper and the envelope with all the Foundation documents.

"Are you saying no?" I ask. I peg him with a stare, a silent reminder of how much money I pay him.

"No, I'll do it, but—"

"Great! Thanks."

I leave without giving him any further chance to lecture me.

Later, I'm sitting at my kitchen counter, staring at the phone in my hands. I spent the whole afternoon writing a letter to Mackenzie that I hope she doesn't have to read. And now there's nothing left to do but set the wheels in motion.

I tap out a text message to Eli and press "SEND" before I can change my mind.

You crossed the line going after my girl. I want this to be over for good. Everyone has a price—what's yours? Name a number and a meeting place.

38. MISTAKES THAT GOOD MEN MAKE

Mackenzie

I keep telling myself to try and enjoy this time off from work, but I'm still unused to hanging around in my room on a random Tuesday afternoon. The weather is scorching, and my poor little window A/C unit is losing its battle against the heat. Which is why I'm sitting here perched atop the covers of my bed in only a sports bra and a pair of pink spandex yoga shorts so minuscule I cringe to think I used to wear them out of the house.

My phone rings, the display showing a number I don't recognize.

"Hello?"

"Is this Mackenzie Thatcher?" asks a deeply melodic female voice.

"Yes, speaking. May I ask who's calling?"

"I'm Dr. Sade Hadiyah, I—"

"Sade?" I interrupt. "As in *Doc Shady?*"

She lets out a brief husky chuckle. "The very one. I suppose I shouldn't be surprised my reputation precedes me." There's a pause. "I pulled some strings with an old friend at BC to get your number. I understand it's an intrusion of privacy and I apologize, but I just need a few minutes of your time. Are you alone?"

"Yes, I am. What do you need to talk to me about?"

I hear her exhale a long breath.

"I want to say first that I would usually never blur ethical lines in this way, but it felt emergent. I'm afraid for Graham's safety."

"Tell me," I demand immediately.

"He sent me an email that has me deeply concerned, and I've been unable to reach him by phone. The email includes an attached letter; he asked that I give it to you if something happened to him. I fear he's going to do something very stupid, so much so that I'm breaking confidentiality and his trust by contacting you. But I suspect you are the only one who will be able to get through to him if he's set on hurting himself."

I suddenly understand the phrase "blood running cold" because a chill rushes over me. Every inch of my skin breaks out in goose bumps.

"You think he would do that?" I almost whisper.

"I think he's in a very vulnerable place," she replies carefully.

"Can you send me the letter?"

"Yes, I'll forward it to you now."

"Thank you. And thank you for calling."

I give her my email address, and we end the call after agreeing to stay in contact, particularly if either of us manages to reach him.

I try to call Graham. My hand is shaking as I hold the phone to my ear. It doesn't ring, going straight to voicemail—once, twice, three times. He's turned it off. *Graham, where are you? What are you doing?*

I find the email from Shady already waiting in my inbox. I open it with fingers that are still trembling.

‒ ‒ ‒ ‒ ‒ ‒ ‒ ‒ ‒ ‒ Forwarded message ‒ ‒ ‒ ‒ ‒ ‒ ‒ ‒ ‒ ‒

From: **Graham Wyatt** < GrahamWyatt@gmail.com >

To: Sade Hadiyah < DrSHadiyah@edoc.com >

Subject: Favor

Hey Doc,

If something happens to me, can you please make sure Mackenzie gets the attached letter? Just covering my bases.

I'd ask you not to read it, but it's nothing you don't already know.

Thank you for everything, really.

Graham

[1 Attachment]

Mackenzie,

First, (though also last, and all the places in the middle) I love you.

I love you. *Damn, it seems wrong that something so big should only take up eight letters. It feels like it should be Mary Poppins long, or have that math symbol over it that's for numbers whose decimals go on forever. Remember when we had Pre-Cal together? I could barely concentrate because all I wanted to do was stare at you, but I aced that damn class because you were always so responsible and said we had to study before fooling around.*

I loved you so much back then I thought I would explode from it. But it doesn't even compare to what I feel for you now. And no, Professor, it's not some idol worship from putting you on a pedestal all those years in prison. Maybe that was partially true when I first got out, but these past months being with you—the reality of you, with our bickering and those thighs you think are too big and your fear of loving me again—I've fallen in an even deeper, crazier love with you.

That time together as us, again, made the whole rest of my life worth it. Even if it's all we get.

I have a lot of regrets. But loving you has never—will never, could never—be one of them.

I guess what I'm trying to say is the way I love you isn't something I could describe in eight letters or 800 letters. I wish I were a genius or a poet who could do you justice. I'm just me, though. And this is the best I've got.

But this letter is supposed to be about more than that. I don't want to leave unfinished business between us. I'm sorry for everything that happened, Z. If you only ever remember one thing about me, I want it to be what I'm going to say next.

Please, don't go another minute thinking I don't trust you. That's not the reason I lied and kept secrets. I've thought long and hard, and had some talks with Shady, and I've realized the truth ... that it's me I don't trust. A big part of me still sees myself as the piece of shit who was in that parking lot buying drugs in the middle of the night, who didn't deserve to use his daddy's money to hire a lawyer. Shady says I have self-worth issues or some shit.

What it really comes down to is that I knew I didn't deserve you. But I was a selfish asshole and I pushed myself back into your life anyway because I'm not strong enough to stay away from you. So, I lied because I didn't trust myself not to mess things up again. Because if you knew about the stuff with Eli, I thought it would expose how unworthy I am. I never lost faith in you or doubted that you would stand by me—I just didn't want to have to admit that I wasn't sure you should.

I should have given you the chance to make that choice for yourself. I get now that I was being selfish. I wasn't protecting you; I was protecting me. I'm so fucking sorry I didn't figure it out sooner. I'm sorry I didn't stop to think about what you deserved, which was my every truth. That if you wanted it, you deserved to have every piece of me, even the bad parts.

But I pulled my head out of my ass too late, and I hurt you. And I got you hurt. There's no way I can make up for what happened—for my hand in things, in creating a situation that led to Eli causing you harm. I literally had your blood on my hands that day. I'll never forgive myself and I'll never forget, because it was the worst moment of my life. Worse than handcuffs or even you telling me it was over. Because your pain is the thing I can't live with.

I've spent every minute of the last few weeks trying to step up and do the right thing, to be better. The way you looked at me, like I was a good man who was worth a second chance, who deserved the priceless honor of your love ... that's the man I want to be. If I make one last mistake, I want it to be the kind that good men make, when doing the hard thing is what's best for those they love.

Maybe you'll never read any of this. I'd rather all these words I've vomited from my fucked up soul get to stay in digital purgatory, and that I'll have the chance to look you in the eye again and tell you that, fucked up as it is, every bit of my soul is yours.

But if you are reading this, I hope you understand why I had to do what I did. I hope that means I got one thing right and you're safe.

Last, (but still first, and to infinite decimals,) I love you.

Y

* * *

"MARISA!" I scream and run to her room.

She has the day off, so she's lounging on her bed. But when she sees my face, she immediately sits up straight.

"What is it?"

"It's Graham, he—" I'm lost for words, so I frantically shove my phone at her with the email still on the screen.

"Que idiota! Dios," she mutters when she finishes reading.

"I'm so scared." Tears fill my eyes and my voice breaks. "What do I do? His phone is turned off. I was going to try his house ..."

"Get dressed. I'll drive. On the way I'll call Shaina, and you call your dad."

I pause in her doorway. "My dad?"

"He and Graham have been talking."

I gape at her.

"You're lucky that I'm so freaked out right now, because I'm not even going to ask how you know that."

✳ ✳ ✳

"Hi, sweetheart."

"Dad?"

He hears the tremor in my voice, and instantly sounds alert and on edge. "Is something wrong? What's happened?"

"Tell me the truth. Why would Graham write me a letter that sounds like he's about to kill himself, and why would Marisa think you know something about it?"

He sounds far off for a moment, as though he's pulled away from the phone to curse. Then his voice is back in my ear.

"We should have this talk in person."

"Why? What is going on, Dad?"

"Where are you?"

"Marisa and I are driving to Graham's house to check on him."

"He's not there. If you're on the way to Westwood anyway, then meet me at home. We'll talk when you get here."

"What is going on?" I repeat. "I'm really freaking out here."

"It's going to be okay, honey. I'll see you soon."

Then nothing. I keep holding the silent phone to my ear for a few long seconds before lowering it.

"He hung up on me," I say with no small amount of shock.

Marisa is already off the phone, which was short because Griff and Shaina didn't have any insight.

"Where are we going now?" she asks.

"My parents' house."

38. DEAD SERIOUS

Graham

"Do you really think Eli will drop his quest for revenge in exchange for money?"

I hear movement on the other end of the line indicating that Mr. Thatcher is pacing. I almost called him last night but chickened out. I barely slept, so I'm glad he sounded alert rather than pissed off when I called him so early. I'm giving him the details about what's happening tonight. It's supposed to be top secret, but the man deserves to know.

"Well, he texted me back late last night asking for fifty thousand in cash. So, I think he'll show up to take the money and then try to kill me anyway."

I think I catch a low curse.

"And Eddie Duluth is on board with this?"

"Chief Duluth officially handed it over to the DEA a few days ago, and they're the ones who will be tracking me and recording the whole thing. This is going to work." I take a deep breath, my words for me as much as for him. "We're going to get him, Mr. Thatcher. We'll have him for extortion as soon as he takes the money, and I'll be taping anything else I can get him to confess to. The Feds just need something to charge him with so they can lock him up. The goal is to get him behind bars and then make sure he stays there forever by compiling evidence to stick him with the rest of his crimes."

"And the DEA agents will be nearby? You did say you expect him to try and kill you."

"Aww, are you concerned about me, Mr. Thatcher?"

"Don't be a wiseass."

"Sorry, sir. And yes, they'll be close, but we have to make sure he doesn't spot them. They're giving me a bulletproof vest and I'll be wired so they'll hear everything and move in if things get sticky."

"It's not exactly an airtight plan. Tell me seriously, Graham, is this some kind of suicide mission?"

The line is silent for a heartbeat. I've come to have an even deeper respect for this man, and I want to make sure my answer bears no resemblance to a lie.

"No, sir. I hope to God I walk out of this thing. But I won't pretend I'm not willing to die to put this asshole away."

"Now you listen to me, boy. You fix that mindset right now. You never enter a battle anticipating your own death. That's when you get yourself killed. And I don't want to hear you've gotten yourself killed, you hear me? You may be broken up at the moment, but make no mistake: if you die my daughter will be devastated."

"Thank you, sir."

"Don't thank me. Just stop talking like you're a G.D. kamikaze pilot."

I swallow back a completely inappropriate laugh, because this shit is dead serious. Literally.

"I misjudged you," he says in a tone more subdued than his previous army commander voice. "I let myself get sucked into gossip without finding out the facts. I apologize for that." He pauses again. "You're a good man, Wyatt. You live through this, and I will personally make your case with my daughter."

"Thank you, sir," I say again, with more vigor this time.

As I leave the house—I have a shit-ton of cash to acquire—my resolve to live is even stronger. I vow that Mackenzie and I will run the Wyatt Foundation together, and she'll never have to read that letter.

Eli is the bad guy. And bad guys don't get to win.

Mackenzie

"He's going to do WHAT?" I shriek, so loudly that my mom comes running in from the other room.

"What's going on?" she asks, hands held out somewhat awkwardly by her sides. Every year while school is out on summer break, she tries a new hobby, and from the look of her splotchy apron and colorful hands, this year it's painting.

"Mom, did you know about this?" I am fuming, and I want her to be incensed along with me.

Marisa is seated in the corner, but for once she's processing everything quietly, so I can't count on her to be furious at my side.

"About Graham? Yes," Mom replies. "Your father and I have been married for over twenty-five years. We didn't make it this far by keeping secrets."

Her words are a knife to my heart, even though the dig is unintentional. *Thanks for that one, Mom.*

Since she's being no help, I turn back to Dad.

"He can't do this! It's crazy—he's going to get himself killed!"

Dad runs a hand over his face, and the fog of fearful anger in my mind clears enough that I can see how tired he looks, his age more apparent in his face than usual.

"I tried to tell him as much," he admits, shocking me. "But Graham is determined to take Eli down, and he believes this might be his only chance. I hate to say it, but I'm not sure he's wrong. I talked to Ed Duluth after hanging up with Graham this morning, and he says the DEA is going all in on this, even though it may be a long shot, because Eli is slippery and they can't seem to get any concrete evidence against him. He wouldn't tell me details, but it appears that Eli's criminal dealings go even deeper than we realized, and the DEA wants him off the streets. I just wish they weren't doing it by sending Graham in like a pig for slaughter."

"Mike!" Mom chastises as I gasp.

Tears start to fall as I sink onto the sofa, overwhelmed. Today has been such a whirlwind. I couldn't take any time to focus on Graham's letter earlier because I was so afraid he was going to hurt himself. And then I was barely able to process the relief that he's not suicidal before Dad told us about this DEA mission and I was overcome all over again with fear and anger.

"I'm sorry, honey," Dad says, anxiously kneeling down in front of me. He's always been a little squeamish around tears. Soldiers don't cry, but daughters do. "I didn't mean to upset you. I shouldn't have said that."

"It's okay. You were being honest. Thank you for that." I blink hard and try to hold back the flood of tears that's been building all day, which is suddenly too much for the flimsy dam I've been using to hold it back.

"Is there any way we can stop this?" Marisa speaks for the first time since we got here. She looks shaken up too, and I can see fear for Graham written on her face.

My dad shakes his head. "Graham will be prepping with them now. He did tell me that Eli sent the time and location, and that it's happening tonight, before he had to turn his phone off. But that's all I know. This whole thing is supposed to be top secret, so we shouldn't even have as much information as we do. Ed Duluth promised to reach out if he hears anything."

Marisa has to leave to go to work, but I choose to stay. I shut myself in my childhood bedroom, where I pull Graham's letter up on my phone and start to read it again. This time there's no urgency keeping every word from sinking deep down into my soul. The flood of tears is unstoppable, and this time I simply let it come.

I'm barely able to see the words on my screen, but I swipe at my eyes every few seconds and keep reading. Inside me there's an aching need to be close to him, and these words are all I have in this moment.

"I never lost faith in you or doubted that you would stand by me— I just didn't want to have to admit that I wasn't sure you should."

I sob. Remorse threatens to drown me. For weeks I've pushed away any thoughts of how Graham was dealing with our breakup. I couldn't stand to take on his pain in addition to my own, especially considering I'd caused it; I knew it would break me. But now I can't help but think about the man—my boy—who wrote this letter, whose last words to me were ones of such self-recrimination and defeat.

"If I make one last mistake, I want it to be the kind that good men make, when doing the hard thing is what's best for those they love."

Oh, Graham. I wish I could go to him, take him in my arms and tell him he is a good man, the best of men. That has never changed—his heart has always been pure and full of love, even too much love sometimes, as when the loss of his parents cut so deeply it overwhelmed him. His decisions were never made with ill-intent, never with the thought to harm anyone else. If anything, his deepest flaw is a penchant for self-loathing that blinds him to the way hurting himself will hurt those around him. I may never be able to pinpoint when or how his grief morphed into this enduring self-hatred, but now that he's explained it, I can't believe I didn't see it before.

I want to tell him I love him and that I understand. That we're okay. I couldn't make a life with a man who doesn't trust me, but I can make a life with a man who is learning how to trust himself. And now he might not live long enough to give me the chance to tell him that.

"...fucked up as it is, every bit of my soul is yours."

"And mine is yours," I whisper through my tears as I watch the sun set outside my window.

Though I'm sorely out of practice, I pray for the first time in too many years, hoping my negligence won't negate the validity of my request.

"Please, God, keep him safe."

39. MR. CRIME FIGHTER GUY

Graham

Hey, God. It's me, Graham. Long time no talk, big guy.

I'm hoping you can do me a solid. I'm sure you're tired of people only reaching out when they need something—guilty, sorry—but I think you'll get why this one is important.

So, if you're the one with the remote control up there in Heaven, do you think you could change my dad's screen to the Graham channel for a bit? You see, for years I've been hoping that he's too busy watching football to keep an eye on me, but tonight I'm helping take down a bad guy and it's finally something I want him to witness. Crazy, right? Me, being Mister Crime Fighter Guy?

Wish me luck! (You can watch, too, but I figure you've got a lot going on, so I totally understand if you don't.)

Thanks a million! I promise I'll go to church soon.

❖   ❖   ❖

Eli looks like shit. If I had to guess, I'd say he's been reaching deeper into the cookie jar of his own product. Like the last time I saw him, though, I know not to underestimate him.

I've had plenty of time to think about the way he grabbed Mackenzie, and I've come to the conclusion that the only reason she's still alive is because Eli's such a sicko. He wouldn't go straight for the kill shot—or in this case, a fatal wound with his knife—because he wanted to drag it out and have some fun first. He's also too smart to fire a gun in a neighborhood like that, so he probably only had it on him as an intimidation tactic to persuade her into his car. Thank God that didn't happen. I shudder to even think about it … so I force myself to shut those thoughts down. It's not the time. I have to keep my shit together right now.

"Are you packing?" Eli asks.

I give him a cocky smirk. It's not difficult—I just pretend we're talking about my dick.

"Are you?"

He raises one eyebrow *(damn, I wish I could do that!)* and his lips curve into a calculating smile. "Fair enough. Looks like you're not such a good little Boy Scout after all, huh?"

Of course, while I'm certain he's got a gun, I'm only letting him believe I do so he's (hopefully) less inclined to get trigger happy. Though I guess you could say I am "packing" a team of DEA agents. I just happen to be packing them remotely, via the little microphone clipped to the collar of my shirt, the one recording everything and letting the Feds listen in from a few miles down the road.

"Well … *show me the money,*" he says like he's a scrawny white Cuba Gooding Jr. then laughs at his own cleverness. Inside, my eyes are rolling, but outwardly I keep my face blank. I'm shouldering a duffle bag full of neatly wrapped bricks of cash (it's surprisingly heavy). I throw the bag in Eli's direction and watch as he crouches down and zips it open. The sight of all those Benjamin's reminds me

I'm definitely taking a risk here because that's really my money. The DEA couldn't get their hands on this much cash so quickly— paperwork or approvals or some bullshit. Luckily, I'm a rich motherfucker who doesn't actually care all that much about his money. Certainly not more than Mackenzie.

"Why do you need all of this?" I ask as casually as possible. "There's no shortage of junkies these days. I can't imagine you're hurting for cash."

He looks a little smug. *Go ahead, asshole, brag away, you know you want to. Write your own reservation for Hotel Super Max.* I hope they give him a year for every word.

I bet right now he's feeling like a big man since we're on his turf. This abandoned office building is far enough from the road that he obviously feels satisfied we won't be interrupted—even though he chose to meet out here in the open rather than going inside.

Good. I want him to feel safe. I want him to get too confident, because that's when he'll run his mouth and tell all the viewers at home how awesome he is at being a criminal.

"Business is good," he agrees. "My brother always thought small. Me? I'm looking to diversify my interests."

The punk thinks he's some kind of entrepreneur now? Someone must have been listening to a Business for Dummies podcast. Of course, I can't say this, no matter how much I want to. *Keep him talking!*

"So, what? Selling to bored housewives?"

He makes a little condescending noise.

"Oh, I already got a kid with a pretty face selling to all the suburban pill poppers. Those cougars love him. I've already expanded that shit beyond what Curtis could have imagined, but I'm talking bigger."

"But doesn't that kind of grows his legacy more?"

Yeah, his brother is a soft spot, and I'm going to poke that shit until he cracks.

"No one even remembers his name—it's my legacy I'm building," he spits.

"I don't know, you're here, aren't you? Seems to me you're still doing Curtis' dirty work."

His face reddens in rage. *Crack.*

"Curtis doesn't pull my strings anymore—no one does! I'm here with you because of loyalty to my family, and to make sure no one thinks they can get away with talking to the cops. But I'm in charge, you got that?" He's standing now, unable to contain his agitation. "Curtis has shit for brains. He'd still be wasting his time moving product to bored little rich boys like you. No way he could pull off the operation I've got—boys and clients in four states, who know how to push the most expensive and addictive stuff to maximize our revenue."

Now that he's calmed down, I can tell he's starting to get pissed at himself for revealing so much. But I need to keep him talking. I shift my expression to one of surprised admiration and curiosity. I'll stroke his ego, even though stroking anything of his makes me want to take a shower.

"You shoulda gone to Harvard, man." I'm mostly being honest. I mean, this kid can't be more than nineteen, but he's running a legit criminal organization and managing to cover his tracks so well he stumped the DEA. He's got to be crazy smart—it's a pity those brains weren't put toward something better.

As I'd hoped, his chest puffs up a little at the compliment and the recognition that he's smarter than me.

"And waste all that time in a classroom? Nah, I'm about to make money those pansy-ass Harvard kids won't even dream of until they're forty. They'll never have half my business chops, anyway. I'm on the trends the way Curtis never was. Years back ice may have been the big thing, but these days dirty doctors—and I've already got some in my pocket—are where the real cash potential is. But that's only the beginning. I've invested in real estate by the docks, got a sweet little setup down there where we're producing our own shit—owning more parts of the distribution process, you know."

Apparently pleased with himself, he squats back to the ground to examine the cash.

"You understand this means we're square," I say gruffly. "I don't want to ever see you again or hear that you're sniffing around my girl." I want him to confess to the blackmail and to hurting Mackenzie.

"Are you saying you think I'm a man who would go back on my word?" I think that's precisely what he is, actually, but all I do is shrug. I'd rather not piss him off too much because, well, the dude wants to kill me and I don't particularly want to give him any more reason to do that.

"I only count twenty-five thousand here," he says after a minute. Took him long enough to figure that one out.

"That's right. An associate of mine will get the other half to you later tonight, as long as I get home alive."

I think this is pretty clever. It's a little obstacle to keep him from killing me before backup arrives, along with the thick protective vest I'm wearing under my shirt; I'm glad to have it, even though the thick layers are brutal in this heat. I just hope the DEA folks won't mind when I return this thing soaked in my sweat.

Eli's icy blue eyes narrow as he stands back up, glaring at me.

"That's not how this works."

"You do this a lot?" Give me more. I think we've already got some incriminating stuff on tape, but I have to be sure.

"Enough," he answers vaguely.

"What, you don't think I'll come through with the rest of it? You think I'm not a man who keeps my word?" I echo his earlier statement.

"I think you care enough about that pretty little redhead to follow through. And I know you've got the money."

My hackles rise at his mention of Mackenzie.

"You're lucky I'm playing nice after what you did to my girl," I growl.

I'd love to wipe this pavement with his skinny ass for what he did to her, and I have to swallow down the surge of anger.

"Yeah, our shit ends tonight," Eli says. His words have an ominous ambiguity to them, and I hope the DEA guys can hear it too. I'd say now seems like a good time for them to show up.

"Okay." My voice sounds a little nervous for the first time, but I can't help it with the way those pale blue eyes are staring me down. It lasts far too long, then he finally nods once decisively. Suddenly, he's pointing a gun at me. *Shit.*

"I'd rather kill you than get the other twenty-five K," he says calmly. So he was just weighing his options, and I'm on the losing end. *Shit.* The gun clicks as he cocks the trigger. "Guns aren't my personal preference, but I'm making an exception for you. Right now, I just want you dead quick. I brought you to my playground. Now you get to join the other losers I've buried here."

I'm frozen in place, unsure whether to run so I'm a moving target or try to keep him talking until the Feds get here.

"What, you thought I'd let you walk away alive?" He smiles wide, showing all of his meth-ravaged teeth, and then his arm tenses in preparation to shoot.

I spin on my heel and run, ducking and weaving, trying to get to the side of the building so I can turn the corner and put a wall between us. There's a crack—as loud as I remember it—and there's a sudden sharp pain on the back of my thigh. I force myself to continue moving even though it hurts like hell. My pant leg clings to my skin as blood quickly saturates it. Wetness soaks through the fabric almost immediately.

Come on, Feds, where are you?

On my next step, my injured leg refuses to hold my weight, and I fall to the ground. When I roll onto my back, I find Eli standing right there, staring down at me.

Don't look, Dad. Go back to football. I'm sorry.

He grins brightly as he aims the gun toward my heart and fires. The impact knocks the wind out of me. *Holyfuckingshit* that hurts. Then Eli disappears from my line of sight. Movement draws my attention to the side, where I see he's been tackled to the ground by a DEA agent. More armed guys in all black surround us.

Finally.

"You all right, Wyatt?" one of them asks. His dark clad figure looms over me from the same spot Eli just vacated.

"I think so. Bullet in the leg," I tell him as I try to suck in breath. Thank God for the bulletproof vest, because no doubt that second shot would have killed me. They don't tell you how much it still hurts when you're shot with one of these things on; my entire torso feels like a massive bruise, and every breath hurts like a motherfucker.

I hear the agent call for a medic. I can still see him clearly, but he sounds far away. Almost instantly, there's someone crouched down beside me. Fingers touch my wrist and then something is being wrapped tightly around my leg. It hurts, but my chest hurts more. That doesn't make sense. Am I a pansy who can't handle getting hit through a vest? I'm also cold, which is weird, because I was overheated moments ago.

"He's lost a lot of blood. Stay with me, Wyatt."

Again, the voice seems to be coming through a tunnel, but I think it's female. I can't confirm—I closed my eyes at some point, but I don't remember doing it.

"Is that a bullet hole in his vest? Check on his ribs as soon as you get him in the van."

I'm lifted up then they're carrying me. Every small motion of whatever I'm lying on is torture. Inside my chest, my heart seems to be competing for a spot in the Olympics. I'd like it to slow down. It's hogging all the mojo from my lungs, which are screaming in pain and refusing to do their job. Every breath creates a sharp stabbing sensation on my left side. But those breaths are becoming less and less effective because I can't seem to get enough air. *I can't get enough air! Something's wrong.*

"Can't ... breathe ..." I croak, voice so faint I'm not sure if anyone will hear me.

"Someone help me get this vest off him."

Everything goes fuzzy, fading in and out, the pain my only constant.

"He's turning blue. Grab me that oxygen mask!"

Well, fuck, I'm dying.

And then I'm not aware of anything.

40. WAKE UP FOR ME

Mackenzie

I jolt awake at the sound of a crash somewhere in the house. I can't believe I fell asleep! Before I can run out to see what's going on, my mom appears at the bedroom door.

"Get dressed, honey." Her face looks solemn.

"What's happening?" My heart is beating in my throat as the fear tries to take over all of my senses.

"Daddy's on the phone with Chief Duluth. Graham was injured, and they've taken him to the hospital. We're going there now."

I grab shoes, not even bothering to check my appearance in a mirror, even though I must be a mess after crying and falling asleep in my clothes.

"Goddammit!"

The muted shout reaches us from the other side of the house, and I gulp down a bubble of panic. My whole life Dad has seemed unflappable, steady, the one you can always count on to be calm in a crisis. If he's this upset …

Don't you dare die on me, Graham Wyatt.

* * *

Graham is in surgery when we arrive at Massachusetts General. The lady at the front desk won't tell us anything else, insisting that the hospital can only share details with family.

I *am* his fucking family. I'm all he's got—along with Griff and Marisa, who are both on the way, and Shaina, who had to stay home with the kids. We are his family.

"I'm his fiancée!" I blurt out, pushing in closer to the reception window with renewed determination to get past this bridge troll. She eyes me then holds out an imperious finger signaling for me to wait while she answers the phone.

Mom is right by my side and now she shifts closer, hand reaching out to clasp mine. I gratefully take it and squeeze to absorb her offered comfort. When I do, something cool and metal presses against my skin. Slowly pulling away, I glance down to find my mom's engagement ring laying in the center of my palm. I slip it onto my finger while new tears fill my eyes. I can't seem to find any words at the moment, but the look on her face tells me that the gratitude and love I'm feeling for her is shining out of mine.

The lady ends her phone call and turns back to me.

#LifeHack: Need to get past a power-hungry bridge troll? Wave something shiny in her face.

Shortly after, someone comes out holding Graham's file. She's much friendlier than the other lady as she gestures me to the side so we can speak privately. I hold my breath as she starts talking.

Graham sustained a gunshot wound to the thigh and one to the chest that was impeded by his protective Kevlar. Relief surges through me. That doesn't seem too bad, right? But why is he in surgery? Her next words decimate my momentary optimism.

The surgeons are operating on him to remove the bullet from his thigh. They're also treating him for a collapsed lung, which resulted from the close impact shot to his vest that also broke multiple ribs. He lost a lot of blood and went into shock on the way to the hospital, so they're also keeping an eye on his blood pressure and oxygen levels.

What's the point of a bulletproof vest if it can't keep him safe?! Some rational part of me recognizes that his condition would be much worse if he'd taken a bullet straight to the chest, but it's a small comfort in this moment. I want to rage. I want to go find some of those fancy DEA guys and give them a piece of my mind for putting him in this situation.

I manage to remain as calm as possible, but I'm helpless to hold back the tears that begin silently streaming down my face.

There's nothing for us to do now but wait. Again.

※　※　※

The next couple of hours crawl by as our little corner of the waiting room fills up. Griff gets here first. I'm shocked speechless when he walks right up and wraps his giant arms around me in a hug that almost completely engulfs me. This is definitely not a normal occurrence—except with Shaina and his kids, Griff is not exactly a cuddly, touchy-feely guy. I get over my surprise quickly and simply lean into him.

"This is from Shaina," he rumbles quietly after a moment. I just nod against his chest. *Sure it is.*

Marisa arrives, immediately taking her place by my side and staying there.

Chief Duluth comes, and he has a little more information for us. Apparently, Eli shot at an agent during his attempt to get away and got a bullet to the gut for his troubles. He'll live, but shooting a cop basically guarantees he'll never be a free man again. I feel nothing but satisfaction at this news and can't even summon the energy to be horrified at myself for wishing that bullet killed him.

Any other time, I would really get a kick out of watching my mom sit down beside Griff and try to befriend him. Mom patiently smiles and nods at Griff's deep, monosyllabic responses to her attempts at conversation; I imagine it's similar to seeing her try and break through to a difficult second grader.

A bit later, Marisa gets up to find coffee, and my mom takes her place at my side, like they're my own little support tag team bent on making sure I'm never alone. If I had room for any emotions other than fear for Graham right now, I'd be overwhelmed with gratitude.

"I'm sorry for what I said earlier," Mom says suddenly.

I turn to look at her face, which is drawn and tired.

"About how your father and I have survived by not lying to each other," she clarifies. "I didn't mean anything by it."

"It's okay, Mom." I'm telling the truth. At this moment, it no longer matters. That conversation seems like it happened years ago. But Mom shakes her head and goes on.

"No, I saw your face and realized after the words were out how you might take them. I want you to know that your father and I weren't always this solid. We've had our fair share of stumbling blocks. I'm sorry if I ever made it seem that trust was something black and white that magically happened from minute one of a relationship. I suppose I never wanted you to have to learn things the hard way like we did. But now I'm thinking that's the only way it can be done."

I lean over and rest my head on her shoulder, and she reaches up to stroke my hair like I'm a kid again.

More time passes and with every tick from the plastic clock above our heads, my agitation rises. Eventually, my patience snaps. I stand up, ready to storm the desk and demand an explanation for why this is taking so long, when the doors finally open and a man in scrubs comes out asking for Graham Wyatt's family. He has a mask pulled down around his neck and his hair covered with a bandana, like those surgeons on TV (only this guy is definitely no McDreamy). The doctor approaches calmly as Graham's little mismatched cheering squad clusters around him.

I close my eyes and take a breath before he starts talking, but it comes out shallow and my hands are shaking.

Please, please, please ...

✻ ✻ ✻

"Morning, babe," I say in a cheerful voice. "I got up early and went for a walk instead of doing yoga. Sorry, I know you love the little show."

I approach the bed. "That beard is getting out of control. I bet you'll love it, so I'm going to wait a couple more days before doing something about it. You should probably wake up so you have a chance to appreciate its glory."

Graham doesn't respond, and he doesn't stir when I reach out to pet the light brown beard that's grown out during his time in the hospital. I gaze down at him and force myself to look past the pallor of his skin, the intubation tube helping him breathe, the beeping heart monitor, and only see the man I love. I kiss his forehead before sitting down with my coffee. I've got my own little cot along the wall that the nurses brought me once they realized I wasn't going anywhere.

"Come on, babe. I'll give you two days, and then I'm shaving the whole thing off. You'd better wake up and stop me!" My voice sounds a little less cheerful this time, a little more desperate.

I take a deep breath and remind myself that I need to stay positive for him.

I've started fabricating reasons he should wake up that I tell him throughout the day, as though all he needs is the right incentive. As more days pass, I find my entreaties sounding progressively more like begging, and it appears I've now resorted to threats. Although there isn't any solid evidence that he can even hear me, I don't care. I talk to Graham all day long, and at this point I don't mind admitting that it's for me as much as for him.

When Graham went into surgery that first night, it should have been a fairly simple procedure, but he'd lost a lot of blood and his body was in shock. His heart stopped twice while he was on the table and they had to resuscitate him. The doctors were worried about oxygen deprivation causing permanent damage to his brain and heart, so they put him in a medically induced coma.

They told me this wasn't necessarily cause to panic, that it was merely a way to help slow things down and let his body recover from all the trauma—something to do with lowering his body temperature and blood pressure—but honestly, at that moment the only word I could focus on was *coma*.

They kept Graham in the induced coma for a week before finally taking him back to finish the surgery to remove the bullet from his leg. After the surgery they took him off the drugs that had been keeping him under so he could come out of the sedation naturally. His doctor said he could wake up immediately … or it could take a while. I was at his side every second when they brought him back from surgery, afraid to even go to the bathroom in case he woke up while I was gone. My parents and our friends were at the hospital all day as well, waiting.

But he didn't wake up that day. Or the next. And now it's been another week, and he's still non-responsive. No one can tell me when he'll wake up or why he hasn't woken up yet. Every nurse and doctor I talk to tells me "he'll wake up when he's ready," which seems a pretty pathetic bullshit cop-out from people who supposedly work at one of the best hospitals in the country.

I've basically moved myself into his hospital room. I still won't leave for more than ten minutes at a time—twenty max, like this morning when I was restless and needed a walk— in case I miss it when he wakes up. My mom has offered to sit with him while I go and get a good night's sleep at home, but I've politely refused. There's nowhere else I should or would want to be right now. But that doesn't mean the situation isn't wearing on me, that my heart doesn't break a little more every hour that passes with no change.

A new nurse walks in as I'm brushing tears from my eyes.

"Oh, honey, he's going to be all right," the woman says. She's wearing bright pink scrubs and a name-tag that reads "Glenda."

"How can you tell?" I ask, voice a little wobbly. These days I'll take reassurance from anyone willing to give it.

"Oh, I just can. I came in to get his vitals and hang some new IV bags while you were out, so he and I had a couple of minutes. He's a young man who's strong and fit with a big life ahead. I'm sure his body can make it through this."

She finishes fiddling with his oxygen pump and leaves.

I shake my head and feel a real smile break out on my face for the first time in days. Even unconscious, Graham is charming the nurses.

"She was checking you out, babe. You'll love that. Why don't you wake up so we can laugh about it?"

✤　✤　✤

Graham turns twenty-four at the end of his second week in the hospital. Since his birthday is July 5th, he always used to go on and on, bragging that all the Independence Day fireworks and parties were really in his honor. I want to see him be that carefree, cocky boy again, at least a little. When he wakes up, I vow to help him find his way back there. (Yes, *when*, because I refuse to even consider the alternative.)

On the Fourth, I watch the city's huge annual fireworks display from his hospital window. It's actually a great view, if you can overlook the reason I'm here. I can't.

"They're lighting up the sky just for you, because tomorrow's your twenty-fourth birthday. The whole city's celebrating, big and flashy the way you like it. Open those eyes for me and we'll watch it together."

Graham

The first thing I see is a flash of reddish gold. Everything else is white except that beautiful color, exactly the hue of Mackenzie's hair.

So, this must be Heaven. I wasn't sure I'd make it here.

"Graham?"

It's even Mackenzie's voice I hear. Did God find me an angel that looks and sounds like her to greet me? *Dang, dude, you sure know how to make a guy feel welcome.*

I blink, and when I open my eyes again, things are a little clearer. I see shapes, hear beeping nearby. My body is heavy. There's an unpleasant sensation in my throat as though I've got a strain of strep that got a little dose of Hulk juice.

So ... not Heaven, then?

"You're awake!"

Mackenzie's face appears now and takes up my whole line of vision. One soft hand begins stroking along my face, her touch making my skin tingle. I try to speak but suddenly feel like I'm choking.

"No, don't try to talk. Let me get a nurse!"

While I blink heavy eyelids and try to make sense of what's happening around me, more people show up. They poke and prod and peer at me, and then they remove the thing in my throat. It hurts like a mother, which wakes me up more.

I'm in the hospital. It feels like I swallowed a shot of lighter fluid and chased it with a lit match. There's a sensation of lethargy weighing down my limbs.

I'm ... alive.

As doctors poke at me and shine lights in my eyes, Mackenzie is there the whole time holding my hand. She's beaming at me with a brilliant joyous smile that's at odds with the tears running down her cheeks. When the docs and nurses back up a bit, she caresses my head again.

"You have no idea how good it is to see you."

As she pulls her hand away, I catch something glinting in the light. I focus on that hand as it rests beside me on the bed. And suddenly I'm livid. *How long have I been out?!*

"Who put that ring on your finger?" I ask. The words are painful and my voice is completely wrecked, but I need to know.

She laughs a little while still crying. "Well, I guess your brain is fine."

I frown at her. Waking up to find her engaged to some other guy is *not* fucking funny.

Maybe this is Hell, after all.

She dashes away tears and holds the ring closer to my face before whispering, "This is my mom's. I told them I was your fiancée so they'd let me stay."

"Get me out of here and I'll make that true."

She leans down and kisses me between the eyebrows.

"A little lower," I wheeze, and she laughs again. She can't seem to stop, and I'm not complaining because it's a magical sound.

"Good to see you awake and talking. Just take it easy. Your throat will be sore for a while from the intubation," the doctor says. "You've been unconscious for almost three weeks, Mr. Wyatt. And this lady here hasn't left your side the whole time."

My mind clears a little more.

"Does this mean we're back together?" I ask Mackenzie.

Now her laughter turns a little hysterical, on the edge of sobbing. She leans in and rests her forehead against mine. Wetness cools my skin as some of her tears drip onto my face.

"I'm yours. Always have been, always will be."

Look at that, I'm in Heaven. And I didn't even have to die.

41. INCORRIGIBLE

Graham

"You gave us quite a scare, son."

Quick, someone check Twitter to see if anyone's spotted some flying pigs, because Mike Thatcher just called me "son." I have a sudden urgent need to grab my cup of water and take a long drink. *(I'm not crying, you're crying!)*

"You should be satisfied that you accomplished your mission. Eli Markum won't be hurting Mackenzie, or you, or anyone else ever again. Ed Duluth told me that because of your recording, they started digging up the area around that old building and they've already found two bodies. So in addition to going down for trafficking and assault, they've got him for multiple murders."

Mr. Thatcher's voice turns a little stern now, once again the army commander. "But there's a fine line between heroism and stupidity, you hear me?"

"Yes, sir. I don't have plans to do any more hero-ing."

"Good. You're needed here alive." His eyes cut toward the door that Mackenzie and her mother left through only minutes ago.

I nod. She needs me here alive, and I need to be here just as badly, living for her.

Right about now, I'd like to get started with that whole living thing. It's been almost a week since I woke up, and I'm still in this damn hospital room. The doctors haven't discharged me yet because they wanted to keep an eye on me and do all kinds of tests on my heart and my brain. The last few days I've felt more myself, and I'm going more than a little stir crazy.

I am so ready to be out of here.

Things aren't all bad. I get visitors every day—the Thatchers, Doc Shady, Marisa, and Griff have all been here a few times, and Griff and Shaina even brought the kids the other day. Chief Duluth came by once too. The whole thing is surreal. It reminds me of that kid Tom Sawyer—or was it that other rascal Huck Finn? —who staged his own death so he could attend the funeral and see who came. Almost dying sure made me popular. Who knew?

And of course there's Mackenzie, who still refuses to go home. She's here, loving me and planning our future again. Sometimes I have the thought that maybe I'm in Heaven after all. I mean, getting this much love and forgiveness seems nothing short of a miracle.

It's not Heaven—for one, in Heaven I can't imagine I'd be stuck in this hospital bed with my girl so close yet unwilling to touch me because of doctor's orders. This is our epic reconciliation moment … We should be naked! There should be all kinds of wildly passionate make-up sex happening. But no, the only action I'm getting is when the docs feel me up to check on my ribs.

Leave it to me to get a miracle with a cruel sense of humor.

❖　❖　❖

That evening after Mackenzie's parents leave, Doc Shady pokes her head through my open door and smiles at us.

"Hey, Doc!"

She explained the whole situation to me and apologized for sharing the letter with Mackenzie, but I forgave her. That letter was essentially the reason Mackenzie changed her mind about us, so really, I should be thanking the doc for breaking some rules.

"I have something for you," Shady says, rummaging in her purse.

"Burger and fries from Wahlburgers?" I ask hopefully.

Doc and Mackenzie both roll their eyes at me—because that's not something Shady would do and there's also clearly not enough room in her purse. But a guy can dream, right?

She produces an envelope and hands it over to me. It only takes me a second to recognize it, because it's the same one I gave her a few months ago.

"You didn't even open it?" I ask. There's a check for five grand in here!

"You're a patient, Graham. I can't accept your money. I've been holding onto it for you, and now that you have the foundation set up I'm returning it so you can put that money toward your project."

"I was trying to thank you." I might be sulking a little. I thought that was a super nice thing to do!

"I appreciate it. But I'd rather if you show your gratitude by never scaring me like that again."

I nod, guilt an uncomfortable weight on my chest. Until Mackenzie made me re-read my email, I didn't realize it sounded like I was about to off myself. I hate knowing I put them through that on top of everything else.

I hand Mackenzie the check to keep safe in her wallet. She tries to leave to give me and the doc privacy, but we both encourage her to stay. I've already had a couple of one-on-one chats with Shady while I've been here, and while I agreed to continue seeing her for regular therapy, I'm not up to being shrunk right now.

The three of us chat for a while before Doc says she has to go. She gives us a warm smile—damn, they need to bottle that shit up and figure out how to get it into an IV bag, because I swear she's natural Xanax.

"I have some contacts here at the hospital, so if you need anything give me a call and I'll try to help," Shady says in parting.

"Maybe you can pull some strings and get them to discharge me?" I ask immediately, even more hopeful than I was for Wahlburgers. "I'm ready to get the hell out of here."

Shady doesn't have a chance to respond before Mackenzie is up and out of her chair. She points a finger at my face. "Graham Wyatt, you are not leaving that bed until a freaking *army* of doctors and surgeons clear you! You hear me?"

Damn, she's hot when she goes all fiery redhead on me.

"Guess I'm not going anywhere," I say to the doc, a little sheepishly. As much as I want to go home, I don't want it enough to piss off my girl. Not when I just got her back.

Mackenzie

"You're incorrigible," I tell Graham as soon as Shady leaves. My voice is exasperated, but I'm holding back a smile. I'm so grateful that he's awake and feeling well enough to be incorrigible.

"But you love me anyway."

"I do." I let the smile out now. It is simply not possible to love anyone more than I love this ridiculous man.

"Mmm, I like those words coming from your mouth. You wanna say them in a church sometime soon and make this thing official?"

I blink at him.

"I wasn't kidding when I woke up. Marry me, babe."

I won't deny the little tingle of excitement that runs through me at his words and the utterly sincere expression on his face, but I hesitate.

"You know I want to marry you," I start slowly, thinking, "but I don't think now is the right time."

"Why?" he asks. "You want to marry me, and I sure as fuck want to marry you. I don't see a reason to wait."

"We've been through a lot. I think we need some time to recover from all of this. Let's settle in at the new house and live our lives. We don't need to take on something as big as planning a wedding right now."

"And I'm guessing if I say we can pop over to city hall and do this thing today you'll still want to wait?"

He's pouting now. I can tell, even though his mouth is more than a little obscured by the beard he still hasn't trimmed.

I go over to the bed and carefully sit down on the mattress beside him. He's got it propped up to a half-sitting position, so we're nearly eye to eye now.

"The thing is, I want to plan a wedding," I admit. "I want to wear an impractical, fluffy, overpriced white dress and have my dad walk me down an aisle that has you waiting at the end of it. I want to vow our love to each other in front of all our favorite people, and then have a giant party we'll remember for the rest of our lives. I want all of that with you. I just don't want it right now."

"So … how long are we talking?"

"Two years," I blurt out. I'll admit I made that up on the fly, but I suppose it seems reasonable. No need to rush, right?

Apparently, Graham doesn't agree. No longer calm, he gapes at me with his jaw open and eyes wide. "Babe! You're gonna make me wait two years?!"

"I don't want to put a timeline on it. I don't want us to be counting down the days. Let's relax and have this time together, time to breathe—to wake up together in our bed and eat cereal in our pajamas and make love on the kitchen table whenever we want." He's grinning. I knew he'd like that. "Let's just be young and in love."

"Okay. We'll do it your way for now."

He kisses me long, slow, and deep. We keep kissing until the beeping of his heart monitor brings me back to my senses.

⁂ ⁂ ⁂

"Graham! I am not giving you a blow job in a hospital bed!"

He's been campaigning for this all day.

"Please, babe? You've got to be horny too, having to see my sexy ass in this little hospital gown every day. We'll sixty-nine it."

I raise my eyebrows at him in a silent response he'll be able to read loud and clear: *not happening*. It's not that I don't want to touch him and be with him that way again—but I won't risk it. He went into cardiac arrest a few weeks ago—as in, *his heart stopped and they had to bring him back to life!* I can handle being horny for a while, but what I can't handle is losing him. The doctors said to avoid strenuous activity for at least four weeks, so that's what we're going to do.

Plus ... *here?!* Nurses and doctors walk in and out of this room all day long. There's a window in the door, for goodness sake. Anyone could look in! Nope.

"Come on," he almost whines. "I'm dying over here!"

"Well, maybe you should have considered that before you did something so stupid!"

"Am I ever going to live that down?" His petulant tone resembles that of an exasperated teenager.

"Nope. I will retell it to our children every night before bed as a cautionary tale."

"Our children? You hiding a baby bump somewhere under those leggings?"

"No!" I pretend to swat at him with the back of one hand.

"Well, I can fix that ... if you get over here and let me knock you up."

"You've got a screw loose!" I'm swallowing back laughter.

"Nah, I passed that brain function test with flying colors, remember? Got a gold star and everything."

"And how many techs did you have to flirt with to get that star?"

"Oh yeah, I forgot to mention ... I hope you're down for a threesome because I promised Raul in Radiology we'd all meet up once I get out of here."

I laugh because I can't help it. I'm so happy to be bickering with him again. When my bout of laughter fades, he's grinning at me widely. I school my features and walk closer to the bed, preparing to use my stern voice. Because although we're making light of it, this shit is no joke.

"I'm serious. If you ever even *think* about risking your life like that again, I swear I will kill you myself!"

He reaches out for my hands and I let him, stepping in all the way so my legs are pressed against the side of the bed. He looks up at me with soulful hazel eyes, keeping them locked on mine as he slowly kisses both of my hands.

"No, babe, I promise. That part of our story is over. I'm ready to move on and get started with the whole happy ending part."

My heart swells with love.

"That's really sweet, Y." Then I add, "Please don't ruin it by making a sex joke."

"Aw, come on! I had a really good one ..."

42. IN GOOD HANDS

2-ish years later...

THE BOSTON JOURNAL

"SUCCESSFUL WYATT CENTER A WORK OF HEART"

Local philanthropist Graham Wyatt realizes his dream of helping others as the Wyatt Community Center announces upcoming expansion.

BY MICHELLE ANDERSON, STAFF WRITER

Just six months after opening its doors, the Rose and Tyler Wyatt Community Center (aka "the Wyatt Center") is expanding its reach. In addition to continuing their affordable residential drug rehabilitation and cutting-edge halfway house initiatives, the Wyatt Center has recently announced two new programs coming this spring that will focus on youth outreach and mental health.

The Wyatt Center's grand opening six months ago sparked equal parts support and controversy from the Boston community. Unrelated to any existing hospitals or government-funded programs, the center and its colorful founder have both come under much scrutiny. So far, the nonprofit has held up under that scrutiny and appears to be slowly winning over skeptics. Multiple third-party experts in the fields of drug rehabilitation and societal reintegration have extolled the high quality of the facilities and innovative approach to patient care.

"It is on par with what the best hospitals and celebrity programs are doing right now," wrote one researcher from Harvard.

Some in the community are still not convinced. Most local criticism has targeted social issues rather than treatment practices, particularly the unique hiring philosophy. Taking nondiscrimination to a new level, the center accepts and even encourages convicted felons and recent parolees to apply for employment.

Since opening, the Wyatt Center has created more than forty new jobs, employing local people in positions ranging from therapists and nurses to facilities managers and kitchen staff. To date, some reports estimate that up to fifty percent of those employees have criminal records.

I had the pleasure to sit and talk with Graham Wyatt, the twenty-six-year-old millionaire who is the center's sole founder and visionary as well as its primary investor. Public records show that the Westwood native singlehandedly funded the center's development and construction with a personal investment of ten million dollars. Wyatt himself served time in prison for drug-related offenses committed following the tragic loss of both his parents when he was eighteen—a fact that has also fueled talk from local critics.

Wyatt was more than happy to explain the hiring policy.

"I made some really bad decisions during a hard time in my life that landed me in prison for five years, so I have firsthand knowledge of how good people can end up in situations that don't reflect who they want to be. A lot of guys can't get back on their feet because most employers won't hire someone with a record. If they don't turn back to crime to make a living, they get stuck in minimum wage jobs far below their skills. And that doesn't sit right with me."

His passion for his work came through with every word. The Wyatt Center—which he named after his parents Rose and Tyler—is clearly a personal project for him. Unpretentious and relaxed in dark jeans and a green sweater, Graham—he refused to let me call him Mr. Wyatt—sat on the edge of his seat as he talked animatedly.

"What it comes down to is that I believe everyone deserves a second chance, and that's what we're doing. If you're the best person for the job, we hire you. Period. Then it's up to you to prove yourself. We have a one-strike rule for violations, but I'm happy to say we haven't needed to let anyone go since we opened."

We then talked about the new mental health program that is part of their announced expansion plan. It is clear that mental health is one of the cornerstones of the Wyatt Center; both their rehab and halfway programs already include therapy. Graham spoke candidly about why this issue is so important to him and why he's chosen to focus such a large portion of the Center's resources to these services.

"I've personally struggled with depression—it was one of the things that led me to use drugs as a teen. I was spiraling after my parents died, and it was the therapy I received in prison that helped get my head on straight."

The new mental health initiative will open up the psychological services currently available as part of the Center's rehab and halfway house programs, making them available to everyone.

"It's not only about the therapy services and pharmaceuticals," Wyatt told me. "We also want to raise awareness and decrease the stigma associated with mental illness. At eighteen I didn't know that was the kind of help I needed—and even if I had understood I was depressed, I honestly can't say if I would have decided to get therapy on my own. I want to tell people that quarterbacks can be depressed too and that's okay."

Conversation then veered to a topic for which his passion is even more obvious and fervent.

"It just so happens that my fiancée—cross your fingers for me that's what she is by the time you publish this … I'm asking her tomorrow! —is completing her Master's in Psychology. She's going to oversee the psychological services across all of our programs once she graduates in June and officially joins the team as our Head of Mental Health. I say 'officially' because Mackenzie Thatcher (soon to be Wyatt) has been a pivotal part of this project from minute one. I can say with complete certainty that the Wyatt Center would not exist without her— from all those nights she stayed up with me drafting incorporating documents and reading resumes to her unending support that kept me going when I had moments of 'What was I thinking? I'm not qualified to do this!'"

Graham consistently deflected praise and shrugged off my references to his generosity in donating more than half his personal net worth to the Center. He adamantly asserted that he couldn't have pulled this off alone and attributed the success to his team.

"I'm just here to look pretty," he joked. "Griff O'Brien is the one who really makes things happen. He jumped right in and helped organize things from the early stages when I had a big dream, helping make it a reality."

Griff O'Brien was unavailable for comment any of the times I called or popped in. When I mentioned this, Graham replied, "Ah, he doesn't have time for this sort of thing. He's keeping the place running!"

A quick online search revealed that O'Brien is not only an employee but also a close personal friend of Wyatt's. Social media photos show Graham and Mackenzie spending holidays and vacations with Griff, his girlfriend Shaina, and their two kids. Graham is even coaching Griff's eight-year-old daughter's soccer team.

Deeper digging uncovered that O'Brien and Wyatt first met in prison, where they were briefly cellmates. O'Brien's criminal record is far more extensive than Wyatt's, though by all accounts he's left that life behind. Everyone I encountered had glowing things to say of O'Brien, who is greatly respected around the center and responsible in large part for its day-to-day management.

After walking through the rehabilitation facilities and the single occupant apartments available for their halfway house residents, I was tempted to check myself in! The place looks like a high-end spa, not an affordable community program. Wyatt has truly spared no expense to make the Wyatt Center a welcoming place for people to come and improve their lives. It's working, and the center has been astoundingly successful; within the first two months he and his team found themselves putting people on a waitlist, and they've already had to build on to the original facilities twice.

I personally don't think I'll ever be able to hear the phrase "passion project" again without picturing Graham Wyatt's face. He talked to me for more than two hours about all the upcoming projects and initiatives he has in the works—including career counseling services and some community partnerships encouraging workplaces to open job opportunities to Wyatt Center "graduates," a college scholarship program, and a youth sports league with subsidized fees and donated equipment. We talked for so long we had to order lunch (Graham insisted on paying).

I even got to briefly meet Mackenzie Thatcher—the center's soon-to-be Head of Mental Health and, I'm sure, the future Mrs. Wyatt. I doubt any woman alive, or most men for that matter, could say no to Graham Wyatt. His unique charisma and endearing passion might also be the secret behind the astounding number of individual donations that have already been made to the Wyatt Center, enough to ensure its continued operation for years to come.

"I'm hoping we can do some good, help people who might not be able to get it otherwise," Wyatt summarized.

He also admitted that he wants the center to do justice to his parents' legacy. I think it's safe to say the legacy of the late Mr. and Mrs. Wyatt is in very good hands with their son, who has put not only his money but his heart into their namesake project.

Considering the momentum it's already achieved and more ambitious endeavors on the horizon, the Wyatt Center is well on its way to becoming a permanent local fixture. We'll have to wait and see what it accomplishes over the next six months and the next six years. With such a devoted leader at its heart, the possibilities for the future are endless.

43. THE BDP

Graham

I need to write a "thank you" letter to the previous owners of our house for installing this massive free-standing Jacuzzi tub in the master bathroom. It's been the setting for some damn good memories over the past couple of years, and we're currently in the process of making another one.

This thing is the best wingman I've ever had. When Mackenzie gets home from school or work and claims she's too tired for sex, I can always talk her into a relaxing bath. Which inevitably leads to fooling around.

I present Exhibit A.

Our skin is slippery as our hands roam and tease. I move so I'm on top of her and begin to knead her boobs with both hands. Then I suck on one of her nipples but pull back and make a face when some of that fizzy bath shit gets on my tongue. She giggles and runs her fingers through my hair.

I shift my leg so her pussy presses flush to my thigh, hotter than the water around us. She grinds against me a little, and that's it. I can't wait anymore.

"Gotta have you, babe."

She nods. I shift her back so she's leaning along the wall of the tub then grab her legs and lift them until her ankles are on my shoulders. She bends into the position with ease, and for the millionth time, I bless the wonder that is yoga.

We both moan with my first push inside her. There's something erotic about the warm bath water surrounding us as I move slowly in and out. Every now and then I get a little extra zing of sensation when some bubbles get in on the action.

I thrust a little harder and the motion pushes us closer to the stream of one of the Jacuzzi jets. We're suddenly perfectly aligned so the rushing water hits right where we're connected. I can feel the water running along my shaft as I pull out and massaging my balls when I'm buried inside her. It's fucking magical.

Mackenzie moans again and adjusts her ass a bit. I can tell when her clit finds the jet's path because she spasms around me.

"Yes," she whispers.

Yes, indeed. It's perfect. *She's* perfect.

I enter her again and pause when I'm as deep as possible. I look down at her beautiful green-blue eyes that are currently hazy with lust and love. Love swells inside my own chest until it's on the edge of bursting. *This is everything. She's my everything.*

"Marry me, Mackenzie."

Her body freezes, suddenly going stiff as her mouth drops open in shock.

"Be my wife?" I ask again.

Her shock seems to wear off, and her expression morphs to an entirely new emotion.

"GRAHAM!" she shrieks. "You can't propose during sex!"

... I think I just did.

"Because ...?"

"Seriously?" She sounds exasperated. Not exactly the response I'd hoped for. "What am I supposed to tell my parents? Our friends? Our children?!"

Well, shit. Did I fuck this up? I never had any doubt about her answer, but now some uncertainty creeps in.

"I'm sorry," I say, trying to fix it. "I have the ring, and I was going to take you to dinner or something tomorrow and ask, but then we were having this moment and it felt so good and I just couldn't wait. Do you want me to take it back?"

There's a little bit of panic in my voice, and down south I'm starting to soften. I suddenly become aware that I'm still inside her with her ankles on my shoulders. Maybe she's right and this was bad timing.

"Are you saying no?" I have to swallow down the fear.

Her face softens and the tension leaves her body.

"No. Of course, I'll marry you, you gorgeous, wonderful idiot."

She said yes.

That sure takes care of any hard-on shrinkage—the adrenaline of the moment has me harder than I've ever been in my life. I kiss her, tongue plunging inside her mouth at the same time I resume the motion of my hips and bury myself deeper within her body.

"I love you," I tell her. "I'm sorry."

"I love you too," she replies a little breathlessly, hips pushing back toward mine. I can tell I'm hitting that spot on her inner wall and that this isn't going to last much longer. Good, because the thought of her as my wife has me ready to blow.

"I'll make it up to you," I promise, my own voice less than steady as my balls start to draw tight.

"I know you will," she gasps.

We climax together.

We're getting married!

Mackenzie

The elevator climbs up, up, up, and I take a deep breath trying to steady myself. In a minute that door is going to open and I need to act surprised to see Graham with our family and friends. Supposedly, I think Marisa and I are simply grabbing drinks at the Top of the Hub, one of the nicest restaurants in Boston situated at one of the tallest points in the city, the top floor of the Prudential building. It's fancy and coveted for its amazing view; there are windows on every wall that allow you to look down on Boston. It's a place Marisa and I would never go for no reason. Of course, if this was actually a random BFF night out, I also wouldn't have gone shopping for the perfect dress or spent hours prepping my hair and makeup.

You've got to love having a heads-up about your own "surprise" engagement.

Marisa's eyes meet mine, and we burst out in giggles. I have to turn the other way to avoid eye contact. I try to compose myself, but I can still hear her laughing and that makes me start all over again. We don't need to say anything. It's clear we're both thinking about my actual engagement. She and Shaina are the only ones I've told the story, which we've dubbed "The Balls Deep Proposal" or "BDP."

I mean, I've been waiting a long time for Graham to propose. I never actually expected him to wait this long, and for the last year I've been secretly hoping he'd pop the question earlier than the perfunctory two years I mentioned that one time. I figured he had some big plan in the works or was waiting for something special. So, when he finally asked me to marry him in the midst of sex (incidentally, sex that was arguably among the best of my life), I was incredulous.

In retrospect, it was such a Graham thing to do that I shouldn't have even been surprised. I'm well aware that he isn't romantic in the traditional sense of red roses and candlelight. I'd take the way he loves me any day because it comes straight from his heart. Graham's style of romance looks like surprising me with tacos when I've had a long day, turning off my phone alarm on a Saturday so I can sleep in while he goes to the grocery store for me, giving me three orgasms before he lets himself come. Every day he looks at me like I'm the most miraculous thing he's ever seen, and he never stops showing how much he loves me.

So, he asked me to marry him while we were basically having a threesome with a Jacuzzi jet. In the big scheme of things, it's something I can live with. I would have been fine coming up with a solid cover story or a low-key do-over at my parents' house. He's the one who got ambitious with this thing, renting out the Top of the Hub and inviting so many people. Truthfully, I suspect it's *Marisa's* dream proposal I'm about to enter.

The elevator dings as we reach the top floor, and even though it's not a real surprise, my insides flutter with excitement. It's been sort of fun being secretly engaged for the last couple of weeks, but I'm ready to share the news with my parents and start wearing Graham's mother's diamond ring outside the walls of our house.

The doors open and my eyes immediately lock onto Graham. He's dressed up in a perfectly cut suit, sans tie, with his hair pulled back and beard trimmed short enough to emphasize his perfect jawline. My parents are right beside him, Mom already crying. There's a group behind them of our friends and more of my family, all eyes focused on me as I step out of the elevator. Toward the back of the crowd I spot Griff towering a head taller than everyone else, and though I can't see them I know Shaina and the kids must be nearby. I also catch sight of Derek, whose eyes are locked on Marisa as always. We've all come a long way since he first introduced himself as "Officer Schwartz," and while he's more than earned his first name status by now I doubt Marisa and I will ever stop calling him Officer Guapo.

Graham walks toward me, stealing my attention again. He takes my hand and leads me to the center of the room before getting down on one knee.

"Mackenzie Elaine Thatcher," he begins. "I'm already the happiest man alive, and the luckiest, because I have you in my life. But I've been wanting to marry you since we were sixteen, so I hope you'll agree to take me as your husband."

Even though it's technically just for show, I cry anyway.

Honestly, when it comes to spending the rest of our lives together, saying yes to this man twice is no hardship.

44. FERTILITY FUCKFEST

Another year later...

Mackenzie

My IUD is going to expire right before my twenty-seventh birthday. I've been aware for a while now that its "effective until" date was approaching, but I've managed to sidestep those thoughts—similar to the way I've sidestepped my husband's attempts to talk about baby making.

Let's be honest. Graham has been wanting to get me pregnant since … well, I can't remember a time he *hasn't* wanted to, and his enthusiasm has only grown since we got married six months ago. I secretly suspect at least a small part of his eagerness comes from the caveman part of his brain … you know: "Me man, put seed in my woman and watch her grow big."

All joking aside, I know he's genuinely excited to be a dad, to start a family of our own. He loves being Layla and Harry's "Uncle Graham," and he's simply itching for some kids that we don't have to give back to their parents at the end of the weekend.

Don't get me wrong, I want to have babies with that man too. I want to be a mother. Every now and then, when Graham isn't home,

I'll sit in one of our currently under-utilized extra bedrooms and imagine it redecorated for a little boy or girl. I've already decided that the bedroom closest to ours on the second floor will be best for a nursery. Until now, I've always been okay letting those be "someday" dreams.

We've already been through a lot in our lives, both separately and as a couple, and sometimes it's easy to forget that we're still very young. But we are. Maybe a little selfishly, I've slowed things down because I wanted to have these years to ourselves. Not getting married and having babies right away also allowed us to put all of our focus on the Wyatt Center. For all intents and purposes, the center has been our baby for the last three years. I'm so proud of what we've built, and beyond proud of Graham for not only rising above his struggles but using his own experiences to help others. As the charity and the community programs thrive, I've noticed something settle inside him, the proof of his success soothing his lingering self-doubt. With every passing year, I see him reclaiming more pieces of the happy, confident boy I once knew.

It's been a wonderful time in our lives that we'll look back on fondly.

Now, the expiration of my IUD seems to be a cosmic sign. My little contraceptive friend and I have officially run the course of our seven-year relationship. It's the end of an era, and thus seems a natural time to begin the next one. I make a doctor's appointment to get it removed, and I don't plan to replace it with anything.

I should tell Graham, but I decide to surprise him. I just *know* he'll make a huge deal of it, and I'd rather avoid having him count down the days like a kid looking forward to Christmas. (In this scenario, I suppose my body would be the chimney, and the baby would be

Santa? ... *Oh my God, I've been spending too much time with Graham!*)

The day of my appointment, I come home and tell him the news. To say my husband is ecstatic would be a gigantic understatement.

You'd think I came home wearing edible underwear or sporting nipple rings from the way he jumps me. I'm not exactly complaining, but I do briefly consider calling Shady for a little personal consult. I mean, it can't be normal for a man to get insta-hard at the very mention of impregnating his wife. Right?

Without asking me first, Graham pulls rank at work and schedules us both for a three-day vacation that just so happens to be the exact timeframe during which I'm ovulating. (He's the one who told me this, by the way, because apparently the man looked it up and has been tracking my cycle more closely than I have.)

At first, I'm kind of pissed off at him for this crazy alpha man move, but it's not possible to stay mad at him for long. Because he's Graham ... and because we spend those three days naked.

The whole thing is reminiscent of the first few months when we got back together, a heady blur of sex and insatiable need and constantly feeling drunk on orgasms. We make love in every possible way on every possible surface in our house, barely taking breaks to eat or sleep. In truth, we cover all those bases more than once, because in addition to the lovemaking, there's a lot of what can only be called fucking—hard, sweaty, raw.

It's the best vacation I've ever had.

"Oh crap." We're sprawled out on the bed in a state of exhaustion toward the end of the third day. "I hope I'm not pregnant at Griff and Shaina's wedding!"

Yep, our best friends are finally making the thing official. I choose to think our wedding inspired them, but Graham says that Griff (who is secretly a huge sweetheart) wanted to wait until he could give Shaina the wedding of her dreams. They're finally at that place financially, now that they've moved their family into a nice house only a few minutes from ours—a house that conveniently became available at a surprisingly low rate right as they started looking … I told Graham I don't even want to know what kinds of strings he had to pull to make that one happen.

"I hope you are. We did good work here!" Graham protests.

"But what if I'm all bloated or have morning sickness?"

"I'm sure it will be fine, babe."

He's probably right. I mean, I've met people who tried to get pregnant for months or even years before conceiving. I'm sure I have some more time.

✻ ✻ ✻

Maybe I jinxed myself. Personally, I choose to blame the fact that no part of Graham (even his sperm) can ever resist a challenge. Graham says it was a simple matter of mathematical probability after our "fertility fuckfest." Regardless, a week later we are the proud owners of a urine-covered white stick whose digital display reads "pregnant."

That's right … *insta-pregnant.*

Which is how I find myself knocked up at Shaina's wedding a month later, running off every few minutes to puke into some bushes while the poor photographer tries to take pictures of the bridal party. The photos were planned for noon, which is apparently the time my body has deemed the "morning" part of this whole "morning sickness" situation.

Shaina is really sweet about the whole thing, asking the guy to take some other photos while she comes to the bathroom with me. I puke some more then rinse out my mouth while she attempts to reassure me.

"I was so sick during my first pregnancy too, and then with Harry it was barely anything."

I start muttering how I'm *'never doing this again'* while trying to use a paper towel to remove some vomit from my bridesmaid's dress.

"Fuck," Shaina says, drawing my attention to her. I've been so caught up in my own little crisis that I didn't immediately notice she's gone silent. I look up to see her standing there staring off into space, wearing a very strange expression.

"What's wrong?" I'm up on my feet, suddenly feeling better and ready for bridesmaid duty. Honestly, right now I'll gladly deal with any emergency as long as it has nothing to do with my gag reflexes.

"I think I'm pregnant," Shaina says, shocking the hell out of me. She looks pretty shocked herself.

"What?" I gasp, but I don't think she hears me.

Moving toward the door, she growls, "I'm going to kill Griff!" Then she runs off toward the room where the guys are getting ready.

I don't even try to stop her or worry about the whole "can't see the bride" superstition. Griff and Shaina are as solid as it gets. That is, as long as Shaina doesn't kill him since, apparently, he's knocked her up for the third time.

45. #DADDYSGIRL

1 (more) year later …

Mackenzie

I'm in love.

It's still new, but the first time our eyes met, I knew this feeling was on a different level from anything I'd experienced before, even for Graham.

Her name is Violet, and she's ten weeks old. The crown of her head is covered in the finest layer of strawberry blonde hair, and she has her daddy's hazel eyes. I can't get enough of her—of those chubby cheeks and the little rolls on her arms and legs. This baby has me one hundred percent brainwashed with love chemicals, and I wouldn't have it any other way. Fortunately, Graham isn't upset that he's no longer the sole love of my life, because he is just as smitten with our daughter.

Currently, I'm gazing down at Violet adoringly while trying to pay attention to Marisa, who is pacing back and forth in our living room. She's been doing this for a while now—I don't think I've ever seen her so worked up.

"I mean ... his last name is Schwartz. Schwartz! *Schwartz*. Oh my God. Every time I say it, it gets worse. It's like someone decided to make a name by shoving all the most awkward consonants together!"

Violet reaches for a strand of my hair and smiles. I can't help but coo at her and tickle her tummy, which is covered by a pink onesie with the words "Sorry ladies, he's mine. #DaddysGirl" on the front (one guess who got it for her).

"Are you even listening to me? Ugh! I should have gone to Shaina!"

"She wouldn't be any less distracted," I remind her. If anything, she'd be much worse. She has three kids to wrangle now, one of them only four months old.

As it turned out, Shaina was in fact around three months pregnant at her wedding. It seems that with everything she had going on—raising two kids, planning the wedding, and her apprenticeship with a local tattoo parlor—she simply hadn't noticed.

Although she quickly got over her initial shock and dismay, she forced Griff to have a vasectomy shortly after their daughter Sky was born (apparently the threatened alternative was never having sex again). For my part, I love that we have kids so close in age. I hope that Sky and Violet will be best friends the way Shaina and I have become.

"Hello?!" Marisa calls. I force myself to focus on my other best friend and her current crisis.

"Okay, so you can't marry him because of ... consonants?"

I'm trying to take her seriously—truly, I am—but it's hard not to laugh at the panic she's worked herself into since Derek proposed yesterday.

The reason I find this drama laughable? I know Marisa, and I'm certain Derek is perfect for her. He's strong enough to handle her, but soft enough to balance out her sharp edges, and always stays levelheaded when she gets carried away. He also not only keeps up with her quick wit and dry humor but actually holds his own and gives it right back. I've never seen her as happy as she's been since she finally let him catch her after making him keep up the chase for quite a while.

So, I'm well aware she's going to say yes. Inside, she realizes it too. Her current rant is merely a nonsensical concern she's fabricated because she needs somewhere to direct her anxiety.

"It's not just the consonants!" she huffs. "But I mean—it's a terrible name, isn't it?"

"So, marry him but don't take his last name," I suggest evenly. "Or you could always go with Mrs. Guapo."

She lets out a sound of exasperation and rolls her eyes dramatically. Her accent always comes out more thickly when she's agitated, and it's in full force right now.

"*Of course* I'm going to take his last name!"

"Don't you think you should tell him 'yes' first?" I sound smug, but I don't care.

"Violet, I hate your mommy," she tells my daughter.

"You love me."

"I'm only here for baby therapy. Give her to me!"

Marisa rocks and cuddles Violet, who is already under the enchantment of her child-whispering aunt.

"I bet Derek will be more than happy to give you one of those," I tell her.

She glares at me, but I sense her resistance softening. Though she won't readily admit it right now, she's itching to have a baby of her own. Marisa loves kids, and she'll be an amazing mother.

"I'm scared," she whispers, looking only at Violet.

"The best things in life are both terrifying and amazing. I think you're the one who told me that."

"I stole it from a quote I saw somewhere," she admits, a bit miserably.

"Well, it's still true. I get that you're nervous, but you don't have anything to worry about with Derek. If he hasn't been scared off yet—despite your best efforts, I might add—he's not going anywhere. That man loves you as much as we love chocolate."

That makes her smile. Marisa and I still have girls' nights where we binge on our favorites: brownies, tacos and guacamole, and tequila when I'm not pregnant. Sometimes we let Graham join, but often we send him away so we can have quality BFF time.

Then she sighs deeply, and in that exhalation I hear defeat. "I know."

"Maybe you should go see him and put him out of his misery?"

I can only imagine Derek is on pins and needles. He's probably a little hurt too since Marisa's reaction to his proposal was far from ideal.

"Yes," she agrees sullenly, handing Violet back over to me.

"I love you," I tell my best friend.

"I love you too, even when you piss me off by making sense."

❖ ❖ ❖

I've just gotten Violet to sleep when I hear Graham's car outside. He's been gone since the early afternoon, busy with some errand he wouldn't explain.

He enters our bedroom minutes later sporting a huge grin and a bandage on his arm. He wastes no time proudly showing off the new tattoo on his right bicep—it's his first ink on this arm and very different from the grayscale design of his half-sleeve. The tattoo is a delicate flower in shades of purple, white, and yellow ... a violet. It's done in a style that looks like the artist used watercolor to paint right on his skin. It's gorgeous. Almost too pretty for a big tough man, but if anyone can pull off the look, it's my husband.

"I love it," I tell him as my eyes fill with tears. (I'm a lot sappier these days.)

When I was pregnant, we considered naming our daughter Rose after his mother, but Graham decided it would be too strange. Instead, we kept with the flower theme. I suspect that somewhere in our house Graham has a little list stashed away of floral baby names for the future. (I know I do).

I love that Graham is so proud of our daughter that he wanted to honor her this way. Whether he realizes it or not, this tattoo also means so much more—it represents how far he's come from the colorless grief in his past. It's a symbol of the fresh chance on life we have together, a blank slate we're filling with vibrant joy and love.

I wrap my arms around Graham's waist and his hands come to rest on my back, folding me into his embrace.

A bit later as we get ready for bed, he tells me that he plans to add more ink to the arm as we have more children, so someday he'll have a whole garden. And yes, he follows this statement with extensive innuendos about planting, ploughing, seeds, etc. I stay quiet and let him get it out of his system. I figure he's probably been waiting all day to share these little gems with me.

Because that's Graham Wyatt. Heart-wrenchingly sweet and hilariously strange, often within the same breath. Strong and vulnerable, sexy and goofy. The most loyal person I've ever met. He still makes my pulse race when he walks into a room—and he's still the only man who ever has, as though my body and my heart recognize that he belongs to us. My love. My best friend. My first, and last, and forever.

I no longer try to question it or explain it away with science.

I've long since accepted that while there are many things about the human experience that can be rationalized and categorized, there are others that defy quantification. Some things are simply too extraordinary to be anything but magic.

Like soul mates.

True love.

Fate.

EPILOGUE

Graham

There's a reason the phrase isn't "perfectly ever after." Life isn't perfect and neither are we.

We argue. Mackenzie can be a control freak, and I can be a caveman. I complain that she overthinks things, and she accuses me of being reckless. I prefer the word "spontaneous"—I mean, we hosted an animal rescue's adoption event at the Center… who *wouldn't* come home with a puppy?

For the most part, we manage to leave our past behind us, where it belongs. Sometimes life throws us inescapable reminders that bring up old hurts, but we get through those tough times together.

It works because our respective flaws balance each other out: Mackenzie loves that dog almost as much as she loves our kid, and though I grumble, I'm lucky that she keeps our life organized.

She's still the beautiful girl who caught my eye the first day of ninth grade, who I watched from afar for a year before finding the courage to ask her out. (Yeah, so maybe I've always had stalking tendencies when it comes to Mackenzie. But, really … look at her. Can you blame me?) She's also the remarkable woman whose strength and compassion inspire me every single day. A woman I get to call my wife.

Not a day goes by that I don't thank the big man upstairs for everything I have. That's one thing our past has done for us—we don't take anything for granted. Mackenzie and I didn't come by this life easily, and I like to think that remembering how close we came more than once to *not* having it makes every beautiful moment a little sweeter.

In short, I'm the luckiest son of a bitch alive. *(No offense, Mom!)*

I still wonder if I deserve to be this happy, and often suspect I don't, but those thoughts have very little power over me nowadays. Because what does that even mean? Who decides what we do or don't deserve in this life, what invisible hoops we're supposed to jump through before we earn the right to happiness?

Life is about choices. Good ones, bad ones, and all the little moments in between. Every day, Mackenzie Thatcher Wyatt wakes up and chooses me, chooses us. And instead of questioning it, I accept her love and I choose her right back.

One day, we'll have to tell Violet and her (hopefully numerous) siblings our story and about my past. I won't lie—I wish I wasn't the guy who has to admit to his little girl that he went to prison. It would be nice if her parents' love story didn't include death and drugs, mistakes and broken hearts (or, you know, comas).

But that wouldn't be our truth. And our truth is something precious that I won't hide, because somehow it all turned out pretty damn wonderful.

So, we'll tell our children what's true about life: that sometimes bad things happen to good people, and sometimes good people do bad things.

At bedtime, the fairy tales in our house will just be a little different. They will include a princess who's her own knight, and a prince who causes his own imprisonment by opening the gates to dragons that scorch his castle. A prince who tried to take on that hoard of dragons all by himself and almost didn't live to tell the tale.

Once in the not-so-distant past, I let my inner dragons win. Those assholes haven't disappeared—they'll probably never go away completely—but these days, they're the ones who lose. I conquer them now, because I've learned that not every battle has to be fought alone, and I'm lucky to have an amazing wife and friends who will always have my back. I guess that will be the moral of the tales we tell our children—that asking for help is one of the bravest things you can do, and that they'll never be alone. The best armor is love, after all, and we're going to raise our kids wrapped up in it head to toe.

So, perfectly isn't in the cards for us as we live our ever after. But happily? Yeah, we've got that shit on lockdown.

The End

ACKNOWLEDGEMENTS

Honestly, I never thought I'd have an Acknowledgements page. Writing was always a solo, personal thing for me, and up until December 2018 it had been *years* since I'd written anything that anyone else read. But in putting myself and my writing out there, I found a support system I didn't even realize I needed so badly.

I began posting chapters on Wattpad thinking that if my book was somewhere public it might keep me accountable and force me to actually finish the thing. It quickly became so much more than that; I discovered a community of readers and writers whose enthusiasm and praise for *Us, Again* not only gave me the motivation to finish writing it but the confidence to follow through with my goal of self-publishing.

So this is a shout out to every Wattpader who read, voted, or commented on *Us, Again*. Thank you for the amazing comments, telling me I'm funny (I still find this shocking!), and helping me choose epic chapter titles. You made me believe in my own writing and your love for these characters helped me connect more deeply with them as well.

All of my love to the readers and bookstagrammers who read and reviewed advance copies and helped promote *Us, Again* on social media. Thank you for making me feel like a "real" author! I can barely express how much I appreciate every photo, message, and piece of feedback.

Now let me raise a glass to my "Best Of" Instagram ladies. Thank you for the camaraderie, the feedback, all of the GIF's, and the endless hot man photos (keep an eye out for those thumbs!)

Danielle Paul: Without you, this book might not even exist. (I've already told you this a hundred times, but it's only official if it's in the final published version, right?) Thank you for being reader #1 and for all of your encouragement, comments, and enthusiasm as I wrote this. You are, and forever will be, Graham's Fairy Cougar Mother. (But they made it official with rings and babies and everything ... so maybe it's time you stopped trying to steal Graham from Mackenzie?)

And a million thank you's to Shauna McDonnell, the very first person to pre-order the eBook, my first Goodreads reviewer, and my one-woman cheering squad as I angsted endlessly over the process of self-publishing. Your belief in me means more than you will ever know. Shameless plug time: Shauna is a first time author, too! We initially connected because she was also writing a second chance romance (only hers has an Irish Rockstar). Check out Luck, book 1 in her 4Clover series, releasing on Amazon December 1, 2019.

ABOUT THE AUTHOR

Elle Maxwell decided to be an author at the age of nine. She then spent the next twenty years letting life and self-doubt push that dream to the backburner, until she realized she was about to turn thirty and needed to get her butt in gear. Just to be dramatic, she self-published her first book on her 30th birthday.

When she's not writing, Elle is a dog mom, artist, binge-reader, and chai latte enthusiast. She is also in a long-term love affair with her adopted city of Boston.

Us, Again is her debut novel. (But definitely not her last … keep an eye out for Marisa's book, coming sometime in 2020!)

CONNECT WITH ELLE ONLINE!

visit ELLEMAXWELLBOOKS.COM

TO SUBSCRIBE FOR EMAIL UPDATES ABOUT FUTURE BOOKS AND ACCESS TO FUN STUFF LIKE EXCLUSIVE BONUS CHAPTERS

♥

Reviews are everything to indie authors, so if you loved Us, Again please consider writing a couple of nice words on Amazon and/or Goodreads. It's an easy way to win the author's eternal love and some major karmic brownie points!

Made in the USA
Middletown, DE
11 November 2019